W9-AVR-925

Push of the Sky

Push of the Sky

Short Works by

Camille Alexa

HADLEY
RILLE
BOOKS

PUSH OF THE SKY

ISBN-13 978-0-9819243-7-3

Published by Hadley Rille Books
Attn: Eric T. Reynolds
PO Box 25466
Overland Park, KS 66225
USA
www.hadleyrillebooks.com
contact@hadleyrillebooks.com

the author dedicates
this book to her parents,
of course

Contents

Foreword
by Jay Lake

There are people to whom one is introduced, and there are people whom one simply realizes one day that one has come to know without being quite sure how or why. "You know Camille, don't you?" "I'm sure you guys would love each other."

For many years, Camille Alexa owned and operated a resale boutique four blocks from my house in Austin, Texas. We shopped at the same stores, hung out at the same coffee houses, quite possibly saw one another in passing, but never met. I moved to Portland, she moved to Portland. It took more years here in the Northwest for us to come to know one another, but already it's as if we've been friends a decade gone by, in a hotter, dryer place.

Likewise her fiction. You'll read this book, and the stories will feel familiar. Some are love at first sight—for me, that was "Shades of White and Road." Others creep up on you, an acquaintance become an old friend all unknowing. These stories are delightful, complex, sharp-edged and beautiful.

Camille Alexa is a stylist par excellence, with a magical vision of the mundane and a straightforward way of describing the fantastic. I read her fiction and think of Karen Joy Fowler, of Gabriel Garcia-Marquez, of Maureen McHugh, of Ray Vukcevich. Stylists all, but with deep rivers running through even the lightest channel of their words. They've charted a course that these stories follow in their own, distinct ways.

The only real mystery is why Camille's work isn't already better known. You'll come to know her fiction quite well through these pages. Pass the word.

Jay Lake
Portland, OR

The Butterfly Assassins

His Majesty's necro-alchemist clutched the dead man's jaw with one hand and dug long bony fingers into the cadaver's mouth. He scooped a mid-sized handful of material and dumped it into the porcelain basin held by his assistant.

He scooped again and again. With every flick of his hand into the waiting basin, a soggy mass of riotous color splatted into the bowl. Fuchsia brighter than the most prized of the Queen's freesia, scarlet more pure than the royal gardener's best roses, purples deeper than the prettiest violets ever grown in the conservatory of the eldest princess: the colors mingled together, stark and vivid against the cold porcelain white. If Pelton leaned very, very close he could make out the shapes of individual wings in the mass; tiny antennae and bits of segmented, spindly leg.

Pelton's uncle, the King, hung back. He wrinkled his royal nose in disgust and annoyance, and Pelton couldn't help feeling relief that for once, the expression wasn't directed at him.

The King snorted. Turning to Martzel, he said, "You're the necremist. Is it actually possible the man was choked by butterflies?"

The necro-alchemist straightened. "Hmmm. More like dry drowned, Sire. These particular lepidoptera secrete an ichor causing paralysis; in this case, of the lungs. Under ordinary circumstances the humors of a man's body are enough to overcome such tiny traces of poison, but if Fenris is like the other three we will find traces of the animals even deep in the cavities of the chest."

The King's nose wrinkled even further. Pelton had the irreverent thought it looked like an enormous walnut perched on his countenance: bulbous and wrinkly, and split down the middle.

His Majesty turned, his heavy robe swinging into a small table arrayed with shiny, wicked-looking implements which clattered across the flagstones as they fell. "Bah! Fenris is the fourth! The fourth Court alchemist I've lost in as many weeks. They don't grow on trees, you know!"

The head necro-alchemist cleared his throat. "Actually, Sire, there is one scholarly project in the mountains rumored to be experimenting with just that very—"

"Bah!" repeated the King and stomped from the room.

Pelton looked at the necremist. "I s-s-say, Martzel, is that t-t-tr-true? Are they really growing men on t-trees?"

The man shrugged. He stooped over the bowl of sodden scraps pulled from the dead man's mouth and throat and poked at them with a slender, silver wand while his assistant gathered the other implements off the floor. "I don't know, Pelton. This is a wondrous age for the scientific magicks. If a talented man sets his mind to it, he can accomplish almost anything."

Late into that night, Pelton turned the necremist's words over in his mind.

"*A talented man...*" he whispered into the darkness, "*...can accomplish almost anything. A talented man....*"

His tongue rarely betrayed him in the dark, rarely stumbled over itself and made him seem the fool.

Through the narrow window in his turret bedchamber he could see the first blush of pink-tinted grey which heralded the coming dawn. He almost never slept. He and this particular sky were old friends.

He slipped from his bed and pulled on breeches and boots—piled on the floor where he had left them the night before—and went to peel back the linen drape from his worktable in the corner. He leaned close to each of the four lanterns in turn and whispered: "*luminarium statim.*"

Pelton hated the incantation triggers of the scientific alchemies. Some nights, when he was tired, it might take him five or six tries to get a lantern to light. Earth and Sky help him if one of the princesses were near, or the Queen. He'd rather just live in darkness.

Seating himself on the bench, Pelton gazed across the table's array: the softly gleaming burnished bowls, the iron arm clamped to the edge of the table with the single, staring eye of a massive magnifier, the black velvet box with the amber clasp. His hand hovered over a small bowl of hammered silver. The bowl was divided, each segment looking from above like the wedge of an orange or the spokes of a carriage wheel. Deciding, he plucked two tiny gears, their gold teeth glinting in the lanternglow. Taking a minuscule pair of tongs, he separated an even more minuscule spring from the others in the bowl and placed it on the tray before him beside the gears. He reached for the velvet box and, opening it, took a moment to stroke the smooth petals of polished wood within.

Pelton looked up from where he sat and gazed at the sliver of light, stealing now across the still-dark sky. "A talented man," he told the dawn, "can accomplish anything."

And with that, he began his day's labors.

"Ah, Pelton, there you are. Late for dining, as usual. And is that soot on your face?"

Pelton tried to answer, hastily rubbing at both cheeks in an effort to rid himself of whatever offensive smear or streak vexed Her Majesty. "I-I-I-I'm s-s-s—"

The three youngest princesses tittered, and the eldest turned from him in cold embarrassment. The two dozen dinner guests and sycophants who had the exalted privilege that evening of dining in the Royal hall hastily turned to each other and began brittle, artificial conversations. Their gazes slid from beneath powdered lashes and alchemized curls to stab at Pelton with covert, darting glances.

The Queen's expression softened. "No, I'm sorry, Pelton. Of course, it's of no consequence at all. Though I wish you'd lay aside your silly bits of wood and cog. It's not seemly for a member of the Family to spend his days playing with attomo . . . autumnals . . . autorificals."

"Automata, Your M-Majesty," said Pelton, taking his place at the table.

Her Majesty fluttered her fingers in the air, the equivalent of her husband's nose-wrinkling.

The Queen called for more heated wine. Dinner resumed. As always, wine did help somewhat to melt the icicles in Pelton's stomach, which usually formed in the presence of his family, the Royal Court. His true parents had died of Frost Fever, two years before the med-alchemists developed their spagyric panacea. He should have been grateful to his uncle and the Queen for keeping him here at the Palace and raising him as their own, and he was. Any unhappiness he felt was his own failing, he knew.

After dinner, the guests and Family retired to private chambers to take refreshment and to gossip and to, unintentionally he was sure, torture Pelton. That particular evening his main torturer was the head transmutationist's new mistress.

Seated beside him, she leaned across Pelton's arm and smiled. He tried to ignore the rounded globes of her bosom pressing into his sleeve. The Court gossips claimed the woman had once lived under the protection of a med-alchemist, and it was rumored that before her tenancy with the man, her endowments had been considerably smaller. Magickal alchemy was truly wondrous, Pelton thought, if sometimes abused. The image of the damp, crumpled silk of dead butterflies came to his mind, and the way Fenris's lips had looked: swollen, purple, and covered in festive flecks of wing.

As though she read his mind the woman at his arm shuddered, the pale expanse of flesh above her gown quivering as she did so. "Poor, poor Fenril," she said.

"Fenris," corrected Pelton.

The woman fluttered her fingers in an affected imitation of the Queen's habitual gesture. "Yes, poor Feckris. I hear he died the same way as did my dear Chollie."

Of course, thought Pelton; Cholland had been the first of the butterflies' victims, and the med-alchemist who had purportedly enhanced this lady's . . . charms.

"I hear there've been over a half-dozen alchemists *done in* the same way!" She shuddered, and again her mounds of unnaturally-proportioned flesh quivered. "Horrible!" she said. "Just horrible."

Pelton frowned. "M-m-m-my Lady, there have b-been b-but four. Four lepidopteran d-d-d—"

"Deaths?" She leaned back, having decided, perhaps, that her primary power was wasted on him. Her eyes narrowed, and she took another gulp of wine. Pelton could practically see the shift in her mind, as though the woman's brain were truly made up of cogs and wheels, gears and springs, like the innards of one of his automata. She smiled, and trotted out her secondary power: information. It was gossip that made the Court go 'round, as any social climber worth her salt or other minerals knew.

"It's said," she began, and Pelton knew better than to ask by whom, "that in addition to the four alchemists His Majesty has lost here at Court, two more in the profession have been found near the Dragonwood, and one in town. The same way: all stuffed with butterflies. It makes one quite rethink one's opinion of the creatures!"

More strange deaths, outside the Court. That was news to Pelton.

"It's also said, that they were all from the same coterie at the same Order, initiated into the alchemical mysteries the same year! It's *also* said. . . ." Here the woman pressed even closer against Pelton's arm, though he could tell all pretense of seduction had fled her behavior. The excitement of the potential conquest of an underling relative to the King paled in comparison to the excitement of speaking, in hushed and juicy tones, of the misfortunes of others. "It's *also* said, that there's but one left of the original coterie." Her eyes glittered, and her gaze slid sideways toward the necremist.

"Martzel?" said Pelton, and the woman made shushing motions with her hands, including the one holding her wine. A few drops of burgundy sploshed onto Pelton's sleeve. He watched the red blossom quickly on the white linen, and again he was reminded of crushed scarlet wings and purple lips. He looked across the room at Martzel, who stood near the King by the great hearth.

The transmutationist's mistress leaned back against the velveteen cushions in triumph, satisfaction evident at dire news dispensed and speculations divulged. "It makes one wonder, does it not, whether His Majesty will soon also be searching for a new necro-alchemist, as well?"

The next three nights Pelton did not sleep at all. He didn't even emerge from his room, and when the Queen sent her private med-alchemist to visit him in his chambers, he wasted a good two hours assuring the man he suffered from nothing more serious than a burning need to finish his work. The man asked to see the object of his fixation, and Pelton attempted to describe the relationship of the miniature cogs to the tiny hammers, pins, fulcrums and levers. But the med-alchemist simply shook his head.

"My boy," he said, "of what possible use can these mechanical automations be, when with a few simple words I can achieve the same animation for a stone or a block of driftwood?"

Pelton looked at the piece in his palm. It was almost done, and it was a thing of beauty. Its wings were smooth and flawless, the wood grain fine and even, the amber insets and tiny silver legs glistening softy in the lanternglow. He toggled the release pin on its undercarriage, and the sliver of panel on its narrow back sprang up, exposing the miraculous and perfect innards of its works, finer and more delicate than anything he had ever made. He looked into the face of the other man, willing him to understand.

"S-s-s-ssometimes, even a f-f-few words are anything b-b-b-but simple," he told him.

The med-alchemist met his gaze and held it. He held it for a long time before reaching to place a hand on Pelton's shoulder. "All right, boy. I'll tell Her Majesty she has no cause to worry . . . and that there's no magicking to be done for you, unless it's to hasten the change from youth to man. No, no!" he laughed, seeing the look of interest flare in Pelton's eyes, "there's no such formula yet, though in this age of wonders, I wouldn't be surprised if there were one soon."

He turned to pack his bag and leave. "If only," he said, "I could feel as confident about my other patient. Martzel took to his chambers the very same night as did you, and he won't even let me past his door."

Pelton knocked on the thick planks of the necremist's door. "Martzel," he said, "P-p-please let me in. I've got s-something to sh-show you."

Receiving no answer, he reached into his pocket and pulled forth what looked like an unusually large beetle, practically the size of a man's fist. Glancing both directions along the corridor to make sure he was alone, Pelton held the beetle over the keyhole and gently stroked one of the creature's mandibles. Instantly, the legs clamped onto the door, digging themselves into the wood, scrabbling to straddle the doorknob and fix themselves around the lock. The carapace lifted, spread as though prepared for flight, exposing its spinning works. A whirring noise arose, and Pelton winced at the over-loud clatter as the picks descended from the beetle's proboscis, thrusting themselves into the iron keyhole and rattling in the lock. *That one needs a bit of finesse*, he thought, and vowed to work on it later. After this other business had been taken care of.

The lock tumbled, the beetle retracted its picks and its carapace. Pelton reached out in time to catch it as it detached itself from the wood and fell from the door. Pocketing the mechanical creature, he winced again to see the six fresh gouges in the ancient wood ringing the round iron flange of the doorknob's stem, like a halo of splintery stars.

Silently apologizing to whichever member of the Palace staff would be assigned to the repair, Pelton turned the knob and entered the chamber. The necremist was nowhere to be seen.

The place was considerably smaller than his own turret rooms, but just as considerably tidier. Martzel rivaled Pelton in his collection of books, but whereas Pelton tended to leave his in towering stacks and randomly-heaped piles, these stood in neat rows on dustless shelves, each encased in crisp white linen. Pelton examined the titles stenciled on each spine in a careful hand. He slid the nearest volume from the shelf. *Magickal Metallurgy for a Modern Age*, it read. Its neighbors were *Lepidopterics: a Study in Faunic Spagyrics*, and *Noteworthy Advances in the Quest for Aqua Vitae*.

Pelton eased the book back into its slot. His fingers brushed along the spine of the *Lepidopterics* title. Though he'd heard of the experimental use of lepidopteran ichors in transmutation and healing alchemies, he had not until that moment considered the study relevant to the recent deaths. Of the variety of theories he'd heard posed on the matter, divine retribution seemed the least likely and a localized imbalance of ecological humors the most. What man had not at some point witnessed the mysteries of nature? The wonders of man-made magicks and even his most complex mechanicals paled in comparison to the inscrutable workings of Earth and Sky and the beasts which dwelled between.

A sound made Pelton start. In the corner against the far wall he could just see the rounded edge of the toe of a man's boot and the dark, wool-draped shape of his leg rising from behind a tufted chair. He approached slowly, taking care to move in such a manner so as not to startle the man. "Martzel?" he said.

The boot scooted back even farther under the hem of the necro-alchemist's robe.

"Martzel? It's m-m-me. It's Pelton."

The man looked up. Pelton was shocked by his appearance. In the days since Pelton had seen him, the necremist had visibly withered. His complexion was sallow, wan, and the hollows of his eyes sat deeper than Pelton remembered. In all, he looked like a man who had not slept or eaten in a week. He looked like a man cursed, or haunted.

"I'm the last," he said, and buried his face in his hands.

Pelton pushed the chair aside and sat, cross-legged, on the floor beside Martzel. "I-is it the b-b-b-butterflies?" he asked.

Martzel groaned. He lowered his hands from his face and stared up at the high window of his room. Following the path of his gaze, Pelton could see the rectangle of beautiful azure summer sky, framed by whitewashed palace stone.

"Pelton, I swear to you, we didn't know. By Earth and Sky, we *did not know*."

"Martzel, why are the m-m-members of your Order c-coterie d-dying? Is there s-s-something you c-can tell me?"

The necremist closed his eyes. One hand stole to his chest, and Pelton could make out the shape of the Alchemist's Order medallion beneath the weave of the wool where his fingers rested. "Our initiation test. We were a brilliant group, so sure of ourselves. Several of us knew our places were already secured here at Court. We thought we could do anything. . . ."

Pelton smiled. "A t-talented man c-can accomplish alm-m-most anything."

Martzel smiled in return, but his smile was sad, and small. "Yes, Pelton. We'd already learned that mantra by heart. But just because a man can accomplish something, does it mean he should?" He paused, his face taut. "We thought to dazzle our superiors. We wanted to produce for our initiation exams something so spectacular, we would take our places at the head of a new generation of magickers: we would make a man fly!"

Pelton's face lit up. "Y-yes! I've b-b-been working on a s-similar idea! A machine of automated w-w-wings, a huge b-bird, w-which w-will carry a man across the sky as a sh-ship might b-b-bear him over the s-sea!"

Martzel shook his head. "No. No, and not some mere alchemically-levitating carriage. The King himself keeps a dozen such in the royal stables. And we certainly would never have considered mechanical automations."

Pelton's enthusiasm deflated at the tone of the last words. Even Martzel, whom he almost considered a friend, made clear his scorn for the gear-driven beasts of Pelton's imagination. He wished he could explain that the miraculous result of spring and key and hammer was as magical as any incantational alchemy practiced by the Orders.

"No, we wanted to *grow* a flying man; to orchestrate a creature which from birth would be as agile and as airborne and as beautiful as. . . ."

"A b-butterfly."

Martzel nodded. "Our opportunity came. We acquired a likely subject: a woman who, through an unfortunate carriage accident, had suffered an injury to the brain. Med-alchemists could not wake her, though her body lived. It was only a matter of time before even our alchemies would no longer be able to sustain her life. She was eight months with child."

The necro-alchemist's hands tightened to fists. Pelton saw the muscles in the man's throat tighten as well, the cords of his neck standing out as though he pulled a great weight.

"What reagent better suited to our purpose than lepidopteran ichors? We killed them by the thousands . . . the tens of thousands! Earth and Sky help us . . . the *hundreds of thousands*! We extracted their ichors and by alchemical means, fused the lepidopteran humors with those of the unborn child. It was madness."

"And the ch-ch-child? He f-f-flew?"

"She. No. Her mother did not survive the birth, despite our

efforts. The child never woke, though her body responded to feeding and care. She looked like any ordinary human child; our experiment had failed. Her eyes never opened, she never cried, never laughed. Cholland finally hired a woman to care for her, and we buried our shame, our guilt and our secret deep in the Dragonwood. Arrangements were made when I took my position at Court fifteen years ago. The last I saw of the child she was swaddled and silent in the arms of her nurse as the two of them were borne off into the trees."

Martzel sobbed openly. Pelton placed an arm about the necremist's shoulder and tried not to think of him as anything other than a man who, when young, had made a grave mistake. "It's p-p-probable she would never have b-been b-b-born, if you hadn't k-kept her mother al-l-live."

The necro-alchemist gazed at him through tears. "It would have been better, thus," he said. "Instead, our careless experiments gave rise to an unanimated shell with only the semblance of life: a thing alive, yet not living; neither completely formed human nor fully-realized beast, but some sad limbo of the two. And after all this time, it's as though the lepidoptera seek revenge for the murder of their kind." Martzel gripped the lapels of Pelton's jacket, the knuckles of his bony hands stark against the dark weave. "Or perhaps Earth and Sky punish us for our meddling. Did we reach too far in our arrogance? I'm the only one remaining of the original coterie."

Martzel released Pelton and rubbed his hands across his face. His eyes were red, his cheeks and brow pale and damp. His breathing came in ragged, agonized heavings from his chest. "If only I knew!" he said. "If I could make amends, right whatever wrongs I've committed! Set straight whatever force of Earth or Sky we bent in our pride and folly. . . ."

Pelton thought, but did not say aloud, that if a talented man set his mind to it, he could accomplish almost anything. "C-could you f-find this place in the D-Dragonwood where the child s-s-slumbers?"

Martzel shook his head. "Only Cholland knew. The rest of us who procured positions at Court refused to be told. We hid the event even from ourselves, hoping to forget, and in forgetting, believe it had never happened."

Pelton thought he could borrow one of the King's levitating carriages, and even a necro-alchemist should be able to form the proper incantations for its operation. He'd show Martzel his automaton and explain his idea when they were aloft. Martzel couldn't hide and wait for the butterflies to come for him, no matter what force drove their bizarre and fatal behavior. No, *he* had to go to *them*. The man said he wanted to make amends. And his recent confession seemed to have done him good; already, his face looked more human.

Pelton stood and brushed non-existent dust from the seat of his breeches. He held out his hand and helped the necremist to his feet. "Come," he said. "I have a p-p-plan."

The closer they got to the Dragonwood, the more buoyant their spirits became. Facing fears must be good for a man, Pelton decided. And action was always better than paralysis, though he didn't say that aloud. He'd not forgotten paralysis was the method of death for the other alchemists of Martzel's Order coterie. Paralysis of the lungs. Death by butterfly.

Instead, he closed the windows of the carriage, which sailed like thistledown across the plains and moors. Farms and freeholdings looked like children's toys from their vantage, people and their field beasts like slow-moving insects.

Pelton drew forth a small, cloth-covered box from his pocket. Carefully, he opened the lid, and when Martzel saw the unmoving thing inside, he snorted. "A mechanical," he said, disappointed. "If you could build thousands, perhaps they might fight off an attacking swarm. But what is this? Nothing more than a plaything."

Pelton reached to stroke the back of the butterfly, and it rose. Its smooth wood and amber wings beat with strokes too fast to follow with the human eye. It fluttered about the interior of the enclosed carriage, sometimes alighting on a cushion or window-ledge, finally coming to rest on Pelton's knee. Its wings slowed to a single beat every few moments, as might a living butterfly's, warming in summer sunshine. Even Pelton couldn't believe the thing ran on springs and coils, though he had built the works himself.

"N-n-no," he said, "It is so much m-m-more. A beacon! It s-seeks air p-p-patterns, responds to m-motions like its o-own. It will find large c-concentrations of other b-butterflies. B-b-battle's not always the only s-solution, nor the r-r-root of every c-conflict."

Pelton wanted to add that now was the time to face fears. He wanted to remind the necremist that he'd wanted to make amends. If his theories were correct, the recent deaths, the butterflies, and Martzel's guilt all stemmed from the same source. It was time to find that source, and do whatever they could to set things right.

He looked into Martzel's face, wondering how to convey so much within the limitations of his tripping tongue. But from the other man's expression he saw there was no need: his jaw was set, and his eyes were bright, alive.

The necremist leaned forward. "Open the window," he said.

It took even less time than Pelton had thought it would.

Martzel was able to direct the magicks of the carriage to follow the automaton, though he experimented with several words and phrases before stumbling upon the proper incantation: *secutus comitar machinatio*.

For some time, Pelton leaned far out the window, trying to keep in sight the beautiful creature he had made as it fluttered across the brilliant blue. But after his third near-tumble from the carriage, his headlong flight thwarted only by Martzel's quick thinking and a grab at his belt, he agreed to stay in his seat and let the magick do its work. He occupied himself by looking down into the forested depths of the Dragonwood, which rolled beneath them like a green and undulant ocean. When the carriage began to descend abruptly into the forest, he experienced a moment of alarm. He pictured them crashing down through branches, irreparably damaging their ride home and possibly outraging the ancient forest, not to mention his royal uncle.

Martzel, however, seemed unconcerned. It was his turn to lean out the window. Pelton heard him muttering alchemical incantations under his breath and felt the carriage respond to his directions like a plow-beast to a farmer's stick.

Slowly, gently, though branches and leaves brushed along all sides of their conveyance like the feathers of enormous birds, the carriage came to rest in a small clearing. Pelton unlatched the door and jumped down, feeling the solid ground beneath his boots with relief. He craned his neck, looking up at the canopy of the great forest. The trees were so ancient, so massive, their branches had all but obscured the clearing from above. Only a small aperture to open sky—roughly the size and shape of the smallest air-carriage in His Majesty's stables—allowed a bright shaft of sunlight past the green. Following the slant of the sun's rays down through the trees, Pelton saw the mottled thatch roof of a tiny, tidy cottage.

Pelton's automated butterfly was nowhere to be seen, but as he neared the cottage, he saw that what he had taken to be discolored thatch were actually the wings of butterflies, overlapping and intermingling. There were more butterflies clinging to the cottage roof than Pelton had pictured existing in the whole realm. As he neared, their thousands upon thousands of wings beat and whirled, as small tufts of living butterflies rose and fluttered in the air a moment before resettling down amongst the sedge and heather of the roof.

Pelton glanced over his shoulder at Martzel, afraid the man might lose heart at the sight of his potential assassins. But the other man's expression remained neutral, if slightly determined. Together they approached the cottage.

At Pelton's knock a small, wizened woman answered the

door. Her clothes were clean and of nice quality, though countrified and well out of fashion by Court standards. Her face was wrinkled and dark, like a baked cinnamon apple, and her eyes were kind. She curtsied low, but the necremist lifted her to her feet.

The woman smiled. She cocked her head to one side, squinting as though she viewed them from a distance. When she spoke, her voice had an odd lilt, its tones more those of a young girl than an ancient. She bobbed her head in Martzel's direction. "Sir Alchemist. I know you, though it has been some time. My Lord," she said, turning to Pelton, "you honor me. It has been long since I've had visitors. Provender is usually left by the door, though its absence of late did unsettle my mind." She stepped aside and motioned toward the dim cottage interior with one pale hand. "I beg," she said, her words coming almost as song rather than speech, "you will join me for honey tea."

As the old woman moved about the silent room, pouring hot water into cups of soft honey, Pelton's eyes adjusted to the low light. He noted the worn gentility of the fabrics on the settle; the cleanliness of the white stones of the hearth; the faint, pleasant scent of lavender and herbs, bundles of which hung tied with faded ribbons, dangling from the ceiling by small iron hooks. Martzel sat beside him. Pelton could feel unasked questions radiating from the man, almost sparking from him like charges from a lightning eel.

The old woman set a cup before each of her guests and sat. "With only the child to speak to," she said, "one rather forgets—"

Martzel went rigid. The old woman again cocked her head and viewed them askance. "Ahh, yes. Of course, you seek the child. The child, and the butterflies, as the one is never without the other. When she thirsts, they lead my hand to water. When they light upon food, I know her to hunger. And when she is lonely, they flutter about my head and show me no peace until I go to her and sing all the songs I have ever heard and tell all the tales I can ever think to tell, though her own tongue knows nothing but silence, poor thing. Silence, and sorrow, that one so lovely should be stillborn, and forever."

Martzel had become still as granite beside Pelton on the settle. Pelton leaned forward, drawing the old woman's gaze from his companion. "The child l-l-lives, though she n-never s-speaks?"

The woman set down her tea. "Aye, if such could be called living. In all these fifteen years and some, I have never seen her move, nor sing, nor speak. She lives on honey and water I feed her. When she opened her eyes for the first time some weeks ago, I rejoiced. . . . But her stare shows only the sky. I do not see even myself reflected in those depths when I cry over her at night. Only the butterflies speak, like a garrulous twin translating a mute twin's silence."

"Th-the b-b-butterflies speak?"

She laughed, a sound like glass bells. "Only in the way they do. I've come to understand their collective ways these past years, though they do not seem to understand mine. Perhaps they cannot. See."

She stood and crossed to a small door at the back of the room, crooking one finger in the direction of the men by the hearth as though she could drag them along behind her stooped form by invisible string.

Martzel jolted to his feet and stumbled after her, moving like an ill-made automaton. Pelton followed, and when they reached her side she smiled again, more broadly this time, and turned the knob beneath her hand. The door swung silently inward, and Pelton blinked against the brightness of the room after the cool dark of the rest of the cottage. When his eyes adjusted, he could make out the chamber. The rear wall slanted away, built completely of windows, open so the angled beam of sunlight he had seen piercing the canopy of the forest outside shone down directly into the room and illuminated the sparse furnishings and simple white walls with an almost blinding brilliance.

On the bed lay a figure draped in what Pelton first thought was the most wondrous gown he had ever seen. Its fabric—

somewhere between the finest-spun silk and the softest iridescent velvet—was a shimmering field of impossible blue. Such a simple word as *blue* didn't do that color justice, thought Pelton; but neither did any other word or hue he had ever heard or experienced. It was bluer than sky, bluer than ocean, bluer than sorrow.

He stepped to the edge of the bed. The blue fabric fractured itself into hundreds of butterflies, which fluttered, lifted themselves and engulfed him as he stood still, letting their antennae and the edges of their wings brush against his lips, his cheeks, the lashes of his eyes. After a moment, the azure cloud rose. The creatures wheeled as one, ascending through the open window above and dissipating into the single patch of sky. Looking down, Pelton saw the occupant of the bed, her gown now a simple thing of white linen, her black silken hair falling away to both sides of her pale face and spilling onto the floor about her form like an enormous split cocoon spun of midnight. Upon her throat rested the tiny creature of wood and metal that he had built. Its polished, amber-tipped wings pumped in a lazy motion, keeping time with the movement of the girl's pulse beneath its little silver feet.

Pelton felt the others behind him. The room was so quiet he was sure he heard the beats of their hearts, though his own sounded as thunder in his ears. Leaning across the inert form before him, he held his finger above the automaton. The mechanical butterfly fluttered the few inches from the girl's neck to alight on his outstretched finger, and when it did, the girl turned her head to follow its flight and met Pelton's gaze with her own.

Pelton heard the sharp intake of breath from the old woman at the door. In her peculiar sing-song lilt, the woman began to croon a prayer to Earth and Sky, while whispered words of apology or appeal began to trickle, then gush from Martzel's throat as the man fell to his knees.

But the girl looked only at Pelton, though nothing showed in her eyes but the blue they were.

"Did the little ones tell them? Did they tell the Makers?" she said. Her voice was soft, like finest vellum brushed with dry feathers.

Pelton found he was holding his breath. He exhaled as slowly and quietly as he could. "The b-butterflies have been k-killing alchemists," he said.

The girl frowned, the translucent skin about her arched brows sliding into hitherto untraveled planes. "My wings," she said. "They've just been trying to explain: they gave me everything else, but I have no wings."

The mechanical creature on Pelton's finger rose. Following the flight of its thousands of living fellows, it wheeled up and out of the open window, making for the sun.

Pelton looked down into the eyes of the girl on the bed. Blue, blue, blue they were: bluer than sky, bluer than ocean, bluer than sorrow.

"I think I can fix that," he said.

The Italian

In my dreams, I flew.

I'd never pole vaulted in waking life. But for the past thirty-two months, three weeks and two days, in dreams I vaulted over pit and crowd and sky at the end of a pole. At night, the slender stalk of aluminum and fiberglass in my chalky grip planted itself—an extension of my spine and lungs and the muscles of my arms—in the ground and shot me through the air, and I flew. Beneath, the garish motley of spectators in over-bright tee-shirts undulated. All sound ceased except the pumping of my heart. The zenith moment was not brief, but elastic, sustained. My body hung suspended, in absolute success and physical perfectitude, without weight.

And then I would twist and fall. When my back slammed into the mat I would wake, gasping with the impact: crying, struggling upright, sucking breaths between sobs.

John would quiet my flailings, my beating heart, my despair. Often, neither of us could return to sleep. He'd lift me into my chair and wheel me to the kitchen. He'd make coffee, and dawn would creep across the sky, apologetic.

When John assured himself I was fine, he would wheel my chair into the den, where I spent mornings reading while he took his own wheels—the beautiful Italian bicycle he loved as much as he loved me—and they would ride the fresh morning trails together amid the dewdrops and the opening petals of wildflowers. That was their romance: dew and flowers and unfettered sunshine.

At dinner John served salad, then poured me another glass of wine.

His bicycle leaned against the dining room wall. He claimed it was easier to wheel it here, through the sliding-glass patio doors, than take it all the way around to the garage. Sometimes he forgot to put it away, and at night, when I wasn't sailing through the sky at the end of a pole, I could hear the bicycle all the way from my bedroom.

"You all right, Catherine?" asked John. "The anniversary's coming up, but it's been nearly three years. I'd hoped. . . ."

"Thirty-two months, three weeks and three days," I said.

He reached across the table and placed his hand over mine. "It was nobody's fault," he said. "Just an accident. A stupid, horrible accident."

I looked at the rumpled napkin in my lap, corners sticking out like the wings of broken doves. "I didn't mention fault," I said.

John hadn't driven in thirty-two months, three weeks and three days. Nothing, since the crash, but the bicycle. I turned my head to watch it lean against the wall. My chair looked stocky and reliable next to the Italian's streamlined curves.

After dinner, John wheeled me to bed. He helped me undress and laid the sheets across my body; across the thick dead logs of my legs. He and the Italian went for an evening ride; "Just a turn about the field," he said.

They left by the dining room patio door. Even from the bedroom, I heard the click of the latch. My chair sat by the window, motionless, staring in the direction of my departing husband and his wheels.

That night I woke gasping for breath into darkness, clutching my breast with the hand which moments before had gripped the slender tower of fiberglass and vaulted me high above the bar like a rocket, like a shot, like a meteorite.

My breathing calmed. The beats of my heart resumed their ordinary rhythm. The scent of freedom and success faded from my nostrils and I lay quiet.

I saw the outline of John's body in the dark. He faced away, his breathing unhurried. The window, where my chair usually waited, was vacant.

I closed my eyes and listened. I could hear my chair in the dining room by the sliding patio doors, its rubber wheels pressed against the glass.

Without waking John I rolled myself onto the floor. I'd felt nothing below the waist for nearly thirty-two months, three weeks and four days. If there were going to be bruises, they wouldn't pain me. If bits of floor dragged and scraped my thighs where my nightgown rode up, I might bleed but unless I looked, I wouldn't know.

My palms were tingly and raw by the time I reached the dining room. My shoulders ached. By moonlight filtering in the patio doors I saw the spokes of my wheels and those of the Italian, glinting, side by side.

The last few feet were the hardest. It took me a moment to catch my breath, but the wheels were patient, and silent.

I fumbled open the lock on the sliding door, pressed both palms against the glass, and thrust it as wide as I could. My chair bounced back from the rough motion. The Italian shuddered, but didn't fall.

The screen was light, and easy to slide aside. The wheels trembled on the threshold, then the Italian shot past and sped to the edge of the yard, where it hesitated. My chair, heavy and safe, waited.

"Go," I said. "It's all right, really."

The chair bumped over the aluminum threshold and rolled across the night-soaked grasses and curled-up leaves of clover to stand beside the Italian. They then wheeled as one, veered away, and I soon lost sight of them in the tall growth of the field behind the house.

Rather than drag myself back to bed, I slept slumped against the wall. This time, when the pole cracked the whip of itself and vaulted me above the crowd, I flew higher than ever.

I spread my arms. My body soared over countryside and the sprinklings of cities. Flattened against invisible currents, I watched anonymous landscape pass below, patchwork cornfields and the mottled greens of forest. On the edge of the horizon near the rising sun I caught the twinkle of spokes, spinning across the earth as I shot, unapologetic, across the sky.

The Clone Wrangler's Bride

"*Thirty-two non-planetary standard seconds to critical impact.*"

Matty Johnson swore as she pounded the control panel in a windmilling motion of frustration and rage, her fists and long red braids flying. "Star-blasted piece of spaceturd! Avoid! Avoid, dang you!"

"*Unable to avoid asteroidal collision due to prior damage sustained. Recommend life pod launch. Pod launch sequence activated.*" The ship's computer voice paused. It made a sound like a hiccup, or a tiny electrical sob with no emotion. "*Nineteen seconds to critical impact.*"

Matty swiveled to face the mandroid sitting in the next seat. "You!" she said. It turned its expressionless silver face toward her. Its unblinking eyes were like large golden marbles. "You! Do something. You're supposed to see I get safe to Mars Dometown Eye-Vee! Do something!"

"*Fifteen non-planetary standard seconds to critical impact. Pod launch in ten . . .*"

Matty and the mandroid stared at each other.

"*Nine . . .*"

Until then, the Echo 3000 Series Fully Automated Mandroid had moved with a shuffling, gangly slowness that had driven Matty to the verge of several verbose rages. Now, its right upper appendage moved lightning-quick, flashing like a hopped up muleskinner's knife, slicing through her seat harness as though it were butter.

"*Eight. . .*"

"Oof!" said Matty as the Echo 3000 flew past her seat, taking Matty with it in a tackle that would have earned any steer wrangler back home his rodeo buckle.

"*Seven . . .*"

"Wait!" screamed Matty as she and the mandroid sailed through the air into the open life pod behind her and the hatch began to spiral shut. "My dowry! I need my dow—"

"*Six . . .*"

"—ry!" She jabbed a slender finger repeatedly in the direction of the velvetite satchel slung over the back of her chair by the control panel.

"*Five . . .*"

The Echo 3000 cracked its left upper appendage like a telescoping whip. It lashed through the diminishing pinwheel opening between the life pod and the small ship.

"*Four . . .*"

The Echo 3000's appendage, wrapped around the small velvetite bag, whipped back through the opening just as the hatch swirled shut and the life pod's shields locked into place.

"*Three . . .*"

"Dang-it-all to a wormhole's anus! My best hat's back there on the floor by the control panel. Dang!"

"*Two . . .*"

The mandroid and the woman stared at each other, one's lash-fringed brown eyes with the nigh permanent scowl above meeting the smooth, golden, mercury-cool orbs of the other.

"*One.*"

Matty barely had time to press herself hard into the automolding foam behind her and grip tight the straps on each side of her head next to her red braids.

"Dang," she said, as the whole world went blacker than a wormhole's anus.

Matty opened her eyes to hot, dusty, and red.

The Echo 3000 sat nearby on the rocky sand, its two lower

appendages folded in the spot that would have been its knees had it been human. Without speaking, it reached over and dabbed a damp, neatly pleated cloth onto her forehead.

"We made it," said Matty, though her voice croaked out of her like a bullfrog's after an all night rut.

The mandroid unclipped a canteen from the belt slung low across its chestbox. It unscrewed the top and held the thing to Matty's lips. She slurped a few slurps, letting the water slide down her throat. "Thanks," she said, but the mandroid simply stared, then recapped the canteen and clicked it back onto its tubular middle.

Matty struggled to a sitting position. Beyond the temporary emergency bubble tent lay the mangled, blackened wreck of the life pod, the trail of its landing stretching back as far as the eye could see like a big lumpy scar on the rusty plain.

Matty snorted. "Well shoot; this don't look too different from back home, excepting it's a tad redder, and my arms and legs feel like they got little balloons in there, 'stead of blood and bone. And double-dang, but my head feels sore: feels like my cranium met the business end of a prize bull."

The mandroid sat on its folded appendages and met her gaze with its unwavering globes of gold. Silent, it offered her the small velvetite satchel.

"My dowry! Thanks, erm . . . do I call you Mister 3000? Manny Droid?" Matty regarded the mandroid as she stretched out first one leg, then the other, massaging the muscles of her calves with hard-knuckled fingers. "I'll just call you Echo, then. Thanks, Echo, for my bag and my life and all."

The mandroid's appendage reached behind its silver body and brought forth a breathing helmet for Matty's pressure suit, standard life pod issue. It handed that to her as well. She nodded her thanks and set both things in the sand.

Matty stood as much as she was able within the confines of the tiny clear dome, scrunching her neck down onto her shoulders. Reaching her arms out to her sides, she could almost touch her fingertips to the smooth surface of the temporary plasti-shield. Sighing, she plopped cross-legged onto the ground in the dust next to the helmet and the velvetite satchel. The bottom edges of the dome hummed where the barrier fields met the surface of the planet, their emergency seals decaying by the minute.

"So, Echo. What's next? How do you plan to do what my Daddy bought you for and get me to my wedding day?"

The mandoid sat; silent, rigid. The life pod medi-kit and the bit of damp gauze the Echo 3000 had used to wipe Matty's brow lay beside its folded lower appendages. The dust around the gauze formed a little ring, as the dry soil sucked the moisture from the fabric.

Matty sighed. "Look, Echo, I'm going to need your help if'n we're going to get me to the altar. I know, I know," she held up a hand as though to halt any forthcoming argument, "Daddy done arranged this whole thing his own self and neither you nor I had not a hoot nor a holler to say about it. We both been bought and sold; me to wife for some back planet clone wrangler and you to get me delivered to him like a sack of planting potatoes. But Echo, we got to make the best out of life, and I plan to make the best out o' mine. So can you help me?"

Silence fell heavier in the tiny dome than a boulder off a cliff into a dry gully. Matty sat. The mandroid sat. Matty sighed.

"Echo, if you can't talk, this is going to be a long, long, sad-long day. Can't you speak to me? Can't you say anything? Anything at all?"

A noise like the sound of tiny tin butterflies fluttered in the chestbox of the Echo 3000. The noise got scrabblier and scrabblier, like that bunch of little butterfly feet and butterfly wings were scrabbling against the insides of the metal man. The noise rumbled from its chestbox, up through the cylinder of its throat and into the region of its smooth metal mouth. Finally, it spoke.

"Yes, Matilda Johnson."

* * *

Matty turned to look back the way they had come. The slug-like trail of her shuffling, big-booted footsteps and the jagged ridges left by the mandroid's appendages sliced back across the dusty plain, clear and sharp and almost painful in their singularity upon the vast empty sweep of red desert and dust and rock. The mangled pod and its landing trail were far behind them now, not visible as even a fly speck on a bubble dome.

Matty lifted her gloved hand to scratch at the rim of the helmet where it fused onto the neck of her pressure suit. The best she managed was a couple bangs on the plasti-matter near the rim seal. The dome of the helmet rang when she rapped on it, dull and thunky like the sound of a cracked church bell. "Dang it!" she said. She half turned to look at the mandroid trudging beside her. The suit and breathing helmet made her motions stilted, difficult.

"I mean, it's great the pod had all its breathing equipment and stuff, 'cause we sure didn't plan for no crash landing, right? But Echo, I tell you, this mother's itch-freakin'-y. It's itchier than a wormhole's—"

"Yes, Matilda Johnson."

"Echo! I told you eight million times; Matty. M-a-t-t-y. A body can't help what her parents name her, but she sure can dump the parts she don't like, if she's a mind to. If you're so set on the Johnson, well I suppose I can live with that, though you'll have to get it through your thick metal brainpan my name's probably going to change when I get hitched for good. I know my suit-com's working, so I know you hear what I'm saying. Cantrell: I'm going to be Missus Matty Cantrell by this time tomorrow, and don't you forget it. You hear?"

"Yes, Matilda Johnson."

"Gah!" Matty kicked a large pebble with the rim of her oversized boot. It spun from the rounded toe and glanced, hard, off the thick lower appendage of the mandroid. "Matty!" she said. "M, a, t, t, y!"

"Yes, Matil—"

"Don't you dare!"

The Echo 3000 fell silent. So did Matty, though her silence was broken by the huffing wheezes of her annoyance and by her periodic grumbled curses, too low to be adequately relayed by her suit-com's pickup.

Another hour passed in silence and dust.

Matty slurped on the recirculation tubes of her suit, drawing her own stale fluids back into her mouth. "I just got to pretend this is plain old water, Echo, or I'll just go crazy with the gross-out. So, I'm drinking pure fresh Earthside mountain water from the tube in this suit, right, Echo?"

The mandroid seemed to hesitate. It slid a golden-orbed glance at the woman by its side. "Yes, Matilda Johnson," it said.

Everybody walked on and nobody said anything. Another hour passed in more silence and a whole lot more dust. The landscape gradually began to change. Every once in a while, a huge, flat-topped boulder rose from the edge of a rocky dune. In other places the ground was riddled with holes, some smaller around than a woman's clenched fist, some big enough for a mandroid to fall into if it wasn't careful, and all of them deep enough to show nothing but the darkest blackness, like little wells of hot tar, or puddles of starless space.

"Echo?" said Matty. The mandroid turned its chestbox and head to face her, but neither slowed their forward motion. "Echo, you sure this is the right direction to Dometown Eye-Vee?"

"Yes, Matilda Johnson."

Matty scowled out past the smudgy clear curve of her helmet's breathing dome. "And you're sure we're not nearer to Dometown Eye-Eye, or Dometown Ecks? Eye-Vee is the closest one?"

"Yes, Matilda Johnson."

"Well. Well okay, then. If you're positive. I just thought maybe—"

A rubbery tentacle, supple as the whip-like attachment of the mandroid's upper appendage and just as quick, shot from the hole nearest Matty's foot and wrapped itself about her ankle. A quick tug, and Matty toppled heavily to the ground. She clasped the velvetite satchel to her chest with one hand and began to beat her suit-gauntleted fist against the tentacle on her ankle with the other.

Tentacles of varying thicknesses and shades of dull, oily green began to emerge from the holes littering the ground, which looked like a giant, rusty-red prairie dog field.

"Get off! Get off me you dang, you dang—"

Matty's curse ended in a sound most approximated by the phonetic utterance "eep," as a larger, oilier tentacle slapped and slimed its way across the field of her vision. Inches from her face, held off only by the thin plasti-matter of her helmet, the underside of the soft-suckered tentacle undulated and writhed, as dozens of tiny, rubber-like rings spasmed repeatedly against the slick surface, trying to gain purchase.

Whip-like tentacles shot from at least a dozen more holes. The soft wet plopping sounds of tentacles sucking at the surface of the Echo 3000's metal shell gave way to high-pitched squeals, as the mandroid unsheathed its blades from the ends of its upper appendages. The blades twirled in circular motions, faster and faster, slicing like sawblades through the green gristly limbs and the rubber rings of suckers, which flew to all sides from the mandroid like coins tossed to bare-breasted revelers at Venusian Mardi Gras. Dark, oily ichor rained to the red dust in splatter patterns like so many broken strands of gaudy beads.

"Get your dang-dunged sucker-punchers offa me!" roared Matty. One-handedly, she beat at the largest tentacle until it slid from the face of her helmet with an audible hiss. Kicking, she managed to bring the heel of her boot down against the tentacle wrapped about her other ankle sharply enough that she heard the wet, slick splosh*pop!* as the thing ruptured under the force of the blow.

Scrambling to her feet, she saw the Echo 3000 several yards away. All around, slick, rubbery, squid-like appendages writhed, rising from the dozens of holes in the ground like enormous, rotten stalks of overcooked asparagus. They wiggled, soaring straight up, impossibly high. To Matty's Earth-gravity-trained eye, they seemed to defy the laws of the natural universe. They looked like a massive, slimy forest of tubular Earthside seaweed, forced straight up through saltwater by the fiery heat of the planet's core to dance by the glow of underwater volcanoes. At the center of the writhing oily mass glinted the ichor-stained silver of the mandroid and its whirling gore-slick blades.

"Echo!" yelled Matty, but as she stepped toward the oily-asparagus forest, the tentacles began to recoil, whipping back into the black holes in the ground like so much slurped spaghetti.

In mere moments, Matty and the mandroid stood alone on the plain. The once-dry dust and gently-pebbled slopes seemed even stiller than before. The dark green fluid arcing in twisting splatters away from the mandroid began to congeal, to coalesce into little globs and rivulets and to slither toward the nearest holes.

Matty ran to the side of the solitary metal figure. With the hand not gripping the velvetite bag, she reached to encircle one of the mandroid's upper appendages, exactly where the wrist would have been on a man. She carefully avoided the unmoving blades at the end of the segmented metal. "C'mon, Echo. Let's blast out of here before those prairie squid get their turds together and come back for round two."

Matty gulped the stale, recirculated breath inside her suit. She watched the slime on the mandroid's chestbox, which, like the stuff on the ground, seemed to seek itself out, running together in thicker and thicker rivulets as it trickled to the planet surface, until the holes scattered about them brimmed with pulsing arteries of living ooze.

"Echo," said Matty again. The mandroid's golden orbs rotated and clicked once, the mechanical equivalent of a blink, and the blades at the ends of its upper appendages slowly retracted into their sheaths. "Let's go," she said, gently tugging the mandroid's appendage.

The Echo 3000 stumbled after Matty. With every step they took, little beads of gore and slime fell from their bodies like drops of viscous black rain and rolled, slithering in the gullies of their footsteps, back the way they had come. After Matty could no longer see the holes in the ground when she glanced over her shoulder at the plain behind them; after her chest stopped almost visibly thumping with the beat of her own heart; after she lost her initial gratitude for the flat, metallic, recycled water from her suit's drinking tube; after all that, the mandroid halted, and Matty with it. It lifted its appendage between them, holding it aloft so Matty could see her own fingers still encircling it just above the telescoping digits at the end.

Matty reddened and dropped the appendage as though it burned her through the hyper-metal of her pressure suit. "What? Never held hands with a girl before? Jeesh, Echo."

Matty whirled as best she could in the stiff, crinkled confines of her ungainly suit. Her long red braids thumped against the inside of her domed helmet as they flopped outward with the force of her motion. She stomped through the dust and the red and the dimming light, not looking back to see whether the mandroid followed.

"Jeesh!" she muttered again, and then louder, "you are one kooky mandroid, Echo. You know that?"

The com-speaker of her suit crackled, but Matty didn't slow her march nor turn to look behind her. The sky ahead was deepening to a purple hazy glow, and the ridge she had been using as her navigational guide looked farther away than ever.

Her com-speaker crackled again, and then: "Yes, Matilda Johnson."

Matty and the Echo 3000 camped that night on top of a large, flat rock. "Find me a place to sleep with no dang-dunged holes in it," Matty had said, and the mandroid had complied.

Matty lay stretched out, back flat against the smooth, massive rock underneath. She clasped her hands behind her neck and pillowed her head awkwardly against the firm convex shell of her suit's helmet.

"Echo," said Matty, "I know it's just my imagination, this suit being rated to stand four times this temperature up and down, but I swear; lying here, looking up at this big old wide sky with nothing for a blanket but a blanket of stars, and nothing beneath me but the surface of a living planet; I swear I can feel the warmth of this old rock leaching up into my bones. It's just like when I was a little girl; there was a rock pert'near exactly like this one at Old Man Miller's pond."

The mandroid, which had been standing at the edge of the rock facing the direction of their destination for twenty-six non-planetary standard minutes, turned its attention to the girl on the ground.

"Yessir, Echo. We'd go swimming in the millpond all day long, 'til our toes were ice and our lips were blue. And then, when we was so wrinkled up you might of thought our fingers was gen-modified albino prune sticks, we would all lay out flat against that old limestone sun rock, and all the day's heat would just soak into our skin like we was johnnycakes on a big, warm skillet. Yessir, just like that . . . ."

The mandroid folded its lower appendages, positioning itself so one golden orb could swivel toward the horizon. The other orb swiveled to focus on the prone form of the girl, small and rumpled, her lightly freckled face glowing pale in the abundant starlight.

Matty sighed. Her eyes drifted shut. When she spoke, it was with the slow, dreamy drawl of a tired country girl on the cusp of sleep. Her accent thickened, as it tended to do in anger or stress, or in unguarded moments. "Yep. Haven't been to Old Man Miller's pond for years . . . . Nope. Always thought I wanted to go pond dipping once more before I died. But there's no ponds on Mars, that's for danged sure."

Matty's glove-clad fingers wriggled from their position beneath her head just enough to stroke the velvetite bag, the cord of which she'd wrapped about her wrist so she could grip it, even in sleep. She sighed, and the sound transmitted over the suit-com like a rustling of summer leaves. "But Daddy needed the money; needed the money for them new gen-modified cows they all got up out there these days. You know, them ones with the four hundred and sumpin'-sumpin' teats and all those udders? Those ones." She opened one eye and squinted up through the starlit dark at the silhouette of the mandroid. "You know them ones I mean, Echo?"

Both golden orbs swiveled to fix on the girl's face. "Yes, Matilda Johnson."

Matty nodded and re-nestled her head inside her suit's helmet. "And tomorrow—wait, we get to Dometown Eye-Vee tomorrow, right?"

"Yes, Matilda Johnson."

The girl reclosed her eyes. "Good, 'cause I'm hungry enough to eat me some slimy old squid asparagus stalks." She smiled, eyes still closed. "Well . . . maybe not quite that hungry yet." Her smile faded. "So Daddy gets his cows, and the Eye-Vee clone wranglers get their new power-mod generator," her fingers wriggled again against the velvetite satchel, "and tomorrow, I get me a new husband: youngest son of the youngest son of the richest man in the twelve Dometowns of Mars. I figure the youngest's youngest won't be so rich, but that's just fine with me. There's more important stuff than security and money credits and clone farms and over-teated cows, Echo, you know what I'm saying?"

"Yes, Matilda Johnson."

Matty's face relaxed. The fingers of her hyper-metal gloves curled slightly to accommodate the positions of the living flesh inside. Matty's mouth looked soft and full, a little slack, like that of a sleepy toddler. When she spoke, it was so softly, the pickup of her suit-com barely registered her words. "Echo. . . ."

"Yes, Matilda Johnson."

"There *is* more important stuff, right. . . ."

Light snores from the suit's occupant transmitted to the mandroid's receivers.

"Yes, Matilda Johnson," said the mandroid, but not before turning its volume way down, so as not to wake the sleeping girl.

"Dang-dung, Echo; that may not be the prettiest sight I ever seen, but it sure is the most welcome." Matty shielded her eyes against the glare of full Martian day. The hyper-metal of her gauntlets cast dark shadows across her face beneath the smudged plasti-matter of the helmet's breathing dome. Both girl and mandroid stood at the crest of the rise, staring down into the wide, shallow crater at the sprawling collection of dome-covered buildings. Hamster trail plasti-matter passageways connected the haphazard array of impermanent-looking corrugated structures and rickety, bubble-domed sheds. Grey, bilious smoke pumped through the semi-permeable seals at the tops of the smokestacks, which rose like thick, dull church steeples from the roofs of the clone vats.

"I seen pictures of Dometown Eye, which everybody's starting to call Dome City nowadays. It looked kind of nice, with hanging gardens and paved streets. But this. . . ."

Matty dropped the arm shielding her eyes. She looked up into the smooth, blank face of the mandroid. Both its golden orbs swiveled to meet her gaze. Matty turned to squint again at the squalid sprawl in the crater below, and she bit her lip. She bit so hard, a tiny trickle of blood appeared at the corner of her mouth, and when she reached to wipe it away, her gauntlet banged into the plasti-matter of her helmet. She let her arm drop and licked at the corner of her mouth instead, and squinted some more at her future home.

Something tickled, tentative, at the wrist of her suit above the cuff of her gauntlet. Looking down, Matty saw the telescoping digits at the end of one of the mandroid's upper appendages encircle her wrist, just as she had clasped it after the fight with the prairie squid. Matty twisted her hand to hold the mandroid's metal digits. Hand in appendage, they turned and descended to the town below.

At the fourth building Matty banged on with her fist, a face flickered onto the vid-screen panel inset by the door. The man on the screen was skinny, and unshaven. He had the sallow cheeks and pinched features of a third generation clone. His ten gallon hat loomed over his bulbous forehead like a gen-modified buffalo perched atop an unripe cantaloupe.

"Yeah?" said the man. "Where'd you come from? We don't want none."

Matty opened her mouth to speak, but the vid-screen blinked off.

"Hey!" Matty let go of the mandroid's digits and used both fists to pound on the door. ""Hey! I'm coming to marry the youngest Mister Cantrell. Hey! I think it's my wedding day, so you better open up in there!" Matty kicked the base of the door and the vid-screen winked back to life.

The clone in the ten gallon goggled at Matty from the vid-screen. "Did you say you came for Mister Cantrell? You have the new power-mod generator? For real and for serious?"

Matty lifted the velvetite bag and shoved it against the vid-screen. "I got it right here, now open up."

Matty and the mandroid waited for several minutes. Around them, figures scuttled through the tubes connecting the scattered buildings like piers in an Earthside wharf town. The plasti-matter of the covered passageways was pitted and scarred; outsides abraded and made opaque by the basalt sands of the desert planet, insides smudgy from the oil and sweat of a hundred human palms, smeared across their surfaces a thousand times. The figures scuttling through them now sounded like giant cockroaches running from a kitchen's overhead light.

When the door swung open, Matty and the mandroid stumbled into the airlock chamber. Matty turned and shut the massive metal hatch behind her, and the mandroid helped her crank the wheel until the green light appeared above the doorway. Matty scrabbled at the neck of her suit, but the Echo 3000 gently brushed aside her trembling fingers from the release clasps and removed the plasti-matter helmet from her head.

Matty heaved air into her lungs. She bent over, hands on her knees, and vomited just as the youngest son of the youngest son of the richest man in the twelve domed towns of Mars stepped into the room. She only narrowly avoided splattering his shoes.

Matty heaved once more, then spat two or three times and steadied herself with a hand on the mandroid's chestbox. It stood, her suit helmet tucked under one appendage, the other telescoping appendage lightly holding the ends of her braids where they would be safe from her spew. She wiped the back of her gauntlet across her mouth, and for the first time tasted the salty, tangy, blood-like flavor of the dust of Mars.

"I take it you're the courier from Earth. You have the power-mod generator?"

Matty looked into the pale, watery blue eyes of her betrothed. "Are you the youngest Mister Cantrell? If so, I'm your future wife. Pleased to make your acquaintance." Matty wiped her gauntlet on the crumpled hyper-metal of her suit covering her thigh and held out her hand. Her other hand rose to tip the brim of the hat she always wore, but encountering nothing on her head, smoothed back the red tendrils escaping from her braids, instead.

The youngest Mister Cantrell eyed Matty's extended hand as though it were a rattlesnake, only, as though it were the most boring rattlesnake in the universe. A rattlesnake so boring, even being afraid of it was boring.

The hallway behind the youngest Mister Cantrell was crammed with man-bodies. Lots and lots and lots of man-bodies. Matty could smell her own self, her scent rising up from the neck of her suit, mingling with fifty times re-drunk water and a thousand times re-breathed air. She could smell the iron salt of Mars from the dust on her tongue, and she could smell the sharp tang of sun-heated metal, her suit and the exterior shell of the mandroid. But most of all, she could smell the decades-long smell of bored men, and the slightly sweet, artificial smell of the cloned tissue of the hundred bodies out in the hall. She only just then began to notice they all had the same dishwater eyes and unripe cantaloupe foreheads of the man before her.

The youngest son of the youngest son reached out, not to take Matty's suspended hand, but to point to the velvetite satchel at her side. "Is that my power-mod generator?" he said. "I believe it's been paid for, with five hundred clones of the most current gen-modified cows available, with a guaranteed minimum of four hundred and twenty-one milk-producing teats per."

Matty's hand dropped to dangle limply in its glove. She slid the satchel from her shoulder, lifting its strap over her head and handing the bag to her betrothed. "If we're to wed, I don't rightly figure how things between us have to be bought and sold," she said.

The young man rolled his eyes. "That oldfangled Earthside conceit? Our negotiator said he had to offer the generator's courier permanent residency at the compound, though I don't know what we'd do with a woman around here. Now that," he pointed his chin at the Echo 3000, "we do have need for. A conveyer belt in section twelve needs some new parts, and I think that mandroid might contain a few bits and bobs we could use for repairs."

Matty opened her mouth, but shut it again. The young man turned his attention to the satchel, and ran one ragged fingernail along the edge of the zipseal. He gingerly pulled forth a squat cylinder, its gunmetal grey glinting dully in the stifled light of the small room.

A collective sigh ran through the ocean of similar faces lining the hallway behind the youngest Mister Cantrell. Only the hats visibly differed from man to man. It was as though each tried to imbue his hat with all the individual personality of a living entity. Some ten gallons rode high and wide, like the prows of ocean liners. Some sat cocked to one side or the other. Some, ludicrously small, rode the crests of bulbous cloned foreheads like fishing lures bobbing on Old Man Miller's pond.

"But I've come to get married. I've come to settle here, build a life. . . ." Matty's voice was small, soft.

The young man replaced the cylinder in the velvetite bag,

and a collective groan ran up and down the edges of the long hallway behind him. "Yes, yes," he said with a dismissive flutter of his fingers. "We've got the papers, and my lawman already has all my necessary signatures. Once you sign, our transaction will be legally concluded, and you can do whatever you want. I'll keep the mandroid for parts, if it's just the same with you."

Matty glanced out of the corner of her eye at the Echo 3000. It stood behind her left shoulder, rigid, silent. The tip of one of its appendages rested so lightly against her hip, she hadn't noticed its presence until she looked down and saw it there.

"No, it is not just the same with me." Matty clasped the end of the Echo 3000's appendage. She felt its telescoping digits intertwine with her fingers. "In fact, this whole deal's a bum . . . deal. If you're not interested in me, I'll just sign your dad-gummed papers and Echo here and I'll go set ourselves up at Dome City."

The young man handed the velvetite satchel to the clone behind him in the perched-buffalo hat. "That sounds like an excellent plan. With our new power-mod generator, I'm sure we could spare some supplies, as a courtesy. And with your mandroid, you'll have no trouble getting to Dometown Prime. Dometown Four and Dometown Prime are only two days' walking distance."

The crowd began to shuffle in the hall behind the young man. Their hats bobbled and jostled against each other and around each other like decorated tumbleweeds rolling around a melon-headed desert.

"Wait!" said Matty as the young man turned away. "Maybe I'm at the wrong place? I'm supposed to be at Dometown Eye-Vee, and I'm supposed to get married. And I can't go back home, so I've got to make the best of things here, if this is where I'm supposed to be."

Slowly, in a manner which clearly indicated his extreme boredom, the youngest son of the youngest son of the richest man in the twelve domed towns of Mars pivoted on one booted heel.

"This is Dometown Four," he said, pointing above his head to the big roman numeral on the wall above the airlock entry: IV.

"After those papers are signed, you're fee to go wherever you want." He snapped his fingers and the lawman at his elbow handed him a thick ream of papers, which he then handed to Matty. "I can hardly be blamed if you arrived here laboring under a misunderstanding of the nature of our transaction. I don't have the slightest notion where you are *supposed* to be, and this is as good as things get around here."

With that he turned, and the milling ocean of near-identical faces behind him parted, then flowed shut in his wake as he passed. When every last hat-wearing clone had filtered from the hall and all that remained was the lawman and Matty and the Echo 3000, the lawman handed her a pen.

Matty signed each and every indicated section on every single page of the four hundred and fourteen page document. ("What," she had muttered midway through the proceedings, "they got one page per cow teat?") The Echo 3000 bent into a table so she could rest her arms against its solid back as she signed. When her hand cramped, the Echo 3000 slid it from her glove and gently massaged her palm until the pain melted and the tingling stopped. When the lawman began to tap the toe of his boot in ill-concealed impatience, the Echo 3000 fixed him with a beady, unblinking, golden-orbed stare, until the man cleared his throat and looked away. And when Matty was done, the mandroid stood behind her and let her small, rumpled body lean against it. She sagged so low, she wouldn't have kept upright had it not been for the firm metal chestbox at her spine.

A clone arrived bearing two satchels of food and water and a bedroll. Matty didn't look up as the Echo 3000 flipped open first one pack and then the other, inventorying food and water and the slender envelopes of Martian money credits.

Matty stood on her own as the Echo 3000 slid both packs onto its appendages, minutely modifying himself to suit the task. Papers signed, foodstuffs delivered, the lawman turned to go.

"May I ask you something, Mister Lawman?" said Matty to the departing back.

The man turned.

"Don't y'all . . . well, don't y'all *need* a woman around this old place?"

The man blinked. He removed his glasses and wiped them on the hem of his grubby shirt. When he put them back on, fresh smears streaked the front of the lenses.

"I'm sorry, Ma'am. I'm not sure what you mean. We are a fully self-sustained community, with our own air and water and food recyclers. We have all the clones we can produce, all the manpower we want. Why would Dometown Four possibly need a woman like you?"

Matty looked at the floor and nodded. The man exited the airlock and wheeled shut the door from the other side. The Echo 3000 helped Matty with the seals of her suit's helmet, and when the light turned red and the airlock reopened, the woman and the mandroid stepped out into the dry and the red and the sunlight. Together, they skirted the compound and crested the rise on the other side of the crater. From there, the main road was clearly visible. In the distance twinkled the glint of sunlight, glancing off the curved surface of the bubble of Dome City.

For a moment, Matty seemed to crumple. She sagged in her hyper-metal suit, falling to her knees. She looked like a wadded up ball of tinfoil discarded after a barbecue. But then the telescoping appendage of the Echo 3000 slid around her waist and helped her stand.

Matty steadied herself on the mandroid's appendage and lifted her hand to shield her face. Not looking back into the crater behind her, she stepped from the shelter of the Echo 3000, giving its appendage a little thank-you pat.

"Well, Echo, it looks like we're moving to Dome City, just the two of us. It's all right; we'll make do. Got to be someone out there who needs a woman like me." She squared her shoulders, took a deep breath, and stepped onto the main road, the mandroid beside her. Her suit-com sputtered as the mandroid adjusted its transmitter.

"Yes, Matty," it said.

Plastic Personality Surgery

I meant to tell you yesterday over coffee
I didn't like your latest upgrade.
"Everybody does it," you said, and showed me
the fresh pink perfect tear-shaped pucker beside your eye.

"One for every upgrade," you explained, and stroked the scars.
I counted five.
"I liked you before," I said.
You smiled and added non-caloric sugar to your cup.

I remember you, my sister once;
that so-imperfect child of five and ten and twelve,
scraping knees and breaking things and throwing tantrums—
you were glorious.

That first upgrade was all right, I guess,
though afterward I missed your clumsy stumbles,
the natural ungrace of any gangly, large-boned child;
I have it still.

Operations—upgrades—two and three I hardly noticed
but four left me bereft, left me missing you.
Because they can alter you with science does not mean
you should let them. I miss the smile you used to have:
          less plastic.

You smile at me now and I see again raw holes
in your surgically-improved personality.
Give me back my sister, I want to say. *Let her out.*
But she's you five yous ago, so I stay silent.

"I'm popular now, and attractive. I fit in."
You look into my face, I don't look back.
I'd rather close my eyes and see you there inside, instead:
puzzled gaze and nervous laughter and self-conscious flutters
          of your hands. . .

No, truly, you were grand.
I miss you. I try to tell myself your fingers on your tear-drop scars
stroke there in some echo of your previous, less perfect self, and
not in conquering triumph over her,
          but I fail.

Cliffs of Cal'allat

Not long after her father succumbed to the salt plague along with so many others, the surviving villagers left Taisin, beaten and broken, on the high cliffs of the cold rocky island of Cal'allat and called her dead. They each spat on her as they shuffled past, one or two giving token kicks to her staved-in ribs. She didn't cry out nor make any other sound, her silence accepted as further proof of the rightness of their actions. *Ill fortune,* they signed above her prone body in ancient hand-speak as they passed where she lay. *Ill fortune, bringing plague down on the rest of us.*

Perhaps she'd have done the same, though had she been more like them she wouldn't have found herself lying in the biting ocean wind on sharp dead grass, cold and bleeding and nearly dead. The island's carrion crows didn't wait for the last villagers to descend the ridge before they moved in to pick at her clothes with their shiny beaks.

Taisin closed her eyes against blood trickling from their corners. She sent silent pleas up into the grey-swept skies that she wouldn't be conscious when the birds ceased to be satisfied with bloody bits of wool and moved to more appetizing pieces. *Just . . . let this not be all there is,* she begged, silent but for the irregular wheezing of her lungs. *Please let this not.*

As darkness fell, so did rain. It spilled heavy from thick clouds in great rolling waves, as though the earth were the shore and the blue-grey above were an inverted ocean. The large black birds flapped away on sodden wings to perch in twisted-limbed salt forests between Taisin and what had until that morning been her village. The people there, like the short gnarled swamp trees, clung to the weathered rock and scraped what life they could from brackish soil.

Let this not be all there is.

When even sharper talons began to pluck at the remnants of her clothes left by the crows, Taisin let out a bubbling sigh. Had her throat not been crushed, she would have laughed. She would have said: *Welcome, hunting creature, whatever you are. If this is all there is, I hope your teeth are sharp, and quick. Those crows would've taken too long.*

But the plucking turned to prodding, which turned to pulling, and when Taisin felt herself rolled onto a sheet of whale hide and trussed like a marsh hare on a spit, she knew those sharp talons had been no night beast's claws, but the crooked arthritic hands of something else. If her eyes had not been crusted shut and her voice not been broken, she would have seen a small hunched figure wrapped in feathers tucking Taisin's bent limbs into the folds of a travois, or she might have asked that figure: *Why have you come?*

Instead, blind and dumb, she felt the movement of the ground beneath her, and at every stone and every dip, the many violated parts of her body cried out, though she could not, until finally she lost consciousness and felt nothing.

Taisin's body felt immersed in boiling oil. Every snapped bone and every rent bit of skin felt as though flames rode through on waves of agony, which crested against her until she writhed, gasping and strangling and emitting no sound louder than a wet, ragged breath.

"Nay, nay, little Moor-mouse. Lie still. They've done what they've done, though it was done out of fear. They'll not come for you while you're here with me."

Taisin willed herself to stillness under the hands attached to the voice which soothed her, which spoke to her in low murmurs interspersed with whispered guttural incantations and the occasional lullaby. The first fires to still were those in her eyes, as cool strips of herb-soaked wool stopped the bleeding. She felt the small woman—who sounded and felt no larger nor straighter than the gnarled trees of the brine swamp—hobble about the dim interior of the dwelling. When Taisin was able she studied the rough, nature-hewn walls of rock. She lay in one of the caves riddling the Cal'allat cliffs, which rose at the edge of the sea like the curved white pelvic bones of dead ocean gods.

Sometimes, when the old woman curled in her nest of gull feathers near the hearth ceased for awhile her croonings and her muttered spells, Taisin heard the crash of ocean echoing down the short passage from around the bend in the cave. At other times, she heard the answering cry of cliffside seabirds in return.

Usually, the chitter and cant of the gull woman didn't shape itself into any speech Taisin knew, but sometimes it did. "Eyes caught up with you, Moor-mouse," she'd say, as Taisin watched her fry gull eggs over the fire, or bubble seaweed soup in a crusted iron pot. "Your dead father's people—oh, aye; I know who you are, little Moor-mouse—your father's people don't well accept what is different from themselves. Those mismatched eyes they consider unlucky, the one green and one brown. Though she was as a queen among her own, your father defied his people to bring her to this island as wife. She died when you were born, her body and her small son borne away by her kin in a fine wooden boat carved like a beast. But those eyes are just like your mother's."

Taisin lay still and didn't answer. *Mothersss motherss mothersss* echoed down the cavern passage, flowing outward toward the sea.

Taisin could walk all the way to the water's edge by the day the ships came

Time had passed. Enough time to make the passing of it no longer meaningful. Though first the weeks had been marked by small achievements of recovery ("*. . . Today you eat all your broth, little Moor-mouse . . . Today you make the fire . . . Today you help me gather eggs on the cliffs, and chase away the gulls as we rob them . . .*"), the season by the sea was all one season. It was an unending season of rock and gulls and grey. Taisin didn't think it strange that the people she'd known all her life, the people who'd left her dying on the cliffs by the edge of the sea, lived just the other side of the briny fens. She sometimes heard dull clanging from the rusty bells their wooly goats wore tied to their short curled horns. She often smelled the smoke of their cooking fires, and if the winds were right in the evenings, heard the mournful hollow wail of their slender stone flutes.

So when the ships came, large dirty sails rising above choppy ocean like the wings of huge drowned gulls, Taisin was the first to see.

The gull woman emerged from the warmth of her cave to join Taisin on the cliff and watch as the sails loomed and the ships dodged the sky-thrusting rocks near the pebbled grey shore. Wind tugged Taisin's clothes, raked long wisping strands of her hair across her face, blew shards of crumbled shore rock, sharp into the exposed skin of her ankles above her short sealskin boots.

By the time Taisin and the gull woman returned to their cave, their swamp reed baskets full of speckled gull eggs and soft ragged feathers, the villagers had emerged in silent clusters from the brine swamp to watch as well. They ranged, quiet and hunched and dressed all in tones of black, along the rim of the cliff above the anchored ships, looking very much like the carrion birds dotting the leafless gnarled trees near their homes.

When they came to the cave in the morning, Taisin met them unblinking. They gathered about the shallow passage, as they had not since Taisin had come to live there. But they hadn't come for her.

"Gull woman," they called from beyond the cave's mouth. "Gull woman, your witchery is needed. Strangers have come, with broad swords and with sharp axes. Take what you will, and make the strangers go away."

The old woman uncurled from her nest of feathers by the fire. She rose like a ghost bird of ashes, like a thick rope of smoke wisps. She did not answer them, nor did she glance at the small bundles of offerings placed in clusters about their feet. There were bundles of black feathers, dark carved fenwood bowls of goat milk, a rare bolt of dull-colored cloth. The gull woman passed all these things. She hobbled to a young mother shrouded in black on black, ignoring the fish-smelling bundle at the woman's feet to reach for the swaddled one in her arms. The young woman stiffened, but the neighbors standing at her sides put their hands on her shoulders. Another stepped from behind her to tug the baby from her arms and hand it to the gull woman.

The young mother stood rigid. "The babe isn't hardy, old woman," she said, her mouth tight. "They say she won't last the week. You'd not have her die alone in a cave, without her mother."

For the first time Taisin could remember, the gull woman laughed. It wasn't a harsh and ragged sound, like her singing or her words. Instead, it was the melodious trill of a young girl. "With me she won't die for many, many years, and I'll be her mother. Pay my price. Do this, and the strangers will leave."

The mother stared at the gull woman with her Cal'allat-grey eyes, then at Taisin. It was the first in a long time anyone but the gull woman had acknowledged her presence. Taisin had forgotten how heavy were the gazes of the people of Cal'allat, how weighted their looks, how cold their stares. And their eyes all the same laden grey color, of sea and of cloud.

The mother let go of the baby, turned on her heel and walked stiffly away, toward the swamp and the stunted trees with black birds for leaves. The remaining villagers stepped back as though one creature, and the gull woman turned to Taisin, the swaddled infant silent and large-eyed in her crooked bird arms. "Go," she said.

Taisin stood, her feet planted like the twisted black roots of swamp trees.

The old woman walked past her into the cave. "Open your mind, little Moor-mouse-who-isn't. You don't have those mismatched eyes for nothing, those eyes of green forests and brown arable soil. They'll see. You'll see. This is not all there is. Not for you. Now go."

Taisin turned to the circle of silent villagers. Letting their glances slide from her, they fell back. Slowly, Taisin limped past them, stepping out onto the moor and into the whipping salt wind.

Her gait was uneven, more shambling since that day on the cliffs. She shuffled along the cold ridge and wended her awkward way down the rock. At the bottom of the curved white cliffs, on the grey crumbled sand at the edge of the sea, crackled campfires ringed with men. Large red-cheeked men, ungnarled and straight-backed, with enormous swords stuck into the sand by their leatherclad haunches. At Taisin's shuffling approach, the tallest one stood. He rose and rose. Taisin was certain he was the tallest thing on Cal'allat, other than the cliffs. Taller than the twisted black trees of the swamp; taller than the roofs of the cramped stone village dwellings; taller, it seemed, even than the low grey clouds which clung to the moors and the cliffs like shrouds of dirty goatwool. His beard was long and red, swinging almost to his waist and braided with yellow twine. A light crooked scar ran across his tanned face, and a torque of hammered gold circled his neck.

And his eyes: mismatched, one green and one brown. Forests and good soil.

Taisin opened her mouth, searching for words for the first time in longer than she knew. Nothing emerged but the strangled scraping of scars deep in her throat.

She stepped close to the man. At her motion the others reached for their swords and rose to their feet. She glanced at them. All these men had green eyes or brown eyes, the colors of fertile brown earth and green growing things she'd seen in dreams but never on Cal'allat. Only the man with the beard had one green eye and one brown.

Taisin knew without knowing, saw without seeing, just as the gull woman had said she would. She hadn't been able to speak since the day on the cliffs, nor did she understand very well the guttural muttered accents of the men around the fire. Instead, she *thought* what was in her mind. She thought it, and gazed into the dual-colored eyes of the redhaired giant with the yellow in his beard and the gold around his throat. She said over and over from inside her mind: *Brother, my brother, my brother. . . .*

Everything became silence. The sound of waves sucking at the rocks on the shore disappeared, and the eternal bitter whispers of the wind, and the ceaseless rending cries of gulls. Everything was frozen, and cold, and lifeless.

Please, let this not be all there is, thought Taisin, first to herself, then toward the man standing before her. She opened her mouth to grind out a strangled *please*, but it dropped from her lips and fell to the pebbled sand at her feet. *Please.*

The silence broke. Wind rushed over her, biting through the loose weave of her garments. Sharp grains blew against her legs, and her hair whipped across her eyes. The large man stepped toward her and folded her into arms the size of tree trunks, straight, and warmer than hearthfire. He murmured into the top of her head, and she felt the shape of his words against her hair.

"Sister," he said, in a language she barely understood. It came from deep in his throat and was too heavy to be carried off by the wind. "Sister, I've come to take you home."

Sailing away, watching Cal'allat fade into grey upon grey upon grey, wrapped in the patterned wool cloak of the man with her dead mother's eyes, Taisin could think only that she'd known. She'd known there had to be something more.

The Taste of Snow

My great aunt Candi-with-an-i is up on the ridge again.

I pull on my boots. I lift my windbreaker from the peg by the kitchen door on my way out, shoving one arm then the other into crinkled sleeves as I trudge across the dustfield behind our house. I see her, a single slender stick curling up from the rock like a spent match, her dyed-black hair looking like the crisp ash of burned wood.

She doesn't move as I climb up to stand beside her. Her eyes gaze off into empty distance, as though seeing something I don't; perhaps seeing something she herself hasn't seen for nearly a hundred years.

Taking her elbow, I'm mindful not to hold too tightly the delicate twig of her arm, the dubious binding of brittle sinew and wrinkled flesh. "Aunt Candi," I say, "it's time to eat. Let me help you down to the house."

She turns to me. The over-dark tendrils of her hair whip about her face, rise on the dry dusty wind and wrap across her eyes like the questing limbs of scraggly black octopi. "It's Candi with an i," she says. "It always used to be spelled Candy with a y when I was a girl. I was the first Candi in my school. The only one." She turns her head to gaze across the stubbled rocky plain with pale blue eyes limned in opal. "Nobody remembers anymore," she says.

I put an arm about her thin shoulders. Carefully as I can, I turn her around. The homestead crouches low against the ground in the gully beneath us. The house, the vacant chicken coop, the shed clutch themselves close to the dirt like bloated desert toads. Everything is dust and rock.

"I remember, Aunt Candi," I say, as we begin our slow, shuffling descent from the ridge. "I remember."

I don't actually remember, of course. What I remember is the lifetime of stories she's told me over the years. Stories about things I've never seen though she and I grew up here in the same house decades, generations, apart. It's funny: that she and I should be the only ones left. Survivors, she would have called us, back when she still thought in terms of here and now, which has been some while. Sometimes she visits her past as though from far away; as though viewing it through a long-distance telescope. Sometimes she slips into childish behavior and mannerisms, though I often suspect her of mere self-indulgence. It's not too much, I think, for me to indulge her also. She has earned it. Earned it with years, decades, a whole century.

But sometimes she goes to a place where I can't follow. Her eyes see some distant time, a time long before I existed; before my mother was born; before even my grandmother was born. Her ears hear the sound of the rain which hasn't fallen on these plains but once or twice for more decades than I have lived; her palms curl upward toward sullen, unaccommodating sky and her tongue, tentative, emerges from between cracked lips. It's then I know she recalls the taste of snow.

She says: "Do you remember, Tiffani, how we'd stand up on this ridge and watch snow fall? We'd build forts under the trees. Mine were always better than yours."

Aunt Candi's sister Tiffani has been gone for fifty years. Most of the trees for miles around died decades ago when rain stopped falling on these hills, the last of them burned up for kitchen fuel by the time I turned ten.

"I remember, Candi," I say. We're in the small kitchen, she sitting at the table, I rummaging through cans in the cupboard. I run my finger along peeling labels, some too faded to see what's inside. Some cans have an unappealing crust of corrosion along their metallic rims. "Beets," I say, more to myself than to Aunt Candi-with-an-i. "Beets can be good."

My great aunt has a moment of clarity. "Your mother probably bought those freaking beets," she says. "Nobody in their right mind would buy canned beets."

She's right. These are what my father would have called "heirloom food." Before he left. Before my sister died in the food riots of 2060. Before my mother was murdered on the road from town, the blood she spilled worth considerably less to her attackers than her truckload of water.

Aunt Candi snorts. "She probably bought those beets about the same time she bought those ugly kitchen curtains. I liked the ones your grandmother had in here better. Remember those?"

I do. I nod. "I do remember those," I say. "Those were nice."

She nods back, her deep black hair making her pale face appear stark and small in the weak evening light of the room.

Knowing I have to make a trip into town fills my stomach with what feels like lead. The cost of refueling will be almost as much as all my other supplies combined. Everything except the water: only clean water costs more than fuel.

Bumping along the rocky, unkempt road to town, I go over my shopping list in my head: potable water; replacement parts for the urine still; black hair dye; whatever food I can afford with the money I'll have left after I fill up the truck. In that order of importance.

As always, I don't stop at the intersection where my mother was murdered. I know those men were hung over ten years ago by the grace of what my father then called *local justice*, but I avoid looking at the small bleached cross hammered into the ground near the intersection as I gun my engine, hurtle past the stop sign. There's no danger of hitting another car; I can see across the dusty rolling plain for miles in every direction.

Town is quite lively today, as the water convoy has made a

delivery from the north. My timing is excellent. If I'd come two days ago the local water silos might have been dry. Our region is allotted only so many gallons per month. The good news is, fewer people live way out here every year. There was a time I had to arrive two days early and camp, just to wait in line for my ration, or purchase used water instead. Used water is all right for some things, not so pleasant for others.

I park. Even for around here my truck looks tired and old. Beaten. Nearby, a few dozen other trucks cluster haphazardly around the main entrance to the L-Mart. It's difficult to imagine a time when these acres of asphalt were covered with vehicles. My father once told me that when he was young, there was so much potable water people washed their cars in it. I try to imagine this parking lot as it must have been in his youth, row after row of shiny cars gleaming in the sun, not covered in dust. I imagine them every color I can think of, and sparkling like hard candies.

Sand has over-swept the outer edges of the lot, making the building appear to rest on an island; an island of black asphalt on an ocean of pale, gritty dust. I suppose the lot once stretched as far as the towering sign way over there, which now looks incongruous, unnecessary. It rises on two enormous, crusted stilts. The sign itself sags at a precarious angle, off-kilter. The metal is corroded, but sound. Two blank spots before the L in L-Mart show where other letters have fallen off or been removed, long ago.

It's a relief to step into the cavernous gloom of L-Mart. I've always loved coming here. It's the only place I've ever been where I can escape for even one minute the sound of wind. It's not the heat I hate so much, nor even the dry: it's the low, ceaseless howl of wind blowing through dusty, empty places, unhindered.

The vendors' stalls form an angular U around the large glass doors of the entryway. No sense wasting fuel for light; of sun we have plenty, though dust clouds have been known to fill the sky for days on end, darkening everything below. Behind the row of tables, off in the echoing recesses of the otherwise empty building, I can barely make out the enormous curving plastic sides of the water silos. They gleam softly to my sunlight-seared eyes. Almost, they glow.

My vision clears, adjusting to less light. I wander along the row of tables, picking up a hammer here, a plastic bucket there. This tarp would be nice to have; it might keep sun off me when I go between the house and the shed. Experience tells me the wind will make short work of such a thing, however. I've spent many wind-crushed afternoons trying to sew up fraying edges of tarps which have flapped themselves to shreds against unchecked invisible fury.

I move on.

Mrs. Jackson is as nice to me as ever. She apologizes even before I reach her table. "Honey," she says, "I'm so sorry I couldn't get your great auntie's color this month. But I got a couple nice ones, might be okay. You think she'd like Midnight Plum?" She holds out a box for my inspection. On the cover is a pretty girl with very white teeth and eyes. I lift the box to my nose and breathe deep, inhaling the scent of big northern cities which still clings to the cardboard.

"Or," says Mrs. Jackson, "how 'bout Effervescent Charcoal?"

She shoves another box into my other hand before turning to assist someone else. This second box has the same girl, or one so similar she might as well be. On this cover her head is cocked to the other side. Her hair is shorter, but her teeth are just as white. I close my eyes and lift both boxes to my cheeks. Their lightly-scented smoothness cools the heat in my face from the outside sun.

I purchase Effervescent Charcoal and the maximum amount of water I am allowed by law. I pay Phil the Fill-Up Man, and hand him my keys so he can fill my truck with fuel while I finish shopping. I buy the few scraggly vegetables I think Aunt Candi will eat, the milk she loves, the cooking oil and the lamp oil we need. Phil the Fill-Up Man returns my keys. My money is spent.

Emerging onto gritty asphalt with my groceries and my water chit I blink several times, re-acclimating to the dryness of the air, the whiteness of the sun, the loudness of the whistling in my ears from the eternal wind.

The wind often seems to form words as it whips past me. Bitter, angry words; hissing words; seductive words, as though the dry wind has a fickleness all its own. It takes me a full minute to realize someone is actually calling my name. A human someone. Jeff.

He motions me toward him, his whole arm scooping the air as though I'm a good scent he can make come his way. "Leah," he says. "Over here. Leah!"

Now he's waving his arm over his head, back and forth like he's flagging down a water convoy. I nod his direction, then place my bundles in the cab of my truck. My water chit I fold once and slip into the pocket of my skirt, where I keep a hand on it, just in case. That wind is devious. If it snatches away my water chit I'm not sure what would happen to Great Aunt Candi-with-an-i.

I cross the asphalt to Jeff's stall. He sets up on the periphery of the L-Mart parking lot in the shadow of a single crumbling cinderblock wall. Some days the legitimate vendors chase him off, some days not.

Jeff's wall provides relief from the sun, but I lift a hand to shade my eyes. He greets me as he always does: "You moving up north to the big cities?" he says. "Or, you going to go down south to that one they have that's all inside, not in the sun or the wind or anything? That has all those tunnel roads and they have electricity all the time and water every day?"

As always, I shake my head. "You know it takes a lot of money to live in those cities, Jeff," I say. "Takes money to get to those places, too. Besides, what would Aunt Candi do?"

Jeff squints a moment, thinking. "Yeah," he concedes, but with the readiness of a ritualistic response to my habitual answers. "Yeah. Candi-with-an-i sure does hate the cities. She sure does."

I finger-poke through the table of Jeff's goods. Trash pickings, items scavenged from abandoned farms. Sometimes he gets something interesting, but the L-Mart vendors purchase anything decent early in the day. I pick up a child's kaleidoscope, hold it to my eye. I try to turn it but sand and grit have clogged the mechanism. I shake it, but the interior pieces are mostly frozen in place. One amber piece grudgingly shifts a fraction with a slight audible *snick.* I set the toy back on the table, pick up a broken screwdriver, a cracked plastic casing for a small stereo with no innards, a pair of scratched sunglasses without arms.

"But Leah. . . ."

I look up at his windburned face, his yellow hair slicked down around his head in stiff, dirty swirls.

"Leah, those city people need other people to work for them, right? And you're pretty enough? And smart enough? People with money need other people who don't have money. Right?"

In my pocket, I rub the water chit between thumb and finger. "No, Jeff. I'm not sure they do."

I drive around the back of the massive L-Mart to the water window. I hand my chit to the cashier, and the attendant runs out with a hose to fill the empty plastic drums in the back of my truck. While he does this, I turn Jeff's gift over in my hands.

Jeff usually has a gift for me. When we were children it was pretty pebbles, or the occasional rare wildflower—the kind that grow up around the edges of urine stills if you keep them outside. Now, it's always some trinket from his scavenging. A bit of colored glass, or a particularly pretty shard of pottery. Once, he gave me a single gold earring, hung on a string.

But this was too much. I'd tried not to accept it but he'd insisted. "Take it for Aunt Candi-with-an-i," he'd said. "She'll like it."

Aunt Candi had been a teacher when she was younger. Schools disappeared from these parts long before Jeff and I were old enough to go. *Lack of funding*, they used to say. *Population density too low to justify the expense*, they'd say: *A drain on our cities*. Nobody bothers to say much of anything like that anymore. Now, things just are the way they are.

But Aunt Candi used to teach Jeff the alphabet in our kitchen. *Q is for Quench . . . R is for Rain,* she would tell him. *S is for Snow. T is for Torrent. U for Umbrella.*

I shake Jeff's gift gently with both hands. It's a globe filled with water. A little cottage rests in the center, and when I shift the globe or turn it upside down, hundreds of tiny flurries eddy about, beating against the rosy-hued windows and the frosted front door and the boughs of the tiny evergreen which stands behind.

All the way home I clutch the globe between my bare knees as I drive. I glance down at it from time to time, the top of the roof and tree just indistinct blobs of color from above. But every time I round a steep corner, or fail to miss a pothole or slow down for a bump in the road, the sparkling flakes flurry up, swirl for a moment in the non-air of the globe before settling back against the curved glass.

For the first time in ten years I pass my mother's intersection without even noticing.

Great Aunt Candi is up on the ridge with her mouth open to the hot dusty air. "Remember," she says to me when I go up to fetch her back into the house. "Remember when we used to stand up here with our mouths wide open to catch the snow before it fell to the ground?"

"I remember, Aunt Candi," I lie, leading her down the pebbly incline to the house.

Jeff's gift does wonders for Aunt Candi's lucidity. It's been a long time since she's addressed me by my own name and not the name of one of my long-dead female relatives. "Leah," she says to me, "you're putting too much salt in those beans. Leah! Don't you let those eggs spoil. Lord knows we get few enough of them these days."

Since Candi-with-an-i is in such a good mood and we have plenty of supplies, I splurge: I light both lamps while I prepare supper. Aunt Candi turns the snow sphere one way, then another, letting out a coo or a laugh every time the flakes inside obscure the little cottage and its single tree. I place one lamp on the table right next to her so she can see the snow better. She has lots of stories tonight, lots of opinions.

"Not everywhere is like this, you know," she tells me. She's slipping tonight in and out of what I call her teacher mode. "Some places," she turns the globe right side up and pauses, intent on the action of the glittering interior; "some places have *too much* water, or at least did when I was a girl. Some places where millions of people used to live, gone. Wiped out by rising tides, or storms you can't even picture. Hard to imagine, here and now. But that's how it is some places. Or at least was. I don't know what it's like anymore." She looks up sharply. I stop dicing the anemic vegetables on the counter to meet her gaze. "Do you?" she says, shaking the sphere in her hand without looking down at it. "Do you know what it's like out there anymore?"

I turn back to chopping. "No, Aunt Candi. I don't know what it's like. You know I've always lived here. Just here."

From the corner of my eye I watch while she holds the sphere to the light, squinting at the glow of the lamp through the swirling white flakes inside. She says, "I remember the taste of snow. Do you?"

"No, Aunt Candi, I'm afraid I don't."

She sighs; a soft sound, and one I'm not sure is in response to my words or to the most recent revolution of the sphere in her palms. After dinner, when I help her to bed, she insists on taking the globe with her.

"Are you going to be okay?" I ask before I leave with the lamp. "Is there anything else you need?"

She shakes her head, but doesn't look away from the globe nestled on the pillow beside her. Lamplight glints off the snowy crystals, the curve of the glass, the opalescent milkiness of her eyes. Her newly Effervescent Charcoal locks curl down onto her powdery cheeks. She looks very young and very old at the same time. Not knowing why, I step back into her room. Kneeling by her bedside, I stroke her hair. But she's engrossed in the world of the snow sphere and doesn't respond. I don't know how far back she's traveled in her memories this time, but it's too great a distance for me. I kiss her cheek goodnight, and leave.

It takes me almost all the next day to dig a grave for Great Aunt Candi-with-an-i. I'm strong, and used to hard work, but by noon my hands are raw and blood red. Not bloody on the outside, but underneath the skin. Blisters form even now, making my task more difficult by the hour.

Jeff would come if I went to get him. He'd help me, I know, and be kind about it. I'm not sure he has it in him to be anything other than kind. And he liked Aunt Candi very much. I consider the things I'd have to spend to fetch him back with me: the time, if by foot; the fuel, if by truck. In the end it is the thought of accepting sympathy which stops me. I'm better off with blisters.

I wrap my great aunt in the quilt her mother made and carry her up the ridge.

I knew she was dead the moment I went to wake her this morning, but only now, holding her small, stiffening body in my arms, is it really clear to me she's gone. As I place her gently in the hole I've dug, I feel one last twinge of guilt for not burying her below the ridge alongside my mother, my sister, my grandmother Tiffani. But then I stand, and there's a bite to the wind I don't recall having felt before. I close my eyes and picture snow swirling around me, as it does around the cottage in the glass sphere. I think: *maybe . . . just maybe. . . .* I let the tip of my tongue emerge from between my lips. . . .

And taste nothing but dry wind and grit.

I open my eyes, pick up the shovel by my feet. Filling a hole takes considerably less time than digging one. Too little time. With the pile of white stones I've gathered I make the shape of a cross over the top of the small mound in the earth. The symbol means nothing to me personally, but I recognize its power as a lost thing from an earlier era. Like Candi-with-an-i. Like snow.

At the bottom of the cross I place the glass globe, twisting its base into the dirt. I kneel on the ground a few moments, one blistered hand resting on top of the curving rise of dry soil. When I stand, when I descend the ridge, I don't look back.

Into my truck I load the water barrels, the lamp oil, the bit of food—even the canned beets. I pack my workclothes, my sturdy boots, my sewing needles. The sun is far down its track when I slide onto the seat and start the engine. It hangs low, the sun, heavy and red the way it gets when there's too much dust in the air, or when something large somewhere is on fire. Of my family home I take nothing which seems it won't be of use to me someplace else.

It's all right; I don't need any hollow reminder of time or place. Pulling out onto the main stretch of highway, the constant moan of wind buffeting the closed windows of my truck, I speak silent words inside my head as I drive away, thinking of snow. *I remember, Aunt Candi-with-an-i,* I say.

And then out loud: "I remember."

Neither Wave Nor Wind

She sang.

Her back ached against the ship's figurehead, the crude points of its carved wooden breasts pressing between her shoulder blades. Her hands and feet throbbed, their bones misaligned, ruined after their recent shattering. Her cheeks stung with the mingled salt of ocean spray and of her own tears. But still Heleia sang.

The hollows of her mouth and throat drew power from the water beneath. The sea's vibrations filled her, echoed through her body, reverberated in the blood of her veins and the marrow of her bones, and were released back into the world as song to shape wave and wind.

As the sun dwindled to a sliver of gold across the rippled waters, Heleia sagged, exhausted. She hung in the ropes lashing her to the prow like a sad withered fruit in a net. The hands of sailors, rough or gentle according to the degree of fear or pity they held for her, dragged her up still in her bindings. They carried her below, passing the mast where a small figure clung, chained ankle and wrist to iron rings sunk deep into the wood. Heleia smiled raggedly at the child as she was carried by, but he met her eyes without emotion.

In her cabin, they eased her onto her bunk. It was heaped with rich tapestries and sea-damp silks, which after the sun and flower-dappled meadows of her homeland seemed and smelled worse to her than gravedirt. Two sailors, their ears packed with beeswax against her song, fed her thick broth smelling over-strongly of fish. They then wadded rags into her mouth, one looking apologetic as he tied the thing tight, the other not quite meeting her gaze. Having gagged her, they hastily retreated while a third, smaller and younger than his shipmates, poured fresh water from a dented pewter pitcher and bathed her face and neck. Though his hands were gentle, Heleia flinched when the cloth dragged across the abraded surfaces of her collarbone, where ropes that held her to the prow left sores prickled with small hempen fibers.

When he was done he bowed slightly, took the plugs from his ears and left the cabin. Shortly afterward, the child from the mast was thrust into the room and the door bolted behind him.

Heleia tried to smile past the gag in her mouth stretching her face into a parody of expression. The boy turned from her, curling himself into a ball on the saltwashed planks of the floor, his shoulders heaving as he sobbed. She felt the vibrations of his sobs travel through the hull of the ship, through the wood of her bunk, through the sinews binding her bones.

Don't cry, she wanted to say, though she couldn't speak the tuneless staccato language these mainland people used. *Don't worry; when we reach the next harbor, you'll be set free. I'll remain to guide this ship around reef and rock and treacherous shallow, but you'll be free. That's the bargain. . . .*

But she could say nothing, not even in the near-wordless melodic songspeak of her island. The small bundle of misery that was the child—urchin or orphan abducted or purchased from among the many living on the streets of the last port's shantytown—radiated his despair. That despair amplified in Heleia's blood as though she were a strung instrument caught in a wind. She didn't mention, even to herself in her imaginary comforting of the child, that the very port which meant his freedom meant the enslavement of another. And another child and another and another, to ensure her cooperation wherever they sailed.

The children were treated decently and fed well, and were eventually released relatively unharmed and with no small amount of gold or gems lining their pockets. Though this bargain hadn't been struck by any formal means, the sailors knew the fate of their ship depended on the fate of the children they carried. That, and never allowing Heleia her unleashed voice.

Heleia rolled to face the wall rather than the boy who feared and probably hated her. She curled her broken, ill-healed limbs in on themselves to form a knot, and thought of her small son Andreo, younger even than the child across the cabin. In her mind she recalled Andreo not as she'd seen him last, his lips blue with cold and lack of air, his limbs twisted in oceanweed and his small drowned body slack and unmoving. Instead she pictured him as he lived inside her still; laughing and golden brown, running through the fields near their home, thousands of flowers littering the cliffside like stars littering the night sky, only showing all the colors of day rather than none.

"Sea witch, wake."

Heleia woke at the sound of the captain's voice, but kept her eyes shut and her breath steady.

"Sea witch, wake to witness the child's release."

Hands Heleia recognized by their gentleness as those of the young sailor who bathed her face slid under her shoulders.

"Please, Lady," the sailor said. "Please sit. Look: the child is well. See how he scampers down the pier; and there—he disappears into the harborfront market. See, Lady? His pockets swing with gold from our last voyage." She opened her eyes to look at the young sailor, who pointed through an open porthole at the afternoon sunshine glancing from shallow harbor waters. Past his arm she saw red clay tile roofs dotting coastal cliffs nearly as vertical as the ones surrounding the island of her birth.

She allowed herself to be partially lifted, though her shoulders and wrists throbbed from the eternal strain of their binding. She knew enough of her captors' words to understand them, but she stared at the captain, past him and through him. She began a low hum in her chest. She could no more draw on the ocean's power without the use of her tongue and lips than she could sprout gull's wings and fly out the open porthole of her cabin. But as she hummed—a simple muted lullaby—fear crept into the captain's expression.

"Enough!" He prodded the young sailor ungently with his boot. "Tell her to stop!"

Heleia closed her eyes and drew as deep a ragged breath as she could through her nose above her gag. Her lungs filled. The note in her throat reverberated in her chest. The tone rounded in her body, thrummed in her veins with no power other than the eerie mournfulness of the sound.

Heleia opened her eyes at the sound of a loud crack. The note swelling in her throat died abruptly at the sight of the young sailor sprawled on the floor, a red splotch on his temple, a thin trickle of blood on his chin. The captain stood above him, hands clenched to fists, his look of fear fading to regret.

In that moment of silence, a knock sounded on the door. "Captain: cargo's loaded and sails set. All hands ready to depart, sir." The door opened and callused hands thrust a small figure hooded in sailcloth sacking into the room.

The captain reached to help the young sailor to his feet. He turned to stare hard at Heleia before he left, but didn't so much as glance at the little form shrouded in canvas which had stumbled to lean against the wall.

The young sailor wiped the blood from his lip and went to unwrap the sacking from the child. "Don't worry, little one," he said as he lifted the sailcloth, revealing a pair of coal black eyes beneath dark glossy curls. "It's only a short trip out, then in to the next harbor. No harm'll come to you."

The girl spat the gag from her mouth as he sliced the rope from her hands. She was small, though probably older than she looked. Nine, perhaps. *Two years older than Andreo would be*, thought Heleia.

"Hah! Harm. . . ." The girl shook the cut bonds from her wrists with impatience and ran to the porthole, watching the red roofs scattered on white scraggy cliffs shrink rapidly smaller in the distance. "Can't be no worse harm than staying in that stinking hole. If you'd've asked me, I'd've come anyway."

She turned, and for the first time noticed the woman on the tapestried bunk, swaddled in silks, her long hair dank and ragged but her eyes fever bright above her gag. Addressing Heleia, she said: "I'm glad to go as far as you want. If I never see that place again it'll be too soon."

The young sailor laughed. "Well, that's a change, little miss. Most of 'em we bring for the Lady have a rough time of it, they do. Poor things. But it's only for a bit, see? Just 'til we gather another load from beyond the Gates. We have a safe landing place where we hides it, then we sets into a port for supplies and lets 'em children go with enough gold to buy their own way in this world, which is more'n most come aboard with."

The child left the window to come stare openly at Heleia. "What about her?" she asked. She reached for Heleia's gag, but the sailor grasped her wrist.

"No, child. Mustn't do that, see. The Lady's a sea witch. If'n you let her sing her song to you, she'll make your ears bleed and your heart stop. Besides, Captain needs her to sing our way through the Gates, so's we can get to the wrecks."

The child's hand dropped away. She turned to the sailor, her eyes large like dark moons in her small face. "The Drowning Gates? With a thousand years of treasure lying under the water; with the thousand pointy rocks no ship can pass? That's one of my favorite stories."

The sailor laughed. "Not just a story, girl. I seen it: piles and piles of treasure, there for the taking with the Lady to sing our way past the rocks." He reached into his pocket and pulled out a pale blue gem the size of a robin's egg and just as smooth. He held it to the child and she took it. "That one's yours," he said, putting a hand on her small head and smiling. "You keep the Lady here company, and when we get to the next port you'll walk off this ship with your pockets full. Just don't you let her get her tongue free, or she'll witch you." He tousled her hair and left.

As soon as the bolt slid into place behind him, the girl pocketed the stone and scrambled up onto the bunk. Looking somberly at Heleia with her dark-moon eyes, reflective as volcanic glass, she said: "Would you ever make my ears bleed and my heart stop?"

Heleia stared into the child's eyes. Just as Andreo's had been, they were rimmed with a fringe of heavy lashes, softer than thistledown, blacker than night. Slowly, Heleia shook her head.

Strong little fingers picked loose the sailors' knots. First her gagged mouth, then her hands, then her legs came free. For a time, it was all Heleia could do not to faint with the pain, as numbness in her limbs turned to tingling and then to fire as blood trickled back into her veins. She breathed deeply the sea air blowing through the open porthole. Tasting salt, listening to the sounds of the ocean, she could tell they'd moved into open waters.

The small girl studied her. "Are you really a sea witch, like in the stories? From islands souther than south, ringed in white cliffs flat and square like a god's teeth?"

Heleia nodded.

The girl's mouth made a round *o*. "Nobody I know ever seen a sea witch. Most people say they got tails like fishes." She placed her brown fingers on Heleia's bare knee below the hem of her tunic. "And there's really treasure under the water beyond the Gates?" At Heleia's nod she pulled the robin's egg gem from her pocket to study it again. Her glance flicked to the claws of Heleia's hands. "Treasure can make people do bad things." She repocketed the gem and took one of those hands in both her own.

The sailors had wronged Heleia. They had bound her and held her captive and bent her to their will, but they could not be blamed for this.

Heleia opened her mouth and began to sing, low and gentle; so softly, the child had to lean close to listen. The power of the sea rose up to her from the waves beneath, and she used it to form misty pictures in the air between her and the girl. There was herself, laughing and running through a field of red and yellow flowers. There was Andreo—beautiful, lovely Andreo—running beside her. And then he was gone. In the shimmering song pictures, there came Heleia looking for Andreo. She wandered the beach, she searched the caves. She trod the green fields, and trampled the yellow flowers, and climbed the white square cliffs until her fingers left red trails against the stone, singing his name wherever she went: *Andreo . . . Andreo . . . Andreo.*

And there lay his broken little body among the water-strewn rocks. Oceanweed twined in his dark hair, sand glittering across his forehead like a crown of tiny jewels. And clutched in his small, stiff fists, shells and gold coins gathered from the rocky shallows, the treasure of sea and man.

Heleia's voice didn't rise, but it began to tremble. The image in the air shivered, wavered, then resolidified.

The song now described Heleia in grief. It showed her standing atop white cliffs, singing a storm out across the ocean. The skies darkened. Lightning struck down around Heleia like stars attacking the earth from the heavens. Her song rose and rose on the storm, rain slicing down with enough force to cut her simple tunic to shreds. The song-image Heleia stumbled down the battered cliffside to the rocky shore. Still singing, she lifted heavy rocks and brought them down repeatedly on her own feet, rolled them with her body over her hands to crush all the bones. Hands and feet wrecked beyond the ability to swim, the song-Heleia crawled into the crashing waves, which subsided as her voice melted beneath the water, until her body washed out with storm-driven flotsam and the receding tide.

The last note of Heleia's song hung suspended in the air, then wobbled and disappeared, taking the shimmering picture with it. The little girl lay back against the silk cushions at the far end of the bunk. Her face was wet, not as though she'd been crying, but as though the salt spray of the misty images had blown against her cheeks.

But that wasn't the end of the story. Not quite. Heleia drew a breath, then softly, softly took the ocean power into the hollows of her mouth and told the rest. She sang nearly inaudibly about the ship blown far off course by her grief-conjured storm; of the sailors who scooped her broken body from the waves, and, recognizing what she was by the way wind and wave responded to her voice, slung her at their prow to guide them back past the drowning gates. That first time she guided them to safety even through her mourning, feeling responsible for their plight, thinking they'd let her drop into the waves when they were through so she could sink to the bottom of the ocean and lie there forever.

But Heleia had forgotten her own people's tales about the ways of landsmen. They sailed the waters in their ships, but controlled neither wave nor wind. So they controlled Heleia instead. They took at each port a child, a hostage. Three times now had Heleia guided them back out among the rocks, shaping wind and wave with her song to steer this ship of men. Three times now some poor landsman child of an oceanside shantytown had been made rich.

"And I'm the fourth," murmured the girl when the song trickled away into nothing. During Heleia's story, the light from the porthole had faded to purple, then to black as night descended. Only a small, sea-phosphor lantern dangling from the ceiling illuminated the cabin. The child slumped down into the cushions, snuggling against Heleia's length for warmth.

Heleia breathed the small heat of her. She closed her eyes against the memory of her son's body snuggled to her breast; against the memory of his soft nighttime breathing and against the remembered sweet clover scent of him.

Andreo. She let the songlike name slip from her lips in a whisper, almost unthinking. *Andreo.*

The girl flung one arm across Heleia's body to snuggle even closer and sleepily muttered, "Chara . . . my name is Chara."

Heleia hadn't realized she slept until the clang and clash of steel meeting steel rang on the deck above. For the first time in weeks, she'd slept without the constraints and gag the sailors bound her with each night. It was a novelty to feel the blood flowing through her limbs, to draw unfettered breath into her lungs.

Chara stood at the single round window. "Pirates!" she said. "I thought those only stories, too, like sailors tell. But there's real pirates!"

Heleia swung her legs over the edge of the bunk, but when her feet touched the floor they were like two lumps of painful lead. Chara rushed to her side and inserted her small body under Heleia's shoulder, saying: "Come see!"

Together they hobbled to the window. Close—very close—a second ship had drawn up. Boarding planks stretched between them and knotted ropes had been secured, upon which pale, russet-haired raiders swung arm over arm, short fat daggers clenched in their teeth and wide heavy axes tucked in their belts. From where she stood, Heleia could just see the strange tall curve of their ship's prow, with its cruel-faced dragon figurehead. Thinking what it would feel like to be lashed to the points of its horns, Heleia sagged. Chara struggled under her sudden weight and Heleia pulled herself upright, bracing against the wall instead.

She experienced a brief surge of elation at the thought that perhaps at last she'd be set free, dropped into the depths and left to sink. She knew she'd been weak. Too weak to join Andreo without rendering herself incapable of swimming back to shore. Too weak to let the children of landsmen die. Weak. So weak.

A small hot hand clasped hers. She looked down into Chara's round dark eyes.

Voices sounded in the passage. Splinters flew as a heavy axe battered through the door. Three pirates, raiders, their red beards forked and their golden hair braided, tumbled into the cabin. Their shirts were bloody, their faces lit with the blaze of battle. At the sight of the woman and the girl, they stopped. Above, thumping and clanging continued.

The smallest of the three, who stood taller than any man Heleia had ever seen, strode to her bunk and slashed a few cushions with his thick blade. One of his fellows behind him took a brief glance about the room. "Gold. Bah! There's no gold here." His words were rough, with sliding tones slurred by the accent of the northern kingdoms. "What tales we were told! Is there gold aboard, girl?"

He reached to grab Chara's shoulder but before he could, her small hand darted to his waist, grabbed a knife from his belt and buried it to the hilt among the golden hairs of his thick arm. He bellowed with surprise and staggered back, but though sharp, the knife was only a small one, of a size used for eating rather than fighting.

His shipmates laughed at his expression as he pulled the little blade from his arm. "That one's a warrior," said one. "They could have used her above decks."

Two raiders continued searching the cabin as the third herded Chara and Heleia to the deck. It was slow going, the wrecks of Heleia's crumpled feet dragging across the boards. Chara was a lithe, firm crutch, tucked against Heleia's side with the woman's arm wrapped about her small neck. They emerged into morning light made dim and hazy by heavy clouds of oily smoke roiling from fires set by the raiders. Muttering rose from the subdued sailors at the sight of Heleia's unbound mouth. Where they sat under guard, several who had until that moment borne expressions of resignation or anger began to cower. Some made warding signs against Heleia, and one began to audibly pray to landsmen gods. A few were beyond such reactions, their corpses lying bloody among slashed rigging and torn sails. She recognized the captain's unmoving figure, and that of the slender young sailor with the gentle hands.

At the sailors' mutterings and the warding flickers of their fingers, the leader of the raiders stepped close. He smelled of man-sweat, and of some not unpleasant spice or liquor unfamiliar to Heleia. In his guttural tongue he said, "These men don't seem happy to see you, Lady. I don't know the habits of these southern, dark-eyed folk. You look like them, but are not of them, I think."

Heleia met his unblinking northern gaze, his eyes the color of ocean ice. She barely understood his words, but read his meaning through the vibrations in the sea air; through the hint of ocean power traveling through the salt-wet wood beneath her bare, broken feet.

When the raiders departed the ruined ship, they set fire to the sails, the deck, the rigging. They unbound the sailors, who scrambled to subdue flames, keeping too busy to fight against the departure of the raiders and whatever small caches of personal treasure had been unearthed from private quarters. They took with them also the brighteyed nimble shantytown child and her silent crippled companion, followed unrelentingly by the wary gazes of sailors who seemed to fear the limping woman more than the flames they battled, though unchecked those flames would mean death. Even after the ship had grown quite small in the distance, far across the chopping waves Heleia felt their eyes upon her still.

Chara quickly became a favorite with the fierce northern men. They had other pets aboard, gathered during travels and raids of warmer southern lands. A marmoset; a tailless parrot; a three-legged dog with yellow spots and rheumy eyes, and a strange upright ruff about its bony shoulders. All these scampered and played across the deck with Chara between them, causing the northmen to laugh and pat their heads as they passed. Though Chara didn't speak their tongue, they taught her ribald drinking songs by sound alone, and laughed as she sang back to them, a mimic only, their own tales of wenches and foes vanquished.

Nights, Chara and the marmoset would curl against Heleia's chest, the dog with his strange fur against her back. Why these men had added them to their onboard menagerie Heleia couldn't guess, and didn't try. In the dark she sensed the thrumming waves and their ocean power beneath her, untapped. She often woke from strangling dreams, feeling the press of a ship's crude figurehead between her shoulder blades rather than the soft muzzle of an aged dog-beast. She'd glance at the wooden dragon curving high above the prow, then resettle her arms about the small girl nestled against her, whose dark curls smelled of sunshine and unspent tomorrows. The girl lived one day to the next, each day for itself. She never mentioned the story Heleia had sung to her on their first night together, nor any detail of her own short history before then.

The northern raiders were much feared along the coasts. They swept into village harbors, taking food and supplies but little else. It was their reputation for fierceness rather than their actual ferocity that caused people to flee at the sight of their ship. More often than not, residents of an entire village would simply fade into the jungle, or into shallow caves up a cliff face, or clamber to the tops of enormous trees with sheltering, wide-leaf fronds, leaving the tall pale men with red-gold hair and heavy axes to refresh their water and food from the empty huts below. The raiders might take a trinket or few, but only if they were met with weapons would they strike back, and brutally. Chara and her fellow pets and Heleia would watch from the deck with the few men left to guard the ship.

One night, Chara whispered to Heleia in the dark: "Sea Lady, why do you stay? I think I'm like these northmen, who always push farther to find the next warm place and taste the next sweet fruit." She pulled out the robin's egg gem she kept in a small sailcloth sack about her neck. It had been much admired by the northmen as a very pretty thing, but it was neither gold nor drink, and so was of limited value in their eyes.

Starlight glinted like ocean phosphor on the girl's face as Heleia looked at her. "But you're not like us," said the child. "You're of a soft green place with yellow flowers, and white cliffs rising from the sea, enormous like the teeth of lost gods."

Shame flooded Heleia's limbs like hot tar. She'd not thought of her home or Andreo in days. Weeks had passed with no more awareness of his loss than a low dull ache in her stomach. She had failed: first him, then the memory of him. *Weak.*

"Oh, no, don't cry, Sea Lady!" Chara hastily pocketed the gem and wrapped her arms around Heleia.

Heleia hugged the girl in return. Though she'd raged at Andreo's death, though simple brine tears of pain and grief had sometimes slid down her cheeks in the weeks which had followed, she'd never sobbed. She did so now, uncontrollably. As though bindings had been broken from around the thick part of her heart, she sobbed. Sounds surged from her throat, her mouth, forming on the ocean air with swelling power as her wails rose in rounding notes of tortured song.

The sky darkened. Stars blinked out one by one as clouds thickened. The ship began to rock back and forth on increasingly choppy waves, and the northmen began to grumble and wake in their bedrolls scattered across the deck.

The pitch of Heleia's keening rose, and with it, the wind.

The northmen scrambled to their feet. They hurried to adjust their sails and to secure their goods against the sudden squall. The power of wave and wind swelled in Heleia's chest, focusing in a tight spot in her center.

"Sea Lady!" The sudden driving salt rain plastered Chara's curls against her small head. "Sea Lady, wait! Don't go!"

But Heleia slipped from Chara's grasp. She rose on a gust of ocean wind, which bore her up like a loose, empty sail. The northmen froze in their motions, blinded by raindrops sluicing across their pale faces, their golden-red beards and braids whipping in the unnatural gale. Heleia rose still, vibrations of power and song filling her lungs, her blood, the empty portions of her mourning soul where her son's love had once resided. Below her, the small curved shape of Chara lay curled tight about the shivering marmoset and the raggedy dog, the sodden parrot a small blue lump of feathers huddled at her head. The pale faces of men turned up toward her in the dark like ghostly flowers, the centers of each possessing the single black spot of an open mouth.

Heleia's head fell back into the wind. She lifted her arms straight out at her sides, willing the daggers of rain to pierce her flesh, to drive her limbs downward into the ocean, to hammer her into the depths of the sea where she meant to follow her small son.

A single sustained note of seasong carried Heleia's body beyond the rail of the northmen's ship. Even in her recollection to grief, even in her determination to this time not fail Andreo, she wished no harm to anyone aboard. Especially not to the small girl who struggled to her feet as Heleia retreated, and who now gripped the side of the ship, watching with one arm outstretched as the raging wind bore the woman beyond reach.

The northmen's sails slackened and they rubbed water from their eyes. Rain continued to drive against Heleia's outstretched arms like tiny arrows. She let the song fade in her chest. She felt the ocean ebb from her veins, its power sink beneath her into the froth. Her body hit the water just as the last chopping waves driven by the sudden winds subsided into nothing.

Saltwater filled her ears. It pushed past her parted lips and filled her mouth. The eternal blackness of nighttime ocean stung her open eyes, though tiny phosphorescent creatures whipped to action by the storm now began to twinkle all around her like elusive, drifting, pale green stars. Face down, her arms spread, she felt her legs ease downward into cold. Her body bobbed, floating, but soon it too would sink. She cupped the dark ocean in her arms as though in embrace. *Andreo....*

Sharp scrabbling fingers tugged at her neck. They tangled in her long hair, pulling sharply. Eddies of water swirled against her body, generated by the frantic kicking of small feet against the downward drag toward the distant ocean bed. Rhythmically, those kicks and those fingers caused her to be jerked upward by small degrees. Too small.

The kicks grew feebler, the eddies of water weaker. The fingers tangled in Heleia's hair made one last effort, turning her over so she faced up rather than down. Her eyes open, she saw the outline of Chara's face, minute phosphorescent ocean creatures gathered along her cheeks, her lashes, the arches of her little brows. Her silhouette glowed dimly in the ocean-dark. She was like a ghost girl, limned in pale green glow. And she was dying.

Heleia let the last of her lungs' air bust from her lips in a rush of bubbles filled with song. She reached for the drowning girl and wrapped her arms around the still figure. Their downward drift slowed, then reversed, as they rose on an upswell of power originating from deep beneath them.

They broke the surface of the ocean as one creature. In the distance, what seemed an improbable, even impossible, length away, Heleia sensed on the vibration of waves the northmen's ship speedily departing across the water. In her arms Chara sputtered and retched, salt water rising from her lungs to stream from her mouth and nose.

Fury filled Heleia that men could be so cruel as to throw a small girl overboard into the sea. She opened her mouth to sing them death; to call up wave to crush the thin hull of their craft; to direct wind to drive them into the depths to which they'd consigned a helpless child.

Drawing deep, shuddering breaths, Chara clutched her with fingers colder than slivers of ocean ice. "No, Sea Lady! Don't hurt them! I came after you! I did! I!"

The song faded from Heleia's throat, and the wind stuttered in the air around them and died. Clouds overhead rolled away on fresh natural breezes, warm against the night chill.

She rolled onto her back like a mother sea otter, drawing the shivering girl to her, settling her along her chest. As they drifted she sang a soft, lilting melody. Warm currents flowed around them as they bobbed in the still night, stars glittering above and phosphorescence glittering below. A sea tortoise rose as company and fixed one large eye on the pair, trailing a flipper lightly beside them in the glowing green water. If they began to sink, it would roll beneath them to buoy them up onto its enormous rounded shell. If they began to drift, it would correct their course with a placid flapping of its great flat forelimbs.

As the sky began its gentle purpling in the early hours of morning, a trio of dolphins joined their small procession, adding from time to time their songs and their small wild powers to Heleia's own. As the sun crested the curve of the ocean, golden in a pink sky above silver waves, Heleia and Chara drifted into the shallow cove of a small island shaped like a crescent moon.

The dolphins slapped water in farewell and sped away, twining around each other as though braiding the waves between them. The enormous tortoise pushed them up onto the soft white sandy beach, and there the three of them lay, warming in the morning sun.

After some time Chara rolled onto her side to look at Heleia. White sand ringed her dark brow in a parody of the halo which had wreathed the dead Andreo. Her hair hung in damp salty ringlets, echo of the oceanweed twined about Andreo's neck.

"I think, Sea Lady, this is just about as far from my old home as I need to get. For now, at least." She squinted up at the sun above the white dunes. "This is a good place, a warm place. I'd bet it has the sweetest fruit you ever tasted in your life, so far."

Chara stood on shaky limbs, steadying herself against the mound of tortoise by her side. She brushed sand and crusted salt from her arms, and shook her hair into a frizzy nimbus. "I'd also bet, Sea Lady, that just over those dunes is a green field of sweet grass." She smiled. "It probably even has flowers, maybe yellow ones." She reached down, palm open toward Heleia.

Heleia met the girl's dark gaze, unblinking. Slowly she raised her pale, wasted hand, and placed it in the agile brown one, and smiled in return.

Poor Little Things

"Dammit, not another one," says John.
"But darling look how cute, how sweet—"

He rolls his eyes and points,
I shuffle nervous feet.
I follow his finger with my gaze
across the parlor floor.
I know just what he means, of course;
I know we don't need more.

"Just this one; he's *tiny*," I say,
hold the bundle to his cheek.
But he sighs with resignation,
and I'm too annoyed to speak.
I carry my little burden,
curled fluffy in a ball,
step over thirty, fifty of its cousins
through dining room and hall.

All the time I wander thus,
pick my way past tail and snout,
I hear the rumble of their purrs,
feel loved and cared about.
"You need me, sweeties—you poor little things—
never mind you're thought a scourge.
I'm *glad* you came to visit Earth;
don't think about The Purge."

The Purge: Earth's answer to Cuddly invasion.
They call it cure.
Murder, I'd call it!
Atrocity, I'd call it!
Xenocide, I'd call it!

My heart is racing now,
beating fast within my chest.
But one stroke to a berry-scented fluffball
soothes my anger into rest.

"Of course, my babies, you are *so* right.
I won't let them get me down.
And I'll get that fancy food you like
if I have to drive all over town!"
And so I thought I would but when
I fetch the car to start, there are Cuddlies
in the engine, wheel wells, seats, trunk and—
. . . well, they're in every blessed part.

"You silly little things," I say, and stroke
and pet a few. "You guys are welcome any time;
anything mine is yours," I say,
and shut the doors and
when I get out and trudge away
I feel just fine.

It's heavy slogging, in truth, to travel
since Cuddlies came to Earthen shores.
Avoiding their numerous deposits
is one of life's less pleasant chores.

But their joyous hues sustain me
on my trek both in- and outward bound,
and when I've bought each can of tuna and salmon,
each potted meat I've found,
I arrive back at the house
to the sixty/one hundred stares
of the two/three hundred eyes—
more, at least one thousand pairs.

They rumble out their purrs to me,
they rub against my legs,
'til even my smallest worry's gone.
It's only afterward that I find John, face down—
well, no face, of course: just bone.
I look at him, his ivory interior,
so much cleaner in death than life.
I think of what they've done and I, his wife,
lie on the linoleum, and as they
begin to mew and chew, I close my eyes
and imagine their distant, berry-scented, alien sun.

Kingdom at the Edge of Nowhere

The girl in soft moth-drab clothing lay unblinking on the floor along the edge of a tunnel filled with people. She watched them churn past, each filled with a conscience, a will, a purpose; not identifiable as entities individual from each other but rather operating as the undulating noisy surface of a roiling ocean of limbs and hair and synthetic cloth. If she'd ever stood at the brink of an active volcano she may have pictured them as rivulets of lava, at times explosive, at times sluggish, bubbling and rushing and crushing with impersonal force.

But this girl had spent her eighteen, nineteen, sixteen years (one of those, she wasn't sure which) pressed against the edges of the only city on the pale, still surface of Earth's only moon. She lived with artificial air, artificial gravity, artificial cycles of light and dark, and with the ebbing, flowing human ocean, which sometimes threatened to drown the mothgirl and often left her gasping for breath, scrabbling at the curved glass and metal walls of Luna Prime to keep her head above the tide.

Gil gazed from the round portal into the velvet black of space. Here in the thick of the Belt, light from the sun glanced off the faceted landscape of his fractured kingdom. The iceteroids beyond the portal, hundreds, thousands in varying sizes and shapes, all moved in the same slow, lazy-orbiting spiral, their motions too measured to be detectible by a mind as ephemeral as that of a human man: even that of the Prince of Ice.

Gil's fingers strayed across the panel. He toggled appropriate switches, having decided which iceteroids to harvest that day, which to let lie. He watched the slender shining arm of the catapult unfold from its groove in the side of his vessel, straightening to become a rigid lance. From where he sat, the cable nets dangling from the arm looked as delicate as Earthside Venetian lace, and as billowy.

Slowly, everything fell into place; the net scooped its free-floating mountain of ice, the catapult chose its trajectory according to Gil's instructions and with silent, Herculean force, the lance arm swung and the cable net released its burden.

Gil watched the iceteroid tumble through brilliant darkness, glittering like a black diamond until it grew too small for him to see with his naked eye. When it reached its destination, years from that moment, credits would be deposited into databanks to reflect its arrival, and numbers would mount in his accounts. Slowly.

And so passed another day of the longest twenty-two years any man had ever lived. It passed as though trapped in molasses; in the wax of cold candles; in melting ice floe; in whatever might be used to describe the pace of a life spent in space, alone, the wealthiest man in the System of Sol.

During those times his vessel designated as night and his body recognized as such after years of convincing and of discipline, Gil played cards.

He entered the room of cryochambers and activated small holograph cells at the base of each glassine coffin. He woke each of his six subjects in turn and lastly, his father. Their bodies remained frozen in the slender tubes, their holo-faces animated by the minds of the sleepers within. The deck of cards with which they played their nightly games was also holographic, projected above the small table in the center of the room.

Sometimes Gil wished the bodies of his subjects and his sire could be projected along with their faces, but other times even the thought of such a futility and a sham drove him to helpless rage.

Rage in slow motion was a hard thing to bear. Gil's rage wanted to rip fierce and hot through his heart and mind; it didn't want to slog through his veins at the pace of a glacier.

When the cards were played out and Gil was tired, he bid his subjects goodnight. One by one, he flipped switches at the ends of the clear cylinders holding the frozen remnants of their bodies: the icicled cell tissue and frosted follicles and the tubes running from the cryo-machines to what viable scraps of human brain remained. Gil could tell which of his subjects were failing; which, through cellular decomposition and lack of mental fortitude and the long, slow beat of time had deteriorated past the point of waking. His mother's coffin lay dark in the corner of the room, a miniature mausoleum of glass and metal. Only his father remained sharp, and as alive as a man can without the benefit of a living body.

Sometimes Gil left his father's holo on for awhile. He'd pull his chair to the edge of the cold coffin, and they'd speak, face to holo-face.

"This is wrong," said his father some nights. "I wronged you, son, bringing you here to the edge of nowhere all those years ago. A little boy should run with his own kind, and a grown man should know more than dusty fairytales in books we thought of as ancient even before he was born."

Gil shook his head. "No Sire," he'd answer, his speech tinted by his favorite books and by a thousand private daydreams. "You left me a realm vaster than any other. You and my mother the Queen and our loyal subjects journeyed far and long to reach our kingdom. Its treasures are the right, and the responsibility, of your heir. I uphold your legacy."

The holo crackled, trying to align its projected planes and angles to portray emotions. The computer struggled to interpret the mind of the man; no matter how long it dwelled in the grey matter of his brain or flowed through the ventricles of his unbeating heart, it struggled. If Gil had seen more human expressions in the preceding ten years—not merely human expression as interpreted by machine—he might have understood his father's holo-displayed emotion to be one lingering somewhere along the road between guilt and regret.

"There's other wealth than credits, Gil. There're other landscapes than this cold one of ice and stars. And there's other realities than those in your fairytale books, though I don't begrudge you your fancies. I'm just sorry we all up and died on you like we did. There's only so many accidents a man can think to predict, and only so many things he can do once his body is gone."

Gil shut his mind against memory of the accident; against memory of his twelve-year-old self dragging the inert forms of his parents and the six members of their crew from the vacuum-breached rooms of the ship, struggling to roll their bodies into the cryochambers on the medi-deck. The ship had long since repaired the damaged portions of itself, but Gil rarely passed through those sectors. There was plenty of room, with him the only perambulatory occupant.

He bade his father goodnight and switched off the holo. He walked the halls of the ship, darkened to enforce the ideas of sleep and of what Gil had always called night. He performed his nightly ritual, washing his body and his teeth and his face just as his mother had taught him long before the accident. When he was done he crawled between his sheets and as always, reached to select a volume from the shelf of tattered books by the bed.

There were other books in the ship's library, but these were Gil's favorites. Gleaned from the rest over years of reading, the cream that filtered to the top and came to reside permanently on the shelf by his bed had certain similarities from volume to volume. Each night, Gil read of Princes and of Dragons; of Vast Kingdoms and of Beautiful Ladies in want of Rescue. Each night, he fell asleep alone in his kingdom, sole heir to its wealth and beauty and solitude. After ten years alone, he dreamt of nothing other than the worlds between the pages of books.

The next night—though Gil never thought of each night as

the next, merely as *night*—two of his father's subjects failed to materialize when he activated their holos. Nothing Gil or the computer tried could resuscitate them.

"Poor Cooper," said his father's holo-image. "Poor Jones. They were good men."

Gil bowed his head. "They were loyal subjects," he said.

That night after cards, Gil rolled the two newly dark cryochambers into the corner. He didn't glance toward his mother's chamber, though in earlier years he'd come each night to sit by the side of the opaqued black glass.

Gil wished the others good night. One by one he deactivated their holos, haunted by a sense of potential finality to the process he'd never felt before. When he reached the switch on the cryochamber of his father the King, his finger trembled at the toggle. He lowered his arm.

"Son, don't mourn us," said his father's holo-face. The features crackled, shifted, tried to align themselves in an accurate portrayal of the lingering mind's intention. "We all died over ten years ago along with your mother. We only do our best each night for your sake. You deserve more."

Gil said nothing. He reached again for the switch.

"Son. You have to go. Go toward Earth. Go live among men. This is no life."

"Sire, I have everything I need here."

The holo-face closed its holo-eyes. "No, son, you don't. Just because you've never met anyone outside the occupants of this ship—the dead and the not-as-dead—doesn't mean you don't need more." The eyes flickered open. "Don't be afraid, son. Don't let this emptiness, this nowhere, be all you get for a life. It's not right. It's not a human way to live."

The next night only two of his subjects sputtered to life. The other cryochambers remained dark, their glassy tubes opaque, inscrutable. The following night nobody woke at all and for the first time in ten years, Gil went to bed without playing cards.

He didn't sleep. Not for days. He read and read and read; he read every book on the shelves by his bed and when he was done he got up, naked in the dark empty ship, and padded barefoot through vacant corridors and past yawning doorways to the library he never visited. By the small blue running lights along the edges of the floor he read some more, until the main lights of the ship's next day-cycle came on and he returned to his empty chamber to dress and begin his morning rituals of ablution and feeding, which were much like his nighttime rituals, but in reverse.

Dressed, Gil traversed the empty corridors to the control deck. He programmed a course for Earth, following the trajectories of the thousands of ice boulders he'd captured over the years and sent hurtling through dead space.

It took a mere ten months to reach Luna Prime at full speed.

If Gil had ever before thought life moved in slow motion, he found the months of his inbound journey another matter altogether. He sat in his chair by the round portal and watched space go by. He found he could turn off his mind. His body suffered, but his mind slumbered. All sense of ritual, of day and night, of feeding and cleaning and breathing and sleeping, dissipated from him like water from a damp rag in an unshielded chamber. He simply *was*, and even that became a tenuous state of existence.

Transmissions began filtering into the ship's audio systems while Gil was still some distance from inhabited places. He began receiving random bits of transmission pollution, flotsam and jetsam of culture and information and advertising and so-called entertainment. It came from The Miracle, The Marat, and The Minaret; all three of the overcrowded space stations orbiting Earth, their dozens of flexible solar panels arrayed like the enormous silver petals of fantastic marigolds, their elongated habitat stems impossibly dainty against the swirled blue backdrop of the planet.

Transmissions came, too, from the fledgling colonies on Venus and Mars: the floating bubbles in the upper atmosphere of the one and the deep underground cave-cities of the other. Mars was Gil's only true rival for potable water, but their product couldn't match the purity and quantity of his iceteroids, flung from the belt and caught in immense gravity nets on the Martian moons, Phobos and Deimos. There could never be enough water to slake the thirst of humankind.

But mostly, the transmissions came from Earth. Earth, that incredible sphere of life and mayhem and madness and money. As Gil approached from space, Earth's beauty was so fierce he was forced to close his eyes, turn his head from its brightness. He, who had gazed into the sun, couldn't endure the sight of naked Earth. For the first time in his life, Gil wept.

The mothgirl played her silver flute in the tunnels and warrenways of Luna Prime.

She played for food, for warmth, for air. She played for whatever charity could be wrung from a citizenry inured to the sight of spindly-legged beggar children and large-eyed waifs. She danced her odd, funny little dance, the stripes of her stockings shimmering as her legs kicked and twirled. Her silver flute flashed, and her smile, when she remembered it. In eighteen, sixteen, nineteen years of living in the tube-like streets, her smile had grown creaky, underused. But it had not grown glib or smug, or predatory. Unlike many, she'd never learned to slit the fabric of another's pocket, slide her nimble stick-like fingers past the lining and pull forth, unseen, whatever contents it held. She'd never stolen the breads and fruits and candies lying so temptingly in vendors' open carts, displayed for all to see but only for those with credits to buy, or those with desperation or deceit enough to thieve.

The mothgirl allowed herself neither desperation nor deceit. Desperation was emotion, and emotion had been held at bay from her fluttery heart for almost all the years it had beat. Deceit involved more action than emotion, but it required too much of the latter to elicit the former. Better if she just slept at night where the pillows of her twiggy arms folded, the gossamer blankets of her tattered, layered garments draping across her face and body like the ruined webs of large spiders. Grey upon grey upon grey, her garments; and her hair and eyes the deep black of space.

One day as on countless others, the mothgirl played her silver flute in an intersection of tunnel and tunnel. The glassine arched over her head, latticed with metal and welded tight shut against airlessness with clear lumpy sealant. Beyond the arch stretched the motionless dustplains of Luna, sometimes brighter than bright, sometimes darker than dark. When Earth and its only moon were in proper alignment, she could glimpse the swirling beauty of the vibrant blue and white orb below—or above, depending on how she thought of it and her mood at the moment. Moods were not emotions. Of moods, she had plenty.

As always, the constant stream of traffic and human bustle flowed past her, around her, and over her—sometimes brutally. She was accustomed to the occasional credit chip pitched her direction; the occasional castoff garment laid by her side; the occasional bit of pastry or bottle of recycled water tossed at her feet. What she wasn't accustomed to was the undivided attention of a fellow human being.

On this particular day, as she twirled and whirled and flittered her flute, she felt the intense, lingering regard of another.

She lowered the flute from her lips and lifted her head to study the never-ending river of life and color and noise flowing by. He was obvious, amongst the rubble of human bubble and turmoil and anonymous haste. He was still, and calm in a way coming only when ice freezes deep in the veins, forming crystals around the heart.

"Hello," she said, though it was only a flutter, like beating mothwings against a pane of smooth glass.

And though he couldn't possibly have heard her across the ocean of teeming life between them, he mouthed his response: "Hello."

This time when she raised the silver flute to her lips, she imagined that the notes flitting from the slender tube flew out on quivering wings, to eddy around the watching man. He was the deep cold spot in the river, dark though his clothing shone soft and white in the glow of reflected sunlight glancing off the surface of Luna and filling its only city with soft, diffuse rays.

For once, when the mothgirl danced with her skippety grace, no one pushed her aside in haste or inattention. No one wandered across her path, or accidentally barred the progression of her steps. No elbow jostled her, no foot tread too close to her own, nobody intruded into the space between her and the still man in white. As she danced closer, drawn to his unflickering light, she imagined she felt the cold emanating from him, and the stillness of the air about his head. *Ahhhh*, she thought, *there it is; his icicle soul.* How could a flame that burned so bright burn so cold?

That night, when the day crowds had turned to night crowds, bodies still crammed, pressing and moving ceaselessly through every inch of Luna Prime, the mothgirl and the frozen man slept huddled together under the arch of the main square's dome. Here, all the tunnelways and warrenways and pathways converged. Above, the silicate glassine hemisphere with its spiderweb lattice rose, puffed and protective, sheltering the homeless and the aimless and the loveless of the city. This was where the mothgirl had been born. This was where the mothgirl slept. This was where the mothgirl, when she thought about it at all, assumed she would one day die; for real and for good and forever, and not just on the inside where no one else could see.

The frozen man was frozen in the same places the mothgirl was dead, which were only interior spaces. His body was warm enough. Huddled near him, the mothgirl slept more deeply than she had for as long as she could remember. Next to the frozen man, her dreams—which she suspected usually pittered from her head like tiny stars with wings and beat their featherlight antennae against the dome-clad sky above/below—instead folded gently around her in a protective cocoon.

These dreams whispered into her ears throughout the night. The tale the whispers burned into her heart was of a Prince of Ice, who lived in a cold, empty castle and lured huge dragons of frozen water from their lairs of black space. He caught them with his pointed lance and net, and sent them tumbling toward the sun and all humanity. Though the people lauded his bravery and his prowess with the coal-black beasts of ice and space, they did not love him. In fact, they didn't think of him at all. Their gratitude came in the form of credits, and nobody, including the Prince of Ice, ever questioned the quality of the bargain.

When the mothgirl woke it was to see the man sitting true to his nature: frozen, still and quiet as a small mound of ice. He hunched over his knees, wrapping his long bony arms about his frame. He watched the endless stream of human passersby, and listened to the tumble and mumble and screech and croon that hovered above their daily existence, a cloud-cover of noise and bright, painful colors.

The mothgirl stood and held out her hand to the man. She didn't know the places of the city existing without the press of bodies and breath and sound. It never occurred to her that the man beside her might hold in his name the wealth of a small kingdom. It wouldn't even have occurred to her that such wealth existed; enough wealth to purchase privacy and silence.

So instead she led him to the public garden. There, the presence of hundreds of other bodies was mitigated somewhat by the company of Earth-grown trees and Luna-grown flowers. Both towered overhead, the fronds of palms and the waxy petals of gigantic, impossible blooms.

Neither the Ice Prince nor the mothgirl thought those top-heavy spindles of chlorophyll and stalk impossible. Neither thought anything at all, except that in one another's presence each found the right balance of stillness and life. For the first time in sixteen, nineteen, eighteen years, the mothgirl felt the powdery wings of her heart tremble, and for the first time in twenty, the man smiled.

"My name is Gil," he said, "and I think I love you."

* * *

Gil didn't want to let go of the girl's hand. When their fingers slipped once or twice, he felt his moorings shift. His feet suddenly felt too small to hold the height of his frame, and the ground beneath him seemed to slide sideways and recede.

He walked quickly from the garden and along the passageways of Luna Prime. So many people. So, so many. Everywhere: on Earth, on Luna, even on the new colonies of Mars and Venus. Too many mouths and ears and eyes and wills. Too much breath and movement. Too much . . . possibility, everywhere he'd journeyed.

But his quest had drawn him all the way to *her*. During his journey to her side he'd squeezed through the dark, cloying, overpolulated underground caveways of Mars. He'd braved the sardine can metal tubes of humans on The Miracle, The Marat, and The Minaret. He'd waded through the choked streets of Earth, and languished five days in a small overheated box on stifling Venus. He'd danced as close to the sun's fire as his ship would tolerate, and when he was able, he'd used his catapult to ensure each of his six loyal subjects and his father and lastly, his mother would never be cold again. He'd watched as their icy chambers sped, swift and true, to the center of that glorious fire, whose heart was as bright as his own had been dark.

Through all this he'd searched, because a kingdom without a king was a useless thing, but a king without a queen seemed worse.

Gil led the girl by her hand through the crowds of Luna Prime for three days until he found the place he'd left his ship. "What's your name?" he asked her over and over, until finally she manufactured for him an answer: "Tinea Noctis."

He whispered the name again and again to himself. With every repetition he felt the tightness in the center of his chest thaw, until he led her up the ramp of his ship and let go her hand, and could breathe.

Gil knelt. "Milady Tinea," he said, "would you come live with me in a far-off empty kingdom between planets? I can teach you to play cards. And any time you like, we can visit your home and come down and wander the warrenways of Luna Prime, so long as you don't let go of my hand. I think it would be all right if you didn't let go. Will you be my queen, and help rule my kingdom at the edge of nowhere?"

The mothgirl closed her eyes. She breathed the stillness and solidity of the ship. Behind her lids danced images of the Prince of Ice, capturing his frozen dragons in the service of humanity and casting their ice carcasses at the feet of the people. She saw without looking the warmth at the thawing core of the kneeling man, and weighted against that, she rolled on her tongue the flavor of a life lived amid the ceaseless writhing bodies of countless strangers.

Without opening her eyes, she pulled her silver flute from the folds of her dress. The notes wobbled forth a moment as if testing uncharted currents, then rose with fluttery tones. In the mothgirl's imagination the notes in the air beat their wings against the metallic curves of the ship, every feather-soft brush against Gil's cheeks and eyelashes as they passed him warbling *yes* as her answer, before disappearing into echoes down the hall.

Inclusions

"Where you going?"

"'Sploring."

"Not supposed to."

"Don't care."

She watched him take one last drag, then flick his single stolen cigarette into the damp clumpy dirt and shove his fists deep into tight coverall pockets. His surly shoulder blades stuck out like the stubby wings of a cubist angel, all rounded angles and foreshortened planes.

He kicked a stone, and they both watched it roll some distance before it bumped up against the base of a fruitloaf tree and stopped. Without looking at her, Danton turned and stumped off down the overgrown path.

Marta glanced back toward the dig site and the crew camp. From here, her mother looked like a tiny beetle, her slick black rain'brella mounted to her back, bobbing with the motions of her shoulders as she combed through damp, loamy soil for planet-native artifacts. The 'brella shifted, caught the feeble off-hue light and reflected the iridescent colors of the mineral rain, keeping the drops off Mom with its shiny carapace.

Mom didn't need her; wouldn't even know she was gone. Turning her head, Marta could barely see Danton's back, all ochre canvas and too-long hair, disappearing around a bend through the trees.

She wiped the damp from her eyes and ran to catch up.

When she reached him, he slowed a bit and she was pleased. Maybe he didn't think she was as useless a bit of cargo as he'd pretended on the voyage out. Blasted stars, but there was eff-all to do on an interplanet archeology ship. Coming with Mom always sucked, no matter how good the onboard vid'brary was, and having a fellow arkie-kid on the trip should have been a relief, should have been fun, could even have led to . . . well, more of the stuff she'd gotten a sample of with Mike last year, back Earthside. Her own archeological dig . . . or would that be more like biology? No; zoology, definitely: Mike turned out to be a total animal in the end. Wild and beautiful and willing to experiment with just about anything.

And here she was, stuck with surlyboots engineer's boy: not really an arkie-kid at all, and obviously less than interested in her.

He glanced at her sideways and shook his head to dispel rain. Fat, slick raindrops wended their way along the ridges of his curls and dripped from their ends, and when he'd shaken his head the droplets had pelted her like tiny, soft, glistening stones.

They trudged for awhile, silent.

Marta began to hum in her head, an accompaniment to the *squelsh squelsh squelsh* of her boots in the crumble-mud. Danton said nothing. And nothing and nothing and nothing until finally Marta broke. "So what are you exploring? Not enough at the actual dig to interest you? Have to break rules, have to sneak into off-limits jungle? They haven't even surveyed the whole planet yet, you know. They think it's empty like the rest, but you never know."

He glanced at her again; that sidelong look of oblique impoliteness, with its air of sensibilities offended and personal boundaries encroached-upon. "They're all empty, excepting Earth. Ruins, bits of bone, random tools . . . never anything not dead less than ten thousand years. Anyway, you don't have to come," he said, indicating the way behind them with a jut of his chin. "Path leads straight back to safety-ville."

Eff you, thought Marta. She almost said it aloud. But what was the point? Was she going to go back, sit like a good, bored little girl in the landed arkie ship, watch the same vids for the umpteenth thousandth time? No thanks.

But it was safe there. This particular oily-rained, red-sunned, over-vegetated rock—Planetary Mass Number 327—wasn't cleared for civilian exploration past scientific campsite boundaries. Camp and ship might be boring as eff, but out here beyond the pink-plasticked stakes driven to mark the edges of the safety-zone, the dank, mineral-smelly jungle felt less harmless. Not menacing, exactly, in the broad, salmon-colored, muted light of day, but unwelcoming. It was like the whole planet felt toward her the same way Danton seemed to. *Go away*, rustled the almost-feeling in the back folds of her brain. *Leave me alone*.

The path narrowed until finally there was no path at all and the uneven, slick yet crunchy ground beneath threatened to trip and harm.

Danton didn't slow, didn't pull his hands from his pockets. Marta could see the hard, irregular spheres of his bunched fists under the yellowish canvas of his coveralls, the fabric stretched tightly enough so that she could make out the knob of each individual knuckle where it strained against the cloth.

Squelsh squelsh squelsh.

He had to pull his hands from his pockets now, to push aside rough tubes of heavily sagging vine and sharp, tiny leaves of spiky undergrowth trees. Her mother—the enthusiastic scientist mother who never thought how tedious life in her wake must be for her teenaged daughter—her mother had told Marta about the vegetation here; how it wasn't composed of the same organic compounds as the stuff on Earth. Mineral-based, she'd said. It made the jungle sharp, the bark of the trees abrasive, silicate. It sliced the fingers and rubbed raw the palms, if you weren't careful. Marta could see rough abraded sections on the delicate webbing between Danton's finger and thumb as he lifted a low branch. It snapped off with a mild protest of a *crack!*, and he threw it aside.

She tugged the sleeve of her under-tunic down to cover her fingers and used the back of her hand to hold back branches and thick, arterial-looking vines that looped down across her way. Danton certainly wasn't looking back to make sure she was all right, and he didn't seem to be going to any particular effort to ease her route through the tough undergrowth. She found herself pressing closer up against his back than she would have, using the shield of his body to protect her from the slapping and whipping and slicing of leaf and stem as they crunched and squelched along. Danton wasn't wide: his scrawny, gangly frame was narrower than her own. But he was tall, and he didn't seem to care if she sheltered in his wake. Didn't seem to care that she was there at all.

They came into the clearing with such suddenness, Marta bumped into Danton's back before she realized they'd stopped.

"We're here," he said, not turning around.

Behind her, the slick-dark crystalline vegetation rose, a chaotic but well-fortified wall. Not invincible, though. She could see the way she and Danton had come; the growth behind them bore the scar of their passing. The silicate-based plantlife was less resilient than the softer organics of Earth. It took its injuries more permanently; the slices in Marta's hand from the tall slender stalks behind her would heal before the leaves regrew, no stronger than chlorophyll-colored icicles. It was as if they only played at being plants, but when injured, remembered they were bits of stiff, breakable stuff. Ephemera, masquerading as solidity.

Danton walked to the center of the clearing and began to kick away branches and piles of stalk from a rounded bit of ground.

"You've been here before," said Marta.

He did look at her now. He'd shoved his fists back into his pockets, and she could see a small flower of blood blossoming through the canvas.

"Your hand—" she pointed to the red.

He shrugged, looked away, didn't pull out his hands, didn't stop pushing aside broken leaves from the edge of the mound with his boot. "It'll be all right in a minute," he said.

Marta didn't feel like giving him the satisfaction of asking him what he meant. She walked over, squatted down beside the space Danton had cleared along one side of the mound. "Holy eff, that's a . . . . "

She looked up at him and he nodded. Rain showered down on her from his hair, from his eyelashes. "A door," he said.

He squatted beside her and took his fists from his pockets. She watched as he traced the outline of the opening in the air above its edges, his knobby, big-boned hands invisibly sketching the parameters.

"Here," he said, pointing, "the top edge, the sides . . . and here, the handle. I think."

"It's so small," she said. "Too small to be a door, really." She thought about the dig back near the ship, of the rough, uneven angles of low, cut-stone walls. She pictured the lumpy carvings of plants and small, ovoid bodies with too many limbs all the arkies said were renderings of the long-gone inhabitants. "My mother says the people who lived here never had advanced buildings, certainly never forged metal like this."

Danton shook his head. "Not metal," he said. "Look closer."

He leaned forward and began to brush crumbled, tumbled bits of pointy leaf and twig away and Marta reached out with the end of her under-tunic sleeve to help wipe off stray clumps of dirt. He was right. The door, though perfectly square and regular in a way she associated with the advanced technologies of Earthside manufacturing, was not metal. Maybe not even manufactured. "Grown?" she asked, looking into Danton's face. "This is vegetation, isn't it? Well, plant, or whatever plant *is* on this rock."

They had completely cleared the outer edges of the doorway, barely a meter across and a meter high and absolutely, perfectly, rigidly square. He ran a finger along the small u-shaped tube of a handle in the center of the door. "Cool thing is, I thought I knew what square was, until I saw this. No human-made, machine-made thing was ever so . . . perfect, you know?"

It was, too. Perfect.

Marta was aware they were almost touching, she and this awkward, unmannerly boy, along thigh and edge of shoulder. The parts of her closest to him felt warm, muddled. "How does it open?"

"Don't know. I've been back here three times, tried plenty of different stuff, but can't figure it out. But watch." He stretched his hand out and placed it flat against the door. Marta heard him suck his breath in sharply, heard the air of him whistle past his teeth, but then his grimace relaxed and he held his hand out in front of her, palm up. It was pink and fresh and smooth.

"The cuts, the blood?" she asked.

For the first time Marta could remember since meeting him at the Lunaside away-dock five months ago, he smiled. "Gone," he said, looking at his hand.

She took it in her own, turned it. The back: still lacerated, grass and leaf-whipped skin cross-hatched with tiny slices. The palm . . . She ran a finger over his palm, and just as she was thinking how warm and heavy and smooth it was, he pulled it back. His smile disappeared, and the habitual frown replaced whatever expression she had thought she'd seen there for a moment. She remembered it as pleasure.

"What did it feel like?" she asked.

He shrugged, looked away; his usual. "Try it yourself."

Marta poked her hand up out of her sleeve, a fleshy turtle emerging from its fabric shell, and gingerly reached out a single finger. She pressed the tip to the door, just to the left of the tubular handle. Frowning, she looked at Danton. "Nothing," she said.

He reached out as though to take her hand but stopped. Instead, he said, "Is there a cut there? An injury? I think it needs blood to work."

"What, some kind of vampire door?" She laughed. He didn't.

She inspected her hand, but it wasn't nearly as bad as his had been. She flipped it over and pressed her sliced-across knuckles to the door and gasped.

A hum sped through her body. Honeyed lightning. Her lips parted, she threw back her head and closed her eyes and by the time Danton managed to knock her away she was panting with the crazy, surprising, joyous heat of it.

Marta opened her eyes, smiling, still breathing hard. The edges and points of leaves and bits of bark were pressing into her back, but she didn't care. Danton was leaning over her, gripping her shoulders. Why hadn't she ever noticed how pretty his eyes were?

The rain had subsided from its drizzly state to its misty one. It never stopped completely on P-Mass 327, so this was as good as it got. Marta watched the peach-fizz ambient light refract through the water caught in Danton's eyelashes. Yes, she thought; his eyes were very, very pretty, and so she reached her face up and kissed him.

He didn't kiss her back, but he withdrew gently. He closed his eyes for a moment, took a deep breath, exhaled slowly through taut lips. "I thought you were getting electrocuted," he said, helping her into a sitting position.

She shook her head, smiled again. Danton lifted her hand and held it up.

"Cuts are gone," he said. "And the blood."

She leaned forward across the door and pressed her palm to the pale green surface. Pressed both palms.

Nothing, not even a tingle.

She pressed her cheek to the faintly emeraldine smoothness beside the handle. Light grit and oily-rain mist and the faint, sharp green scent of the planetside vegetation—a scent she'd come to think of as chlorophyll-salt—mingled in her brain. Just as earlier she'd felt the nudge and whisper of *go away*, now she felt the lure of *come in*.

"We have to get it open," she said.

Danton rubbed a hand over his eyes and grunted. The touch of his hand left a thin smear of blood across his brow. "Your hand," she grabbed at his arm; "this one's still bleeding. Do it, see if it opens. Do it!"

But he rocked back on his heels, stood up. "I'm done," he said. "I'm going back." He turned to leave.

"Great. I'll do it myself." Marta reached for a pile of long, slender stalks. They were so fine they looked like spun-sugar threads she'd once seen at an Earthside fair; splintery and willowy and delicious-looking, only these were pale green and the ones she'd tasted at the fair had been pink.

Marta bit her lips as the vegetation sliced into her palm, razored into her layers of skin, drew threads of crimson from beneath. From inside.

Danton reached forward and tried to pull the stuff from her grip.

They struggled, lost balance, fell as one onto the grit and oil-rain-slicked surface of the perfect square alien door, and as they both threw out palms to catch themselves and the blood from their mingled cuts kissed the door with simultaneous ungentle pressure, it opened and let them in.

Danton fell forward first, smacking his face against the edge of the square doorway with enough force to stun. Marta's fall was blocked, mostly by the back of Danton's head, and she cried out as she felt her tongue split under the sudden force of her own teeth. She sat back flat on her rear with a heavy crunch.

She spat a couple times onto the ground and watched the globs of red sit atop the clods of dirt and crunkled bits of leaf and grassy stem. She looked at the still form of the boy in front of her, stretched out long and flat and lean, his arms folded somewhere out of sight beneath his body, his longish hair obscuring his face. He lay across the threshold into an open tunnel.

She spat a couple more times into the mud, then crawled forward, squeezing through the opening to lift the unconscious Danton's face. He looked younger than she'd thought before. Seventeen, maybe? It was hard to tell. It was like looking at a different person without the resident surliness marring his features. A lumpish, eggplant-colored bruise was forming on his temple, and a sickle-shaped gash rode right through the center of it, seeping but not quite bleeding.

She said his name a couple times, pushed back the hair from his eyes and willed them to open. They did, and she helped him sit as he had helped her before, and together they examined the open door—which no longer showed any interest in their blood or anything else—and at the roughly rounded wall of the tunnel under the mound. It sloped sharply down, then gently around a bend, away from the coral light of red-tinted day. A golden glow reached up to them from below, around the curving wall.

There was no question of turning back. The sting in Marta's tongue and the swelling of her mouth were nothing to the afterglow of the feeling which had coursed the rivers of her veins when the door had taken the blood and wounds from her hands. It was all she could do not to stretch out and purr. This was better than anything she'd felt last summer with Mike, and the idea that there might be more just down the corridor, just out of sight . . . .

She'd almost forgotten Danton and when he groaned, she had to force her eyes to focus on his face. Though the door was small and square, the tunnel was oval, and tall enough for them to stand. She helped him to his feet.

"Are you hurt badly?" she asked. "You sounded like you were in pain."

He smiled, in an embarrassed way but not surly at all. "It wasn't pain," he said, and shoved his fists into his pockets again. "It was good before, but not like that. Not even close."

"The door?"

He nodded, and smiled again. She decided she liked it very much when he smiled. "Come on, then," she said, and on impulse, held out her hand.

They made their way along the dim passage, holding hands on one side and each trailing their fingers along the wall with the other. The walls were like sandstone; the same adobe-ish color and crude-smooth surface of the squatty remnants of wall and pit and floor her mother sifted through every day. Shaped by hands less agile, perhaps, than human ones, but not less purposeful.

Marta felt a twinge of guilt at the idea of invading an untouched site better left to official arkie teams. But she was the bored and angry daughter of an absent-minded, academic mother. *I was dragged out here on a stupid dig,* she thought, *as I have been on a dozen others over the past ten years since Dad died.* And it had been boring, boring, boring. At last, something interesting was happening, and she'd gotten here first. Well, she and Danton. Besides, what exactly would she tell her mother? It would have been a little hard to put the feeling from the door into words. Describing it to her mother might have been . . . awkward.

They rounded the curve in the path of the tunnel. Marta raised her hand to shield her eyes from the goldy-tinted light, but lowered it as her sight adjusted.

Danton released her hand, stumbled forward. She could see his face bathed in warm, pale light; light so different from the rain-bright gleam of outside or the hard, linear wash of shipglow.

He crossed the room to place a hand on the edge of a large enclosed pool in the center of the underground structure. Marta walked the perimeter of the room, touching the surfaces of beautifully flat, upright, angled tables and what she was sure were chairs, though of odd dimensions.

The surfaces were smooth to her fingers, radiating malachite coolness into the otherwise warm air. Like the door, they were perfect in line and form . . . so perfect, she never would have pictured them, nor even the idea of them; that nature would form something so straight and true.

Danton whistled. "Man, those Earthside arkies would just kill to get their hands on artifacts like these." He walked to a table and pressed his palm to its green top.

Marta drew a finger across the crystalline surface. "Not artifacts: biofacts," she said, "or ecofacts. Not fashioned by intelligent labor, just grown, then found or adopted for use."

He looked at her and snorted. "This stuff just grew here and it happened to make itself into furniture?"

Marta shrugged. "It grew, anyway," she said, running her finger along a table edge. "Like the door. It's perfect. Natural, and more beautiful, somehow, than something manufactured would be . . . . "

"The pool there's even better." He pointed to the source of the light in the center of the room.

Marta walked to the edge and knelt. Like the rest of the pieces in the room the pool—a large tub really—rose straight and perfect, and somehow blatantly, organically, minerally *grown*, up from the dry sandy dirt of the floor. It was aggressively octagonal, the squared rim of it came to about the top of her thigh and was filled with the clearest golden liquid she'd ever seen. It was like illuminated honey, if honey could be the most perfect version of itself in the Universe. The light seemed to radiate up from far beneath the level of the floor.

"It's like the phosphor oceans of P-Mass Twelve, only golden instead of green," she said. She peered into the depths. "No . . . more like Earth amber, but with its own light."

Danton leaned over the edge of the tub. "Amber's solid, though, tree-sap fossil, right? That stuff looks . . . well, not watery, I guess, but definitely not solid." He straightened, pushed his hair back from his face, thrust one fist back into his pocket and gesticulated with the other. "Besides, doesn't amber have bugs and stuff trapped inside?"

Marta thought about it for a second. She'd seen beautiful amber in Earthside museums with insect inclusions, small leaves, once even a lovely and absolutely perfectly preserved frog, tiny, enfolded forever in clear gold, suspended in time and space for millions of years. "Sometimes stuff gets encased, preserved: inclusions. Not just bugs, though, all sorts of things." She smiled at the glow and reached to touch it.

"No!" Danton lunged forward, caught her sleeve. "You don't know what that stuff is."

She raised an eyebrow. "This from the guy who makes sneak trips into prohibited jungle to feed his blood to some alien-grown bit of architecture?"

He withdrew his hand, frowned. "Different," he said. "That was different."

He turned, wandered away, began to run his hands across the walls. "There's carvings on these walls, you know," he said, "Pictures. It's kind of like the pieces your Mom's been finding at the site; all potato-people with bunches of arms. But they're doing stuff . . . look, here's potato people . . . I'm not sure, planting something? Here's potato people, uhm, hunting maybe? Or what? Dancing? And look—these ones are swimming in the pool. I guess they were smaller than we thought."

With a last look at the thick, unrippled surface of the heavy golden fluid Marta stood, dusted off her knees and joined him. They both ran their hands over the surface of the shallow-carved rock, following with their fingers the tiny non-human figures engaged in inscrutable activities. "Braille archeology," said Marta. She traced along the smooth-etched edges of the frieze.

"Bas-relief," Danton said, "Like in the Creswell Crags, or ancient Egypt back Earthside, or the third moon of P-Mass Sixty-seven." Marta turned to stare at him. He stared back. "What? I read. I might not be an arkie-kid, but I'm not stupid."

"I didn't think you were stupid."

"Fine."

"Fine. . . ." She turned away, ran her hands along the wall, followed the cut stone and the tiny ovoid people-shapes. Her eyes, well-adjusted now to the dim honey glow of the light coming from the pool, made out patterns in the pictures. "Not pictures," she said softly to herself, "Pictographs."

Danton came up behind her. He was standing close enough that she could feel his breath on the side of her neck. The hairs there ruffled slightly with his exhalations. "What's that? How is it different from pictures?"

She cleared her throat, moved a little bit away, regretted it. "Pictography. It uses symbols or pictures to represent concepts or events or activities or a special place or something. It's more like writing than art is. Art shows ideas, pictographs show . . . well, actual things. Instructions, warnings, histories, etcetera. Like . . . a radiation sign telling you why parts of the ship might be dangerous or like . . . ancient Egyptian writing using repeated pictures to describe events or what people believed."

"So what, this is like a how-to manual? 'How to live like a Potato'?"

Marta reached the end of the frieze. She put both her hands flat against the dry, sandy stone and laid her cheek against the slightly irregular surface of the wall. She closed her eyes and breathed the honey air and the papery dust-scent of the rock. "They weren't potatoes. More like . . . more like . . . moles."

"So this is an overgrown molehill?"

"I didn't say they *were* moles, just more like moles than potatoes. They weren't moles at all. They were peaceful, underground dwellers who minded their own business and knew how to coax the local plantlife to grow into shapes of incredible beauty and function, and they loved children but had a really hard time conceiving them and *that* was their tragedy and their downfall as a race."

It was his turn to stare at her. "Now how the blasted stars would you get all that, just from a bunch of... cave scribbles?"

She took a deep breath and held it for a moment. She let it out slowly and turned to face him. "First of all, this is not a cave, it's a building . . . maybe even a very special building, like a temple or something; I don't know. But somebody carved out these walls, shaped them and decorated them and lived their lives inside them. As for the rest . . . . It's just what the story says. Stop giving me that look."

"I'm not—"

"You are! Stop it. I've spent more 'tween-space hours on archeology ships in my life—inbound and outbound—than most kids our age have spent in regular schools, and there's never enough to do. I've spent hours . . . weeks and months and years-worth of hours watching arkie-ship vids and reading arkie-ship books and listening to boring-ass arkie-talk, and I've picked up on a few things. That's all."

He wasn't looking at her like she was an idiot anymore, but he wasn't looking like he believed her, either.

She stomped across the room to the beginning of the frieze. "Look," she said, pointing, "this, where you thought they might be planting, but they're growing stuff, see? They aren't planting it, just asking it to grow in certain ways. It's related to their praying."

"Praying?"

"Well, I don't know if they believed in any god we've ever heard of, but look, this pictograph—the one where they're all joined together—is repeated, in conjunction with this one, and this one, and this one. They were very spiritual . . . they prayed to the planet, or communed with nature, or whatever you want to call it, whenever they did important stuff. Especially this." She placed her hand over one of the scenes with the tub. It was obviously the same octagonal tub that held the thick, silent honey-stuff in the middle of the room, and several of the small, roundish figures were conjoined within, immersed in the liquid. "They're trying to make babies, see—the smaller versions of themselves appear only after that, over and over, but never enough of them, until finally, no small ones at all. And look how sad they seem . . . . "

Danton leaned over, pushed her hand aside. He squinted at the carved rock and traced the edge of the pool carving with a finger. He glanced over his shoulder at the real tub, vegetation-green and taking up the center of the room, very inviting with its seductive glow and impression of radiant heat.

"Do you think . . . " he trailed off, refused to meet her eyes. "Could the wanting to make babies be . . . uhm . . . related to the feeling at the door?"

She saw he'd shoved both fists back into his pockets. The bruise on his forehead was even more livid than it had been when they'd entered, though it wasn't really bleeding. She reached out and pushed back the lock of hair which fell across his eyes and before she knew what she was doing, she stood on her tiptoes and blew gently on the bruise.

He held his breath, and when she lowered herself back onto the balls of her feet, he let it out in a *whoosh*, yanked his hands from his pockets and grabbed her arms to pull her close, and they kissed the teeth-clacking, awkward kiss of two people who hadn't meant to.

Marta winced at the sear of pain in her tooth-bruised tongue and mouth and Danton let her go and apologized and stumbled backward until he bumped up against the tub.

"Sorry . . . I'm really sorry," he said, running his hands through his hair, and tried to sit on the crystalline green ledge behind him. Tried, but failed, as he tumbled backward into the pool.

Marta ran to the edge and reached in with both hands to pull him out. She could see him beneath the surface, looking up at her. His eyes were open and she watched his expression change from alarm to ecstasy as the bruise on his head faded and the cut closed up. The liquid felt like honey, too. Warm and viscous and sweet.

Until Danton had fallen in, Marta hadn't been sure the pool was so deep. It had been impossible to know, looking down into the still surface, though as far as she could tell the lighted amber stretched down forever, welling up from some point as far beneath the surface of the planet as the dimpled orange-peel clouds floated above it. She watched as Danton sank slowly backward, down, away.

She braced her feet against the outer base of the tub as best she could, took a deep breath, and plunged her head and shoulders into the pool. She flailed, slow-motion, in the clear, beautiful gold, trying to catch hold of the boot and coverall cuff that would lead her to the rest of the boy attached to them.

Her eyes were shut tight against the fluid, but it made its way into her nostrils and her ears. It seeped into her mouth between tightly-clenched jaws and pressed-together lips, and when the amber met the wounds and cuts of her teeth-bit tongue she moaned inside with how good it felt, and how frustrated it made her to be distracted from her task.

Then she felt him grab her wrist, wrap his long bony boy-fingers around her hand. For one panicked moment, she feared/hoped he would try to pull her in; in to the deep honey well with its entrapped, ancient, distilled desires of a long-gone people and all the pleasure she could take if only she stayed there forever and ever and sank and sank into nothingness and into the center of this unexplored, alien planet with its inexplicable alien *otherness.*

But no, Danton was pumping his legs against the pull of heavy liquid. She could feel the rhythmic motions of his kicks, could feel the progress he made against the drag until finally, they broke the surface of the pool together and he scrambled up over the lip and out of the tub and turned to help her. She had been clinging only by the toes of her boots, and by the time they both managed to plop out onto the floor of the room they were exhausted and drenched in moist amber mess.

She scooped as much fluid from her eyes as she could, flat on her back, gasping into the warm, quiet room. She was afraid it would hurt, or sting her eyes. But it didn't. It didn't hurt at all. Nothing on her hurt: every scrape and bruise and ache, even ones she hadn't known existed until they disappeared, were gone. She felt good and golden and alive. She started to laugh.

Pretty soon, Danton was laughing too. The two of them laughed so hard, lying on their backs on the sandstone floor, Marta got a stitch in her side and remembered what it was like to hurt and had to stop.

Danton raised himself up on one elbow and leaned over her. His hair was slicked back from his face, though the amber was drying quickly in the warm air. It dissipated into nothingness, leaving no evidence at all it had ever been there. Only absolute perfection of feeling and state of physical being were left behind, and the same intoxication Marta had felt the couple times she'd gone further with Mike than she'd meant to.

This time, when Danton kissed her, it was right; better than right, and when Marta looked into his eyes, she saw he, like her, wasn't exactly sure what came next. Whatever it would be, Marta was certain of this: it would be perfect.

It would be more perfect than any manufactured thing could ever be.

Paperheart

- 1 -

M'graithe watched the trail of flickering torches wend its way up the side of the rocky slope toward her cave: humans from the village below, bringing her the season's tithe of cow or lamb. They didn't usually leave it so late in the evening, preferring instead to come to her lair in daytime, as though blue skies and singing birds were some talisman against her nature.

She'd never hurt them, of course. Though the enmity ran deep, though she remembered the butchery of her kind by theirs, could taste still their blood on her tongue from the days of her sire and the battles he'd been forced into by rampant human expansion and aggression, she wouldn't break the truce they'd held between them for five hundred years.

They clustered around the mouth of her cave like cattle at a salt trough. One stepped forward from the others, his torch held high. He looked well fed, prosperous like the rest, though she could barely tell one human from the next but for the clothes they wore. To her dragonsight, the blood flowing sluggish beneath their sheaths of skin all looked of the same cool watery thinness.

"M'graithe!" the man called, his voice echoing tinnily down the cavernous passage behind her. "Dragon, come out!"

M'graithe stepped into the circle of light cast by their torches. She changed her shape out of courtesy, shrinking from her dragon form to her woman form, allowing the change to progress just slowly enough that those paying close attention would catch an outline of armored tail slithering along stone at the edge of the darkness, or would hear the flap of large leathery wings. Her eyes glowed like coals, mirroring the fire in her heart, the source of her power.

She knew the nakedness and golden glow of her woman shape made humans uncomfortable, though far less uncomfortable than twenty feet of full dragon and tail with wings to match. When she spoke, the power barely contained within her smaller form rode the timbre of her voice like a leaf an ocean wave. "Welcome, in the name of our treaty and the peace of these last centuries. I accept the tithe you've brought in return for my services."

A muttering ran through the crowd. The man in front waited for the murmurs to subside before speaking. He cleared his throat. "Dragon, we've brought you ten percent of our herds each season for generations, but this will be the last. The time has come for you to go. Your services are no longer needed; we've had peace in these lands for more years than anyone can remember. Our forefathers negotiated this bargain in a different era, an era with different needs, and we—"

M'graithe drew a deep breath and the crowd shuffled backward as one, as though they were all bound together by invisible cords lashed to their ankles. She felt wings longing to sprout from her flimsy human shoulders. She felt the rumble of fire deep in her chest, and saw the reflection of her blazing eyes in the wide stares of the townfolk.

"*You*," she said, ignoring the small spurt of flame that shot out with the word. "You've had peace here for five centuries because I've kept you safe. I've chased the wolves from your doors—both the furred ones and the ones in armor. I've battled other dragons for you, kept those away who would've taken far, far more than a few sheep. Far more." Her gaze rested on a young boy clinging to his mother's skirts. "What will you do when another dragon, one not bound by treaty and tolerance, comes to these hills?"

The man in front stepped forward again. In human form, M'graithe's gaze was level with his. The reflection of her fire in his eyes made his pupils blaze. "There are no other dragons," he said. "The last was killed off when my grandfather's grandfather was a baby. Dragons aren't immortal, M'graithe. They die with a spear to the heart just like the rest of us."

M'graithe listened to the living blood pump through his veins. Her dragon senses, inflamed by the fire coursing through her heart, picked up small sounds of tethered sheep breathing in the darkness; the faint noise of villagers blinking against her light; the flight of nightbirds diving for insects overhead and the sweet, strange music made by clouds rubbing against the sky. She glanced up at the Moon, gravid and silver, then looked into the eyes of the man before her and saw how tiny his life was. All of them, these humans; tiny and fleeting.

She turned. She walked deeper into her cave, leaving them to their night-blindness, to their short lives and their sputtering torches, which smelled unpleasantly of pitch and smoke and not at all like the fire lighting her heart. She let the wings push from her shoulders, and felt the familiar weight of her tail begin to materialize behind her as she walked. Without turning she said, "Fine. Go. I release you from the old treaties. You're free to live and die as you will. I've flown these mountains since before humankind knew of their existence, but you may stay. I'll not bother you or yours, though I'll not stop those who would."

She heard muttering flare again behind her but didn't bother to look. As she grew larger and more dragon-formed—lumbering deeper into her cave, graceless on land in a way she never felt in the sky—the leader of men called after her into the dark: "We'll expect you gone, dragon. By next season you'll be gone from here, or we'll make sure of it."

M'graithe spun and let loose a bellow of flame. She closed her eyes, feeling her heart blaze with her emotion, feeling tongues of fire lick through her veins, heat roiling back through the air of the cave to bathe her scales. Humans by the entrance cried out and ran, though they were beyond range of her flames. Hobbled sheep bleated with fear, scrabbling against their tethers and each other's flanks, some breaking free and crashing loudly down the hill after the fleeing villagers. All other sounds in the night ceased as wild creatures slunk away, flew out of range, or cowered in the scrub.

When the flames died M'graithe felt empty, completely spent. She shrank to human form and staggered to the edge of her cave, briefly resting against the scorched stone wall before venturing out to check on her season's worth of sheep, to round up the scattered ones she could find and lead them to their pen. She suddenly felt very tired, not just from the night's stupidity but from the years, the centuries which weighed her down, made her feel weary beyond the physical.

Perhaps this was what it was like, she thought, to grow old.

- 2 -

The dragon dreamt of fire.

Like all her kind she slept deep, and long. In her younger years, when dragons still ruled the world over men and all other beasts, M'graithe had loathed wasting time in sleep. For a thousand years she'd wheeled through the air, subject to no one and to no thing save one: the power of flames. She'd flown over the countryside, sometimes in her joyous play leaving scorched furrows in the meadows like the trails of enormous earthworms. Dragons blazed like shooting stars through the heavens, above forest, above desert and jungle. They soared between bluegreen ocean and bluegrey sky, dipping low on the wing to scoop schools of writhing fish up into their fire-wreathed jaws.

In M'graithe's dreams, fire coursed through her body, bringing the heat, the power, the sweet pleasure of ashes, the warmth of the sun. In her dreams, men didn't exist. They didn't mate and spawn with the ease and impermanence of mayflies, driving dragons off lands they'd flown for millennia. Men, not content to share the Earth, sent wave after wave to kill dragons, leaving behind their dead human thousands. The very thing that made men weak also enabled them to bring dragons if not to heel, then at least to truce: their ephemeral natures. Human lives lasted a mere span of years. Compared to the natural life of a dragon, the time a man spent above soil seemed no longer than a few beats of a fiery heart, a few licks of flame. Because of this they were compelled to breed, to seed the earth with as many copies of themselves as they could. No matter how many men the dragons fended off, more came. And more and more and more.

When M'graithe's sire had been brought down, the other dragons had fled. They flew away across oceans or deserts, or to other places even farther away which M'graithe couldn't even remember or imagine. She had stayed. She'd made truce with the humans, the enormous ravaged carcass of her sire, the last full-blooded dragon, ripped to shreds and rotting in the field behind them. She'd retreated to her mountain, keeping her word and sweeping the countryside free of marauders, of invaders, of dragons who'd gone wild, crazed with grief over their own dead and craving the flesh of men in vengeance. Some dragons she'd fought had no more sentience left in their eyes than a rabid fox, or a hare with its leg chewed off in a trap. Those had limped away from battles with her, and over the centuries fewer and fewer had returned. It wasn't until the villager had said so that it occurred to M'graithe there were no more left to come.

M'graithe twisted in her sleep. The fire of her dreams turned sharp. Instead of bathing her in heat and glory, it stabbed at her with flames as biting as shards of glass or the tips of swords. As she tossed she felt fire cut deeper into her flesh, rubbing raw the soft exposed parts of her skin between her scales, under her arms and at the base of her throat. Her heart's flame flared in her chest, and she woke straining against chains binding her to the cavern floor.

She thrashed. Her tail flicked back and forth, slashing the air near the rows of humans driving spikes through the links of her bonds. They cried instructions to each other, dragging chains across her heaving bulk, pinning her head so her flames shot harmlessly away into the depths of her cave. Though she was small for her kind, she outweighed any forty of them.

They'd brought a hundred.

She thrashed, flame bursting from her nostrils in spurts, heat washing back across the sweaty, hate filled faces of those around her. When they'd driven iron stakes through all the chains binding her to the cavern floor, the man who'd spoken at the last tithing stepped onto one painfully outstretched wing, a long jagged blade in his hand.

M'graithe strained against the bonds lashing her jaws shut. In her thrashing she'd smashed one side of her face to bloody pulp, and the hard ridges of injured dragonflesh had swollen shut her right eye. With the peripheral vision of her left, she watched the man on her wing lift his arms to get his followers' attention.

"It's as I said it would be!" he said, and everything fell silent but for M'graithe's ragged breathing and the crackle of torches. The man began to pace on her wing, grinding his heels as he walked, treading deliberately on the bones—hollow, made for flying—beneath the skin. He stooped with quick slicing motions to rend the wing under his feet, the dragon straining against her bonds and sucking her breath sharply against the pain. He dipped his hand in her blood and stood, lifting reddened fingers over his head. "The stories were true! Dragons bleed red. They bleed red until they die, just like any of us."

He walked to her wing's edge, finding the delicate part near the dewclaw. "We've suffered her tyranny for generations, working hard on our farms and our homesteads so this dragon might grow fat off our labors. No more!" He jumped, coming down hard with both boots on her fragile bones. At the snapping sound, the villagers let up a cry, and hoisted their torches into the air.

Tears of fire licked M'graithe's cheeks, rolling down her scales, then her skin as she shifted form. Her body shrank, chains falling from her like dead iron snakes. The villagers' cries of triumph turned to alarm as they scrambled away, back toward the entrance of her cave. M'graithe stepped naked and golden from the heap of empty chain, flames licking across her skin, the air around her so hot it shimmered, tears still streaming down her cheeks.

She turned to face the man with her blood on his fingers. The arm which had been her broken dragon wing hung limp and bloody by her side, her fingers splayed at odd, broken angles. The man backed slowly toward the cave entry as she began to grow again, her body expanding into wings and tail, her neck lengthening until she towered above him. Fire gripped her heart. Red filled her vision: the red of flames, of coals, of blood and burning things. She reared back, preparing to blast him with fire.

"Now!"

Dozens of iron-tipped bolts slammed into her with the force of close range. Many bounced off the hard plates of her scales, but others found their way into the soft flesh beneath her arms, on her belly, at the base of her neck.

"Again!"

Another volley struck her and she screamed, fire shooting from her mouth filling the cave, igniting everything in all directions.

The villager ran, his clothes bursting into flame as he went. "Again!" he screamed, dropping to roll in the dirt. "Again!"

She beat her wings, ignoring the bolts bristling from their leathery expanse. She ran a few ungraceful steps to the mouth of her cave and burst into air, past the gauntlet of raking swords and thrusting spears piercing her hide with cold iron. It had been dark as night deep in her cave, and M'graithe blinked into the sun shining high in the cloudless blue sky; blinked against hot tears gathering in her eyes.

"Again! Again!"

She wheeled upward, away from the hundred sharp points flying through the air after her like a swarm of angry bees. Her broken wing slapped feebly against her side, the crushed bones an agony. Blood streamed behind her like the gaudy tailfeathers of an exotic bird, pelting to the earth like hot red rain.

M'graithe flew over fields and mountains she'd protected for more than a thousand years, and as she flew, salt tears rolled off her face, joining the red spatterings on the green, green earth below. She flew under the scorch of the sun, and under the gentle benevolent wash of the Moon. She flew increasingly raggedly as the landscape shifted, her perforated heart leaking its fire through the air in hot red splashes to soak into snow-crested mountains, cold ocean spray, hard rolling grains of desert sand and finally, cold ocean again. When she could fly no more, she plummeted toward the crust of the world, her dragon wings disappearing into nothing along with her heart's blood, as the last of it trailed away behind her into the morning sky.

- 3 -

"Origami Mistress! Origami Mistress! Come quick. There's a beautiful lady, and in the tree . . . there's a beautiful golden lady, and there's a tree, Grandfather Willow, and she's gold and has hair like ripe plums and . . . up in the tree, and—"

"Calm, child, be calm like water. Catch your breath. That's it. Now start again, and slowly, so I can make sense of your words."

The girl, slender as a reed, with graceful hands and plump round cheeks, leaned over and gulped for air, resting her hands on her knees. Her long black braids looped up about her ears, held in place with small jade combs. Her elongated tunic sleeves draped low, weighted to the floor with ripe plums and pretty little pebbles that spilled when she bent to catch her breath. The origami witch, white-haired and dressed in simple cotton pleated in the style of her art at her waist and shoulder, stooped with surprising agility to gather the child's treasures and hand them to her one by one. The girl nodded thanks, returning fruit and stones to her sleeves as she straightened to begin again.

"There's a golden lady, Mistress, draped over a forked branch high in the old willow tree. She's beautiful, Mistress, and I think she's dead."

The origami witch narrowed her eyes. "Hmm."

"Please! I'm not making up stories. Not this time. I promise."

The old woman smiled and extended her hand. "All right, Jade. Show me."

The girl clasped the witch's wrinkled hand and led her through the ornamental groves. They passed the Fountain of a Thousand Beauties, through the Garden of Delights and over the Bridge of Mourning Brightly. They traveled the entire length of Jade's father's grounds, all the way to the far end of the estate where the enormous willow had stood for a hundred years. Jade pointed high, high into the branches.

The origami witch squinted, peering up into the greenery. "Hmm," she said.

It took twelve gardeners to bring the beautiful lady down from the tree, and three of the least squeamish to pull the dozen bolts from her cold flesh at the old woman's instructions. The origami witch ordered her carried, wrapped in white silk and borne gently, to her cottage at the opposite end of the palace groves. When the gardeners laid the woman on the origami witch's own sleeping mat, the white silk was sodden, the deep red a vibrant counterpoint to golden skin and plum-colored hair.

Jade watched as the witch dabbed at the golden flesh with small cloths steeped in herbs. "Is she dead, Origami Mistress?"

"Hmm. Not yet: dead blood doesn't flow. But she will be soon if you don't give me some privacy, Jade. You may come back tomorrow, though not before noon."

Jade's shoulders fell. "Yes, Origami Mistress. After noon." She turned to glance once at the still, pale figure on the mat before sliding the screen shut behind her.

When the origami witch was certain the girl had gone she stopped dabbing at the cold skin. With speed that belied her stooped figure, she pushed the blood-soaked silk aside. She rose and moved about the small room, gathering herbs and medical instruments and cotton bandages from cupboards and drawers. When she had everything laid out in a neat row on a tray, she stoked the fire in her small brazier, threw some dried petals into the flames, and turned at last to the most important element of her craft.

Pulling two dozen small squares of golden paper from a drawer whose spring catch was hidden in the twining necks of cranes carved into the wood above the mat, the old woman began to speak to the prone figure on the floor.

"You'll never be what you were, my girl. I apologize for that, though perhaps in this day and age it's for the best." She laid the golden squares beside the scalpels and the herbs. "I waited for you. I waited three hundred years. That's not so long a time for your kind, I know, but my old bones do ache at night."

She paused. Her hands stilled and she sank down to rest on her heels, kneeling before the mat and the golden woman. "You'll not thank me," she said. "I don't know how far you've come, scattering the blood of the ancients across the land like dregs of plum wine, but with that hole in your heart, you've used all your fire to keep yourself alive. You'll never have fire again, girl; never be able to let it blaze hot enough in your veins to turn you to that other shape you were born with. Not without it killing you. I hope you can learn to live with that."

She reached to stroke the arch of the still woman's brow above one bloody, swollen eye, then turned and began to fold her paper.

- 4 -

The dragon dreamt of ice.

Cold daggers of it slicing into her chest, filling her nose and mouth, choking her. It was hard and unyielding like iron, without the malleable beauty and nimbleness of flames.

She tossed, remembering cold chains weighing her to stone floor; feeling again the crunch of hollow bones—bones designed for flight and the defiance of gravity—beneath her skin. She cried out as she thrashed, protesting the stabbing of her wings, the piercing of her heart, the slow flow of her hot dragon blood into the cold blue ocean and into the unyielding dirt beneath her as she'd flown as far from her home as her damaged wings could take her. She remembered her dragonform sliding from her like water from the feathers of a goose, and she only dimly remembered falling through the grey haze of clouds, falling though rain and ice crystals in the air, falling without wings or tail to check her descent.

She woke flailing, her arms struggling to keep her aloft. When they met the resistance of soft silk instead of daggers, warm herbscent in the air instead of ice crystals, she ceased her thrashing and her cries.

"That's it, girl. Calm. Be calm like water, calm like deep still pools of meditation. Calm like cool stone."

M'graithe gulped air into her lungs. Her chest felt heavy and wet, but hollow. Her limbs felt weak and fragile, like brittle twigs after an icestorm. And all over she felt cold.

"What," she gasped, her words rasping from her throat, her gaze casting about the room into the shadows, trying to see past the deadness of her fireless eyes, "What have you done to me? I've no heat at all. I'm dead. My heart is cold."

"Hmm. Yes, it might feel cold, after millennia of fire in your heart, to suddenly be without. Don't worry, girl. It's still there, your fire, running deep in the ichor of your veins. Yes, I know what you are. I'm old enough to speak your language, though not by much. I was a young girl when my parents died, both of them the watered-down stock of the ancients. I've used what small magics their blood granted me mostly in waiting for you, my girl, these three centuries. That, and in saving your life."

M'graithe lifted her hand. It twisted in on itself, and ached like ice. A jagged red scar wound the length of her arm, beginning at her wrist and ending near her shoulder. The raised welt was purple and ropy. Her injured eye was tender to the touch, but intact. Her skin, instead of golden, was a faint human tone, pale like peach blossoms.

M'graithe turned her face into the small hard pillow beneath her head and let cold flameless tears slide down her face, unheeded. From the small hearth across the room, the woodfire mocked her with its distant, puny warmth. "You say you've saved me, but you've killed me. You've practiced some witchery on me and made me human."

The old woman laughed. "Not human, girl. Never that. I'm lucky there was enough human blood in your veins to fix you into the form you have. But you've got to be careful never to let the fire take you back. That would kill you for certain, and the purest dragon blood left in the world would be gone forever. Are you quite ready for that? If so, let your rage get the better of you. It'll be a quick end." She turned to poke the meager hearthfire with a charred willow branch. "It was the unchecked rage, the vengeance, that drove them to their destruction, the other dragons. The fire in a dragon's heart brings great power, but also, it consumes. That's now doubly true for you, with the heart I had to give you."

M'graithe looked up. "What heart did you give me? With what cold dead thing did you replace my flames?"

"With the only magic at my disposal." The origami witch reached for the tray on the low table. Beside the single remaining golden square were bloody blades, fine enough to slice a human hair in two equal halves lengthwise. Near these knives lay dried blossoms with their petals folded into miniscule origami pleats, and two or three burnt willow twigs. She lifted and began folding the edges of the gold paper, looking not at the dragon as her fingers worked but into the flames of the hearth. "I made you a heart of human magic—"

"*Human magic.*" M'graithe spat the words like a curse or a bad taste. "Humans have no magic. They're cruel, empty creatures, devoid of honor. I should roast them all on the spits of their own spears until their eyes run down their cheeks like curd."

The old woman continued as though M'graithe hadn't interrupted: "—Human magic, of art and culture, and an appreciation of beauty coming from a lifespan not much longer than a butterfly's, to a dragon. I made you a heart to replace the one charred and emptied of ichor, which crumbled to ashes when I touched it and blew away in a small draft from the hearth. I made you an origami heart, a heart of paper, which if you ever let the dragonfire in your veins get the better of you will consume you for good, and this time forever. Learn to love humans and you can live in this world which has become theirs. Paper cannot withstand the heat of dragon vengeance, or rage, nor even of hate, which is cold."

She met M'graithe's gaze and held up the folded paper in her hand, a golden origami dragon so intricately wrought it seemed it would take flight from her wrinkled palm. She turned and tossed the tiny dragon into the fire, and they both watched in silence as its wings crisped and curled to ash.

- 5 -

"That's enough for today, Jade. You may come back tomorrow, but not before noon."

Jade tucked one last blossom into the plum-colored braid she'd just completed. Pulling a jade comb from her own hair, she pinned the loop up over the still, prone M'graithe's ear. "There. She's so beautiful, every man in Father's household will love her if she ever wakes."

"Hmm."

Jade rose from kneeling by the still figure on the bed, stretching her arms over her head before turning to hug the origami witch. "Thank you, Mistress. I'll see you tomorrow just after breakfast."

She spun and rushed out the open door, tripping down the path with her ears covered, laughing as the old woman called "*Not until after noon*!" at her departing back.

The origami witch shook her head as she shuffled to fill the teapot by the window with warm water. She was still chuckling when M'graithe opened her eyes abruptly and sat up, asking, "Why does she come here every day?"

"Why do you play dead every day? For weeks you've let her prattle in your supposedly-sleeping ears about princesses and handsome warriors, about bridal fashions and pet kittens and the colors of treeblossoms. You could ask her to stop. It would take only one look from those steely eyes—yes, that's the look—to quell her interest in you forever. Well, perhaps not. Jade's a stubborn little thing. It's her own brand of magic."

"Witch?"

"Hmm?"

"When I woke, shortly after you ruined me with this sad flimsy thing you call a heart, you said something: you said you'd waited for me for three hundred years. What did you mean?"

The old woman stopped with her cup raised halfway to her lips. She lowered it and looked at M'graithe. "Paperheart, I don't know what cave or forgotten corner of the globe has sheltered you these last centuries, but the world has changed. The ancient blood is disappearing, diluted beyond detection even in those who claim it. You're old enough to remember the last of the true dragons—"

"My father."

The origami witch nodded. "That explains much of the mystery of you. The true dragons were finally killed off in their wars with humans. They may seem recent to you, those wars, but to people alive today they're distant history. Even the world of my childhood seems little more than fairytales to those living now. Once dragons were gone, men turned their attention to the rapid development of trade, of agriculture, of social advancement, of art."

She turned the teacup in her hands, a delicate pale thing like an unfolding lily. "Such beauty men are capable of. Did you never wonder why dragons, who ruled the earth for millennia, never thought to build a thing like a bridge, or a garden, or a road? Or a teacup so thin you could hold it to the sun and see its rays through the bottom?"

She drained her cup and lifted it, holding it up against the light streaming in the open window.

"Bridges," snorted M'Graithe. "Gardens. What needs a dragon with a bridge, when it rules the skies by wing? What needs a dragon with gardens, when it can scoop prey from the air with a crook of its talon? Or see whole forests at a glance from on high?"

The old woman stood. She unfolded slowly, looking greyer and smaller than M'graithe had thought her before. She shuffled to M'graithe's side and pulled the comb from her hair. "Humans feared your strength, but they should have pitied you your weakness. Perhaps dragon and humankind are not so very far apart, after all."

She lifted M'graithe's hand and placed the comb in her palm. "Just remember, dragon; your blood is of them, just as their blood contains much of you. The two are mingled. If you listen closely you can hear the dragon ichor sing in their veins. If you look closely you can see the magic in them. There's enough power still pumping through that paper heart of yours for that. When I'm certain you've understood, I'll be at peace, knowing the last being in the world more dragon than man has learned to love."

M'graithe stood, flexing her ruined arm as though it were a stiff wing. "What needs a dragon with a frail human thing like love?"

"Hmm." The origami witch shuffled toward the door to the garden, her back looking even more stooped than it had. "What indeed? Love is just another sad little human magic after all, dragon. One which will save your life as surely as your paper heart."

- 6 -

"You're awake! Oh, Lady, I still can't believe you're awake! When I first saw you high up in Grandfather Willow, your back bent over his top boughs and those pointed sticks prickling from your chest like a porcupine's quills, I was certain you were dead! I told Mistress so, didn't I?"

"Hmm."

Jade returned to her task of tugging a sandalwood comb through M'graithe's hair. "And then you slept all those days. Day after day until I thought it was forever, though I suppose it was very few weeks. But I came every afternoon. I sang you songs and read you from my lessons, and told you all about everyone in my father's house. Didn't I, Origami Mistress?"

The origami witch didn't look up from her scroll. "Hmm. Jade, I think it's time for you to go now. You may come tomorrow, after—"

"—Noon. But Mistress! Can I show the Lady the Grove of Beautiful Sorrows? We could walk past the Fountain of a Thousand Beauties, through the Garden of Delights and over the Bridge of Mourning Brightly . . . that is, if the Lady's not too tired, from being asleep all that time."

M'graithe sat stony-faced, as she had the entire afternoon. The origami witch glanced at the dragon from the corner of her eye. "Hmm. Yes, Jade. I think a walk would do the Lady very well indeed. She's shown amazing recuperative powers. Yes, I think a walk is the perfect thing."

Jade leapt to her feet. "Thank you, Origami Mistress. Come, Lady!"

She tugged the dragon to her feet and hurried them both out the door before the origami witch could change her mind.

All through the gardens, M'graithe let herself drift above the endless river of chatter flowing from the girl. Her stories of lapdogs and of the latest style of embroidered slipper and of the sleeping habits of her father's court streamed around her in warm currents. She'd grown so accustomed to the girl's voice it was almost effortless to allow herself to be carried along by the child's buoyancy. As with all her kind, languages came easily. Especially human languages, which were after all descended from the ancient universal dragon tongue. She nodded when the girl motioned toward flowers and artificial waterfalls and flimsy ornamental bridges. She looked up when the girl pointed to a funny cloud in the sky, and crouched beside her when the child squatted to show her an enormous beetle, markings on its back like spilled ink. When they reached the end of the garden with the palace, far from the origami witch's tidy herb-scented hut, M'graithe looked up. At the sight of the figures crouched on the scrolling roof framing the entryway to the palace, her breath caught in her throat.

She looked down at the mosaic tiles scattered in the clay along the path under her feet, and saw the same familiar sinuous winged shape, twisting its way toward the steps. Beyond, stretching away in rows like sentries on duty, crouched two dozen topiaries sculpted into similar serpentine curves.

"Dragons," she whispered.

The ancient word was close enough to the girl's language for her to recognize. "Yes! My father's descended from true dragons, from years and years and years ago. They call him the Dragon Lord."

M'graithe began to burn. She felt her blood simmer. Her shoulder blades itched where wings should be, and her eyes grew hot. She felt a slow smolder begin in her veins, felt the mounting flame which would burn her paper heart to ashes.

How dare they? *How dare they*?

Simple, cruel, pitiful humans, with lives no longer or more meaningful than a flea's or a gnat's. By what right did they claim the blood of *Dragon*, the title carried by her own sire, dead these five hundred years with a spear of human metal shoved deep under his scales? Dragons bore the blood and magic of the planet itself. In their veins ran the same hot fire coursing deep below the thin crust of water and mud riding the world's shallow surface. Dragons were the old masters of the world, and its true children. And humans? Shallow, empty creatures of mud and water, magicless.

How dare they?

M'graithe felt the edges of her origami heart begin to fray. In a moment the golden paper of her insides would succumb to dragon rage. It would ignite, and she would burn to a cinder, though perhaps not before she could blast the palace to the ground, to nothing more than a scorched pile of clay and metal. She didn't care. In fact, she craved the fire. *Burn me*, she thought. *Burn through me and of me. Burn!*

Jade tugged her sleeve. "Lady, are you all right? You look flushed. It's my fault for asking you to walk so far, and for talking too much. I'm sorry. Here, come sit by the Pool of the Dragon's Tears."

M'graithe looked down into the child's face. Her vision was clouded rage red, dragon power filling her sight and her mind. Senses ignited, old power coursing through her, she suddenly noticed what she had not before. As the girl led her, stumbling and numb, to a stone bench by a pool, she forced the rage to ebb from her crisping heart. She let it seep from her vision, but used its lingering presence to hone in on the thing she'd glimpsed in the girl's veins, running beneath the sheath of her translucent human skin as a current flows beneath the ice on a winter river. She allowed herself to be lowered onto a bench, and Jade dipped her long tunic sleeve into the pool—emptying it first of three large snail shells and a glazed clay marble—and began wiping M'graithe's hot brow and cheek.

"There, Lady. You look better."

M'graithe nodded, mesmerized by the glow of dragonblood flowing through the veins of a fragile human child. M'graithe herself was of mixed descent. The origami witch also. In a way, humans were her brothers and her sisters many times removed; or perhaps, her children. Dragons bred so rarely, eons could pass without a new one opening its eyes to the sun. But humans—these delicate, ephemeral creatures, who made countless more of themselves every day that passed—would keep dragons alive in the world. As long as humans lived, so would dragons.

Jade bent to scoop water into her cupped hands. "Lady, do you need a drink? It's not really dragon's tears—that's just a name.

My father says real dragons, full-blooded ones, don't even cry."

M'graithe tilted the child's palm and took a small sip. When she raised her head she wiped the backs of her hands across her face, feeling cool water on her lips from the pool, warm water from her eyes on her cheeks. "No," she said, meeting the girl's gaze for the first time. "No, I suppose they never did."

The Beetle Eater's Dream

Long after water became more valuable than human blood; long after oil became virtually useless; long after time ceased to have meaning for a dying planet's ordinary citizen; long, long after that, there lived a girl.

A woman really, for who has childhood when there is no time for that or any other mundane thing? So there lived a woman, who waited outside the door of her simple scavenged hut built on the bones of dead machines and covered with the hides of well-tanned longpigs—(her home an artifact of previous tenants: our girl-woman lives on the meager flesh of tiny beetles whose carapaces slice her tongue and stick between her teeth like large husks of ill-ground pepper)—outside this hut, she waited.

She'd dreamed, in the half-dream way of lazy shamans and ill-fated third daughters, of a prince from the stars to take her away. She squatted in dry sand, turned her face to red-sunned skies.

And picked beetles from her teeth.

And squinted into searing winds.

And one day, he came.

As in her dream, he fell from the sky in a golden ball, which cracked open like a lizard's egg and spilled him forth as yolk.

"We've returned," he said, "from your long-ago colonies, bringing goodwill to Earth—Planet 441—from her far-flung children—"

—Not a word of which our beetle eater understood. But he smiled, and she liked that, though his teeth were like nothing she'd seen in her life: so shiny, so white, and so clean.

He held out his palm (as he had in her dream) and she took it (it was just as she'd seen) and together they stepped into his egg.

This woman who had never been a child became looked upon as something rather more and less than one. The few children she met seemed like an alien species. They were more alien to her than the three-thumbed sloths of Planet 311. They were more distant in nature than the binary meta-minds of Planet 297, and far, far more foreign-seeming than the hermit platypus sect of Planet 319. The beetle eater gave these beautiful planets new names—secret names, which she quietly hummed each night in her dimly illuminated shipsteel cabin as she studied their images on tiny pixelated screens: Floshelleth of the Shining Jewels; Litellatella of the Thousand Flowing Startrees; Plethiia With the Multitude of Fishes. Having never had a name, she ached, mourning the namelessness of other things. Numbers were not the same, though numbers suited the children of the children of the children-hundred-times-children of her foremothers. They were clever and pale, rarely speaking to one another and never to her.

Nights, Johnston Eighty-two, he of the golden egg, would come to her cabin. "JohGegg" she called him. Reading and understanding came quickly, but clear speaking eluded the beetle eater, her tongue and throat too often lacerated by hard-edged beetle wings.

So each night Johnston Eighty-two came to her cabin and each morning he left. The beetle eater began to feel the closeness of shipsteel walls, the dullness of shipcrew glances, the staleness of thrice-breathed air.

One morning, as Johnston Eighty-two rose from bed to clothe himself in the garments she hated, the beetle eater caught his hand. She pulled it to her cheek, pressed his knuckles to her skin.

"JohGegg," she said, ignoring his slight frown; "JohGegg go Gearth."

He slid his hand from beneath her cheek. "Earth? Planet 441? It's been catalogued and reclaimed. There are no plans to return anytime soon."

The beetle eater stood. The blankets slid from her unclothed body and Johnston Eighty-two looked away. He bent to pull on his boots.

"Go Gearth," she said again, and held one hand toward him, palm up as she'd been taught, to show she concealed no weapon. She pointed to her bare breast with her other hand, to the space over her heart. "Go Gearth."

He frowned again, shook his head, and left.

Days became weeks. Johnston Eighty-two ceased coming to her cabin at night. She wandered sleek halls of shipsteel. "Go Gearth," she said to everyone she met. Their eyes, especially the eyes of children, were flat as they stared at her, silent. She would stand tall as she could, barely reaching chin height of the shortest of them. "Gearth," she would say, and point to herself.

The day came when he came back. He didn't look at her. She smiled and pulled Johnston Eighty-two's hand to her cheek.

He led her to the docking bay. They strapped into one of the dozen eggs lining the shipsteel wall, gold against platinum. The ship spat them out, sent them spinning toward the planet and its great amberine sun.

A sliver of light cracked the egg. It expanded, until the beetle eater spilled onto hot sand with a tumble and a laugh. She clutched her stomach and rolled across the shallow dune, her skin soaking warmth from the sun, the ground, the air. When she remembered, she sat up and looked at the egg. Johnston Eighty-two stood in the center of the crack, unsmiling.

"I'm sorry," he said, and stepped backward as the crack closed around him.

The beetle eater shaded her eyes against the glare from the egg as it rose. She watched until there was nothing to see in the sky but the cloudless forever of it. Still smiling, she stood. Lifting the hem of her tunic to let the sun and wind and blowing sands of

Earth make their acquaintance with the slight swell of her abdomen, she began to hum to the baby inside her belly. The song's words—sung in her head where only the two of them could hear—were a litany of beautiful names.

Floshelleth of the Shining Jewels.

And Litellatella of the Thousand Flowing Startrees.

And Plethiia With the Multitude of Fishes.

She didn't yet know the name of her child, but she would.

And you, she hummed into hot wind in the wordless, half-dream way of lazy shamans and ill-fated third daughters: *and you.*

Milky Way Meat Market

Jingle-jangle nerves and alien jukebox rhythms swing
a syncopated beat, my one heart, your three.
"Well hello, baby," you say, slick back your hair
with your third antenna.

"Don't baby me, you one trick pony." See? I've got your number,
I know your type. I've been led down love's
shiny primrose path before.
Have you ever seen a primrose, you outer-rim sleaze? I bet not.

"But," you say, "You Earth girls are so often so willing—"
"Oh, yeah, I know, and so very delicious."
You look hurt.

"No eating, I promise. Just tasting—no more."
"No more?"
"No more."

I'd like to believe you, I would, I would.
I curse the universe and the alignment of stars
that the hottest guys in the galaxy are also carnivorous.

Shades of White and Road

It came to me that I should run away from home taking nothing but myself and so I thought I would and so I did. I'd not gone ten turns of the spiral before a small leathery suitcase began to tag along in my invisible wake. "Take me! Use me! Fill me!" it said. "Please, please fill me; I need to be filled."

I scarcely spared it a glance. "Sorry," I said, my voice as firm as the clist clist clank of my heels striking sparks against the metal of road beneath me. "Sorry, but I've no use for a thing needing filling. I'm on my own."

I had to admire the thing; had to give it some credit, for even on its tiny legs it managed to keep pace with me for another hour. It kept its silence, but I felt its sorrowful gaze tugging at my skirts like younger brothers. By the time I stopped for lunch, it was breathing hard but still looking determined. I pulled an apple from my pocket and began to peel the green green skin away with my small pointy teeth.

Suitcase gasped. "An apple!" it said. "This whole time you've had an apple in a mere *pocket*, when it could have been filling me in service of yourself!" Its eyes narrowed. "What else have you, stuffed in those pockets? What else?"

Under its accusatory scrutiny, I sighed. I carefully buried my apple core under small mound of earth by the side of road. Averting my eyes from little green apple grave, I reached to the lining of both pockets and turned them inside out until seams screamed their violation and balls of lint fell to earth like evicted tenants. Along with lint fell three hairpins, a hard roll, and a dead pewter penny.

Suitcase gasped. It opened its mouth and closed its mouth several times like an air-drowning fish, then unfastened its top and popped everything from my pockets into itself. Even lint, which squealed with delight at being included and snuggled down into lining and creases and sang a little fuzzy chorus of grateful thanks.

I harrumphed as best I could and stood. I dusted off my skirt, cleared my throat, straightened my shoulders, and resumed my march in an ever-increasing spiral away from home. Suitcase, emboldened and full of purpose, had no trouble keeping up. It was only after blanket and three-legged stool joined somewhere along the third bend in the whorl that suitcase began to slow down, distracted, I believe, by the clattery clattery clatt of three-legged stool (though perhaps it was the sussely-sussely of blanket slithering along metal road).

"No room, good sirs," said suitcase in all officiousness. "No need for your services, thank you very much goodbye."

Little three-legged stool looked as if it would leave off, but blanket drew itself up in confident array. Addressing me rather than suitcase, it said: "Come night, you'll have need of the likes of me. I desire nothing in this world so much as to wrap myself around you."

To which short speech I could take no offense, as it was delivered in all sincerity and with a boldness I found charming. "Well," I said, stopping to consider. "I suppose sun will be setting soon enough, and night is sometimes sharper than the teeth of saws. Especially when road is out of temper and freezes over like river."

Three-legged stool waved one leg in the air, teetering on the other two. "Ooo, oo!" it said. "I'd be happy to slip beneath you for a spell while you rest and consider. And tonight, when you make camp, and fold blanket next to fire, I could be there too, holding you off cold ground and assisting while you make meal."

I gave my patented harrumph. "This is getting much more complicated than it should be," I said, eyeing in turn suitcase then blanket then three-legged stool. "When I left home this morning for good and forever, I swore I would take nothing but myself and so I did."

"Aha!" exclaimed blanket. "You didn't take us; we took you—"

"For a sucker," grumbled suitcase beneath its breath.

Blanket shot suitcase a glare. "I took you for someone who could provide what I've always wanted: a person of my very own to wrap around, to keep warm and safe against night and cold."

Said three-legged stool, "—And I for someone who would just let me hold her—"

Added suitcase, all begrudging, "—And I for someone who could fill me in any small way with things, both necessary and un."

I breathed deep and counted to twelve. I lifted my hand to shade my eyes and watched as tangerine sun dipped beneath distant indigo mountains, allowing crepuscule and gloaming to scuffle before twilight and darkfall. Glowfruits lit trees lining rural road, their interior fires illuminating night like round paper lanterns strung for festival. Blanket, proving itself more than just another pretty quilt, slithered over to the glowing globe of a fallen fruit and rolled it back toward us, bumping it along the soft blades of dew-damp grass with silken binding. Three-legged stool rapped smartly on the hollow sphere, so crack split down its middle and halves fell to each side. Flames leapt from the shallow bowl of hollow shell, crackling merrily, causing shadows to jump into stark relief despite the continuing violet of sky not yet quite black.

Stool scuttled close to fire. Blanket rolled itself out neat as a bed, and suitcase arranged itself nearby, showing its willingness to play temporary table by propping itself on end with the hard roll on top. A sense of camaraderie settled upon our small camp with the comfort of heated milk.

I sat upon stool, which purred with satisfaction beneath my weight. I ate the hard roll, brushing crumbs off proud suitcase with a murmur of thanks. After dinner I curled next to fire, snuggling into blanket as the first drops of evening dew fell on ground and nearby road. On road, dewdrops glistened in light from fire's dying embers, glimmering like small scattered beads of amber and mercury.

Next day was quite like first, except by the eighth spiral out on the whorl which led from the city to the end of the world, I trailed behind me a strange menagerie, which clittered and clattered and whoosh-whoosh shooshed along the flat steely surface of road like a kite-tail of cans and ribbons tied to the bumper of a bridal carriage. Blanket and suitcase, carpet and frying pan, bucket and fishingpole and three-legged stool. Suitcase had filled itself with glowfruits.

I'd explained to each as it joined our procession: *No thank you. I've left home with nothing more than myself, and I travel alone.*

Which made me the most obvious of liars.

By the third night we'd slipped into comfortable routine. Suitcase would make fire while carpet helped three-legged stool and blanket make camp. Fishingpole and bucket would stroll together to nearby river, which everyone knows runs parallel to road in outward spirals at least as far toward eternity as anyone has ever traveled the whorl. They'd be gone for some short while, then return, giggling and filled with private happinesses, bucket brimming with water and fishingpole carrying a modest evening catch. Their romance was delightful; they made everyone cheerful who came into the orbit of their contentment. With the assistance of frying pan and, by the end of that fourth night, the company of harmonica and deck of cards, we were a jolly little crew. It was on the fourth night we met a traveler coming from the other direction.

"Lo, outward-bound! River and road." He was beautiful. His teeth were clean the way I like them; pearly and smooth as polished nickels. His skin was lovely-dark, and burnished like ebon bark and scented like the vanilla bean which grows deep in jungle between spirals of whorl.

I lifted my hand in return. "Lo, inward-bound. River and road. May your feet never never slip from metal and your head never never slip beneath water."

I'd forgotten what it was like to be in the company of another person, and that night at the fire my tongue seemed to tie itself in bows and make untidy ribbons of my words, which fluttered from my mouth like brightly colored things to be quickly collected by magpies and buried in nests. Shiny things are not always useful things, and that's how my words felt.

I don't know what he replied to my colorful senseless ramblings. I do know his name was Crispin (which I thought very pretty) and I told him my name was Sethily (which it was). All my companions of travel and camp kept silent, as is their custom around people plural. Person singular is a different case entirely, of course, and though I understood and respected the parameters of their conventions, I missed the easy comfort of our previous nights. Even bucket and fishingpole lay limp and silent by fire, though their wooden edges touched upon each other, lightly.

Crispin hefted frying pan with masculine confidence and indelicacy, his large slender frame crushing three-legged stool, his enormous dusty beautiful manfeet splayed out across poor rumpled carpet, grinding it into dirt. Harmonica and deck of cards took refuge inside suitcase, which lay at an awkward angle across damp ground. I briefly missed their cheerful contributions, but was soon distracted by the play of firelight on Crispin's smooth, blue-dark skin.

"Why are you outward bound?" he asked me. "Why leave the city to walk the spirals of whorl?"

I looked into his beautiful grey eyes. "I left, taking nothing but myself. I've had my fill of things. My mother is an architect," I said, "She builds the tallest spires in the city, and fills them with as many beautiful objects as my father can grow in his gardens. He grows many, many things, and my mother fills and fills her spires. Her house was so full when I was born, my mother designed an additional tower just to accommodate me. Of course, it was crammed with so many wondrous baby things that I had to go live in the garden under the ivory vines and the looming fruits of my father's beautiful furniture and sculptures and other gardenworks.

I lived under a slow-ripening pianoforte for nearly three years before it matured. It's in the living room of the fourth spire by now, or perhaps the ballroom. I forget which."

Crispin's eyes glowed by the embers of fire. "Things, yes. I grew up at the outer edges of the whorl where nothing exists. No truly beautiful things grow away from the city; fewer and fewer the farther one goes. I'm from a spiral so far out the whorl, I was lucky to find anything growing at all, even wild little things such as this blanket, this frying pan, that bucket. My father's rumored to have been a bicycle, so I suppose traveling is in my blood. I could never be sure, though, since my mother died when I was born."

The thought of a free-wheeling father and a dead mother brought me indescribably low. That I'd seen my own parents scarcely above one day in twelve since the day I was born seemed of a sudden a petty thing.

"I'm sorry," was all I said. I didn't trust my clumsy tongue to say much more than that. But Crispin seemed not at all saddened by his own story. He laughed, and fished fishy fish from hot frying pan with naked fingers and breathed on them to cool them and held food to my lips which I couldn't help but take. His eyes were simply too beautiful not to; his limbs simply too lithe. We fell asleep curled like twin questions on top of blanket, though long after Crispin's light snores began to ruffle the hair on the back of my neck, I lay awake in dark, missing the chuckles and sighs of bucket and carpet, of fishingpole and harmonica.

The next morning I woke alone. Completely alone. There was empty husk filled with dead embers of last night's glowfruit fire, but gone was bucket, suitcase, carpet. Gone was beautiful man named Crispin.

I bunched the hem of my skirt in both fists. My feet pounded road as I ran back along spiral toward the city. *Clank clank clank clank*. Soon the staccato of my boot heels hitting road were joined by the sound of my panting, syncopated like a lazy rhythm section or a constipated metronome. I clank clanked slower and slower, gathering all my skirts into one hand so I could clutch the other to the stitch threading itself between my ribs. My heart beat in the roof of my mouth, my lungs heaved in irregular, gasping halftime to my panting.

I stopped and stood stooped, hands on knees, head hanging down. When I caught my breath, I straightened and lifted my skirts to continue toward the city with as brisk a pace as I could manage when something caught my eye. There, off to one side, half buried in spindly grass, was one of the legs of three-legged stool.

I plucked it from the growth. Nearby, I spotted the rest of three-legged stool, and I ran to scoop that up too and clutch it against my breast. "Oh, little three-legged stool! What happened?" I tried to fit its broken leg to the corresponding hole in its seat, twisting it into the rattly place where it had once rested so snug.

Three-legged stool drew a ragged breath. "It wasn't his fault," it said weakly, words interrupted by its own feeble cough. "He was simply too big, too heavy, and didn't possess the more delicate sensibilities."

Anger flared in me like the flames of a dozen overripe glowfruits all tossed into a pile and ignited at once. I set three-legged stool on road beside me as gently as I could. I lifted the hem of my skirt to my mouth and used my teeth to start a tear in fabric. I tore two strips from the bottom of my overskirt and used them to bind the damaged leg as best I could. Cradling three-legged stool to my side, I set off at a decent—though more sensible—clip, spiraling ever inward back the way I had come toward the city at the center of the world. Before I'd completed even two turns I came across suitcase, battered and bruised, a deep dent disfiguring the top of its once-proud exterior.

I gritted my teeth as it told me Crispin had used it as a substitute for three-legged stool, only to find its sides were not meant for such abuse. Against my breast, it sobbed: "You know I'm willing to volunteer for additional use. You *know*!"

I rocked back and forth, crooning, "There, there. Of course

you are. You're an excellent little suitcase, really . . . top notch . . . a lovely little thing. . ." and so on, until its sobs hiccupped into subsidence. Gently, I unfastened its latch and peeked inside, whewing with relief to see deck of cards and harmonica cowering in the bottom alongside inert penny and lint. The three hairpins were nowhere to be seen, nor was there any sign of glowfruits.

Neither suitcase nor three-legged stool objected to the indignity of riding together in my arms as I set my feet once again on road in the direction of the city. By nightfall I'd come across and gathered up carpet, bucket, and frying pan. I treated their wounds and scrapes as best I could, and continued to grit my teeth against their dogged insistence that the man on road before us didn't mean to be callous or cruel or insensitive; he simply used things up with complete disregard for their physical or emotional well-being. Unanimously, they maintained that he acted out of carelessness rather than neglect or disregard.

Since I carried suitcase rather than allowing it to walk, I loaded it with frying pan. Carefully rolled, carpet lay across my shoulders like a thick woven boa. Bucket felt well enough to bump along at my heels, having been abandoned more out of a lack of perceived usefulness rather than any real physical damage. In some ways, its hurt ran the deepest. Apparently, only blanket and fishingpole had been deemed useful enough to travel with the beautiful, careless man.

I didn't stop for the night. Metal road was easy to follow even by starlight. Without campfire to ruin my night vision, river and road glittered, near-identical ribbons of reflected starfield, silver-white on silver-black sparkling like long swards of diamond-headed moon poppies, furling in tightening inward spirals as we approached the city.

Denser and denser grew buildings, my mother's handiwork less apparent at the impoverished outer rims but dominating neighborhoods closer to city center. Her style had been so heavily copied, her designs had become ubiquitous. Pale towers with ballooning attachments and slender spires soared overhead.

Melodious wind whistled through carefully orchestrated archways and vaulting, curving, bone-colored walls. Sown between buildings and along edges of ever-narrowing road, my father's gardens displayed tidy white-on-white rows of lamps, of dining chairs, of coffee tables and teaspoons and dinnerplates and mailboxes. Here and there, a massive divan or enormous four-poster bed dangled, heavy on the end of its ivory stalk, full with its juices and nearly ripe for picking after what had been a most excellent growing season.

I didn't stop. I knew where Crispin, whose father was a bicycle and whose mother didn't exist, would go; he would go to the very center of the only city in the world. I also knew what he would find there: the house of my mother and father, at the very middle of the very meeting of all the spirals of the whorl of road.

Me sore and dusty, bucket rolling unevenly on its rims and poor suitcase, carpet and three-legged stool considerably worse for wear, we limped through open gate to largest garden in the only city in the world. All was shades of white and ivory and bone, with the deep polished chrome of road running below and the creamy arching spires of my mother's constructions rising into clouds above.

I limped to door. Balancing suitcase on my hip, I unlatched door one-handed, propping it open with my foot to allow bucket to enter behind me. On all sides towered stacks and stacks of the most beautiful objects my father could grow. Pale bisque ewers and platters and vases and sculptures tottered and teetered, piled row after row alongside the whites of tables and chairs and trunks and draperies and everything a person could think to use and want; all of it shades of the palest cloud-white to the smoothest milk-white to the softest powder-white. Only a narrow path wound through the towers of beautiful junk, just barely wide enough for a girl and her carpet and her three-legged stool to limp through, with their bucket following closely behind.

The path spiraling through the rooms crammed full of beautiful things wound around, mimicking the spiral of the whorl of river and road. At the very center of my mother's house was a large open room, calm and empty like the eye of a hurricane or the exact midpoint of a tornado. In this room crackled fire in white marble fireplace. Three enormous damask wingback chairs clustered about an ivory table covered in delicate china, teapot steaming and platter heaped with small crustless sandwiches cut into triangles.

I stopped. "Mother," I said. "Father. Crispin."

The three seated in high chairs turned as one to face me. My mother spoke first: "Sethily, is that you, darling? We've been entertaining your delightful friend. He's a huge fan of our work, you know; came all the way to the center of the city just to meet us. Come in, dear. I feel as though I haven't seen you in years. Is that dirt you're tracking all over my floors, leaving those horrible sooty smears wherever you go?"

"Sorry, mother. And it has been years. Three years. We had tea once then. Before that it was four years and before that, two."

My father was frowning at the things littering the floor at my feet, their browns and reds and greens somehow shabby rather than vivid against the starkness of my parents' pale neutrals. "Sethily? You couldn't possibly be Sethily. No daughter of mine would traipse such common little weeds through this house; such ragged wild growths from outside the city, polluting the air and my gardens with their pollens of questionable provenance."

Bucket, suitcase, three-legged stool and even carpet, rolled as it was, crowded close against my legs. A clattering sounded from the corner by the fireplace as fishingpole, in its haste to reunite itself with its beloved bucket, fell from where it was propped against the wall and skittered across the flagstone floor. It came to rest at bucket's side, wooden surfaces meeting with a sloppy, lightly splintery kiss. I stepped forward to lift the limp, poorly folded and sadly creased blanket from the back of the third chair by the fire. "Hello Crispin," I said.

He smiled up at me. In the middle of all those thousand shades of white—the walls, the marble, the floors, the furniture, my parents—his gleaming blue-black skin and long lanky limbs and pale grey eyes were more beautiful than ever. I remembered the warmth of him against my back the night before, and the gentleness of his breath upon my neck.

"Why did you take those things?" I asked.

His smile faded, replaced by what looked like genuine confusion. "But you said you wanted no things, and nothing but yourself. I thought these random things had just gathered themselves about you."

"Well, yes. I suppose they did."

"And you said you never wanted to see another thing. You said that's why you left this wondrous city."

"Hrmph. I guess I did say that."

"I just wanted to get to the place where beautiful things grow." He swept his hand in a gesture which included not only the orderly arrangement of the carefully appointed room, but also the tottering piles and stacks and towers and gardens full of beautiful things existing beyond the walls. "It didn't occur to me they were anything special. I didn't know you wanted them."

Little murmurs wafted up from the folds of my skirt where bucket and three-legged stool and suitcase and all the rest clustered. *We told you*, they said. *It's not his fault. He doesn't understand. He's the son of a bicycle and a dead woman, and in his own way grew up wilder than we.*

I cleared my throat to avoid harrumphing. "Yes. Well. I may not have thought I wanted anything, but it seems they want me, so. . . ."

Crispin's smile returned, hesitant. "So. . . ."

My father, master of the harrumph, harrumphed. "Your friend here wishes to apprentice to me. He'll grow you new things, considerably more wonderful, more appropriate things."

My mother turned to look sharply at him. "Now, now! He's agreed to apprentice to *me*. He'll build Sethily a beautiful new spire to warehouse her ugly little objects. And another to house all manner of beautiful, perfect things, plucked fresh from the vine."

"He'll be a master gardener!"

"An architect!"

"Gardener!"

"*Architect*!"

I gathered together what I could of my little crop of wayward objects and we turned and limped toward the door. At the doorway I paused to glance over my shoulder. Crispin, the only beautiful thing in the room, sat in his chair, holding his pale bisque cup of white tea and watching my parents argue over him.

I left, my odd little procession clumping and clattering and shoosh shoosh shooshing behind me. All along that unwinding spiral, out through the house crammed full of soulless objects a thousand colors of pale, I thought about the house I would build, somewhere out there beyond the city between river and road. I'd live by myself but I wouldn't live alone; I'd have the company of a bucket, and a suitcase, and the cheery blather of a harmonica and a deck of cards. I'd have a blanket to keep me warm at night and a carpet to soften the floor for my feet. I'd have a frying pan and a fishingpole to make sure I ate well every day. Even humble lint would be welcome in my home.

All the way outward bound I scoured road for little lost hairpins, just in case they turned up, needing a ride.

Baseball Trophies, Baby Teeth

Uncle Babatunde had only one leg, but many stories.

He wasn't really Monifa's uncle. He wasn't even her uncle's uncle. Mother said he was her uncle's first wife's grandfather, and no blood-relation to her at all. She also said he was an old man, and a sad one, and that nobody respected the elderly anymore.

Monifa didn't necessarily respect Uncle Babatunde, but she did love his stories and his heavy plastic leg. After he moved into their basement, Monifa often sat with him, massaging the soft pads of callused flesh, sore from rubbing against the leg's leather straps. He claimed everything ached too much to be dulled even by rum and Twinkies.

"Uncle Baba," she'd say, "tell again about the souls of the men in your flask."

He'd chuckle. It wasn't a happy sound; it was a sound like the crushing of dead, dry leaves, or the grinding of glass. "Child," he'd say, "there's not near enough rum and Twinkies in this house to dull the ache of that burden."

He'd shake his head, tilt his drink to his lips. Monifa would look over his shoulder at the glass case against the wall which had once held her brother's baseball trophies. On the top shelf rested the dried head of a small animal, red beads sewn where the eyes had once been. On the bottom shelf lay the knife with the handle Uncle Baba had carved when he was younger than Monifa, with a blade the size of his bigger thumb (the longer thumb, which stuck out straight from his fingers like a broken twig from an arthritic bush). On the middle shelf—dented, tarnished silver sides gleaming like dull wet riverstones—was the flask.

Sometimes, after Monifa's parents had gone to bed and her brother was old enough to stay out all night without telling Mother where he went (causing her to cry, and reminisce about his days of baseball trohies and baby teeth), Uncle Babatunde would drain too many glasses of nutmeg and rum. He'd put out his hand just so, and Monifa would stand perfectly still while he levered himself to his feet, leaning onto her small, sharp shoulder. Together they'd waltz a three-legged dance across the wide, low-ceilinged basement of Mother's home.

Monifa would steal glances over her shoulder at the plastic leg, pale pink, nothing at all like Uncle Baba's rich leathery skin which was dark like the soil in Mother's garden where the best flowers grew. That pink plastic looked too lonely and too raw, lying by itself on the grey nubby weave of basement carpet.

Uncle Baba would hand Monifa his empty glass, the outside still cold and wet with the ghost of ice. One hand heavy on her shoulder, he'd fumble open the trophy case with the other.

She always held her breath when he drew out the flask that lay, curved and narrow and shiny-dull, on the middle shelf. Uncle Baba would hold it to his nose, inhale at the edge of the screwed-on lid and squeeze shut his eyes, tight and wrinkled. Sometimes he'd sing, low and soft in a language she didn't know.

"What's that song?" she asked him once, after he stopped singing and they both stood, stooped from so-long standing beneath their weights.

"Child, that's no song. It's an apology to the men whose spirits live trapped inside this flask."

The slender, beaten thing in his grasp was from an older era, an older generation and one not often emerging from basements and obscurity. "But they were very bad men," she said. "They killed your young wife, and cut off your real leg."

Uncle Baba nodded. He'd told her many times of the village where he'd been born; where they drank water straight from the wide, wide river, and collected feathers from enormous birds the colors of everything, and sang shopping lists to remember them all the way to market where people fell in love with each other over piles of plump purple tubers.

"Yes, little one; all true. But should the spirit of any living thing be locked forever in a metal bottle which a young man happened to trade a traveling Belgian for two raw diamonds the size of his thumbnails?" He rattled the tarnished flask. Monifa considered the wide flat plains of his thumbnails: quite large thumbnails, after all.

In the damp quiet of the sleeping house, she heard soft rustlings from the flask in his hand. It was the sound made by beer bottles filled with cigarette butts when she found them in her brother's room and shook them: soft rattling, like the ragged shells of dead beetles knocking together.

When Uncle Babatunde died, Monifa was nearly sixteen. She'd not had much time for an old man and his plastic leg for some while. For a long time by then she had stayed out most nights, tasting sex and other illicit things with the tip of her tongue. Mother, after years of crying over Monifa's brother's baby teeth and baseball trophies, didn't spend much time crying over Monifa.

Monifa helped pack Babatunde's things into old cardboard boxes. "A whole lot of nothing and nothing for a life to leave," said Mother into the empty room.

The heavy plastic leg leaned in one corner. It glowed, mellow and warm in the dim basement, looking less forlorn without Babatunde's presence rather than more. Monifa walked to a half-filled box and pulled out the flask, wrapping her slender fingers around its dull, hammered-metal sides and screw-threaded top. She slid it into the pocket of her dress, where it lay warm and hard against her thigh. When she moved, it rubbed along her skin through the cloth. When she knelt, its hard, rounded edges pressed into her flesh.

That night Monifa didn't go out. In the quiet house—brother long gone, father long gone, Mother asleep with the aid of blue pills—she lay in bed. She shook the flask gently, holding it to her ear, listening to soft clacking. She lifted it to her nose and breathed, unscrewing the lid to the scent of nutmeg, rum, and Twinkies.

She turned the flask upside down and shook its contents free, certain Uncle Babatunde would have been glad.

I Consider My Cadaver

I worry too much for my cadaver,
that future unliving she,
who spent some too-few decades as this
one I consider me.

Is she all right? Does she remain intact?
(How exactly did I go?)
Does she lie on hot asphalt or cold metal slab?
These are things I need not know

and yet

I consider them. I consider, too, this
bag of flesh, this sack of meat and bone,
though when my cadaver does turn up I'll
consider the considering done.

Flaming Marshmallow and Other Deaths

I'm so freaking excited I can hardly stand it.

Tomorrow. Tomorrow is my birthday; *the* birthday. The birthday everybody waits and waits for and until you get there you just hate that all your old friends already got theirs and you're the only one without it yet and sometimes you think *holy-freaking-eff I'm never going to turn sixteen*, but then you do.

At first I'm afraid I won't be able to sleep. I turn off the light, but after lying in the dark for half an hour I turn it back on. I look at the calendar hanging on the wall above my bed. I reach up, lift it off its nail with one hand and snuggle back under the covers, taking the calendar with me and running a finger over all the red Xs marked over all the days leading up to this one. It's a little cold out, and the last thing in the universe I want to do is catch an effing cold the week of my birthday, so I snuggle down into the warmth of my flannel sheets even more. I know there's going to be parties this weekend, and I'm going to want to go.

This is what I've been waiting for all these months. All these years, I guess, though before my friends started getting theirs, it didn't seem like such a big deal. We were all No-Knows then.

Tomorrow, I'm finally going to feel like I belong.

Tomorrow, I'm going to find out how I die.

"Carolyn! Yo, grrrl, wait up!"

At the sound of my name I turn around. It's Patrice. I can see her bounding up across the commons toward me. Her super-long hair is braided today, and as she runs it whips around at the sides of her head like two angry red snakes with ribbons tied to their tails.

"Hey, Patrice," I say, and clutch my books closer to my chest. I try to walk a little faster, thinking maybe she'll get the hint. She doesn't.

"Today's the Big Day, huh?" she says.

I nod.

She turns her head away, bites her lip. "Lucky," she says.

I shrug, speed up even more. It's not my problem she's one of the smartest kids in our class and they moved her up a grade like, four years ago. It's not my fault she's going to be a No-Know for another whole year.

Out of the corner of my eye, I see Brad Binder. He is so effing cool—a burner, they say. *That's hot*, I think, and then I laugh to myself.

"What's so funny?" asks Patrice. We're at my locker, so I balance my books on my knee with one hand while I fumble my combo-lock with the other. I pretend I don't hear her, but she sees me flicking sly glances Brad Binder's direction.

"Not *him*," she says, rolling her eyes. "You can't be serious."

"Shhh!" I try to shut her up. I wish I had some kind of freaking superpower or something. I wish I could just concentrate really hard and make her go away.

Brad Binder pulls his letter jacket out of his locker, which is so close to mine, three other girls have asked to trade with me. He shrugs his perfect—so effing perfect!—shoulders into his jacket and takes out just a notebook with a pencil shoved in its rings. No computer, no books, no nothing. God, that's so effing cool. Just like a burner.

As Brad walks away, Patrice fixes me with one of those stares of hers. "He's not that great, you know. I heard he kisses like a dead lizard."

I guess you'd know, I almost say, but I stop myself. I don't want to stoop to her level, be so childish. I'm sixteen today and after school my dad's taking me to the mall to get that slip of paper and then I'll know where I really belong. So I shrug again instead, let it slide off me, like egg off Teflon. "He's a burner," I say. "They're pretty cool."

Patrice snorts. "You know what his slip said? 'Death by Flaming Marshmallow.' That doesn't sound like a real burner cause-of-death to me, no matter what he says. He should probably be hanging out with the chokers, instead. You wouldn't think he was so tough then."

I've had enough of Patrice. "You wouldn't understand," I tell her, and walk away, toward Geometry class. Maybe Cindy Marshall will be nice to me today, it being so close to me getting my c-of-d slip. Maybe I'll end up being a crasher, like her.

If only!

I'm almost late getting to class. Mrs. Tharple looks at me extra sour, but I don't give a flying eff. I slide into my seat right as the bell rings, and catch Cindy Marshall's eye. I smile.

"Don't even look at me, you No-Know," she says to me, low under her breath as Mrs. Tharple starts handing out our pop quiz. The other two girls behind her snicker. I feel their eyes darting against my skin, sharp like the teeth of weasels.

"It's my birthday," I say.

She turns in her seat and looks at me full-on. I try to understand the look in her eyes, but I can't. I feel like it's something really obvious, like she's trying to tell me something so, so, so obvious, I should already know it.

I feel really stupid.

Mrs. Tharple walks between us, places our blank quizzes face up on the desks in front of us, glides on by to the next row and toward the front of the room again.

I look down at my Geometry quiz, try to concentrate. Try to ignore the heat in my cheeks and the tips of my ears and on the back of my neck.

"Hey, you," hisses Cindy Marshall.

I look up.

"So did you get your slip yet?"

I shake my head. "After school," I tell her.

She narrows her eyes. I sense the other girls, crashers both, also watching me, but I play it cool. I hope.

She nods. "If you get your c-of-d, and it's crashing—anything: plane, car, bike, hot-freakin'-air balloon, whatever—you come talk to me again. Tomorrow."

I have to bite the insides of my cheeks to keep from smiling. I try to look like this isn't the best offer I've got all morning. I try to look tough. I want to be crasher material, I really do.

"Tomorrow," I say, and she nods again, once.

Not a one of those girls acknowledges my existence the entire rest of the class, but I don't care. Everything will be different tomorrow.

Tomorrow, my life can begin.

Lunch isn't what I'd hoped for.

I've spent all this time counting down to my birthday, thinking, *this is the day everything changes*, but it isn't. I don't feel like a No-Know anymore, even though technically, I still don't actually know. I'm under eighteen, so I have to have my parent or legal guardian with me to get my slip. If I could've, I would have ditched lunch today, gone to the mall, gotten the whole thing over with. Instead, I have to wait for my dad to get off work. It's so unfair.

So, even if I get my slip tonight, nobody but me is going to know my cause-of-death until tomorrow. Well, my parents will know, and my little brother, I guess. And I'm sure I could call Patrice and tell her, but why? After tomorrow I'll have new friends to hang out with.

But for today I'm still stuck in No-Know-ville.

I grab my tray and slide onto the bench at the end of the table. Patrice waves me down further toward her end, but I pretend I don't see her. I line up my eight extra packets of mustard and start tearing the corners off one by one, slowly squeezing out the sharp yellow and gooping it all over the top of my synthesized proteins and pressed vegetable shapes.

Covertly, I scan the room, wondering, fantasizing about where I might be allowed to sit tomorrow. Who's going to welcome me with open arms? It all depends on my c-of-d.

A ruckus is going on over in the corner. Of course it's the burner kids, cracking each other up, starting a food fight. The burners, the drowners, the crashers, the live-wires and the fallers . . . all the violent accidentals; they sit in mingled clumps along the two tables in the corner. That's the coolest corner, and I'm pretty sure I'll get to sit there tomorrow, or at least close. The next couple tables out wouldn't be so bad; you've got the med-heads and the sharpies and the bullets—mostly malpractice and murder, right?—though some kids sneak in there who should probably be over with the suicides. I can see those from here, all dressed in black and with pale faces. They look like a bunch of crows, pecking at their food.

Just please don't let me be one at one of the last two tables, sickness and old age. Ugh. They look boring even eating lunch. That would be my c-of-d if I was forced to sit at that table: Bored to Death.

"Happy birthday, Carolyn."

I'm so startled I squeeze a mustard packet too hard and it squirts all down the front of my dress. I start to dab it with a napkin, but I'm just turning bitter yellow clumps into bitter yellow smears.

"I'm, I'm so sorry, Carolyn . . . *eff.* I—I—"

I look up into Jamie's face. We used to be friends, a long, long time ago. He lives just down the street, and we used to ride bikes together every single day. I can still taste the sun and summer dust on my tongue, just looking at him. We stopped hanging out when his parents joined the Anti-MoD League. Sometimes on the way home from school, I see his mom standing out in front of the mall with her placard and her sandwich board. "Lives are for Living" say her signs some days. Others, "People Against Machines of Death" or even, "Don't Ask: Don't Know—You Have a Choice!"

Jamie's almost eighteen and he's still a No-Know. I'd just die if that were me. I'd just die.

"It's okay, Jamie," I tell him. "Don't worry about it."

He has a couple napkins in his hands, and he's dipping them in his water and holding them out to me. He started to dab one on my breast, but figured out in time it probably wouldn't be such a good idea.

I try to stifle a sudden memory of me and him kissing behind the convenience store dumpster. I was probably about twelve or thirteen, and he was fourteen or so; right before his parents joined the League. I remember he tasted like strawberries.

I hope Jamie doesn't see my ears and neck turn red. He's one of the few people who knows me too well for me to hide it.

"Your mom picking you up after school?" he asks.

I keep dabbing, shake my head. "My dad."

He nods. He's watching the motions of my hands as I rub the damp napkins on my lap, on the fabric stretched across my ribs, but he's not really seeing me.

"I'm sorry," he says again, and I don't think he's talking about mustard.

By the time Dad picks me up, I'm mentally exhausted.

He kisses the top of my head when I get into the car. "Hey kid! Happy special day."

"Thanks."

I throw my stuff in the back seat and fasten my lapbelt.

Dad's just sitting there with a loppy-sided smile on his face. "You want to go get an ice cream first, or something?" he says. "You want pizza? A movie?"

How can he be so-freaking clueless? I want to tell him what a moron he's being, but when I look at him something feels like it slips sideways in my stomach. For the first time, I'm looking at the forty-something man with the glasses and the stubbled cheeks and the ugly sweater, and I don't see my dad.

I mean yes, of course, I see my dad; the middle-aged med-head c-of-d (accidental overdose) with the over-expensive house and the boring job and the two kids and last-year's-last-year's car, bought cheap with high mileage from a rental fleet. . . .

But I also see a guy. I see a guy who loves me so much, he can't even put it into words. It never occurred to me to think this might be a big deal for him, the day I get my slip. He looks tired, I think. More tired than usual.

I reach out and put my hand on his where it's resting on the steering wheel.

"Sure, Dad," I say. "Whatever you want."

He covers my hand with his other one, so it's kind of like a hand-sandwich, my fingers and knuckles pressed between two layers of his. His eyes look a little bright for a second, but I decide it's only my imagination as he places my hand back in my own lap and starts the car and pulls out from the curb.

I watch the school get smaller and smaller in the side mirror as we drive away.

I finish off the last of my ice-cream cone, and so does Dad. We wipe our sticky fingers on the wet-wipes and throw those away, and I get up from our food court table and gather all my bags as I stand. Dad's bought me a new pair of shoes, two new books and a hat he says I look great in but which I know I'll never, ever wear again in a million billion. All I'm missing is the partridge in a pear tree.

"So. . . . What next, Birthday Girl? Need some new gloves? Music? You used to love the music store."

He's walking over to the mall directory, studying the list of stores. I walk up to him, set down my bags of books and shoes and touch his arm. "Dad," I say, "It's time."

He doesn't look at me right away. He takes off his glasses and starts to clean them on the edge of his sweater. I can see he's just making them all linty and smeary, so I take them from him and clean them on the inside hem of my dress, instead. When I hand them back they're considerably cleaner, and I pick up my bags and start walking the direction of the slip kiosk. I don't have to look up the location on the mall directory; I know exactly where it is. There's not a fifteen-year-old in the country who doesn't know the location of her nearest machine. I know its hours of operation (regular mall open-hours: ten a.m. to nine p.m.), I know how much it costs (nineteen-ninety-five-plus-tax), I even know the brand (Death-o-Mat, by DigCo.; "*We Give the Same Results—For Less!*").

The only thing I don't know is what's going to be on that strip of paper when it scrolls out of that slot.

It's getting kind of late, and the mall's going to close soon. Most of the stores are empty. It's a school night, so nobody my age is around. It's mostly straggly-haired moms pushing heavy strollers, and tired-looking shop clerks with achy feet.

The machine kiosk is in a darkish corner over by the restrooms. The janitor has the door propped open to the ladies', and even though I kind of have to go, I'm not about to brave the janitor and his stinky mop. Besides, I don't want to put this off anymore. I need to know.

Dad pauses when we get to the machine. He fumbles with his wallet, pulls out his identity and credit cards. He clears his throat but doesn't say anything, doesn't look at me.

I thought Dad's hand shook a little when he slid his cards into their proper slots and keyed in his and my social security numbers and other information, but I'm sure I was imagining things. It was probably just my brain buzzing. That's what it feels like inside my head right now; like all the curves and loops and folds of my brain are buzzing with tiny bees, or maybe electric currents. I guess brains are, after all, though. Filled with electric currents, that is, not tiny bees.

The machine's green light comes on and an arrow points to the small, shiny, self-cleaning divot in the otherwise dull metal. I set my bags down at my feet, slowly reach one finger toward the indention—

"Carolyn!"

I jump, look up into Dad's face.

He pushes his glasses back on the bridge of his nose, fumbles it a little, blinks.

"Uhm . . . for an extra five dollars, it will tell you your blood type, your glucose levels, and whether or not you're pregnant." He points to the list printed on the machine's face. Then he frowns, distracted. "Hey, there's no way you might be pregnant, is there?"

I close the tiny distance between us and wrap my arms around his waist. He hugs me back, and for a second, as I breathe in the warm fuggy-sweatered dadness of him, I feel like the most precious and important thing in the universe.

Without letting go of Dad or giving him any warning, I reach behind him and jab my finger into the shiny divot. Dad flinches, and presses my face closer to his chest.

A tiny slicing pain flits across my finger, then numbness as the machine sprays its analgesic and disinfectant.

I pull back from Dad, and he clears his throat and lets me go. The machine spits out Dad's two cards from their slots, and my slip scrolls out from the single slot below. Dad and I both reach for it, but when I freeze he pulls back. I've got to do this, and he knows it. He plucks his plastic from the machine and slides the cards into his wallet while I uncurl my slip and read.

I read it three times. Four times. I'm on my fifth when Dad, unable to contain himself, gently tugs the paper from my stiff fingers and reads aloud.

"Death by Millennium Space Entropy," he says.

"But. . . ."

Dad wraps both arms around me and swings me up into the air like he hasn't done since I was a very, very little girl. I keep my arms stiff, but let my legs and body go limp, and Dad twirls me in a circle, laughing, joyous.

He finally sets me down, and I have to reach out a hand to

steady myself against the edge of the machine. I'm a little dizzy. Dizzy, and confused.

"Millennium Space Entropy," says Dad, shaking his head, unrolling the slip and reading it again. "That's amazing, Carolyn. It's fantastic! You'll be nearly a thousand years old by the next millennium. Maybe you live to *be* a thousand! Just think, medical breakthroughs all the time, vastly extended lifespans . . . it could happen, sweetheart, it could really happen."

Dad, grinning, crushes me to his chest again, and I can hear the rumble of his happiness somewhere deep inside. "I just want you to have a long and happy life, Carolyn. A very long, long, long and happy life."

"But Dad," I say into the nubby wool of his sweater, "Where will I sit tomorrow at lunch?"

Weird Fruits

When the largest volcano on Mars erupted, people of every nation on Earth watched the live satellite feed as plumes of fire and dust and the very stuff of the planet itself roiled into the Martian sky and filled its heavens. Tiny machines, which had roved the rocky red surface of Earth's neighboring planet and faithfully transmitted back through intervening space images of unfathomably deep craters, majestic mesas, and countless photos of seemingly endless rubbled terrain, recorded and relayed the massive eruption in all its beauty and terribleness. The little mechanical rovers and wanderers and data gatherers recorded and sent, recorded and sent; the Martian skies grew brighter and brighter, then darker and darker, as ash and particulate matter boiled into the atmosphere, filled it, and finally choked it.

For a brief time Earth's scientists were united in speculation and observation. They shared data and collaborated on notes, thrilled to have been able to witness, even remotely, an event of such magnitude. Especially exciting was the thought that it may have mirrored Earth's own geologic history; if Mars had had any dinosaurs, it was observed, they certainly would have gone the way of the dinosaur.

But that brief time of peace and undivided interest ended. Earth's customary bickering and squabbling ensued. Movie rights were scrambled for, transmitted footage from Mars was bought, borrowed, stolen. Theories flew across oceans like missiles, and scientists the world over had to be separated like scuffling schoolchildren when their arguments came to blows. Only one thing was agreed upon by all: the force of the Martian eruption, certain unexplained atmospheric phenomena, and the mysterious makeup of the erupted matter had combined to cause an enormous cloud of uncertain composition to separate from Mars's orbit, and it was headed directly for Earth.

Nobody was frightened. This was, after all, just a cloud. A big cloud, true; a strange cloud, which seemed to be traveling through space with inexplicable, increasing speed. But not a frightening cloud; not an *alarming* cloud. It was, agreed most scientists, merely a Gaseous Spaceborne Event.

Events, like rodeos and rock concerts, are successful only as long as hype is sustained. If the Gaseous Spaceborne Event had managed to reach Earth in a timely fashion—say, the first few weeks or months after it had caught public attention—its arrival might have been the Event of the year, the decade; even of the century. As it was, by the time it reached the planet, three years after it had faded from the front pages of Earth's virtual newspapers, Earth's citizenry had already seen the movie, read the subsequent book, and bought and discarded all the Mars-inspired Spring fashions. In fact, by the time the Gaseous Spaceborne Event reached Earth it was last-year's last-year's news, and interesting to hardly anybody at all.

It reemerged as briefly interesting when, upon hitting Earth's upper atmospheric strata, the cloud dissipated, spreading evenly enough to cover nearly the entire planet with a thin veil of tiny Martian particles. For a day and two nights, by North American reckoning, the sky glittered and twinkled as billions of tiny bits of that alien world traveled the last small portion of their interplanetary journey. Everywhere but the icy poles, people around the world glanced up for a moment or two to appreciate the sight of a sky sparkling as though sprinkled with fairy dust. It was generally admitted to be very pretty, but also generally said to be not quite as spectacular as the movie detailing the same event, released the previous summer to great acclaim and massive box office profits. No one, not even the scientists, thought any of the billions of little grains of Mars, shot deep from the bowels of that planet and propelled across the empty nothing of space, would survive intact to actually land upon Earthen soil.

Jennifer Jay Johnson, aged thirteen and three-quarters, was the first to find a doppel seed.

Jenny, as her parents insisted on calling her over her increasingly strong objections, actually saw the doppel seed fall. Unlike her older brothers, she was outside watching the glittering Martian dust in the evening sky; watching the glorious dancing of a million pinprick embers sparkling against deepening violet twilight. One seemed to glow brighter than the rest, then a little brighter, then much brighter. She followed its path, openmouthed and silent, as it fell to Earth. Directly into the earth at her feet, to be precise.

It made a slight *plop* when it hit, as though it fell into water rather than dirt, and then a hiss. Jenny squatted on her haunches beside it. She didn't touch it. Even in the gloaming she could see faint wisps of smoke or steam rising out of the little hole it had made in the ground. Smoke or steam: either way it would be too hot to touch, Jenny decided. She leaned over the hole and blew gently into it, closing her eyes and breathing deep the burnt spice and hot salt scents rising from the hole to greet her. *This is how Mars smells*, she thought.

She pushed a little dirt with her finger until it fell into the hole and filled it up.

At dinner, Jenny tried to tell her parents about the tiny piece of Mars which had buried itself in the dirt at her feet. Her brothers heckled. Her mother sighed. Her father laughed and said she'd be the next great scriptwriter for movies about things from outer space, only she'd have to pick a planet other than Mars because everybody was tired of it. Nobody believed her until after her father answered the knock on the front door. *Damned Green Peacers,* he'd muttered as he passed under the large archway which was the only demarcation between the dining and living rooms; *Damned religious nuts, or people wanting to mow the goddamn yard, or whoever that is asking for goddamn money in the middle of goddamn dinner.*

But it was none of those things. When Jenny's father opened the door, an unclothed Jenny stepped in from the front porch.

Nobody said a word. Even Jenny's brothers fell silent, though there was a naked girl in the living room. Jenny, sitting at the table, was grateful for the thick ropy vine coiling its way, leafy and slick, from the navel of the naked girl. It twisted down between her legs and disappeared into the darkness behind her, enough leafy growth sprouting from it to cover at least the lower portion of the naked Jenny's torso.

Jenny's mother got up from the dining table, took the blanket that was always draped over the back of the living room sofa, and went to wrap it around the shoulders of the naked Jenny. The naked girl looked up into Jenny's mother's face, then grasped with both hands the thick ropy vine attached at her navel and gave it a two-handed wrench. It fell to the hardwood floor with a loud wet smack, and the girl turned to push it with her bare foot until it was on the other side of the threshold. When it lay just outside the open door on the painted boards of the porch like a huge dead snake, she closed the door behind it with a solid slam. Jenny's father, standing stock still and gaping, turned slowly and stumbled to the living room sofa.

Nobody finished dinner that night.

By the time the sun rose over New York, ten million Americans had doppelgangers: by noon, thirty million. And twenty-six million people living in South America, and forty-two million in Africa and eighteen million citizens of the European Union and sixty-seven million from Asia. New Zealand and Australia had an undisclosed number of doppelgangers, but Canada had virtually none, outside a smattering on the west coast. The doppel seeds didn't seem to like cooler temperatures.

Twenty-four hours after Jenny Jay Johnson's copy invited itself to dinner, nearly half the population of the United States of America had doppelgangers.

They did not seem to eat. They did not seem to produce waste. The thick twisted vines which bore them pushed up out of the ground like enormous blind eels. They unfurled large hairy leaves veined in orangey red, and sprouted small gourd-like growths at their ends, with little nubby warts which rapidly swelled and grew into arms, legs, fingers and toes. As soon as the weird fruits were as large as the nearest uncopied human they reached down, detached themselves from their parent vines, and sought out the human they resembled. Scientists called this, for lack of a better word, *imprinting*. All over the world, families went about their daily business—working, eating, defecating, sleeping—with a host of doppels silently observing, like mute out-of-town relatives come for an unexpected visit of no certain duration.

No one ever had two doppels at once. The only difference between the copies and the originals, other than the eerie silence of the former, was in their eyes, which instead of containing whites and irises all the eyecolors of all Earth's people were nothing but a field of pale gritty orange-red, the color of Martian dust.

Doppels could not be cut or abraded, crushed or sliced. As governments around the world discovered in their secret laboratories and out of the sight of their own peoples, no technology or material or weapon at human disposal could rend or damage any portion of the doppels' bodies. The vines and leaves from which the doppels grew withered to dust as soon as their produce matured and disengaged.

Communities around the globe reacted differently, based on any number of cultural and personal preferences, tempered or inflamed by local attitudes and beliefs. In some places the doppels were greeted and treated as lost children, or unfortunate but not unwelcome relatives. In others, doppels were attacked on sight, though they never made any move or retaliation against the ineffectual efforts of their human counterparts, other than to stare unblinking as people tried without effect to run them over, shoot them or set them ablaze. In some places people did their best to ignore their doppels, which seemed compelled to remain near the people they specifically resembled. In a few places the mute, red-eyed beings were honored and treated as ambassadors, as kings; even as gods.

But other than physical space, they took nothing. Once people grew accustomed to their silent, staring presence and complete indestructibility, most of them simply continued the routines of their daily lives. In more than one household, after just a matter of days, doppels of multiple family members were ensconced in darkened dens, propped on faded cushions in front of eternal television reruns as though they had always been there. More than one household took to standing their doppelgangers in broom closets, out of the way along with skis and mops and unused toys. That was why, when the deaths began, they were already there.

Jenny's mother was one of the first to die. Throughout the day at the hospital, test after test came back as *inconclusive*, as her mother's body shriveled and dried, the creeping orange tint visible in her veins through the sallow paper of her skin. The vivid streaks covered more and more of her wasting body as it sank into itself and dried up, until all that remained was a small mound of rust-colored dust.

It happened so quickly; the unnatural orange tint of the veins showing like blood poisoning but running its course to death and dust in just over a single day. By dinnertime, ten million North Americans had begun to die, and Africans and South Americans and people all over Asia and Europe. Even Canada had its share of deaths.

Jenny and Jenny's brothers and Jenny's doppelganger sat at the dining room table. Mr. Johnson was still at the hospital while doctors ran tests on the dust of his wife, and Mrs. Johnson's doppel stood in the kitchen, silent and inelegant in its parka and apron. Unlike with some families, the Johnson doppels, though there were only two of them, wore clothing at all times. The very first night, Jenny's father had laid down the law. He'd said: *No-goddamn-body's going to see my wife and daughter walking around in the goddamn nude.* After the first awkward dressing, it was easy. The doppels were perfectly capable of mimicking simple behaviors. By the second morning, they helped themselves to clothes whenever the ones they wore became soiled or torn. Their choices were erratic and without human logic, but at least they allowed for what Jenny's mother would have called *minimum decency.*

Jenny rose from the table and went to her mother's doppelganger. Meeting its strange red gaze, she reached past it to the cupboard. She pulled out a box of macaroni and cheese. She filled a pan with water and placed the water on the stove and turned on the burner. Every move she made was watched in silence by her brothers and the two doppels. When the macaroni and cheese was ready, Jenny divided it into three bowls, and she and her brothers ate in silence as the two sets of odd red eyes watched, unblinking.

The next day at school, Michael Turner's doppel came to class without him. It was waiting in his seat when the bell rang, its hair combed, its books piled on the corner of Michael's desk. Mrs. Frample only stared at it a moment before proceeding with the day's lessons. When class was over, it rose and left the room along with the other children. The next day, three more of Jenny's classmates didn't show up, and by the end of the week a quarter of the class was made up of doppels. Class time had become very quiet and productive, but in between classes the remaining human children became riotous, uncontrollable, as though to counterbalance the silence and stillness of their red-eyed classmates.

That Friday, Jenny walked home by herself. She usually walked home with Laura Sheffield, but Laura hadn't come to school that day. Laura's doppelganger looked like her. It wore her clothes, and her mother had sent it to school with Laura's lunch money, though everyone knew doppels didn't eat. It carried Laura's books and wore Laura's shoes. But it didn't come to meet Jenny at the bench by the flagpole after school let out. So after waiting for a short time, Jenny had headed home alone.

That night, Mrs. Johnson's doppelganger made the same macaroni and cheese it had made each preceding night that week. After the second night, when Mr. Johnson had lurched up from the table and vomited orange shell pasta all over the combined living and dining room hardwood floor, dinner had gone quietly and smoothly every evening. Shown once, Jenny's mother's doppel had known how to load the dishwasher and put away the milk. If it still wore mismatched shoes and bikini bottoms with pajama tops, at least Jenny took some small comfort in having a mother which was indestructible.

When Jenny finished dinner, her mother's doppel cleared away her dishes and began to load them into the dishwasher. More tired than usual, Jenny rose and clumped heavily up the stairs to her bedroom. She switched on the light, and turned to shut the door behind her doppelganger, which had followed her up the stairs silent and close as a shadow.

"First," she said, taking her doppel by the hand and leading it to the edge of the bed where she pushed it gently until it sat, "you've got to stop dressing like an idiot. Nobody wears underwear on the outside of their clothes, and nobody—I mean it—wears one hiking boot and one slipper at the same time."

She went to her closet, flinging the door wide and glancing back to make sure her doppel watched. She pulled out a nice sweater and her favorite jeans. "This is what you should wear Monday. And this . . ." she rummaged through the pile of clean clothes on the closet floor for a cool tee shirt and her good corduroys with the embroidery on the hip ". . . would make a nice outfit for Tuesday. If it's cold on Tuesday you can wear this green jacket with it."

She lined up three more outfits, pointing to each and saying *Wednesday, Thursday, Friday.* "Weekends you can wear whatever you want so long as you don't leave the house. And so long as the shoes match, I guess you can wear whatever you want on your feet."

Leaving the outfits lined up on the floor like a policeman's suspects, Jenny went to her bedside table and fished a few objects from the tumbled chaos in the drawer. She sat on the bed next to her doppel, and its shoulder brushed hers with the motion of the mattress dipping under her weight. "This is my grandmother's locket, which I wear to school every day, and this is the book I'm reading right now. It's kind of stupid but it's pretty good, especially page one-forty-two with the makeout scene. And here's some money I've been saving up just in case. I've got about forty dollars."

She put the book in the doppel's lap, and placed the money and the locket in its cupped hand. "I sit third row from the back in Mrs. Frample's homeroom class, and I don't like Jimmy Kemper, who sits on my left. David Mapps sits behind me, and I do like him. I like him a lot. I don't think he knows. And . . . and my name's not Jenny. It's Jennifer."

The doppel looked down at the things in its hand, then up at Jenny's face. In its customary silence it stared into her brown eyes with its strange solid red ones. It reached the hand not holding Jenny's grandmother's locket and Jenny's forty dollars and placed it on her arm, partially covering the sharp orange veins which crept, stark and visible, beneath her pale skin.

To Heroboy, From Tiffani

Yo, Heroboy; it's me, Tiffani. S'up? I hope you check your messages, because like, well, I just do.

It's been a long time since you called, right? I think you might've lost my number, might've forgotten where I live. I think what I'm saying is: I kind of miss you.

I know my friends weren't so nice to you. Sorry.

I know Barb laughed at your limp cape. And I heard Veronica make that unnecessary crack about your bulgy tights: totally uncalled for. But hey, just think what it's been like for me. It isn't easy being popular. It's even harder staying that way. I mean, most girls like me wouldn't have given you the time of day, right? Probably wouldn't have touched your ten-foot pole with a . . . well, 'nother one, right?

But still: I'm totally sorry. Really.

I want you to know I kind of liked the way you kissed; all tongue like molten lava, and faster than a speeding bullet, when it had to be. It really was kind of nice.

I wish now I hadn't sort of pretended not to know you in the halls and on campus. I hoped you wouldn't take it all that hard, but maybe you did.

I also know I said some things I shouldn't have when you asked me to the dance? But like I tried to explain earlier: I'm not sure you're Gamma Gamma Phi-dating material. I know, I know; we made those jokes the first time we hung out. I do remember. All that stuff about how we're both Gammas? Only with me, it's all about getting invited to the best parties, and with you it's like, those rays that shoot from your eyes or whatever. I always meant to tell you your eyes were totally hot. No, I mean *really hot*.

But then your picture showed up in all the papers. I stopped seeing you in Brit Lit 101. (Did you drop that class? I kept the handouts, just in case.) I watched that news footage? Of the asteroid and everything? I saw how you managed to deflect it into the Moon. I know some people are kinda pissed about the new crater, all visible to the naked eye and stuff. But I think it's really pretty. Whenever I see it I think of you.

And then that time you saved that whole busload of nuns? When that was all over TV, Barb said your cape looked really good; totally billowing in the wind and everything. And Veronica mentioned the bulge in your tights again, but this time kind of jealous, right? But I swear, I haven't told them anything about that night on Mount Vesuvi-whats-us. Well, I told them very little, anyway. What happens inside a live volcano, *stays* inside a live volcano, right?

. . . But you've been off-planet for awhile now.

I know you're saving Earth from the latest threat to all humanity and whatever, but can Intergalactic Space-Slime Menace really mean so much to you?

I obviously don't.

I'm just saying.

Author's Note: This story dedicated to S.H.

Droidtown Blues

For the last fifty miles of plodding across the rusty pebbled dunes of Mars, the Echo 3000 had dragged his limbs beneath the weight of failure. The slight, crumpled form of the girl he carried on his back weighed as nothing, but her exhaustion, her helplessness, her vulnerability dragged at him like anvils strapped to his chestbox.

Ahead of him, the last fading starlight before dawn glanced off the curved surface of one of the twelve Domed Cities of Mars. From his vantage up on the mesa overlooking the plain, Dometown IX glowed in the glittery darkness like the huge gelatinous body of a bioluminescent Earthside jellyfish. With slight adjustments to his ocular calibration he could make out the peeling planks of synthawood, the wide rutted Main Street bisecting the town, the tall false fronts of angular buildings. Gaudily painted signs nailed above entryways announced such establishments as *Carbon Lil's Cyber Saloon* and *Doc Janglebits: Surgeon, Barber, Cryofreezer* and *Clanker & Sons Drygoods (Clones Not Welcome)*.

His receptors crackled as the girl shifted, her spherical helmet rubbing the back of his cylindrical torso. Her voice, slurred with sleep, came across the open transmission line: "Echo, we almost there?"

The Echo 3000 shifted the angle of his appendages slightly so the sling they formed adjusted, conforming to the girl's movements as she snuggled closer against his back. "Yes, Matty Johnson," he said in his flat monotone.

Faint, her voice murmured in his head as she sank back into dreaming. "Good. I'm so hungry, I could eat a ding-danged purple-cloned mule. With a cherry on top . . . an' maybe some whipcream . . . an' just a dollop of that maple syrup ol' Granny Miller used to make. You know what I mean?"

The Echo 3000 returned his ocular calibration to desert travel mode and clanked lightly toward the passable incline down the mesa's edge to their left. "Yes, Matty Johnson," he said.

The food the clone wrangler had given them back at Dometown IV was almost gone. It had been clone rations, dry and flavorless. Only dimly could the Echo 3000 understand what that meant to the girl he carried. She'd spent the entirety of her most recent meal trying to describe to him the taste of an orange, and of her Granny Oompa's corn fritters back home. The mandroid was well versed in branch-lineal human ancestry recording, and while he wasn't certain why Matilda Johnson seemed to have as many Grannies as she had offshoot digits on her appendages, he said nothing. Perhaps there were advancements in human gene modification not yet downloaded into his information systems.

He stopped before the Dome's only entry. By his calculations, the girl's oxygen admixture had sunk to dangerously low quality levels, barely adequate for the retention of human consciousness. He was surprised when she came awake with a startled snort and slid from his back to stand unsteadily on her own lower appendages.

Matty banged her silver-gloved fist on the glittering barrier field covering the portal. "Hello? Hello, Dometown—" she glanced at the looming IX stenciled above the entry's synthawood lintel "—Dometown Icks? This is Matty Johnson, from Earthside Farmstead Number 31122440? My air recirculators ain't working so good, and we—me and Echo here—we'd be awful grateful if you'd open up so's we can come in."

After a brief pause and a slight whirring, an image winked onto the screen beside the portal. A man, heavy-jowled, with large muttonchop sideburns, squinted at them, his teeth clamped deeply into the soggy end of an unlit cigar. "Carpetbaggers not welcome," he said.

The Echo 3000 rolled one golden ocular orb toward the girl by his side as she drew herself up and threw back her shoulders. "Dang it all! I ain't no flea-bit carpetbagger!"

The heavyset man leaned back in his synthawood chair. The worn brocade of his waistcoat stretched across his ample middle, bulging at the buttons and the shallow watch pockets. "No bluestockings, neither," he said.

"Bluestocking! Why, I oughtta. . . ."

The mandroid slipped his upper appendage into the satchel slung across his chestbox. The distinctive clink of hard credits in the envelope he withdrew caught the man's attention and he leaned forward in his chair, as though it would bring him closer to the pair standing on the other side of the screen.

For the first time, the man looked more closely at the mandroid than at the girl. His eyes narrowed. "Credits. Well, that does change things somewhat. I suppose it'd be all right to let y'all in."

He leaned forward suddenly, causing the girl to flinch, though his image remained flat on the two-dimensional screen. He pulled the cigar from his mouth and stabbed the air with it, punctuating his words. "But we don't need no flesh-selling here, girl," he said. "This is a droidtown. We don't need no scrawny, freckled, redheaded bonebag fem stealing none of our regular flesh customers away from honest hardworking cancandroids, y'hear?"

The Echo 3000 watched the girl's face turn from a reddish shade to one approaching purple. He wondered if her air had finally given out, if he'd failed the mission programmed into him by the girl's father. He watched her silvery suit gauntlets curl into fists, then loose again. His audio pickups barely registered her voice as she counted under her breath from one to ten.

With relief, the mandroid watched her color fade. If anything, the girl seemed even paler than before, her freckles sharp and pronounced across the bridge of her nose. Softly, articulating one word at a time with uncharacteristic clarity, she said: "I won't be selling my flesh, Mister. Not to nobody."

Everything went unnaturally quiet. The man on the screen sat as though frozen. The girl at the mandroid's side stood still as a cryochamber. The flat reddish plain behind them was motionless, the landscape empty but for the cresting sun distant and solitary on the horizon.

Though the mandroid's chronometer registered only a few seconds' passing, it seemed an eon before the man in the straining waistcoat broke into a wide grin, slipping the cigar again between his exposed teeth and leaning back, his chair creaking as though for mercy beneath his weight.

"Well then," he said, "welcome to Dometown Nine."

The glittering barrier dropped into nothing on the red sand, and the airlock hatch swung open.

The Echo 3000 held the girl's spherical breathing helmet tucked under one upper appendage and her long red braids in the other, keeping both clear of the spew from her mouth as she vomited behind a clonemule trough off Main Street. When she was done, she wiped her silver-clad fist across her mouth and spat a couple times into the trampled ruts of red dust.

"Sorry, Echo. You know what recirculated air does to me."

She stood straight as she could, her small shoulders squared, her pointed silver boots planted firmly on the pebbled ground. The mandroid tucked her braids behind her ears one at a time and said, "Yes, Matty Johnson."

She reached up and patted him on the juncture where his upper left appendage met his chestbox. "Thanks, Echo. Say: you hungry? You need you some of that oily stuff they feed you people down at the factory at Luna Colony?"

The mandroid clicked his golden ocular orbs. "No, Matty Johnson."

The girl scratched her head. "Well, just say so if you change your mind. Looks like we might be able to wrestle up some good grub for you 'round here. There's a bunch of your kind." She gestured into the wide gritty avenue of Main Street, at the passing mailmandroid with his bulging satchel of letters; at a deliverymandroid clattering down the street behind his clonemule, his rear appendages supporting the cab of his truck, wheels at the ends of their telescoping lengths. "What do they call you metal folks these days in the cities? 'Tin Persons'?"

The mandroid swiveled his ocular orbs and telescoped an upper appendage to dust off the knees of the girl's suit where she'd knelt on the ground. "No, Matty Johnson."

"Well. Okay, then." She reached to wrap her fingers around the end of the dusting appendage.

At the light grip of her little silver-gauntleted fingers, a small tight spot fluttered in the Echo 3000's chestbox, right where his main cylinders fired. As she led him out into Main Street, he scheduled himself an afterhours all-systems maintenance check and reboot. He hadn't run one since their crash on Martian soil. He'd been afraid to shut himself down before they'd reached their original goal of Dometown IV, but doubly so after they'd been turned away, unwelcome. The mere thought of leaving the girl unguarded at night on the Martian desert left him restless, uncomfortable. She was so soft, so fragile; her parts so easily broken and so difficult to replace.

"Echo, you listening? I said: do you think that's a good idea?"

He realized with something near alarm that he'd not registered the girl's most recent verbal datastream. She often articulated arcane human concepts and, to him, unfathomable queries and propositions, the totality of which he'd assimilated into his view of her as a unique construct of flesh and bone and organic synapses. But rarely did he completely fail to attend her articulations. "Yes, Matty Johnson," he said, hoping it was what she wanted to hear.

She wrinkled her nose and scratched at the root of one red braid. "Well. All right then. If you really think so," she said, veering sharply to their left, tugging him behind her, clomping as much as was possible in light gravity up the wide synthetic planks of the mockwood steps.

The mandroid, having spent time on Luna Colony and on the farmsteads of Earth, was impressed by the genuine look of the synthetic products beneath them, by the realistic sag to the center of the steps, the weathered grey splintering edges, the small, star-like marks where countless spurs had gouged the planks. As he passed beneath the gaudy banner, drooping and nailed off-kilter above the door, he decoded the data printed there in binary. *Droid Pair-a-Dice*, it read, *Fun With All Pistons Firing (clone entrance in rear alley).*

The girl leading him didn't even slow when she reached the slatted, swinging saloon doors at the top of the stairs. She thrust one palm flat to the front and marched through the entryway as the half-doors banged wide.

The mandroid tumbled after her into a chaos of smoke and noise, a riot of color.

Data overload . . . Data overload, blinked the warning in the upper left corner of his metal brainpan. He swiveled and clicked his ocular orbs, trying to recalibrate his assaulted systems. Slowly, his sensors regained equilibrium. He filtered out the low, heavy haze hanging in the room, rising from cigars, spiraling outward from rings wreathing the brainpans of dozens of mandroid varietals reclining at scattered tables. A clatter and jangle of notes from a piandroid in one corner coalesced into a lively dance number as the Echo 3000's aural sensors auto-switched to music mode. The jarring hues—orb-stabbing purples; pinks hotter than a tin cowshed roof; greens more poisonous than a millipede's bite—sifted, filtered down into a readable map of waistcoats stretched across hollow cylindrical middles; of wide, curly-brimmed hats sliding off perfectly spherical brainpans; of flounces and ruffles of multicolored petticoats swinging about the lower torsos of the dozen cancandroids up on the room's long stage.

He'd never seen so many droids assembled in one place. He

supposed he must have once stood in a factory row of fellow series-members, but he'd come to consciousness in the small drab parlor of Mister and Missus Johnny Johnson, with its spindly-legged, well-polished furniture; with its oldfashioned wallpaper printed with drooping heads of massive cabbage flowers. The first action the Echo 3000 had taken upon gaining awareness was to analyze the impurities in the air: human sweat, and minute particles of cow manure, and an intriguing combination of condensed animal fats and disassembled grains and heated iron he later understood had been pancakes and butter, frying in a pan in the nearby kitchen. And Matilda Johnson: the sweet, subtle tinge of scent which always rode near her in the air, the scent the mandroid had never allowed himself to fully break down into its composite parts. Matty.

Matty seemed to have shrunk. Her eyes were enormous in her thin pale face. Her mouth hung slightly open as she looked around the narrow dancehall of the saloon. She licked her lips, gripped a little tighter the Echo 3000's upper appendage.

The barmandroid, a hover model, whisked over the top of the counter. The faint hum from beneath his apron reverberated even through the crash of music, past the jangle of jewelry on metal, cutting through the stomp and swirl of the completely synchronized cancandroids on stage, each one turning with identical jerky motions to expose the backsides of their torso boxes, then bending at their hip joints, flipping as one their full flouncy skirts to display the delicate lace ruffles of bloomers beneath. Painful purple, hot pink, poisonous green.

"Welcome, sir!" boomed the barmandroid above the din, wiping his two appendages on his bar apron. "Augustus P. Roach, at your service!"

The Echo 3000 swiveled both ocular orbs toward the droid and moved closer to the girl.

"Sir!" the barmandroid broadcast from the slot beneath his bristly metallic mustachio, "Would you like your clone serviced out back while you relax?" he gestured toward Matty without looking at her. "The Pair-a-Dice Saloon offers a full range of hard oils and soft greases, games of true chance, and the loveliest cancandroids this side of Dometown Prime! Everything a discerning gentlemandroid like yerself might require for gen-u-wine relaxation, recuperation, and recalibration!"

As if on cue, two cancandroids whirred up on hoverjets, air pulses sending their skirts ruffling upward in suggestive swirls. The haze of oily cigar smoke hanging about them in great cloying clouds rolled away in roiling puffs. Matty huddled even closer to the mandroid, her eyes slotted against the artificial wind, her braids streaming out behind her like red ribbons from the tail of a kite. "I'm not a clone," she said, her unamplified human voice nearly inaudible in the smoky hall.

The music clanged louder. The cancandroids blasted their jets in synchronized rhythm, circling with hypnotic gyrations their jointed lower torsos, so unlike the Echo 3000's own solid cylinder. Someone thrust a tumbler of hard-oil whiskey into the end of his appendage wrapped around the girl, and suddenly the lights seemed brighter, more garish, more disorienting to his fatigued ocular components.

"I'm not a clone!" Matty repeated, to no visible effect. She then yelled at the top of her lungs: "I . . . am . . . not . . . a . . . *clone*!"

Every mechanical being in the saloon went silent. The nearby hoverjet cancandroids fell to the floor with two simultaneous clanks. The piandroid halted its raucous key-banging mid note, and the click and drone and murmur murmur murmur of dozens of other droids ceased abruptly, as if the saloon had been struck by an electric pulse.

Matty's braids fluttered down against her head. They swung slightly at the ends, their diminishing momentum the only lingering proof of their recent motion.

Slowly, she straightened. She released her crushing grip on the mandroid's appendage, which felt as light to his alloys as a butterfly landing. She cleared her throat, and reached with a habitual gesture to straighten the hat she'd lost in their crash landing only days before. Finding nothing atop her head, her fingers moved to slick back loose tendrils curling about her forehead in a soft red halo.

Ignoring the beady orbs of silver and obsidian and malachite trained on her from around the room, she patted the mandroid's chestbox. She cleared her throat. "Echo," she said, "I need to do some scouting, see if there's anything a girl can do to earn an honest living around here. You stay. Get a little relaxation, recuperation, and . . . recalibration? That's it. You get those things and I'll come back, tell you what I find out."

She tugged her helmet from the crook of his appendage. She gave a decisive nod, then stepped around the barmandroid and made for the door. Not a single droid moved: nothing but their ocular orbs, which swiveled to follow her like sentient marbles.

Something inside the mandroid snapped like a faulty belt. He lurched past the two grounded cancandroids and lightly whipped his telescoping appendage, a gentle lasso, barely encircling the girl's wrist.

She turned. Her brown eyes were soft, liquid and warm like puddles of pure motor oil. She smiled at him, tugging her digits from his appendage after a slight squeeze. "I mean it, Echo. You just stay here and wait for me, okay?"

His transmitter whirred inside, but he said nothing.

"Okay, Echo?"

The mandroid drew his appendage back to standard travel length, defeated by her soft human wishes. "Yes, Matty Johnson."

The slatted doors had not even ceased swinging behind her before the music cranked to life. The hoverjets blasted, the greasy cigar haze thickened, and the flounces and ruffles flounced and ruffled all the colors of a garish artificial rainbow.

And underneath the hum and whirr and clangity-clang clang, the mandroid heard a single word murmured, staccatoed, and binary-clicked with all the loathing mechanical hearts could muster. Over and over and over again: bonebag. Bonebag, bonebag, bonebag.

Bonebag.

* * *

Not even one standard hour had passed since Matty left, but there was definitely something wrong with the Echo 3000's interior systems.

His chestbox pistons fired wildly, erratically. His ocular orbs canted off in opposite directions, seemingly without his conscious impulse or control. His appendages felt rubbery and feeble, his aural pathways clogged with glass shards.

And still they plied him with drink after drink; tumblers of dark viscous oil, dank, with a hint of vegetable decay. He'd been aware such substances existed but had never experienced them: substances deliberately engineered to cause disorienting effects not easily flushed from the systems.

At first he'd barely noticed. He'd paid only meager attention to his surroundings, waiting. The cancandroids lowered him into a chair at a gaming table. They'd pressed their curvaceous torsos against him, their metal hot to the touch, the scent they exuded a heady mixture of electricity and copper. The laces of their corsets crisscrossed their smooth silvery surfaces, and their skirts rustled with the ceaseless motions of their jets.

He allowed them to pull the credit envelope from his satchel and convert it to chips for the dice table. He kept one eye on the door, always; waiting, hoping for Matty's return. *Failure, failure, failure,* he chided himself with a low thrum like a faulty engine. The thought spun continually through his brainpan, and the room with it. *Failure.*

Do you like us? The cancandroids clicked and whirred and hummed all around him, pressing their corseted surfaces against his chestbox. *Do you like us do you like us do you like us?*

Yes, he thought. *No. Yesno.* But what came out of his vocalizer box was: "So."

They laughed, delighted, and plucked it from his vocal slot and made a game of it. *So,* they laughed. And spun and sang and twirled. *So so so so. . . . So.*

When the pile of chips on the table before him had dwindled

to zero, the mandroid stood to go. He'd been too long away from the girl. Everything felt wrong.

"So," he said, pushing his chair from the table. He fought the twirling in his brainpan, fearing he'd go reeling, crazed like an off-course gyroscope. "So," he said again, and took a step toward the door.

The room tilted. The floor seemed to scurry away from him like a furry biological creature and he found himself flat on his back, ocular orbs trained on the smoke-stained ceiling. He'd never before seen droids smoke, but here they were, drawing acrid inhalations from oil-soaked cigars into their ventilation systems, expelling from the same vents. He'd also never before seen droids wear human-styled garments, though his experience in the wider universe had been limited. During the course of the evening, one of the cancandroids at the gaming table had slid his appendages into a short fringed jacket. He'd never felt half-naked before he'd been partially clothed.

Lying on his back, orbs clicking, reclicking as they tried to calculate his exact distance from the saloon's ceiling, the mandroid thought of the Johnson kitchen, and of the smell of browning pancakes, and of the feathery softness of red braids as they glinted in gentle Earthside sunlight.

Just before he experienced total involuntary system failure, he managed to sigh a single word.

"So."

Auto-reboot attempt #4.

Auto-reboot attempt #5.

Diagnostic running. Errors detected. Corruption detected. Corruption isolated.

Auto-reboot attempt #6.

The Echo 3000's brainpan felt stuffed with sand and his vocalizer circuits coated in metal shavings.

For a moment he thought he suffered complete ocular

malfunction, but with a small click and swivel, the large golden orbs shifted to pitch-black mode and he dimly recognized the slightly darker edges of a door frame, two chairs, the slab-like table on which he lay. The fringed garment he'd worn in the saloon had disappeared. His satchel was gone, and with it the remnants of Matty's food and money credits.

Some of his sensory systems seemed wholly inactive: his thermal detectors, his audio capacity, his joint and appendage mechanicals—all damaged or temporarily unavailable. When he tried to read the composition of the components in the air, all he detected was smoke. Thick, cloying, greasy ash particles from oil-soaked cigars.

The room's air pressure changed. Even past the ringing and static of his audio pickups, he made out the verbal datastream of a droid in the hall, and the corresponding human response.

"An Echo 3000, boss! Good for parts. Real good for parts, though expensive for the likes of those around here. Maybe we sell it offworld? Maybe get more money from one of them pressgangs? Outer-rim ships always need conscripts."

"Your Pinkerton programming is failing you, Augustus. No; this Echo's too good for conscription. Too good for most anything here on Mars."

The hoverjet hum of the Pinkerton Model 427, known to the public as barmandroid Augustus P. Roach, shifted into an obsequious whirr. "Oh no, Mister Cantrell. Nothing too good for you, boss. Nothing but the best for the oldest son of the youngest son of the richest man in the twelve Domed Cities of Mars. Oh no, sir! Oh—"

"Enough."

"Oh yessir, sir!"

The Echo 3000 dimmed all his systems. He allowed his ocular orbs to swivel in random directions and opaqued them as though in shutdown mode. As best he could with his damaged audio pickups, he tracked the approach of the beings in the hall. The door opened. Though the Echo 3000 couldn't actually *see* the bulging waistcoat, the straining buttons, the muttonchops or the sagging chins of the man who'd granted them entry at the gate, he recognized the wet slap and chomp of chewing on the end of a damp, unlit cigar.

The man rapped his knuckles against the Echo's chestbox. "And you say this came across the desert from brother Cantrell's place over at Dometown Four? I'm surprised he didn't keep it. A clone wrangler can't afford to be picky when it comes to mechanicals."

"Yessir, Mister Cantrell; nosir."

"And it carried the bonebag with it the entire way?"

"A genuine human fem, sir, no clone. It seems she arrived on-planet with a delivery for Dometown Four, but with the misunderstanding that she'd find permanent residence with your brother. He turned her away with a few credits and a satchel of clone rations."

The large man snorted. A small fleck of sodden, oil- and saliva-soaked tobacco hit the curve of the mandroid's chestbox with a tiny *ping*. "A flesh-and-blood fem at Dometown Four, the biggest clone ranch on Mars. That's rich."

The Pinkerton 427 tried to join in the large man's laugher, but its efforts rang hollow and sycophantic.

"Enough!" barked the man.

The barmandroid's tinny laughter ceased instantly. "Yessir. Once she's located, shall I arrange her deportation?"

The large man took the cigar from his mouth and with the hand that held it, wrapped again on the chestbox of the prone mandroid. "Now *that's* the Pinkerton model I hired! But no, Augustus. Deportation's unnecessary. Let's just invite her to leave Dometown Nine."

"Yessir, sir." The Pinkerton 427 spun on its hoverjets to leave.

Without turning, the man, one knuckle still resting on the Echo's cylindrical torso, said, "And Augustus?"

The Pinkerton 427's hoverjets stilled just past the doorway.

"Yes, Mister Cantrell?"

"Invite her to leave . . . without her breathing helmet."

There was only a slight pause. "Yes, sir, Mister Cantrell. Sir."

His chronometer was functioning erratically. The Echo 3000 was certain that had Matty been there, she would have described his time spent in near-total darkness as *forever.* He knew, even with his continuing malfunctions, that the elapsed time was closer to twelve standard hours.

The hours passed with an odd and excruciating slowness, not in small part because they were filled with his contemplation of his absolute, crushing failure to protect the girl. Perhaps, and his pistons fluttered slightly at the thought, she was waiting for him, trying to find him. Possibly, she was even counting on him.

He tried again to bend his lower left appendage. He tried the lower right. Nothing and nothing.

Run diagnostic again.

Run auto-repair sequence. Again.

Again.

Again.

"Yes, sir; Jacob Tinker will transport your cargo to Dometown Eleven. There, its parts will be disassembled and prepared for off-world auction."

Thick smacking. The odor of wet, unlit cigar. "And the bonebag fem?"

The Pinkerton model's jets switched to their low whine. "Not located yet, Mister Cantrell. But close. We've found scraps of food detritus, stolen from an outbound shipment of clone rations, and. . ." its voice dropped a few decibels, ". . . droppings."

The Echo 3000, lying as though helpless, hoped the leap of his chest pistons wasn't detectible to the Pinkerton model.

"A thief, eh?" said the man. "Good. No jury on Mars, be it man, clone, or droid, would convict a fella for inviting a food thief to leave. With or without her helmet."

"No, sir. No they wouldn't."

"Is Tinker here?"

"Yes, sir."

"And the mandroid's ready for shipment?"

"Yes, sir. All operating systems shut down by the nano-whiskey from Dometown Eight."

"Good. Box it."

"Yes, Mr. Cantrell. Sir."

His ocular orbs opaqued to feign shutdown, the Echo 3000 didn't see the entry of the labor droids. But he heard their approach; heard the awkward shuffle of low-sentient creatures. With autonomy and intelligence registering scarcely above a pneumatic hammer's, they shambled into the room, four of them, and proceeded to assemble a synthawood crate around him where he lay. Shaped like a human coffin to accommodate the wider breadth across his chestbox, the box snapped together one pre-fitted plank at a time. Even the synthawood's scent was engineered to resemble pine. It was the first time since he'd entered Dometown IX that the mandroid remembered detecting any odor in the air other than cigar.

He practically ached to spring into action; to eject from the sheaths at the ends of his appendages the whirling blades which could slice through plastic, through flesh, through rubber, through metal. He wanted to explode from the pine-scented planks, to shatter every low-grade joint and empty brainpan of the labor droids.

Oh, how he'd wanted to smash the obsequious hoverjets of the mustachioed Pinkerton model, and though it was against his programming he didn't think he'd have grieved if, during his rampage, a shard of Augustus P. Roach had lodged in some small fleshy bit of the man in the waistcoat. Preferably somewhere painful, and difficult to repair.

But he bided his time. Had his systems been fully functional he would have taken on an entire town of Pinkerton models. An entire army. A planetful. To save Matilda Johnson, he'd have done anything. At the moment, *anything* meant lying low, feigning droid-death, and counting the minutes until he could slice through the side of his coffin crate. Also, presumably, he'd slice through the bottom of Jacob Tinker's wagon and eventually, as soon as he'd found Matty, through the very shields of Dometown IX itself.

The last board of his crate snapped into place. His stabilzers accommodated for the uneven hoist of his box to the shoulder joins of the four labor droids. The Echo 3000 allowed himself to roll as if deactivated, though it bruised his pride to loll and bang about the inside of a box like a piece of mining equipment or a non-sentient motor part. He repeated to himself, in the hollows of his brainpan: *I am a drill bit. I am a core sampler. I am an eggbeater. I am nothing.*

The stilted, unrefined gait of the labor droids carried him, rolling and thumping, out of the building. Even from within the crate he detected the change in air pressure and the sonic alteration indicating they were beneath the dome rather than a low synthawood ceiling. His sensors, energized by the increase in stimuli, sharpened one by one. Fine-tuning, questing past the planks of his crate, he detected the decrease in temperature signaling Martian night; the grease and salt odors of low-grade labor droids; the molecular particles in the air of manure from gen-modified clonemules, of hover-axle grease, of human sweat.

His box hit the ground with a clumsy clunk. He listened for the sounds of droids moving away, but the night remained quiet. Labor droids were so low-grade, they made no sounds in the darkness; their systems simply weren't sophisticated enough to require constantly moving parts.

He increased the sensitivity of his audio receivers. He heard distant clinketings of rival piandroids from various saloons lining Main Street, their clangity-clang-clang even more meaningless when taken together. He heard the soft breathing of napping clonemules, and the periodic gentle jangle of the wagon team's harness. But still he heard no sounds of retreat from the labor droids.

He could wait no longer. With a low *snick*, his blades slid from the ends of his upper appendages. A deft flick, a double whip-like motion faster than human eyes could follow, and the top and sides of his synthawood crate fell away in pine-scented slivers. He sprang forward into a tight crouch, sensing the perimeters of the canvas sheathing arching overhead, covering the Conestoga-style wagon.

Four labor droids stood at the foot of the wagon like fenceposts dressed in overalls. Their smooth ovoid faces were featureless, their stubby limbs sprouting from their denim-clad torsos like nubs from a cactus.

The Echo 3000 hesitated only a moment before lashing out, gathering the droids by the neck joins—two in each whipping appendage. If he acted quickly, while the sounds of escalated nighttime revelry filled the dome as thickly as clinging cigar smoke, he might silence all four labor droids at once and for good. He couldn't risk them triggering automated alarms, and every moment that passed was another moment Matty might be discovered and put out for permanent deactivation.

He tensed his appendages, the droids limp in his grip as rag dolls. He was about to crush all four of them together into a compacted bundle of broken circuitry and scorched denim, when—

"Stop! Echo, Don't!"

The Echo 3000 froze.

Matty scrambled from beneath the wagon. "They're friends, Echo. They're helping us outta this turd-blasted town. They kept me alive, hooked up with Granpappy Tinker. Helped me find you, Echo. *Friends.*"

She placed a hand, tiny and pink without its silver gauntlet, on his chestbox. At her touch the Echo 3000 thought he'd melt. He felt as though all his metal surfaces and all his complex interior components would puddle into a small pool of mercury at her feet.

He thought if that happened, and he knew she'd be all right, he'd be glad to reside there forever.

He slackened his grip on the neck joins of the labor droids and they toppled to the ground as one, their primitive mechanisms too crude to reestablish equilibrium. Matty stooped to assist them to their stumpy lower appendages one at a time, dusting them each off and bending to kiss each smooth ovoid top as she did. "Thank you, Ld-5272," she said. "You've been real sweet, Ld-6197. You're just the best, Ld-9813; don't you let that no-good barmandroid tell you otherwise, y'hear? Thank you, Ld-1312. You take care of these others now, a'right? They need a good leader like you."

The Echo 3000 recorded her verbal datastream for later analysis. For the moment, it was all he could do not to crush her to his chestbox in what would probably have been a grip detrimental to the delicate inner workings of a human girl. She waved to each labor droid as it shambled off into the noisy, smoke-laden darkness. When the last droid was gone she turned to him. She dusted off his chestbox, though he detected no particulate matter on the smooth metal, and stood on the tips of her toes to kiss the flat metal beneath his ocular orb.

"Good to see you, Echo. Real good. Now let's get back in ol' Granpappy Tinker's wagon and hide ourselves under that synthetic hay like he told me to. He'll see us through the gate. Nobody likes that cigar-chomping Mister Cantrell. Nobody."

The mandroid felt his torso cylinder swell with relief, and with what approached gratitude to the infinite randomness of the universe. "Yes, Matty Johnson," he said.

She stepped into the circle of his upper appendages and he lifted her gently—gently as a brush from a hen's nesting feather, gently as a bumble bee landing on a gen-modified flower—into the back of the covered wagon. Together they nestled under the synthetic hay, the mandroid curved as best he could about the soft body of the girl, every sensor set to maximum protection levels, his sheathed blades unlocked and on alert.

A human, which the mandroid deduced from Matty's lack of alarm was her grandsire Tinker—he scheduled himself to update his human genealogical understanding at the earliest opportunity—approached the wagon. He spoke in low soothing tones to the sleepy clonemules, the wagon dipping slightly as he swung up into the driver's seat. Slowly the wagon rolled forward, accompanied by the soft clop-clop of modified mule hooves on the hard red clay of Dometown IX's Main Street.

A night watchmandroid halted them at the airlock and the Echo 3000 tensed. He allowed just the tips of his blades to emerge from their metal sheaths. . . .

But Jacob Tinker's papers seemed to be in order. He had a delivery commission to Dometown VIII signed and stamped by the droidtown Boss himself: Mister Cantrell, the oldest son of the youngest son of the richest man on Mars.

They rolled into the airlock. The Echo 3000 heard the thrum and hum of the wagon's atmosphere barriers activating, and felt the electrical charge in the air as the mobile shield lowered around them, covering the wagon, its driver, its mules and its occupants like a large transparent blanket of dancing sparkles. The mandroid felt the energy of the field skitter along the back of his torso cylinder. It reminded him of the feeling he'd had back at the droidtown, the moment he'd realized Matilda Johnson was alive and safe and had come for him.

It was a long time, rolling with the gentle gait of clonemules as they plodded in the dark across the desert—in some direction unknown to the mandroid; toward some unknown destination, with no certain future—before the Echo 3000 vocalized.

"So," he said into the dark, which was redolent with the scents of sweet hay and redheaded girl. He could think of no better place to be, could imagine no higher attainment of purpose or directive. "So."

The girl curled against his chestbox murmured sleepily, "What'd you say, Echo?"

"So."

She lifted her head. Even in Martian darkness, under the cover of canvas and atmosphere shield, he could see her white teeth as her lips parted in a drowsy smile. "Why, Mister 3000, I think you did learn something in that stinky ol' droidtown after all! I think you've done gone and expanded your—let's be honest here—kinda limited vocabulary. So. . . ."

She nestled back into him. After a few minutes he allowed his blades to retract all the way and lock into peace mode.

"So," he said into the night, answered only by the soft snores of the sleeping girl. "So."

Of Spice and Lime and Tea

Having never met a ghost before,
I can safely say I didn't know what to do,
 exactly.
She wasn't beautiful, nor frightening.
A little old, perhaps: fifteen?
Fifteen, that must be it;
a magical age
 when you're only twelve.

Who are you?
I would have said had it mattered.
It didn't, so I spared myself embarrassment;
instead I said, "How do you do?"
(It sounded very grownup at the time)
and she said "Dead."

I nodded—with aplomb, I hoped—and
offered to share with her my tea
which, surprisingly, she took.
("But where does it *go*?"
I asked and she shook
her pale head
 and breathed a sigh.)

We spent that afternoon at play,
about the garden
behind the house
I've not stepped in now
          for fifty years:
her moth-wing eyes,
her off-hue hair,
her spindly legs and
strange, aged-auntie dress;
soft and faintly clingy,
like spiders' eggs.

Finally, the sun came low.
"I've got to go," I said.
She nodded and she took my hand
          (—a whisper of caress—)
and pulled me close.
"Girls aren't supposed to kiss," she said
          and kissed me.

I looked for her
that next day and
the twenty thousand since.
I looked for her long past
the fading of
          the feeling of
her tongue against my teeth.
(*Is this how people kiss*? I'd thought; *With open mouths?*
How odd! And yet . . . delightful.)

Sometimes still, on simple summer days,
the scent of bergamot catches me.
I feel her lips on mine again,
and taste spice
and lime
and tea.

Three Days Dead

The big woman glanced from the road to smile at Karen. "So tell me a little about yourself, Karen. Your brother said you work for the animal hospital in Dallas." In her island accent she pronounced *Karen* with two syllables of equal weight like two separate words.

Karen shifted, lifting first one sweat slick thigh off the hot green vinyl stationwagon seat, then the other. Her skirt clung to her skin, bunched up around her hips and stuck there. "I'm just a vet tech," she said, gripping the dashboard as the woman veered sharply to avoid a wide rut in the dirt road. "Not a researcher or anything like Brian is. Was."

The woman, who'd introduced herself as Avita, made a soft sympathetic sound. "Your poor, poor brother," she said. "He was a good man. Unlucky, what with him falling off the cliff and strangling on his own blood before we found him. But good."

Karen watched the tall clumping sugarcane straggling off in all directions lick past the open windows of the moving car like green and yellow flames. "Brian and I didn't know each other all that well," she said. "We haven't—hadn't—spoken in years."

"You're family, though. No parents? Nobody else?"

Karen shook her head.

"Well, family is one thing you stick by, even in death. Yes, yes, especially in death." Avita's gaze flicked to Karen's averted face before returning to the road. "His accident is a sad thing, him dying so young and before you could get here. Still time to say goodbye, though; he's only one day dead."

Karen's knuckles whitened as the car careened over another rut and around a curve, unruly rows of sugarcane giving way abruptly to a dirtfield stubbled with yellowing husks. The road took another sharp turn and the ocean unfolded to their right, an endless expanse of blue glass slashed with white near the shore and stretching away to disappear against the indistinguishable blue of cloudless sky. They bumped along in silence and wind and the sharp scent of ripe cane until the dirt road narrowed and narrowed, ending in front of a whitewashed two-story house. Palms with wide ragged fronds shadowed the front porch, coconuts hanging in thick clusters like hairy animals gripping their trunks. Behind, a slight rise cut off the view of the ocean as it curved around the island. Covered densely in poinsettias like crinkled scraps of red velvet, the rise seemed strangely incongruous with the stultifying heat and the thick droning of insects.

Inside, the house was surprisingly cool, with tile floors and open concrete latticework and simple bamboo furniture. White gauze ruffled at the casement windows, letting in the salt scent of the sea. Karen reached to stroke an enormous lizard, its tail a different color than the rest of its body where it draped off the white wall onto the floral cushion of a chair. Before she could touch it, it swiveled a black bead eye at her and slipped out the window in a flash of green.

"Karen," said Avita behind her, "You're in the islands now; you can't go around touching and playing with the animals. These are no puppies and kitties from Dallas, Texas. Island animals have got island ways. With your poor brother laid out in the next room, you don't want go accidentally petting no duppy."

"Duppy?"

Avita mounted the stairs, motioning Karen to follow. "Well," she said, "It's after noon now, so you're probably safe. But don't go petting anything once the sun goes down."

Without waiting for an answer Avita turned down the narrow hall. She stopped at a door opening into a pleasant room, pale and cool like the rest of the house. Narrow slatted shutters led onto a shaded balcony, thickly flowered vines tinting the air with dim green light. Karen dropped her bag in a chair, pushed the shutters aside, and stepped out to a view of sea and sky. The red field with its incongruous holiday vegetation was out of sight behind the edge of the house. The dirt path and the way back through the canefields stretched away to one side like a dusty skein of earth unraveling toward the horizon.

"You'll be wanting to see your brother."

Karen stepped back into the room, leaving the vine and salt breeze behind her with the open sky. She nodded, and the older woman placed her arm around Karen's shoulders. "He's down in the parlor. Le' we go."

Brian in death looked smaller than he had in life, more hairless and somewhat shriveled. She'd not seen him since he'd left the university to study tiny Caribbean reef squid off the smaller islands along the archipelago stretching across the blue, looking from the air like a broken candy necklace.

Karen sat in the only chair. Avita left the parlor quietly without her noticing. Shadows on the lawn grew shorter, then longer. After her flight from Texas to Florida to Barbados, then the trip by small propeller plane, hopping from one tiny island to another, she felt tired and drained. She sat alone in the cool room listening to lizards scuffing along the tiles, to poinsettias bristling in the salt breeze off the patio. She closed her eyes against the sight of Brian, his hair slicked back from his forehead, his fatal injuries hidden from view beneath the unnaturally white starched shirt someone had dressed him in to lay him in the parlor of his landlady in this house on this island in the middle of the ocean.

Without realizing she was tired, Karen slept. Upright, in a chair, beside the body of her dead brother.

Karen's head jerked forward and her eyes opened abruptly. The house was quiet and dark. The bitter smell of salt and sugarcane rose from beneath the heavy incense of a mosquito coil burning on the verandah beyond the open doorway. Through the dark, the lit tip of the coil glowed, a solitary ember of deep unwavering red.

Karen stood and stretched. Her spine popped. Her head felt too heavy, as though her neck were flimsy, inadequate scaffolding for the structure. In the darkness her brother's shirtfront shone white, eclipsing the rest of him like a starched cotton moon. She stepped out past the open doors into the warm breeze and breathed deep, smoke from the burning mosquito repellent incense scraping against the inside of her throat like rough paper. She moved away from the coil and gripped the railing. Ocean wind tugged at her hair. Her skirt, slightly stiff from sweat and travel, scraped the backs of her legs. Overhead, enormous palm fronds rattled against the moonless sky like dried straw, brushed against the roof's edge like twig brooms sweeping a hearth. She was about to return to the dark room when a slight jangling noise reached her, riding the night breeze above the incense and the salt and the stuttering palms.

She squinted into the dark, lifting her hand to shade her eyes as though it were sun she peered into and not the black island darkness of a moonless night.

A bleat, as of an animal in pain. Again the jingle of metal on metal, like clinking links in an iron chain. At the end of the veranda where it curved toward the front of the house sloped a set of wide shallow steps. Stumbling only slightly as she tested their width, Karen followed these down into the yard. Banana trees glinted in cold pale starlight. Massive leaves like elephant ears brushed against her shoulders and caught at her hair as she groped toward the faint sound. To one side squatted the elongated silhouette of the stationwagon. To the other rustled the sugarcane, and between car and canefield ran the road.

Karen judged the position of the road from memory and by the curious emptiness of noise in that direction, the dead spot a road leaves on a landscape like an unhealed scar. The clink and jangle sounded again, and the heavy breathing of an animal laboring for air. In the middle of the road rose a lump, where something hunkered low against the earth as though mired in dry soil.

As Karen neared, the lump solidified into a small spotted calf with a humped back. The night painted everything in colorless ink, flat and two dimensional like a graphite sketch. She crouched by the animal's side and it thrust a blind head toward her. Moving cautiously as she would with any wounded creature, she stroked the calf's head, feeling with her other hand at its curl-covered neck for the dangling end of chain, which jangled lightly with the animal's heaving sides as it struggled to breathe.

"Poor thing," she murmured, petting and stroking. "Good, calm thing. Are you hurt?"

Under her stroking fingers, the calf's eyes remained closed. The flat splots of its black-against-white hide looked like a faintly glowing Rorschach; like viscous India ink spilled on starched funereal cotton.

Light flooded the lawn in sharp angled squares. "Karen, what are you doing out there in the middle of the night? Come in here. Come, so."

Karen stood. "Avita,"—she hesitated only slightly over the name—"There's an animal in the road, hurt. Could you—"

"No. I see, but I don't want to hear any more about that. You just come up here into the house. Come now. Come."

Karen climbed the wide front steps toward Avita, toward the light which illuminated the front verandah while erasing the rest of the night, making it a thick black soup of warmth and scent. When she reached the doorway, she turned to squint back out into the swallowing dark where nothing was visible. No sugarcane, no banana trees, no animal hunched against the road breathing its own blood and rattling its chain. Vaguely, barely, she could just make out two spots of red, glowing like the lit ends of mosquito coil incense, hovering in the air where the calf's eyes would be.

The next day brought clouds and a stiff wind, rolling off the ocean with a dry electric charge which caused the hairs on Karen's arms to prickle and her skirt to spark against her legs. She tried not to gag on the warm pungency of the milk covering her cereal, poured fresh and hot after Avita milked the goat tethered in the yard just out of reach of the poinsettias. Avita stood with her back to Karen, her shoulders hunched as she scrubbed a pan dirtied the night before.

". . .And was I talking to myself yesterday?" she was saying, punctuating her words with sharp jabbing motions against the iron skillet she held. "An' also when I said, 'don' go touching the animals; don' go wandering in the dark lookin' for a duppy to find you, to fix you wi' his stare, to gash you wi' his teet' like fire'?" As her obvious frustration mounted, her accent slid thicker, the ends of her words swallowing themselves as she scrubbed. She turned, her expression softened only by the lines around her mouth. She took a deep breath, held it, let it out. "Karen. I was a friend to your brother, strange boy he may have been. He went out every day to the reefs, or to draw little pictures of those squid he studied. I was happy to have him here, and now I do right to watch over him his three days dead. He's two days dead now, but after that third day I'll bury him deep under ground and not look back. Mourn the dead, Karen. Mourn and move on. Don't encourage a soul to linger after the body goes."

She turned her back to Karen again. When she rinsed the pan, it was gently, dabbing the thing like a baby in the bath. "What you saw last night was the Rollin Calf. You don't need it, you don't want it. You see the Rollin Calf again, you stay clear. It might show itself to you as a dog, or a cat, or a goat or a man. But you always know the Rollin Calf, Karen: its eyes glow like two hard red coals, and its teeth are made of fire."

That night, Karen lay in bed watching layered shadows move against the textured wall, filtered by drawn mosquito netting and the undulations of bleached muslin curtains at the windows. Beneath her, beyond the small woven rug and the scrubbed wooden floorboards and the trapped air between one story and the next, lay Brian. She pictured him in his coffin, stretched out, eyes closed, wearing clothes she couldn't imagine him wearing in life. Ten years was a long time to pass without hearing your brother speak or seeing his face. They'd been children together once, though it was difficult to imagine now. Especially here, though the heat and heaviness of the air was very much like the oppressive Texas summers of their childhood. It was the scent of the wind that made this place so unfamiliar, and the sounds carried up off the ocean, rising from the poinsettias out in the dark.

A soft clinking wafted in the window, riding above the aroma of sugar and salt.

Its eyes glow like two hard red coals, and its teeth are made of fire.

Karen rose. She slid her feet into her thin sandals and, though she was warm, lifted her cardigan off the back of the chair and draped over her shoulders.

At the bottom of the stairs she paused. She glanced toward the parlor where Brian's body lay, the open doorway a small rectangle of black against blacker. She groped her way to the front door without any light and hesitated with her hand on the knob, listening for any sign of Avita. The house remained silent and dark, and emptier than it should have felt with a corpse and two living people inside.

The knob turned smooth and soundless beneath her fingers, and she stepped out onto the front verandah. The night was slightly better illuminated than the previous one, the Moon a cold splinter of white high above. Wide leaves near the verandah glinted, slivers of reflected moonlight arcing to follow curves of grey and black, all color leached in the absence of daylight. In the middle of the road leading to the house stood a spindly figure on four legs, its eyes like dull red marbles lit from within.

Karen descended the steps, her sandals slapping softly against the wood. She held out her hand as she neared the calf, and it nuzzled her fingers as though questing for a treat. Its sides heaved with the effort of breathing. A chain dangled from its neck to trail in the dust of the road.

"Brian?" she whispered, stepping close enough to feel the heat rising from the animal, to smell its yeasty bovine odor and feel the softness of its short curly coat tickle her arm. "Brian."

The calf blinked. Its breathing calmed, its sides ceased to heave. Every sound and scent of the night and the ocean and the canefields disappeared, and all Karen could see were the deep glowing flames of the Rollin Calf's eyes. All she could feel was the brush of its fur against her arm and the heat rising from its skin. It turned as though to nuzzle her, then rolled its lips back from its gums and clamped onto her arm with red, red teeth.

Her breath rushed from her, expelled from her lungs with a startled jolt of shock and pain. She jerked away, stumbling when the beast released her, falling hard into the dirt by the side of the road. She looked down at her arm, dabbed at the glistening wetness with the sleeve of the sweater dangling from her shoulders. When she looked up, the spotted calf was gone. Only the wind remained, and the soft gentle scraping of palm fronds against the house, and the faint shushing of water off the shore of the open ocean at the base of the cliff.

Next morning, Karen wore a long-sleeved shirt to cover the marks on her arm. In the pale golden morning light they looked more like burns than cuts, though they arced in the unmistakable pattern of a bite. Above and below, her arm showed two complimentary halves of a mouth of fiery teeth, upper and lower. She wasn't expert in the bite patterns of different animals, though working in the veterinarian's office she'd seen dog bites and cat bites and the peckings of birds. She'd seen wounds caused by nutria teeth and raccoon teeth and even, once, the teeth of a small alligator. If someone had come into the clinic with patterns like the ones on her arm, she'd have been certain they were the marks of a human bite.

Avita didn't ask why Karen wore a shirt over her sleeveless black dress. All afternoon, people from around the island arrived in pairs and threes, or alone. Some drove up in decades-old cars, which sputtered to stops and disgorged families in somber garb and scuffed shoes. Most bicycled up along the road, or emerged from between irregular rows of sugarcane, tugging at their ties and the tight necks of their good shirts. A donkey was tethered near Avita's goat, though whether someone had ridden it there or brought it with them on the way to somewhere else, Karen couldn't guess. Periodically the donkey would bray, a hard eerie sound, repetitive and plaintive.

Karen sat in the parlor beside her dead brother. She nodded and smiled at strangers who touched her hair or her hand or murmured low soothing things to her she didn't make sense of. At the end of the third day since her brother had fallen from the cliff by the ocean, they pulled the lid over his coffin and lifted him, and everyone filed from the whitewashed house. They wound along the road from the house to the small graveyard, leaving behind the festive red poinsettias and the green-blue mixture of ocean and sky.

The sun sank lower, dipping behind the sugarcane and bringing twilight. Brian was lowered into the ground and words were said. A hymn was sung and people dissipated into the cane and the gathering darkness one by one, nodding to Karen or touching her shoulder as they went. When only the two of them remained, Avita tucked her arm into Karen's and turned toward the path to the house. It was then they saw the man standing in the middle of the road.

His shirtfont was starched white, his hair and pants ink black; his eyes burned like small stoked fires inside tiny ship lanterns. Avita's hand slid from Karen's arm and she backed away.

Karen stepped toward the man, and he toward her. She stretched her hand to him and he took it in his own. "Brian," she said. "Brian, I'm sorry I didn't come sooner. I should have. I meant to."

He pulled her close, folding her into his arms as one might a child. He smelled warm and soft, like an injured animal or like baking bread. His hair tickled her cheek as though it were an animal's soft curly coat. "I saw the calf last night," she said into his white shirtfront, stiff and wide and fresh. "I saw the calf, but it had red teeth. Burning red teeth, Brian, like chips of hot lead."

"I know," he said against the top of her head, his breath ruffling her hair. "I'm sorry." His hand ran along her arm. When it passed over the marks on her skin they burned as though fresh, as though the wound was hot enough to scorch through the fabric of her sleeve.

Her ear to his chest, Karen heard the broken parts of his ribs which had punctured his lungs, and the soft rattlings of blood curdling there.

He pushed her to arm's length and looked into her eyes, the heat of his red gaze burning her, too. The last island light faded from the sky over his head, and the road stretched away behind him like a flat ribbon. "It had teeth just like these," he said, and smiled. "Teeth just like these."

Veilsight

Paloma stepped onto the simulation deck and closed her eyes as the generated breeze blew past her face, ruffling her sensory veil. The sim-scene about her wavered with the veil's movement, like the reflection of a cloudy sky shimmering on the surface of a wind-rippled pond.

The sound of the door opening behind her and the rumble of male laughter meant she was no longer alone. For no reason she could explain, Paloma stepped behind a sim-tree, out of sight. Her sensory veil fed datastreams to her brain, reading the exact placement of every simulated object in the room, the precise distances between them. If she concentrated, she could even discern bits of code, which streamed around otherwise solid-seeming trunks of enormous redwoods, and fluttered past wide fronds of undergrowth ferns. Sometimes it dripped, little trickles of code, off the non-existent vegetation like weeping moss cascading over the limbs of swamp trees.

One man stooped to pick up a simulated twig. He idly snapped the thing one-handed, letting the pieces fall to the floor. To Paloma's veilsight, the bits briefly looked like brittle, broken strings of tiny glowing characters before resolidifying.

"But don't you find it strange?" the man was asking his companion, "for a woman to do such a thing? To have her eyes put out like that, permanently?"

The other man laughed. "You're an idiot. Besides, the surgeons don't even go near the eyes. Just the back of the skull, to get to the brain."

"The back of the skull, yes. That's the other thing, John; shaving the head. A pretty woman like that, bald as an egg. They say it makes it easier for the nanotech to transmit from the brain to that thing she drapes over her face."

"Veil," said the other, reaching to stroke the reddish bark of a nearby sim-tree. "A nanofabric sensory veil."

Hidden from view, Paloma slid to the floor, smooth column at her back—which felt like rough tree bark only if she didn't look at it—providing support. She drew the veil close about her head and shoulders.

"And she's not bald as an egg; under that veil is a nice little fuzz."

"Fine. Bald as a peach, then. And blind forever."

Their conversation moved to other things, other planets, other women. Paloma sank more and more into herself, huddled in her corner behind a tree only she of everyone aboard could see as a naked shipsteel column writhing in code.

She barely noticed when the men finally left.

"*Extrasensor Dalton, Shuttle Bay Three. Bay Three, Extrasensor Dalton.*"

Intercom noise rained down on Paloma. With veilsight, it felt like being pelted with tiny pebbles from above. She hadn't yet learned to filter all the input, to tune it to manageable levels. She tended to shy away from walls. Funny how she'd never noticed before how close to walls people actually walked, especially in the narrow halls of a ship. It took concentration to move through corridors without trailing the fingers of one hand along the wall like a . . . like a blind woman.

Paloma keyed the pad by the bay door and it whisked open. Her veil began transmitting streams of new information to the nano-receptors in her brain. She tried to ignore useless detritus: the body temperatures of the people in the room, the chemical makeup of trace fuel exhaust clinging to the hull of the small shuttle, the waves of cold heat emanating from the flat overhead light panels.

Keeping her eyes open took effort. It felt more natural to close them when she concentrated, but she'd been told this made others uncomfortable. Nano-sensory technology was so new, the practitioners so few, most people had never met a blind person. Pre-natal genetic manipulation and inexpensive surgical techniques made for a homogenous population. And someday, the Institute would learn to make Extrasensors without the embarrassing irregularity of blindness. Then she'd be completely irrelevant. To everyone.

Paloma greeted the captain, touching one hand to the triangular medallion hanging from the chain about her neck, emblazoned with the all-seeing eye logo of the Institute. Recognizing the dark-haired man in shuttle pilot coveralls from the sim-deck, Paloma gripped her medallion tighter.

The flight to the planet surface was mercifully brief. In the cramped two-person shuttle, the silence grew increasingly oppressive. The pilot, introduced by the captain as Johnathan Campion, maintained a professional spacer's demeanor of casual boredom.

They landed near the planet's only ruins. A great city once, it now hunkered, empty and quiet, at the edge of a vast, planetwide desert. High stone mountains rose on three sides, dry, sandy fingerhills reaching down to encircle the ruins. Paloma could sense nothing beyond the shuttle walls, but she'd studied survey data, knew the city's layout and the formation of the mountains, which cradled the once-mighty metropolis like a dusty gem in cupped, rocky hands.

The pilot landed with finesse. He exited the shuttle, and Paloma heard him sinking anchors into the sand. She unbuckled her harness and stood, pulling her veil over her head. The scene around her unfolded, like a curtain being drawn from a window. A precise map of her immediate surroundings etched itself into her brain, as nanotech receptors read information, interpreted echoes of sound and light. The diagram in her mind showed her rounded edges of seats, flat slanted panels of hull, slightly irregular floor with grip-rubber runner for mobility in upper atmo. The open doors of the shuttle yawned onto hot alien sand.

Paloma stretched her hands to the warmth. Her boots made a *splicksplick* sound as she walked across the gripfloor. She stood in the doorway grasping the edges of the doorframe, and breathed the dry, slightly gritty air.

She slid the veil from her face, letting it fall down about her shoulders. She breathed deeply. Dry, sun-heated wind filled her lungs, caressed the bare skin of her face and hands, steadied her.

"Everything all right, Extrasensor?"

Paloma turned toward the pilot's voice. She remembered to open her eyes so as not to repulse him more than she already did.

"Yes," she said. "Thank you, Pilot. And it's Paloma." She drew the veil over her head and jumped to the ground, ignoring his outstretched hand. She would have sensed his shrug even without the assistance of the veil. At least here in the open, the sand, sun, and wind mitigated the impact of veilsight: she was no longer at the mercy of every irregular heartbeat, every stifled yawn, every tinny echo of the ship's intercom as it ricocheted off the interior hull.

She took several steps onto the sand before turning his direction. He stood, one hand resting on his shuttle, the other shielding his eyes as he studied her, head cocked. Paloma had once seen an antique photograph of a cowboy standing in just such a pose, one hand on the flank of his horse, the other shading his eyes from the overlarge Earthside sun.

"All right," he said. "But if you're Paloma, I'm John." He hopped up into the shuttle, his long legs making it appear effortless. He reemerged, large duffle slung over his shoulder, canteen fastened to the hipbelt of his coveralls. Smiling at her as he passed, he began to hike across the desert toward the tallest ruins at the center of the city.

In the open desert, Paloma was more truly blind. Her veilsight ranged several meters in every direction, but outside, the information was more difficult to extrapolate, more complex and less clear. Walking across the flat, sandy plain, only the man before her stood out as a distinct and fully discernable object. She followed him closely, but it was like moving through fog.

The quality of Paloma's veilsight improved as they neared the ruined city. Low rock walls and slabs of carved stone came into range, materializing from the mist in her brain. Briefly, things would appear sharp and clear: a toppled column, its carved bands eroded by the sand of countless centuries, a long, narrow tablet of pitted stone, jagged end pointing to the sky like an accusatory finger, a cairn of small, carefully rounded spheres. Then they would fade again into haze as she passed, disappearing into vagueness beyond the rim of her sensors, back into sand and the gritty warmth of wind.

Paloma was never certain anymore which elements of her sensory understanding came from the nanotechnology and which from her own body. When they entered the shelter of the great portico at the heart of the city, did she smell a change in the air? She felt the cooler temperature on her skin as they stepped beneath the vaulted ceiling. Things sounded different, too. The crunch changed beneath their boots, the area protected on three sides by high stone walls supported by banded columns which rose overhead, out of reach of Paloma's sensors. But she heard echoes. Echoes and whistles of footsteps and wind, and from inside, the sound of her own heart beating.

The pilot stopped. He eased the bag from his shoulder with a grunt. Paloma moved away until she could barely sense him at the edge of her veilsight. Eyes closed, she lifted her face to reflected heat and slid the veil to her shoulders. She imagined people who might have lived here, who walked these halls, carved these massive crumbling columns of stone. Had they looked like her? Had they laughed and danced and sang? *Who had they been*?

"Are you doing it right now?"

Paloma started. Her eyes opened, but only to blackness. She drew the veil up over her face before turning to the man behind her. "Am I doing what?"

He swigged from the canteen he held, then used it to gesticulate a vague arc in the air. "You know, the thing. The ESP thing, with the machines in your brain."

To Paloma's veilsight, his facial expression was all angles and planes. She'd trained a full year before nano-implant surgery, but still her mind struggled to describe things by their visual properties. In some ways, it was easier to understand other people without veilsight, when her perception of them was formed by their voices, the scent of their skin, the pauses between their words.

Paloma reached to hold her medallion. "The Institute prefers the term Extrasensor. ESP carries negative connotations from antiquated notions about extrasensory perception and what it means."

He handed her the canteen. "What does it mean? I'm not sure what you hope to accomplish here. Survey teams have already documented everything. These are the only ruins on the planet, not as spectacular as even Earthside ruins, much less those in a dozen other places more hospitable than this."

Paloma lifted the edge of her veil to take a few sips of cool, metallic shipwater. She tried not to feel the intimacy of pressing her lips to the same spot his had just touched.

She returned his canteen and blotted her mouth with the back of her hand. "It's no secret the Institute's work is extremely experimental. In many ways, this is as new to me as anyone. I'm only the fourth to receive visual cortex replacement surgery."

He squinted past the open wall of the portico. "The fourth to survive," he said.

Paloma turned to face the same direction. Though her veilsight faded after several meters, their voices echoed differently and the breeze carried more heat when it came from the open portion. "Many have dedicated themselves to the pursuit of knowledge throughout human history. The drive to experience something completely new is, somehow, completely human."

He studied her. "To me," he said, "it sounds lonely to be the first, the only one."

She turned to face him, though direction made no difference to her sensors, so long as he was in range. "What do you achieve, Johnathan Campion, by sailing among stars? Aren't you driven to do something new, to experience what no other has?"

He laughed, a short bark with no humor. "Spacing isn't something new to me. My parents, their parents—all lifetime spacers. My four-times-great grandmother captained one of the first colony ships when 'tweenspace drives were invented and people scrambled to get off Earth like rats deserting a sinking ship." He looked at the open sky. "No," he said. "Everything out here is desolate, and empty. Space and stars and most planets. Empty and dead, except where people put down roots and carve a little something out of nothing."

Paloma reached to touch the shallow banded carvings of a stone column at her side. "Like the people who lived here," she said. "They put down roots, built a mighty metropolis, a kingdom between desert plains and mountains. And they're gone, though these ruins stand, a monument to their efforts. If I can use extrasenses to tap into temporal resonance, I might glimpse echoes of the past, and understand what makes us like them, what makes us different."

The pilot snorted. He bent to unseal the ziptab of his satchel. "And *that*, Extrasensor Dalton, is why most find you and your Institute difficult to swallow." He shook his head. "Temporal resonance," he muttered, pulling out three telescoping tripod stands and several small holo-imagers.

"I'm used to skepticism, Mr. Campion. But the Institute has scientific proof of retrocogntion. Even before nanotechnology, retrocogs were quite well studied and documented. My veilsight and cerebral nanotech should amplify resonances. Especially here, without the interference of continuous new noise drowning out the information."

"Forgive me if I ignore what I'll call, for the sake of politeness, your wishful thinking. I have holos to take: a shuttle pilot's pay isn't enough to earn a down payment on an Earthside home without exotic holography to augment his income."

He snapped the telescoping legs of the first tripod into place and moved out of Paloma's sensor range to set up the second. He measured the proper distance to the third triangulation point with a small handheld instrument, and she heard him some meters away snapping the last tripod into place. She moved toward the sound until he came into veilsight. She walked to him, placed her hand on his where he fastened the last holo-imager on its mount.

"Johnathan Campion," she said, her voice soft. "You'll take holoshots of this place where we stand, on this specific day, in this specific time. You'll take this tiny visual of these ruins and you'll travel with it across a vast ocean of stars and space. When you reach Earth, you'll sell this fragment of time and place to a stranger. That stranger will arrange this fragment on his coffee table. Or he'll project onto his walls or hold in his hands this tiny frozen sliver of today, and though he won't be here, he'll see what we see now. This image, this souvenir, may last as far beyond our lifetimes as this city has outlasted its occupants. Tell me, please, why that is any less fantastic than what I intend to try?"

She pulled her hand from his and turned to go. "It's easier if I look for a resonance pocket on my own, Mr. Campion. I'll meet you back here in two standard hours."

She descended the wide steps leading from the portico. Behind her, beyond the range of veilsight, she heard him say, "Call me John. And be careful, Paloma."

She nodded in the direction of his voice, then turned to step out onto the sand-covered plaza ringed in toppled columns and other crumbling remnants of the dead, empty city.

After the first hour, Paloma was more tired and less hopeful than she wanted to be of either. She stopped in the shade of a pillar which rose from sand, supporting nothing but sky. She sank to the ground. She settled the veil about her shoulders, rested her bare head on her knees. Hot breeze dusted grit across her cheeks and forehead, and the deep open vee of her sleeveless coveralls. The skin of her arms felt hot to her touch, and when she ran her hand across her fuzz of hair, small crumbles of sand showered down.

Paloma squeezed shut her eyes. She clasped her knees, held her breath. *Concentrate*, she told herself. *Concentrate*.

The wind died. The sound of bells tinkling, and of beasts bleating to each other reached her ears. The laughter of a child . . . .

Paloma leapt to her feet, drawing the veil over her head. But as far as she could tell, there was nothing but flat open desert before her, bleached grey heights of mountains rising behind, and the gentle shush of billions of grains of sand blowing across the ground beneath.

Paloma pressed her hands over her eyes above the veil. She pressed the nanofabric so hard, it was as though sparks showered in the back of her brain.

Concentrate . . . .

Paloma let fall her hands. She opened her eyes. Light and color exploded around her. Had sight been this bright? Had she never noticed how *green* green was? The replaced parts of her brain that described her surroundings in meters and millimeters and degrees of angles could never describe for her the color of grass.

Where before had lain a desert of dry sand, now rolled an endless field of green. Paloma turned to look at the ruined city behind her but saw only more grass; an undulating ocean of green stretching all the way to the mountains. Even the breeze smelled green, and the sun seemed gentler, younger.

Across the grass toward her raced a human child, her simple white tunic whipping about her knees as she chased a small quadrupedal beast over the plain.

The beast tumbled to a halt a few meters from Paloma. It was goat-like, shaggy and white and small, a single horn rising from the center of its forehead. The laughing child tackled the creature and slipped a cord about its neck, kissing it as she did so. Paloma remained frozen, trying to etch into memory every detail: the child's woven clothing, the exact texture of the animal's curly coat, the soft verdance of the endless field, even the rich clover scent of the air.

The child began to lead the small animal away. In the distance, Paloma made out the peaks of pale tents, and people, who from this far away looked the size of insects. But the child stopped. She turned slowly, rotating on the ball of one bare foot, until she faced the spot Paloma occupied. Leading the goat-like animal behind her, she walked over. She squinted. She sniffed the air. She dropped the cord to touch Paloma's medallion on its chain. As the wooly creature bounded away across the plain, the girl began squeaking in a high, excited gush.

Laughing, the child launched herself at Paloma, flinging her arms about her. When their bodies met, passed through each other, Paloma felt a deep chill, then a sense of falling, then nothing.

She opened her eyes to the certainty she'd been unconscious far too long. But the chronometer of her veil showed no great lapse of time: the rendezvous with John Campion was still nearly an hour away. Laughing aloud, she began to retrace the way she had come, heading toward the tallest ruins of the massive portico, which rose to shade the entrance of a building which hadn't existed for millennia.

Gradually, Paloma's steps slowed. Halfway to the rendezvous point, she stopped. What proof did she have of her experience? What proof, even to herself, that what she'd just seen and felt was genuine retrocognition, not something manufactured by her subconscious, even unconscious self? Perhaps she'd merely fallen asleep. She'd never dreamt in color, not before nor since the surgery, but perhaps this was some reaction to cerebral nanotechnology specific to herself.

Paloma sat on a raised stone slab, which tilted at a crazy angle but still provided an ample seat. Perched on the edge, she ran one hand over the pitted surface of the stone. It was warm from the white-hot sun, as was the sand, and the air, and the dusty breath she drew into her lungs.

She emptied her mind. She pressed her hands across the veil over her eyes and willed herself to concentrate. Vertigo gripped her stomach, and she felt as though she were falling from a great height. This time, she tasted the difference on the air before she saw it. The air tasted of iron and salt, and of tears. She opened her eyes.

The slab beneath her had shifted. It tilted no longer, nor was its surface pitted. It was straight, and flat and smooth, and covered in blood.

The sky above was a rolling, livid purple, dimpled with yellow like a living bruise. No metropolis stood on the green plain, but a circle of stone huts clustered about the slab, hunkered and low, like beasts made of rock crouching around a kill. Small goat creatures bleated from nearby pens, their coats matted, flanks thin, legs like bent spindles. In a ring about the base of the stone slab where Paloma sat, gutted bodies of the creatures lay, ribs cracked wide, entrails spilling open to the sky.

Opposite Paloma stood a man. He wore a great basket headdress woven of bones. The weight balanced on his shoulders, the points poking the sky with thrusting spikes fashioned of animal horns tipped in blood. People crouched in tight clumps before the stone huts. Thin people. Gaunt people. People who did not look each other in the eyes as the man in the headdress raised his arm, spoke curt words unintelligible to Paloma, then brought his blade down to slash open the belly of the animal on the slab between them. Paloma and the goat-creature cried out as one, but the watching people remained silent.

Thunder rolled across the purple sky. Paloma felt electricity in the air but no moisture. Her skin prickled along the sides of her neck, the tops of her arms, the small of her back. The man used his blade, fashioned of horn, to slice through the thin hide of the malnourished animal before him. He cracked open the ribs, which gave with a wet snap. He hacked at the warm, frail insides of the beast, pulled forth some organ or entrails, then pushed the carcass to the ground. Using his horn blade, he etched onto the stone slab in the layer of congealing blood a symbol so familiar to Paloma, she didn't at first grasp anything unusual.

It was the triangle and the all-seeing eye of the Institute, identical to the medallion dangling from the chain about her neck.

The man shouted. He pointed to a cluster of people huddled in the doorway of a squat stone hut. A narrow-shouldered boy detached himself from the others and stepped forward. The man in the headdress stood aside, and the boy crawled up onto the rock and lay down in the blood and the goat muck, staring at the sky.

"No," said Paloma. She pulled herself up onto the slab, standing so she towered over the boy and the man with the blade. "No!" she said again. Nobody seemed to see her, to be aware of her presence. Remembering her earlier interaction with the little girl, Paloma unhooked the clasp at the back of her neck, catching the medallion as it fell. She stepped over the boy, medallion in hand, and stooped to press the triangle of metal against the chest of the man in the headdress. "*No*!" she shouted.

Where her hand met the man's chest, it burned. It burned with cold; with ice; with temperature beyond understanding. The man cried out. He fell to his knees, clawing at his breast. When his hands fell away, the silent ring of people moved closer, until one tiny girlchild reached to touch the symbol branded into the skin of the man with the blade, who now lay sobbing under the crackling violet sky.

Paloma felt cold against her ankle. It was the boy lying on the slab at her feet, who had reached to wrap his bony fingers about where her ankle would be, though his fist closed on nothing but cold air. Dry thunder rumbled across the sky, and Paloma was certain he met her eyes, *saw her*, before she fell again off that impossible, invisible height, and her sight went to darkness.

Paloma opened her eyes. Seeing nothing, she felt about her shoulders for the crumpled veil, which she drew up over her head. She was stretched out on the slab, body tilted at the same crazy angle as the stone. Her mouth was parched. Her chronometer read a seven minute lapse since she'd last checked.

"Paloma! Paloma! Are you all right?"

She swung her legs over the edge of the slab and sat up. Her head felt heavy, and she swallowed a few times to clear the dry lump in her throat. She heard crunching sand as Johnathan Campion moved quickly into her perception range. He unlatched the canteen from his belt and held it to her lips.

She heard the relief in is voice. "You were yelling. I was afraid something had happened," he said.

She drank, not thinking at all about the flat taste of shipwater, the ghost imprint of the man's lips on the threaded rim.

She handed the canteen back, but he reached to snap it onto the hipbelt of her dark coveralls. He helped her to her feet, not letting go of her hand. "You sure you're all right?" he asked. He reached as though to lift the edge of the veil from her face, but let his hand fall after brief hesitation. It suddenly struck Paloma that she'd spent much time feeling herself shut off inside the veil, but no time at all thinking others might feel shut out.

She pulled away and straightened the nanofabric over her face. "Thank you. I'm fine. In fact, I'm better than fine. Just a little overwhelmed. This was only meant to be a test mission, my first fieldtrip. Not of any particular interest to the Institute, other than to see if I could pick up anything."

"And have you?"

She tilted her head. She tried to concentrate on him, what his resonance was, what his history might be. But nothing came to any of her senses: nothing other than the sharp, almost sweet tang of his skin, the sound of his breathing—slightly ragged from running—and the solid, almost magnetic presence of a fellow human being.

"I think so, Johnathan Campion, though I'm not prepared to talk about it yet."

He nodded. He stooped to pick something out of the sand at her feet. "You've dropped this," he said, holding her medallion. "Here." He stepped behind her. He reached his arms over her head, holding the ends of the chain to fasten them at the back of her neck. She moved to lift her hair, momentarily forgetting there would be none. Instead, she lifted the hem of her veil, and felt his warm fingers on her skin as he fumbled to hitch the clasp.

She turned and smiled. "Thank you."

"I'm almost done with my holos," he said. "I was going to triangulate a couple more, but we can leave if you're ready."

"No. No, I'd like a little longer if you don't mind."

He peered past the semi-transparent veil at her face. His fingers twitched, as though itching to flick away the nanofabric. He balled his hand into a light fist and nodded, then turned and left the range of her veilsight, heading the direction of the portico ruins.

Paloma took a deep breath. No iron taste, no clover scent, no tears. No children, no small, one-horned goats.

Paloma's steps felt shaky, her knees weak. She was glad Campion had left her the canteen. She'd gone only a little way when she felt the need to sit, take another swallow of water. Her bench was long and narrow, troughlike. Its shallow-carved length sloped almost imperceptibly, nearly identical to many lengths of similar stone scattered throughout the ruins.

Paloma had much to think about before she returned to the Institute. She was certain she'd achieved some level of success, though the nature of that success was difficult to define. And how valid would her experience be without any way to prove the intensity of her visions, the realness of them?

Her time here was so limited. What if she never found these exact conditions again? What if there was some special component of this particular place that allowed her to tap into resonances, getting true retrocognitive glimpses of the past? She must try at least once more before she left. She must.

She took another sip of water, then closed the canteen and reclipped it to her belt. She sat as still and straight as she could on the narrow strip of rock, calming her breathing.

This time she didn't plummet into the vision so much as slide into it sideways. Her stomach lurched sharply. When she opened her eyes, she gasped.

So much color! So much bustle and energy and *life*!

This was neither the rolling green of the verdant plain, nor the stark bleakness of the stone huts. The city rose all about her, a veritable metropolis, as promised by the enormous portico and the detailed carvings on the massive columns. She stood and turned to face it now, that edifice she had previously seen only to the range of the several meters granted by veilsight. The people passing her on the street wore brightly-dyed leathers, decorated with polished horn and woven, tasseled fringes. Troughs, like the one she had rested upon, rose on stone stilts, crisscrossing over her head like arteries, pumping water, the lifeblood of the city, to buildings and cisterns and fountains and rooftop gardens.

Paloma shielded her eyes from the hard daylight. She barely noticed that in this manifestation, she had no veil. The sunlight burned too fierce. Her eyes watered. Her skin tingled with heat. But the sky was azure, azure, azure, and cloudless, and stretched on forever. The air was so clear, Paloma could see the peaks of the mountains, high and pale, and the stonework troughs—the extensive aqueduct—which rose like latticework up the stony sides to the tops, bringing high waters to the valley and the people below.

And the quarries! Deep cuts ran into the base of the fingerhills. The sandy stone was needed to build temples to the people, to celebrate the glory of their humanity and their triumph over the arid plain. From where she stood on the trough, which ran at an angle over the roof of a granary, Paloma could see carefully tended, starkly regular rectangles of green fields just beyond the city dwellings. Past the fields stretched the relentless bleached emptiness of unending desert. The desert was the only thing Paloma recognized with any degree of certainty from her own time. The desert, and the massive portico these people had built, an entry to the temple erected to their own greatness.

The aqueduct was so extensive, Paloma was tempted to use it to explore the city, like a personal highway. Looking down, she saw water flowing, splashing right through where her boots should have disturbed its passage. Her feet felt pleasantly cool in the midday air, but so far as she could tell, her presence disturbed nothing.

As Paloma wandered the streets, taking care to stay out of the way of the local citizenry, she wondered: how much of what she was seeing was some actual echo of a previous temporal existence? How much was her own imagination, an amalgamation of fantasy and hypothesis and gleaned fact? How much was what Johnathan Campion had called wishful thinking?

As she neared the portico with its towering columns, the crowd thickened. Each time someone had touched her in her previous manifestations, she'd experienced intense cold, then been wrenched back to her own temporal reality. She narrowly avoided a man herding a fat little goat-beast past her in the busy street. She dodged to miss three naked children, who ran by laughing, kicking between them a small ball stitched of painted hide. Everywhere people laughed and shouted and sang, and above their heads streamed the seemingly endless flow of water, stolen from the top of the stone mountains to stave off the encroaching desert. It must have seemed as though it could never end, that water.

Paloma halted in the shade of the looming portico. Looking up at the vaulted entryway, a vertiginous chill began low in her belly, worse than any she'd felt before. Above her—far, far overhead, deeply chiseled in stone at the zenith of the tallest building in the city—was a triangle, and within, the all-seeing eye. Paloma lightly touched the identical symbol etched in cold metal about her neck. She crumpled, and everything became nothing.

She woke with her head in someone's lap. "Johnathan," she said, and struggled to sit, feeling about her shoulders to pull up the nanofabric of her veil.

"Whoa, take it easy. You were walking toward me, and I called out to you a couple times, but you didn't seem to hear me. Then you just . . . fell."

Paloma used John Campion's shoulder as a crutch and stood. She stared upward at the standing remnants of the portico, but it was no good. The carved columns rose the several meters of her sensory range, then dissipated into haze and nothing.

Campion stood at her side, one arm about her waist. She leaned into his solidity. "Johnathan . . . John. Can you see the top of the portico, in the center, between the two middle columns? Is there a carving there? A big one?"

She felt his body shift slightly as he looked up. The veil read for her the exact angle of his head, the temperature of his skin, the rate of his pulse.

"Yeah, there's a carving there. Biggest carving of the whole place, actually, and maybe the best preserved as well."

She heard the frown in his voice rather than read it in the planes of his face.

"Strange," he said. He used his free arm to pull a miniature holoprojector from his coverall pocket. "Hold out your hand."

Paloma held out her hand. Campion set the small black box in her palm and pressed the activating divot. "That's the second holo-image I took, right after you left this afternoon. I got a good shot of the front. Thought it was imposing, impressive. Thought it might fetch a good price. I'm not sure how your sensory equipment works, but can you read that?"

Paloma nodded, studying the miniature strings of code that dribbled and shifted in her hand as the image rotated on its base. The portico: nothing over its front but a blank, sand-pitted expanse of bleached stone. "Is this what it looks like now?" she asked, her voice barely above a whisper.

"No. I don't know how that happened. And I can't believe I didn't notice the carving before. But there it is, plain as night, just like yours." She felt the metal of her medallion chill her skin as he pressed the eye at its center. "But why is it different now?"

Paloma swayed on her feet. She sagged against the man by her side, grateful for the tall firm length of him.

Taking a deep breath, she straightened. She turned her face to his, closing her hand over the tiny projector in her palm. "John," she said, "let's make one more holo before we go. I think this last one could augment a shuttle pilot's income enough for him to acquire a very nice place, a place where he might be able to put down some roots, and try to carve a little something out of nothing. . . ."

They Shall Be as They Know

On the day before the day before the end of the world, Lynn unslung her schoolbag from her shoulder and tossed it onto the kitchen counter. She pressed the Fridge-o-mat lever harder than necessary and it opened midway with a hydraulic squeal. She gave a light token kick to the machine's base and the door hiccupped on its hinges, opening the rest of the way. She pulled out a tray of cocoa derivatives, a bag of saltbreads. She grabbed a can of caffeine-rich Zamola! ("*Caffeine Carbonated With a Kick!*") and used the same foot she'd kicked the fridge with to nudge it shut. Noticing a slight dent in the end of her boot, she wriggled her toes to force the stiff fabric back into shape.

Soda tucked into the crook of her arm, she tore the corner from the saltbread package with her teeth as she made her way to the family room. Her mother and brother sat on the sofa facing the video wall, side by side and with identical slack-eyed stares. When Lynn stepped into the room her mother's head turned slightly toward her, the edges of her lips curving upward, gaze still directed at the wall. The whites of her eyes glowed a healthy-looking pearl.

"Hi, Mom," said Lynn. She bent in passing to kiss her mother on a cheek that smelled and felt like stale baby powder with an undercurrent of rot. "Hey, Jeff," she said, flopping into the only armchair. Her brother grunted. The video wall droned on.

". . .The Manifesto tells us: *At the End of All,*" read the Chief Magistrate on the vid, glancing at his palm screen, "*all citizens shall know Nothing, and they shall be as they know, which is Nothing.*"

The oration paused. The camera panned the Magistrate's audience, zombies mostly, but a full oration hall nonetheless. The audience undulated. The vid-prompter flashed appropriate responses across the bottom of the screen so at home viewers could follow along.

"*They shall be as they know,*" rumbled the sea of larger-than-life faces, individual slack-lipped mouths of state ward zombies forming words out of sync with the overall swell of response. A zombie in the front row with tightly spiraled curls pursed her lips into a perfect *o* in place of the word *know*.

"No-thing," echoed Lynn's mother atonally, the edges of her mouth still curved, gentle, soft. Jeff grunted.

The Chief Magistrate blotted his forehead and continued to read, glancing at text on his palm screen. "*And when the world's citizens become Nothing, so shall come the End; the End of All.*"

"End," Lynn's mother repeated, and blinked once.

Lynn set down her soda. "I'm changing the channel, okay, Mom?" she said, flipping open the panel on the chair's arm and punching numbers into the imbedded remote control. Twelve thousand and two channels, but eleven thousand, nine hundred and ninety-eight of them Nothing Manifesto feeds.

Lynn snapped the chair panel shut and settled back to watch an episode of *That's Family!* on the video wall. It was about a family who, through some twist of unlikely-sounding plot, found a wormhole in their doghouse. All four of them—and the dog—had traveled through time to the previous century; before Zombadril, before the massacres, before the Magistrate had restored order and taught everyone the Manifesto. In the *That's Family!* past there were no zombies and dogs had hair all over their bodies—from days before breeding and insurance regulations eradicated pet fur. Everybody on the show wore ugly clothes and worked all day and drove individual, pod-looking cars of metal and glass. About the only thing that looked the same was school, though their computers were huge, like joke computers from novelty stores; practically the size of two dinnerplates put together like clamshells. The show's family was always explaining to their twentieth-century neighbors why the zombie dad didn't talk much, and they took turns shaving the neighborhood dogs in an effort to help theirs blend in. It was hilarious.

"We're going to watch this for awhile, okay?" she said.

Jeff grunted.

Lynn's mother said nothing.

When Lynn's father came home she was sitting at the kitchen table finishing the last of her homework.

"How's my best girl?" he said, leaning to kiss the top of her head.

"Okay, I guess."

He nodded absently and pressed the door handle of the Fridge-o-mat. He grabbed a NothingBeer ("*Feel Good Without the Guilt!*"), popped the seal, and settled into the chair beside her. He took a deep pull and flicked a seemingly involuntary glance toward the family room. "How's your mom?"

Lynn scooped her palm computer, personal stylus, and other school stuff into her bag. "I don't know. The same. Better, I guess. She smiled at me today."

His eyebrows rose. "Really? Well. That's nice. Good for her . . . good for her."

"Dad?"

"Hmm?" He took another swig of NothingBeer and held it in his mouth a moment before swallowing. "What, sweetheart?"

Lynn picked at the edge of her schoolbag, at the spot where the seam frayed. She flicked the raw, soft plastic edge with her fingernail. "Dad, why did Mom take Zombadril? She could've tried harder to stay the way she was, to keep things the way they were."

He looked at her a moment without speaking, then drew her to him. "Honey, honey . . . you know it's got nothing to do with you, right? You know nobody on Zombadril stayed the way they'd been before? Nobody predicted the side effects of long-term use. It was just supposed to make things easier."

Lynn nodded into his sweater. The fibers were soft and light.

This close, she could practically taste the slick synthetic surface of the fabric's weave.

"It's just that for some people, like your mom, life was hard all the time. They didn't feel they could cope on their own. Lots of people, millions and millions, were prescribed Zombadril. They didn't know it would—"

"Kill everyone who took it." Lynn's voice was muffled by his sweater.

Her father sighed nearly inaudibly. She heard his breath start somewhere deep in his chest, rise out of him like a warm breeze, ruffle the hair on the top of her head.

"You know it didn't kill *everyone*," he said. "Not permanently. But think how fortunate we are; most people didn't come back at all. Half the world's population really did die forever, if not from Zombadril then from social purges before the Magistrate took over to stop the massacres. Besides, your mother's lucky. The Nothing Manifesto tells us that when everything ends, we'll all join her in Nothing."

Lynn pulled from the circle of his embrace. She smoothed her hair to tuck it behind her ears, then lifted her schoolbag. "If it's so great to go zombie, why is Zombadril illegal now? If that's what everybody wants they should just take it and get it over with."

He frowned, an awkward combination of stern and sad. "Lynn, I don't know what to do with you when you say those things. The Manifesto teaches us responsibility, and patience. The Zombadril Rising just showed us the future, not the way."

"Well, if whatever kind of life mom has is the future, I think it's a crappy one."

She passed from the kitchen, crossed the front room and climbed the stairs. She heard her father activate the kitchen video screen behind her, and the voice of one of the twenty-four-hour Nothing Manifesto Magistrates on one of the world's eleven thousand, nine hundred and ninety-eight NM channels wafted up the stairwell in her wake: "*And so comes the End of All, and in good civic conscience we prepare ourselves for the onset of the Nothing. . . .*"

* * *

Lynn woke the next morning to the gentle blue pulse of her bedside clock.

She rinsed her body and her teeth. She pulled a new overtunic from the dispenser. The morning was programmed to be chilly, so she ordered up a sweater and pulled that from the dispenser too; unfolded it and slid it over her head, smoothed her hair with her hands and dialed up lipstick color #327, flavor 52, her current favorites.

She went downstairs intending to just grab a Zamola! and kiss her father goodbye before she left for school.

"Happy World's Eve, Dad," she said.

His smile was extra lopsided, his forehead wrinkled. "Thanks, honey. Happy World's Eve to you, too."

They hugged. They ate breakfast together in the quiet house. For once, Lynn couldn't hear a Nothing Manifesto Magistrate's voice coming from any screen or wall or speaker anywhere. The silence was good.

She rose and slid her bag onto her shoulder. Her father reached for her arm. "The Magistrate decrees you should go to school today, but. . . ." He let his hand drop without touching her and trailed after her into the hall. "Well. Be extra careful out there today, Lynn. You don't know what people are capable of at a time like this."

"I know more than you think, Dad," she said, stepping out onto the front stoop.

He nodded. "I know you do, sweetheart. I know."

When she reached the corner at the end of their street she looked back. Her father stood on the doorstep of their house where she'd left him, looking slumped and tiny from a distance. She waved, watching as he raised his arm once in reply before turning slowly to disappear inside.

Vic was waiting for her at the mechanized slidewalk. He lounged against the public stop, leaning backward, arms propped against the rail. His hair was a beautiful color. Charcoal Peacock #211, she thought. Suddenly Lynn felt drab.

"Hey," he said, narrowing his eyes and nodding, head back, as she approached. "I didn't know if you'd come to school today."

"What else is there to do?"

He shrugged, then pushed himself off the rail and stretched. She glimpsed a sliver of his perfect stomach in the carefully calculated gap between his short tunic and his kilt. Together they turned and stepped onto the jerky, antiquated mechanical slidewalk that serviced their neighborhood. As always, Lynn felt a sideways lurch in the pits of her lungs at the motion.

"You okay?" asked Vic, slipping a pair of shades from his pocket and attaching them to magnets embedded in his temples.

She nodded, swallowed a couple times. She wished she'd worn shades, though the sun above was filtered to a pale hazy gold, easy on the eyes. It hung low and full in the morning sky, distant, like an omnipotent orange.

Three times between the neighborhood stop and school, Lynn stepped off the slidewalk mid-station to help ragged, unattended state ward zombies that had fallen over or gotten stuck. One lay face down, half on, half off the walk, his legs still churning as though he were upright. She righted him, led him to the nearest stop and called the city medicos. Vic waited with her the few minutes it took the medicos to arrive and begin bandaging the zombie's abraded cheeks with anodyne gauze. He removed and replaced his shades, his lips tight and unhappy.

"Why do you bother?" he asked as they stepped back onto the lurching slidewalk. She watched the zombie and medicos get smaller and smaller, until the walk rounded a corner and she couldn't see them at all.

"That guy might be somebody's dad," she said.

Vic turned his head, looked the opposite direction. "Not anymore," he said.

They remained silent the rest of the trip. When they stepped off at the school stop Vic turned, caught her hand and held it.

"I'll see you at lunch," he said.

She looked into the reflective surfaces of his shades. They

were the same color as his hair, his kilt, his boots, the dark, chipped polish on his nails. She nodded, and he let her go.

"At lunch," she said.

First class was Historical Sociotics. Mrs. Fust handed out pop quizzes, keying in the quiz menu on each desk computer as she went around the room, making slight adjustments in difficulty and language to suit each student.

"Lynn," she said when she reached Lynn's desk. "How's your mother? We miss her here at Nothing Manifesto High. She was much loved, by both her students and fellow faculty."

Lynn pressed her thumb to the sensor divot on her desk, activating its properties and allowing it to key in her specifics. "She's doing good. Thanks for asking, Mrs. Fust." She smiled and glanced at the teacher, who seemed as if she were about to speak, say something more. But she patted Lynn's arm instead and glided off down the row.

The quiz was too easy. So easy, Lynn suspected Mrs. Fust of giving her students a World's Eve gift. Maybe she thought it would be a distraction. Maybe she thought it a kindness, or maybe she just thought it wouldn't matter, tomorrow being what it was. What it wasn't.

Lynn ticked answers with her stylus almost without thinking. They were simpleton questions, really: 1) *Which Magistrate first united the world's population under the Nothing Manifesto?* 2) *How many Zombadril victims reanimated at the time of the Rising, and how many died in the Massacres?* 3) *How does the Manifesto describe the End of All?*

And so on, with multiple choice answers. Kid stuff.

Robotics Industries and Unified Manifesto classes were the same old boring dross, but Geomatics was slightly more interesting because their teacher, Mr. Braun, said they should spend the entire class doing whatever they wanted. "I don't give a crap," he told the class. "Go home, for all I care—go get zombified, get laid, get wasted, get whatever you want. What are you waiting for, anyway?"

He pulled a beverage tube from his jacket pocket and slurped it softly, looking out the window, shoulders hunched. The class, after some initial snickering, began to mill about the room. Ballplayers and other popular kids threw their chair cushions in a ring on the floor in one corner and began playing some makeout-roulette game. They'd toss their personal styluses into a schoolbag and draw them out by twos and threes, then those kids would disappear into the utility closet to do whatever it was teens wanted to do with each other in dark, cramped spaces.

After watching awhile, Lynn gathered her stuff into her bag and walked to the teacher's desk.

"Mr. Braun?" He didn't seem to hear her, so she cleared her throat and tried again. "Mr. Braun, can I go early to lunch?"

He swiveled in his chair to face her, taking another pull on the mouth of the tube in his hand. The hot, poisonous-animal scent of genuine unsynthesized alcohol combined with illicit Zombadril wafted to Lynn's nostrils. It must have cost a fortune, that tube, and was completely illegal.

"Sure," he said, wiping his mouth with the back of his hand, "why not? You want a cigarette?" He fumbled in his other jacket pocket and pulled out a slender cylinder of inhalable plastic stuffed with brown crumbs.

Lynn shook her head. Her teacher shrugged and pulled a small lighter from the same pocket and lit the end of the nic-stick.

"Mr. Braun, is there any homework for tonight?"

He sucked smoke and fumes deep into his lungs. The end of the lit tube crackled, flickered, the tip of the white cylinder turning from red to black as it burned. He released smoke from his mouth in a narrow stream of white which fled some distance from his lips before releasing into lazy swirls and loose puffs, finally dissipating into the air altogether, leaving behind only the scent of dead green things and burnt food.

He patted her on the arm, as Mrs. Fust had done but more clumsy with it. "No, Lynn. Don't worry about it. Just . . . just go see friends, or something, okay? Look up at the sky, eat your favorite food, play with your dog if you have one. Just don't worry about it, okay?"

He stood, shakily, leaning heavy on Lynn's arm. He let go, climbed up onto his chair, then his desk. He raised a hand to the class. "Class," he said, drink in one hand, smoking cylinder held aloft by the other as he waved it, got everyone's attention. "Class! Listen up a second. Please note: there'll be no homework assigned tonight, as there'll be no tomorrow."

The laughing and whispering and talking stopped. Two cheerleaders who'd been in the closet—a boy and a girl in matching Manifesto High spirit uniforms—came out and stood, arms around each others' waists, the girl with her hand on the doorknob.

"Please, kids. No homework. Not anymore. No homework ever again."

Mr. Braun took another drag on his nicotine stick, the crackle of its glowing tip sounding loud and harsh in the otherwise silent room.

One of the jocks, a massive kid, star of the Manifesto ball team and darling of the faculty lounge, stood and helped a slender, longhaired girl to her feet. Together they walked toward the utility closet. "That's right, Mr. B.," he said over his shoulder. "What's the point? We'll all be zombie soon. Total zombie; absolute Nothing."

Mr. Braun nodded, stabbing the air with his cigarette for emphasis. He took another gulp from the tube in his hand, smacked his lips. "Exactly!"

Vic and Lynn lay on their backs in the school commons. The sky had warmed to the hue and taken on the consistency of a fizzy peach. The real kind, thought Lynn, with the actual ten thousand hairs—not the synthetic kind, bald and smooth, with flesh tasting of soap.

"But do we *know*?" he said, "How do we know tonight is the end of everything?" Vic took another hit off the stick. Two cigarettes in one day—more than Lynn had seen in months. Only, Vic's wasn't filled with plain nicotine crumbs; she smelled the mild narcotic burning in there. Unlike plain nic, this smelled sweet and mild, and full of promises.

He handed her the stick. She took a drag, pulling smoke into her lungs, letting it fuzzle her insides.

"We know because of the zombies. And the Manifesto. The coming of the End of All was predicted way before we were born, way before the Rising, even." She let smoke curl from her nostrils up into her eyelashes and her hair. "They just know. The Manifesto says: 'And when they achieve Nothing, so shall come Nothing, and the End of All.' You're not some kind of Antisocial Anachronist, are you?"

She leaned over him. He looked at her mouth for a long second before reaching to take the stick from her fingers. Lynn tried not to tremble when his hand brushed against hers. "My father is," he said.

She grew very still. "That's a crime against the Magistrate. A prison-time crime."

"I guess that doesn't matter if the universe ends tonight at midnight like it's supposed to," he said. He smoked the stick awhile in silence, not passing it back to her.

"But what if it doesn't?" she asked.

He handed her the last nub of the lit narc-stick. "Then I guess they can't jail him for being right, can they?"

She didn't answer. She pressed her lips tight together, drawing hard to get the final bit of smoke from the crumpled tube. She dug a little depression in the soft dirt by her side, dropped the scrap of burnt stuff into the hole and smoothed earth back over the top. She tapped it down with the flat of her palm until there was no discernable difference between that small bit of ground and all the ground around it.

She said, "You going to parties tonight? There's supposed to be tons. Zombies, sex, drugs. Everything."

Vic pulled his sunglasses from his tunic pocket, clicked them into place. "I don't know," he said. "Maybe I'll go downtown, wander around. See what there is to see, you know? You want to come with?"

"Maybe."

"Okay. You going back to class after lunch?"

Lynn stood, brushed dirt from her legs and the back of her overtunic. "Why? What else is there to do?"

Vic shrugged. "I don't know. Nothing, I guess."

"Then yes, I'm going back to class."

On her way to class Lynn passed through the old zombie wing, where people still sent their kids even after it became obvious the walking dead didn't learn, didn't grow, didn't do anything at all: were Nothing.

She didn't have to come this way but she did at least a couple times a week, glancing into rounded door portals as she passed classrooms. All were arranged identically, with dozens of rows of neatly aligned desks. Some rooms had bright colorful paper on the walls, cut into shapes of flowers and stars and trees. Others were swaddled in dark crepe, and some were lit and humming with the impersonal overbright sterility of med-centers. Teachers had lots of leeway with zombie classes—officially called *Post Zombadril*, or *Po-Zo* classes—and each was encouraged to try pet theories of maintenance or rehabilitation, though no case of zombie reclamation had ever been reported by anyone anywhere: once people went zombie they didn't come back. Now, on World's Eve, it seemed stupid for Lynn to be pissed off about that. Useless.

Afternoon classes disintegrated into chaos. By the end of the day she was one of just a few students wandering the halls. Even the teachers had left, and the janitors and administrators, and most higher-functioning zombies seemed to have wandered off or been picked up by relatives. It felt weird walking the halls on a regular school day, finding them nearly empty. Weirder than it usually felt, when school was full of people she didn't know and zombies she couldn't talk to.

It was also strange that the kids she did pass, a miniscule and somewhat random sampling of the population of fourteen thousand students of Nothing Manifesto High—boys and girls she'd never knowingly met, would never see again—suddenly seemed like friends. They greeted each other if not quite as friends then certainly with a casual civility she couldn't remember experiencing before. Their faces and their clothes and their walks were ordinary. Within the ocean of students usually flowing through the halls, Lynn would never have been able to identify these particular ones; would never have been able to pick them out of a crowd and wave or say hello to them again. Not that it mattered. Not that it would.

It's okay, she thought. *They wouldn't remember me either.*

Lynne gave up wandering empty corridors. She stepped onto the slidewalk home. Every public vid screen she glided by, every rest stop wall and every corner stoplight and every enormous illuminated billboard showed the same thing. It was as though the Magistrate had consolidated all its efforts, all its twelve-thousand-minus-two channels into one broadcast. The Chief Magistrate shook his fist and addressed the empty city streets with forceful conviction: "*At the End of All, everything shall become Nothing: all the citizens of the world, and all the insects of the seas, and all the plants of the dirt. All the stars in the skies shall be Nothing, and all the waters in the oceans shall be Nothing, and all the planets of the galaxies shall be Nothing. Prepare: prepare for the End of All!*"

Lynn stepped off at the slidewalk stop nearest her house. She closed her eyes and swallowed a couple times, fighting the lurch of her insides and waiting for her mind to right itself.

Her street was empty like the rest. Nothing moved or barked or sang. Nobody called out to her as she walked to her house. She didn't even see the usual local zombies shuffling along the street in the midday sun.

She pushed the door shut with her boot, wiggling her toes to reshape the dented tip. She went into the kitchen, tossed her bag on the counter, grabbed a Zamola! and headed to the family room. It was empty. The video wall was blank, dark.

Lynn turned to call through the open doorway, "Mom? Dad? . . . Jeff? Anybody here?"

She was answered only with silence.

Lynn placed her drink on a flip-down table and walked

through the house. Upstairs the beds were all made, the rooms tidy and white and fashionably sparse. It was another twenty minutes before she thought to turn on the kitchen vid-panel to see if anyone had left her a recorded memo.

Her father's image winked onscreen. "Hey, honey. Sorry we didn't wait for you, but I think your mother would have wanted me to take her to the Magistrate's oration hall tonight. I know it'll be packed down there, but I really think it's what your mother would have wanted. Really. Jeff's coming, so if you'd like to join us you know where we are. Otherwise . . . otherwise, I love you, sweetheart. Goodbye, Lynn."

The memo winked out. Lynn stared at the blank screen another couple minutes before turning it off. The only surprise when the door chime rang was her lack of surprise.

She opened the door. "Hey," said Vic.

She opened it wider. "Hey."

They heard sounds of frenzy in the nighttime neighborhood streets.

They heard sirens, felt a couple blasts rock the foundations of the house. One was close enough to make the plastic window in Lynn's bedroom shatter. It tinkled to the floor in a shower of pale slivers.

"Do you think that was a nuke?" she asked, exhaling smoke from her lungs and passing the cigarette to Vic. No narc-stick this time; just a cigarette. He'd swiped an entire pack from his dad before the guy had headed for the mountains. They'd decided they might as well smoke them before midnight.

In the dark she didn't see him shrug, but she felt the motion of his shoulder roll under her head. "Could be any homemade bomb. Plenty of people crazy enough, and they're easy to make if you've got the ingredients."

Someone was screaming anti-zombie epithets in the street below. *That's Mrs. Parker from down the road*, thought Lynn, but didn't say it aloud. It didn't seem relevant somehow, with the combined effect of the smoke and Vic's nearness making its way through the folds of her brain, filling out the tiny broccoli-balloons of her lungs and the ventricles of her heart.

The screaming stopped. Not abruptly, which may have been alarming, but slowly, fading away into the dark and the explosions, into the sounds of cracking plastic and distant sirens and the *whooshes* of sudden large fires igniting.

Lying in the dark on Lynn's bed, she and Vic listened to street noise drift up through the broken window. Laughter, sobbing, drunken singing, cries of ecstasy—all filtered up from below and got caught, muted, nullified by the cigarette haze in the unlit room.

Vic leaned across her and dropped the cig end into the beverage tube on the floor. There was a bit of Zamola! still in the bottom, and he swirled the thing a couple times, swishing it around until no more smoke rose from the mouth of the cylinder. Lynn heard other cig bits in there, clacking together softly like the carapaces of drowning insects.

"You sure you don't want to go out there?" she asked. "You're positive?"

He nodded. He resettled her body along the lean curve of his, then lay back and stared at patterns on the ceiling. The buckles of his kilt dug into her hip through her overtunic, but she didn't mind. The pain actually felt kind of good. *If I were zombie, would I feel that?* she thought.

In the dim gleam of diffused fireglow coming through the broken window, Lynn could make out Vic's eyebrows. They arched, perfect and fine, above the glints of his eyes.

"Whatever's out there, there's nothing we can do about it, either way," he said.

Lynn traced her finger along the line of his jaw, along the soft spiky edges of his hair where it crushed against his arm and the pillow behind him.

"What if everybody's always been right, and midnight tonight is the end of everything forever?" she said.

"Then I guess we won't have to think about it anymore."

There came another explosion, an incendiary boom like close

thunder. Lynn estimated it came from the same direction and about the same distance away as the zombie-hating Mrs. Parker's house.

When the boom stopped echoing in Lynn's ears she released her grip on Vic, relaxing back into the warmth of him. Things quieted outside in the street, though she still heard sounds of distant revelry and distress. She felt herself becoming drowsy despite all the Zamola!s she'd drunk. Her eyelids felt heavy and thick. "And what if zombies are just some crazy sad accident, and not a preview of the End of All? What if. . . ."

Vic tilted his head until his cheek pressed against the top of her hair. "What if we actually do wake up tomorrow and there are birds in the skies, and waters in the oceans and stars in the heavens and planets in the depths of space. . . ." His voice took on the drone of the Chief Magistrate. Vic laughed a little, and Lynn liked the way her head bobbed, tucked between the concave curve near his shoulder and the convex one of his cheek. He smelled like soil when soil smelled good and full of growing things. He smelled like unsynthetic chocolate, and the leaves of trees in the school gardens.

He stopped laughing and lay still. Lynn, on the cusp of sleep herself, decided he'd dozed off. But when he spoke, his voice was clear.

"Well then," he said, "I suppose in that case we start all over again with something new."

She smiled, though he couldn't see it. "Something new. . . ."

He stroked her arm with the tips of his fingers. Nothing had ever felt so good before in her life as the feel of his breath against her temple. As Lynn gave in to sleep and her eyes drifted shut, she noticed the faint blue glow of the clock by her bed. Sometime during the past hours something had changed. It was everything, and at the same time it was nothing at all.

The clock read two thirty-four a.m.

Vic really had fallen asleep, though Lynn found herself no longer drowsy. She spent the remaining hours of darkness listening to him breathe, and waiting for the first pale hint of dawn to steal into the room.

Flying Solo

Begin Transmission

Dear Jack,

Well it looks like I'm not going to make it to the wedding after all. For that, I really am sorry.

I know you had your heart set on your sister being your best man. It did seem funny when we first thought of it. I guess you'll have to go the more traditional route after all. Ask Cindy's brother to do it; it'll make him happy. He thinks you don't like him, you know.

I was on my way, honest. I rented a two-seater and debarked from Earthside Station without a hitch. The hitch came later.

I know you told me I wasn't ready to fly solo and I guess you were right. It wasn't the flying I had trouble with actually, but the wormhole navigation; fried the ship's computers on the dismount. I hate it when my little brother is right.

I'm not sure exactly where I am: somewhere east of the sun and west of the moon. (Joke.) I actually got as far as the Dimotros moonbelt, I think. That's where I'm pretty sure I am now. You used to tell me about this place. I think I remember you said as many as one in sixty of these planetoids has breathable air. *A miracle there were so many*, you said. *A wonder of the Universe*, you said. Let me tell you, brother: one in sixty doesn't feel like great odds when you've got forty seconds to choose a rock and your ship's going down with nearly total engine burnout. Hah! I bet my chances of even surviving a crash landing were only one in . . . I don't know how many millions, but we'll call it a lot. And as for what happens next. . . .

Excuse me, Jack. I think I have to go throw up. I think I just now understand the full measure of my predicament.

Love,

Katherine

Dear Jack,

I'd like to say I feel better after a long nap. By the barely-functioning ship's chronometer, I slept for something like twenty-three hours. I feel like crap.

I did try going outside. I got back in here as quickly as I could. I know space is big, but when you're out there bobbing around in all that bigness, at least you're protected by the shell of your ship. It's like a floating, navigable, free-standing apartment. It makes all that vastness doable, you know? Gives you at least the illusion of some small shelter against the wonders of the unknown.

Gods, but I always hated even going out on that bloody deep-sea boat of yours back Earthside. All that rolling brown-grey water, stretching away forever and ever into nothing and nothing and more of the same. Forget sea-sick: I always stayed in my cabin the whole time because I was open-sick. Couldn't wait to get back to the safety of my high-rise loft in the Tower Cities. Couldn't stand all that unmitigated wind and air. It was like the sky was crushing down on my head the whole time. Too much weight for me.

I've transferred these letters into my palm-pad. This little two-seater ship was only equipped for a quick hop. With the computer fried like it is, I figure I've got about another day of power and no way to recharge. The palm-pad will last at least another Earth-standard week, maybe two if I don't use it too often, before I wear the charge out. This will be one hell of a letter, Jack. If it ever reaches you.

Love,

Katherine

* * *

Dear Jack,

Well I was wrong. The ship had about six hours of power left.

I feel quite clever actually, as I thought to fill the recirculation suit with the proper amount of water before the condensation stills quit. See? I remembered something from my pilot courses, after all. Not that they spend much time on crash survival training. It's only just now occurring to me that's because they don't want to explain how low the odds are of surviving. So I managed to pull off the miracle and land in breathable atmo. The double-miracle, really, because I'm still talking to you now. Well, *typing*, though these palm-pad keys are bloody small, Jack! I should have listened to you and bought the upgrade.

I won't ignore the advice of my baby brother again, I promise. No flying solo without the full pilot's license. No buying inferior products to save a few credits. No wasting my life behind closed doors. Actually, this last one seems to be giving me a bit of trouble, not quite working out for the best. But you see I'm taking it to heart. I'd better, as the ship's air pumps are off, gone with the rest of the power.

I've got the recirc suit on. I have the recommended amount of water in the bladders. I have plenty of food. Those syntha-meal bars do taste like a dog's ass, Jack, you were right. I thought you were just bragging. I still do not appreciate the mental image of the empirical data-gathering you must have done to arrive at such a conclusion.

At any rate, the meal bars will last way past the water; I've stuffed my pack and all the pockets of my suit. Before the ship ran down I calculated the location of this rock's claim beacon and typed brief descriptions of the topographical landmarks I should encounter between here and there. There aren't many.

So I'm steeling myself for a trek to the beacon to see if there's a way to send out a distress call or a message, maybe even this letter. If the ship's calculations were right I'm nowhere near Dimotros or its moonbelt, after all. I'm on some rock claimed by an asteroid mining company out of West Virginia: Aggregated Minerals Consortium. Class Yellow Planetoid D-Z1282, in case you're curious.

Right, Jack. Signing off for now. Stepping out into the unknown.

Wish me luck.

Love,

Katherine

Dear Jack,

No life behind closed doors here, brother! No life at all, so far as I can tell.

My gods, but this place is empty. Huge empty. Enormous empty. Forever empty. Emptier than empty.

Even the open oceans of Earth have movement and spatter and vaguely threatening shapes glowing beneath the murky surface just out of view. I know you told me they were buoys marking oceanbed strip-mines, Jack, but I tell you they still looked like the gleaming, bulbous eyes of massive sea monsters. And don't give me the speech 'bout how humans killed off the last living ocean creature larger than my thumbnail over sixty years ago. I've heard that particular speech too many times. You and your soapbox! Not everybody cares to live as you do, off in the wilderness of the under-charted extraterrestrial frontier. At least Cindy is willing to be dragged about on your venture surveying expeditions. You've got a good woman there, Jack—better than I. I hope you appreciate her.

I know you've seen some amazing places on your journeys. You've described a few for me over the years. Let me try to describe this one for you.

I think I've already said it's big. Not big by planetary standards, I'm sure. But when I stepped out of that sweet, warm cocoon of synthesized glass and metal I shall henceforth affectionately refer to as my dearly departed ship—may it rest in peace—I felt vertigo.

You've been to my loft in Atmosphere Stratum Three Tower

City, Earthside. Remember when the fashion was to have sporadic transparent wall programming? There'd be opaqued panels which would appear and disappear in the polarized exterior glass on a random cycle, so you could be walking to the bathroom and suddenly the wall would completely visually dissolve to your right? Or you'd be making dinner, and the glassite would suddenly become so clear right in front of you it was like the sink dangled off the lip of a cliff and you were about to plummet over the edge, glass of milk in one hand and dishtowel in the other? It was absolutely vomitous.

You laughed at me then; you can laugh at me now. I know I'm more a trend follower than I should be. You've always said so, and you're right.

But what I'm trying to describe is the first split moment of that feeling of unexpectedly falling over the edge of a high place without warning and with no thought but the panic spasming the muscles of your stomach. You want to grab hold of something, anything, and you fling your arms out to your sides, some dim part of your brain hoping to clutch onto the very air.

Imagine that feeling in your gut, low and tight, and that certainty in the portion of your mind beyond rational thought that tells you you're falling. That's how it was for me stepping out onto the plain of this desolate place.

Desert, I guess you'd call it. Cracked, mottled ground, dry and vacant. Nothing in sight to relieve the monotony of the landscape. There's nothing here, and it's the most horrible feeling. That sky is going to crush the breath out of me, it feels so heavy. Just the visual weight of it, Jack, bearing down on my mind.

I've chosen a random patch of parched ground on which to spend the night. The day/night cycle here is quite fast by Earth standards. I think it's just over eight hours light, eight hours dark. I've been wearing the suit's helmet even though the air's perfectly breathable. If I remove that last bubble of synthesized glass between me and this place, I'm afraid all that empty land will swallow me whole.

It's about to get dark. It's no gradual process here. I can see the shadow of night racing across the ground toward me over the flat plain, though it's still some distance away.

This palm-pad will last longer if I don't use the light function, so I'll tell you more tomorrow. Goodnight, Jack. I hope your pillow is softer than mine.

Love,

Katherine

Dear Jack,

It was incredible! The most amazing thing I've seen in my life! Why didn't you ever tell me what it was like to view a field of stars through atmosphere clearer than glassite?

There were neighboring asteroids up there of course, dominating the heavens. None as big as this one, I believe. From here, they shone like a loosely strung strand of huge baroque pearls in the night sky.

And the stars. I was totally unprepared for the stars. Like a blanket of diamonds, Jack! At night, that huge sky which felt so overpowering in the glare of day felt gentle, benevolent. It didn't seem like it was going to crush me into the ground: more like it was going to sweep me up with it to take my place among uncharted constellations. I've never seen anything so beautiful in my life.

The strangest thing: when I woke this morning the dust around my body had been disturbed, as though I'd been making a snow angel in the thin layer of ochre powder. Remember when you showed me how to make those, Jack? It was one of the better trips you dragged me on, to the snow preserve in Antarctic Glacial Global Park. I know it's gone now. I've always been secretly glad you convinced me to see it before it disappeared forever, though I know I complained something awful at the time. I tried to go once to that theme park they have in Nevada. You know the one, with the generated blizzards and simulated snow for skiing? I tried to lie down on the floor in the flakes and make an angel like we did that day, but it wasn't the same. Maybe the piped-in music had something to do with it. Distracting. Also, the mood advertisements scattered invisibly around the place, making one suddenly ravenous for Shmuggler's Pretzels™ or NearlyBeer™ or VileCorp Bail Bonds™. Quite off-putting, in my opinion.

Nothing theme park about last night! I had to take off the suit helmet to get comfortable lying on my back on the ground, arms out at my sides. I'm glad I did. Somehow, filling my lungs with air directly from that massive sky without filtration or interference between me and it. . . . It was like nothing I've felt before. Or tasted or smelled or *absorbed.* I can see why you've become addicted to filterless breathing, Jack: makes your head clearer.

I left my suit helmet back there on the cracked soil where I spent the night. It was bloody heavy, anyway.

Love,

Katherine

Dear Jack,

It's been two local days since I've added to these letters. I've missed the wedding by now. I'm so, so sorry.

I hope it was beautiful. Did you kiss the bride? How did her brother do as your best man? I'm sure he was great. I bet in your tux you were the most handsome man on the planet. Certainly the handsomest baby brother I've ever had.

I don't want to say this, but I think I'm lost.

Writing it down like that makes it seem more real. Until now I've been pretending I was merely temporarily disoriented.

I've been studying the stars after darkfall to see if I can't remember which direction I was headed that first night and re-orient myself to the same trajectory. But it's no use. I'm not a natural in the out-of-doors. Not like you. You could probably find water in this desert with a forked stick, or tell the direction you wanted by licking your finger and holding it to the breeze.

Not that there are any sticks here, forked or no. Nor much breeze for that matter.

It is strange, but after my initial panic ebbed; after I fell to my knees and sobbed away gods-know-how-much valuable salt and water into this parched ground; after I slept another short night lying palms to the sky and waiting for the judgment of the heavens and the fates to rain down on me in a shower of those cold, beautiful stars; I felt at peace.

I barely recognized peace. I'm sure it's not a familiar feeling. But sitting here; the light from the local sun brushing my skin like invisible feathers of heat; the ground solid and warm beneath my legs; my lungs full of this slightly sweet, peppery air; I have nothing pressing for my immediate attention but existence.

And not a desperate existence, Jack. Not the scrabbling, driven existence of living in the Tower City in Stratum Three. Not the agonized existence of a person in pain or angry at herself or anyone else in the Universe for bringing her to this point.

I think for the first time in my life, I realize how sweet it is to draw breath. How beautiful the firm, gentle sound of one's heart beating in one's chest, pushing the blood though one's body. It is truly miraculous.

And it took this desolate place to show me. I think I must in some small way be grateful, at least for that.

Love,

Katherine

Dear Jack,

The dust angels have appeared every morning now.

It's almost alarming how quickly I've adapted to the short day/night cycle. During the day I make my way toward the ridge of hills I see in the distance. How far away they are, I'm not sure. It's one of the beautiful things about this place, and the most terrifying: that you can see what feels like forever in every direction, but have no true understanding of where the perimeters of forever *are*.

Don't worry I might be lonely, Jack. I keep myself good

company. I can't remember the last time I had a serious conversation with myself, a rational one not full of blame or abuse or regret. There's no room for those feelings here. The simplicity and largeness of this landscape have no tolerance for petty thoughts.

I leave no footsteps. Sometimes I turn to look behind me, to see if I leave a trail stretching across that crackled infinity like the trail of a microbe slug on the leaf of a potted fern. But no: there is only hard-packed dirt, dry and waterless and of an ochre sameness that tires the eyes. There are patches of dusty areas, but those are irregular and thinly-spaced, though the ground less hard. It makes for a slightly better sleeping surface.

One of the lovely things about losing the drive to self-recriminate: you get to sit down right where you are, and close your eyes, and feel the warmth of an alien sun soak into you from above and leach up into your legs from the day-heated ground below. You listen to your heartbeat, and count your breaths, slow and even, to a thousand, or as close to a thousand as your mind lets you before it forgets its task and hums into a soft glow.

I wanted to tell you I've been noticing small things about this place. When I first stepped out onto this flat, cracked ground, I thought there was nothing and all was emptiness. That's not so. What I thought were mottled patches of dirt are actually lichen fields. It's across these sections my steps leave no trace. The growth is more resilient than it looks.

I know modified lichens are used in oxygen production on Earth, and when I lie on my stomach and press my cheek to the dry, nubby, miniscule curls of the stuff here, I'd swear I breathe easier. It is the origin of the mild peppery scent in the air, I believe, and what lends the dust its color. My suit has become covered in super-fine particles. I no longer stick up from this landscape like an enormous, sore silver thumb. I'm now an ochre one instead.

And the dust angels. Last night I stayed awake all night, or thought I did, not moving. I lay, dazzled by the brilliance of the starfield, soaking up the day's stored warmth from the ground beneath me and breathing the slightly peppery air. When daylight rolled across me a few hours later I rose and looked down at the patch where I had lain. I can only think I must have hypnotized myself with that huge beautiful sky, Jack, because I clearly had moved my arms and legs in the night to make a pattern on the ground. For now, it shall remain a mystery.

I believe I'm near the hills. I hope climbing to the top of the tallest peak will allow me to see either the direction of the ship or the mining claim beacon. It is toward this peak I head now. Perhaps I shall write you tomorrow from its summit.

Love,

Katherine

Dear Jack,

Nocturnal butterflies!

Not really moths, and I know you'll know the difference, brother.

Nocturnal butterflies crawl up from small fissures in the ground and crowd around my limbs at night. I hypothesize they are attracted to the water bladders in the suit, as they seem to congregate around the main arteries which run along my arms and legs.

I watched them last night by the light of the palm-pad. I shouldn't have run the power cells so low, but I know you'll forgive me. My drive to study my new friends must appeal to the scientist in you.

They seemed not at all bothered by my tiny artificial light. I wonder if they do not register its existence? I watched them flutter low across the ground and alight at my sides. Not so many: a mere few dozen. I watched as they performed a funny, dignified little dance; a solemn procession that beat against the hard soil, disturbing the layer of fine ochre dust along the outlines of my limbs in a radiating pattern.

And they aren't anything like the ones kept back home as

pets. Someone gave me one once: a beautiful specimen with blue and gold wings. I gave it away the very next day. I couldn't bear to watch a creature I knew would live for such a brief time, and know it would spend its entire life in a glassite box. Is that what you meant, Jack? When you begged me to leave the Tower Cities of Earth? I think I understand better now than I did at the time.

Oh, and good news: I can see the claim beacon quite clearly from here. I reached the tip of this rocky hill this afternoon. Not the highest peak, as I had thought I would, but a perfectly adequate little ridge nonetheless. After my midday meal of thrice-drunk water and dog's-nethers bars, I shall make for the spire.

Love,

Katherine

Dear Jack,

My water's definitely getting stale.

I'm under no illusions about how the recirc suit works or where this water's already been, but a diet of recirc water and synth bars wears even more quickly than one would think. The suit's specs give it a full fourteen days before the water bladders need rinsing and refilling, and that's Earth standard days, not local ones. Either this particular suit is sub-par, or I've got considerably farther to go before I reach untenable quality standards. If my mouth weren't so dry, that thought would make me nauseous. As it is, it just makes me thirsty. Thirstier.

I'm quite pleased with my progress toward the claim beacon. I indulged myself by spending the rest of the day and last night atop the ridge. No butterflies up on the rock, I'm afraid. I was surprised to find myself disappointed at the lack of nocturnal visitors.

But I did mark my position by the stars. I lay on my back up on that ridge and studied this glorious sky. I never really understood the constellations that used to be visible from Earth. I'm sure it would make a difference if they could still be seen with the naked eye. From the Tower Cities, any natural starlight is far outshone by orbiting space-junk and abandoned satellites and free-floating garbage barges. I know there's been a push in recent years to clean up some of that detritus, but people are slow to change.

So I did as our most distant ancestors must have done: I marked the stars. Planets, I suppose they are, and suns. Everything is just a matter of perspective in the end, isn't it? Tonight I shall check my direction. I feel confident, Jack, that I shall have more of note to report tomorrow, which is only some eight hours away. Here unfurls the darkness across the plain, bringing with it my new friends the stars, and perhaps butterflies as well.

Love,

Katherine

Dear Jack,

However could I have thought this place empty? Vast, yes; panoramic, yes. Inhospitable even, perhaps. But not empty.

I've become accustomed to the shapes of the distant hills and the rolling plain. In this landscape, everything has a presence. The patterned soil, which I know must house my lepidopteran neighbors while they sleep during the day; the more distant rises, particularly the three distinctive hills I've come to think of as the Sleeping Giant, the Spire, and the Hook. Perhaps the Hook is actually a massive J? J for Jack. I shall henceforth think of it as your mountain, my brother.

Even the lichen tundra has distinct forests. Granted, these forests grow no taller than the thickness of the tough, rubbery skin of my recirc suit. But still, I've come to recognize the subtle variations in shade and texture which indicate the beginning of one forest and the ending of another. I am a giant, Jack; my long strides clear whole forests, whole ecosystems, whole continents. I am *invincible.*

Love,

Katherine

* * *

Dear Jack,

I cried last night, thinking of you.

A complete waste of water, I know, though the butterflies seemed to like it. They moved their strange procession from the ground near my arms to the area around my head. They never touch me, but several of them crowded close enough to my damp cheeks, I could feel the air moved by their tiny wings when I turned my head toward them. I wonder if my tears are the first rain ever to fall on this parched soil.

I hope you and Cindy are having a wonderful time on your honeymoon. It comforts me to think you are.

When I rose this morning, a looping halo had been added to the angel I left in the thin dust beneath me, where the butterflies had marched in circles around my tears.

Love,

Katherine

Dearest Jack,

My water has become truly foul. I won't tell you what the stuff causes in the way of headaches.

I have reached the claim beacon. I just kept walking toward the Hook; toward your mountain, Jack. I never let it out of my sight, and it led me to my goal.

You shall be so pleased with me when we see each other next. The beacon *does* have transmission capacities. I've already sent a general, pre-programmed SOS, that anyone might find. Until then, I wait.

It is a pretty spot here. Prettier than any other I've seen this whole adventure. And adventure this has been. I regret only that you had to hear about this lovely place second-hand.

Of course I can't say I wish you were here, because I don't. Not unless you had your ship with you, in full functioning order. If that were the case, I would love us to lie beside each other, our backs warm against this bright and beautiful plain. We'd breathe the peppery air, and watch the achingly brief days and nights roll across the patterned soil with a most gratifying regularity.

Time to send this letter. This and all the rest. I promise: when I return to Earth, it shall not be to spend the rest of my life in a glassite box. It's not good for butterflies, either.

Love always, your affectionate sister

Katherine

End Transmission

The Green Infinity

The helicopter's thrumming vibrated through Sharon's body with teeth-rattling constancy. She gripped the handhold and looked out the window at the seemingly endless undulating green jungle which had once been her husband.

California's population had fled. Pockets of survivors huddled on rooftops against encroaching vines and climbing stalks, awaiting airlift rescue. The verdant growth continued to spread, radiating outward in a pattern reminiscent of wildfire, or of contagion.

They'd tried fire, of course, to stop him. Water, fungicide, herbicide, electricity; planes and tankers of all sizes and functions pressed into service to halt the relentless creeping green. Sharon was the Government's last resort. Second-last, actually, though dropping a nuclear bomb on California seemed unfathomable.

"Oh, Gary. . . ." Sharon's words were swallowed by the helicopter's engine. Back when it was still just quickly-spreading cancer they battled, no drug or therapy or voodoo spirit-prayer had helped. Gary had faced death with dignity and courage. It was Sharon who'd urged him to try experimental DNA recombinant chromosomal therapies using gene splices from *pueraria lobata*—common kudzu. Even now, even with this, it was hard to feel she'd been wrong.

Colonel Bradley touched her shoulder. He gestured directly down into the lushness beneath. She saw her reflection in the wide ovoid mirrors of his aviator shades as she read his lips. *Ground Zero*, he pointed again into the green. *Ground Zero*.

Ground Zero was the hospital, with its helipad roof. Her

husband's hyper-rapid cellular growth had ruptured windows, choked all egresses and smothered the brick siding, but he was for the most part a groundcover plant. The rooftop was bare.

Colonel Bradley jumped down and assisted Sharon out. They crouched under whipping wind and noisy rotor blades, Sharon resisting the urge to wave as the helicopter drew up and away.

The silence when her ears stopped ringing was almost painful. Colonel Bradley stood at polite attention, gaze directed elsewhere, granting her privacy. He was brave, she thought, and kind.

Silence of the world smothered by Gary was more complete than the silence of deserted beaches or wild forests. No birdsong sounded, no insect buzz or rushing water. Just the gentle shuckling of Gary's wide glossy leaves brushing against each other in the breeze. The sun was perfect, golden and high; the sky that amazing forever-blue never captured in paint or film, consisting mainly of light and open space.

Colonel Bradley cleared his throat and glanced sideways, apologetic. "Ma'am, our ride returns in exactly twenty-eight minutes."

Sharon wanted to touch his arm, let him know it was all right. She didn't blame him for what was to come. Gary's body, anything remotely recognizable as physically human, had disappeared in the first minutes of his transformation. As she and the medical team watched, his flesh had turned greenish, then green, then shriveled to brown husk as it was sucked into the tendrils sprouting from his pores. Thousands of tendrils, first the size of green hairs, then growing larger with astonishing rapidity.

Sharon walked to the rooftop edge. She closed her eyes and breathed deep, sunlight on her shoulders, chlorophyll musk in the air. It smelled like Gary—the insides of his wrists, the hollow of his throat, his hair and clothes.

She glanced over her shoulder. Colonel Bradley stood across the helipad with military rigidity, hands locked behind his back, facing away. His short hair was stiff, but wind rippled his shirt across his back in a repeating pattern, like sands blowing across a khaki desert.

She turned again toward the green infinity. As far as she could see, all was greenness. Beneath lay abandoned candy-bright cars, dirty black asphalt, billboards and advertisements all stripes and colors. Never had the city looked so serene.

Sharon ran a finger along a legume-like tendril curling up over the roof ledge, a delicate emerald corkscrew. "Gary," she said. It came out softer than she'd intended, and more wistful. "I know *you* are still in here somewhere. Can you hear me? You must stop this."

Warm breezes whipped her words from her lips. She imagined them swirling out across the dappled green ocean, sinking into the rustling stalks and pulpy flesh of questing vines.

"Gary, I'm sorry I didn't listen when you were ready to go. I know you took experimental treatments only for my sake."

Wind flapped her hair across her eyes. Rustling grew louder as the vegetation danced in currents, sunlight glancing off green leaves.

"I couldn't before, but I can now: I let you go, freely. Thank you for staying as long as you could, but you were right. I was wrong. Forgive me."

Without realizing, Sharon had gripped tight the roof ledge before her. At a tickle against the back of her knuckles, she glanced down. A curving tendril pushed into her hand. It looked like time-lapse photography, when a seed unfurls into a plant in mere seconds. She opened her palm and the tendril formed itself in her cupped hand as she watched. She closed her fingers around the fuzzy beanlike thing. The vine detached itself, browned, shriveled, and fell away. She shoved her hands into her pockets and turned at the sound of the helicopter approaching.

Colonel Bradley ducked and ran across to take her arm as the helicopter landed. She allowed herself to be helped up, buckled in. Leaning into the bubble glass window, Sharon saw tendrils questing up toward them as they lifted, corkscrew curls leaping after them into the air like slender green streamers tossed at a parade.

Colonel Bradley studied her face. Keeping her expression neutral, she nodded. He returned the nod and settled into his seat. Twisting to look at the receding rooftop, Sharon watched the brown of dead vine widen from Ground Zero in an expanding ring. As rapidly as the green had initially spread, the brown nearly kept pace with the departing helicopter.

Sharon leaned back in her seat and closed her eyes, her fingers curling tight around the soft slender seedpod in her pocket.

Virgin Soil

I first noticed you the day
you laughed at me in school.
I didn't know you—
I hardly know you now.
Eons have passed and we've stayed friends
I like to think.
Maybe I'm wrong about that
    as about so many other things.

When the time came;
when everyone had to choose, to say:
Do I go or do I stay
here,
on a dying world with smoke-choked skies,
degrees of highs and lows borne only
through the wonders of technology?
    When that time came
I thought of you.

Why?

We hadn't kissed since we were twelve,
nor done the other crazy, wondrous stuff
grown men and women do
and at which we only played till I was
"Too old for that," I'd said.
I didn't know (how could I have?)
that in later years I'd spend nights
sweating, thinking of you,
wishing again we both were ten.

When the rest of us boarded final flights to space
on our optimistic journey to uncertain safety,
I pictured you somewhere on the planet beneath.
One of the stubborn ones, I thought you'd be.
In my mind you had your third-grade freckles still,
and I my third-grade teeth.

We others landed here, so many stars and years
and tears and hates and loves later,
and I thought of you again, though
it had been a while.
I conjured up your face
in the fields of my mind,
imagined I held your hand
as we debarked together onto virgin soil,
and breathed air as pure as you.

Observations of a Dimestore Figurine

Sun angles in through the shopfront windows, low and tight. Dust motes perform their slow lazy dance from *here* to *there*, never arriving, never leaving. The warm morning air is redolent with the scents of optimism, of bug spray, of gently warmed composite plastics. The gum adhesive of my tag itches my base where I stand. I welcome the itch. It is the kind of annoyance which makes one feel alive, and grateful to be in the world.

I stand, plastic robe-draped shoulder to plastic robe-draped shoulder, with two dozen of my kind. I've become accustomed to the taciturn ways of Fade-robe Jesus to my right. He's a good fellow, but silent. He intends well, but is a poor conversationalist, I'm afraid.

Skew-eye Jesus on my left is a somewhat more lively shelf-neighbor. He has a wonderful sense of humor.

"Did you hear the one," he tells me, "about the guy who. . . ?"

I smile, indulgent. It is my way.

Ahhh. The glorious indignity of being grasped about the middle! Of being lifted through the air, set on my side in a tangled heap of hard-edged robes and the frisbee-like rims of polymer halos from my fellows. I taste the shopclerk's minimum wage through the sweat of her palms. I smell the lunchcart falafel on her breath, the stale fruity candies from the aisle closest to the counter, the faint trace of last night's tears leftover from the fight with her boyfriend.

From my sideways angle on the rolling utility cart I can see all sorts of things. I devour the sights from my temporary vantage, hungry for new detail. I do my best to memorize every aspect of the checkout area: the shopclerk's vacant unbuttoned sweater hanging on a hook behind the counter, the rows of off-brand and expired candy in shiny-bright packages, afternoon glare from the front windows glancing from the multi-faceted surfaces of crumpled cellophane wrappers. It's so much information, I try to register the many details, file them away without actually absorbing or contemplating them. Later, when I stand back at attention in Jesus row, I'll savor all these tiny observations, roll them around inside me like the garish pink hard candy on the shopclerk's tongue which smells of watermelon and contentment.

The shopclerk sucks her candy with an involuntary spitsqueal, the sound of moisture and air rushing to fill each other's spaces at the insistence of her tongue, her lips, the muscles of her cheeks as she sucks, sucks, sucks. . . .

I cannot attribute all my sudden warmth to the tilting rays of afternoon sun. I wait for the girl to spritz the display shelf with her commercial grade no-name cleanser, its misty blue tang sharp and sweet in the daytime air. I listen to the sound of her dusty paper towel dragging across metal.

No longer am I able to concentrate on the details seen from my unusual vantage; I'm too distracted by the thought of the shopclerk's hands lifting me once again, of her fingers encircling my waist, brushing against my thighs and the bare ends of my sandaled toes which peek from beneath the convoluted hem of my pale red robe.

"Pssst!"

It is night. The shop is dark but for the hard edges of unnatural halogen brightness tilting in from the streetlamp outside. There's a harsh, eye-achingly pink-tinted glow from around the back of the neon Open sign which the shopclerk sometimes forgets to turn off at closing.

"Psst! You Jesus there! Psst!"

As usual, we've been put back onto the shelf in a slightly altered order. I try to ignore my new shelf-neighbor. He's a vulgar creature of low grade plaster. His head is bulbous, frightening. His enormous eyes goggle crazily from his encephalitic countenance, his grotesquely sausage-like arms thrust from his tight red plaster pinafore. He's obscenely shiny, even in the dim filtered light of fluorescent illuminated night.

"Psst! *Pendejo*, I'm talking to you. You: Chip-Shoulder Jesus! Hey!"

He pronounces it *hey-zeus.* "It is not a chip, Good Sir," I tell him, "But an unfortunately placed bubble, incurred during my delicate casting phase. It speaks ill of you that you would mock another's deformity. We are all equals here in the Shop of Ninety-Nine Cents."

Of course I don't believe it. It galls me to call this disposable slop of yesterday's yesterday's mainstream pop culture an equal. *Flash in the pan*, I think to myself. *Fad.*

My neighbor snorts. "Okay then, Smirky Jesus. We'll all be out of here, and we'll see your sorry chip-shouldered ass later."

He pronounces *later* with a hard d. "My Good Man," I say, trying for all the dignity of my seven point two inches, "Most find my smile soothing. No need for hostility. Let us live side by side in peace."

He makes a rude blowing noise, one I've never heard before.

"Whatever," he says, disgust in his tone. "And I'm not your Good Anything, *punta.* I'm Four-thumbs Hello Gato. I'm practically trademarked."

I glance at his bulbous digits thrust my direction. In his other hand he holds a blindingly yellow plaster flower, ill-painted, the color slopping over his closed fist. *Garish*, I think to myself. *Low grade off-brand imperfection.*

"You're smirking again," says Four-thumbs. This time I hear the hurt beneath his bluster. Contrition floods through me, and shame. I've been known to excel in the shame department.

A few minutes of silence pass. In the nighttime, small incidental noises loom large. The clock on the wall above the shopclerk's cardigan ticks loudly, unevenly. The Open sign hums softly to itself where it hangs by dainty chains in the front window, the tangled string dangling from its underside basking in the pink-tinted illumination of its neon. Outside a car rumbles by, fat rubber tires shush shush shushing beneath the engine's low clackety clack on the nightslick asphalt.

"I'm sorry," I say. I hope this time, my smile is more in keeping with my general mission to spread peace and goodwill.

It's difficult to read his expression. His slick rounded surfaces glow faintly in the dim light. "*De nada*," he says. "Forget about it. By midnight, we're all going to be gone from this place, anyway."

"I'm not sure what you mean."

He glances sideways, away from me, to row upon row of folded washcloths, thin as paper and very rough, and beside those, stiff-starched bandanas. No conversation from that quarter.

He looks again my direction, says: "At midnight, man. I heard them talking earlier today. Shopclerk's ex-boyfriend, he's coming with his friend at midnight, man. They're going to *liberate* us. They're going to *set us free*."

I'm confused. "The shopclerk's boyfriend plans to break in after hours?"

"Listen up, man, listen to what I'm telling you. He's her *ex*-boyfriend, after last night. And he stole her keys, yo."

Four-thumbs begins talking to Bent-fin Leaping Dolphin across the aisle. They're laughing, speaking of escape plans, dreams for the future. But me, I'm not sure any of us understand the full implications, the ramifications of this situation. Though the mood of my shelf-fellows is seductive, infectious, I try to keep a clear head. I try to decipher the hard, sharp-edged feeling in my hollow gut.

* * *

The shelves are humming. Excitement and fear lie over the shop like an itchy wool blanket. Conversation is sustained at a fevered pitch. Anticipation is tangible in the still night air, tasting of sulfur, or wet metal.

"Did you hear the one . . . ?" asks Skew-eye Jesus, still on my left after today's dusting. "Or did you hear this other one, about the. . . ." But he's too excited to finish his jokes. I smile, benevolent. I'm uneasy, but I hide my formless trepidation as best I can.

"Shht! Everybody shut the freak up! They're coming, man! They're coming!"

I glance sideways at Four-thumbs, but his attention is riveted on the front doors. Beyond, I see the swinging glare of headlights arc across the front of the store as a car pulls into the parking lot. When the chugging engine cuts off, the silence is deafening. Even the always-ticking clock on the wall behind the counter seems to be holding its breath.

The familiar sound of a key sliding into the lock is almost comforting. I've come to associate that noise with the beginning of a new day; with possibilities, potentials, chances; with fresh starts. The lock tumbles with a resounding clunk. The heavy glass door opens, its oiled hinges gliding metal on metal without fuss or protest. Two figures dressed in black flicker past the edge of my view, heading for the register and the small combination safe beneath the counter.

"Hey dude, you know the combo to this thing?"

The boy's voice is startlingly loud in the dark room. After the obvious effort at stealth—black jeans, black jackets, black knit caps covering their hair—the boys' unhushed voices are almost an affront.

"Yeah," answers the other, pausing to tear open a bag of expired toffees from the display by the register. "She told it to me once, like for a joke."

I hear him walk around behind the counter to join his friend. There is conversation, inscrutable male-talk. I hear mention of tits. The word *bitch* is used several times. I hear the crinkle of more candy wrappers, the sound of the counter stool moved aside, the ding of the register opening.

Eventually the friend says: "We got the cash, dude. Let's get on with the rest of it."

The ex-boyfriend walks down the next aisle, his tennis shoes brushing the well-swept cement floor with gentle scuffing and the occasional mild squeak. He walks around the endcap display to my aisle, meanders toward me, running one finger along the edge of the metal shelf as though checking for dust. There is none. His girlfriend—ex-girlfriend—is a diligent employee, a hard worker.

He ruffles one-handed through the stiffly folded polyblend bandanas in dayglo colors muted grey by night. He flips up the top washcloth, which flutters to the floor like an enormous, disoriented moth. He rests a gentle fingertip, lighter than a butterfly kiss, against the bulging plaster eyeball of Four-thumbs Hello Gato, and I can practically feel the metal beneath my base thrum with the vibration of my shelf-neighbor's excitement.

But then his attention shifts to me. I feel his gaze brush across me in the near-dark. I feel it wash over the hard folds of my polymer robe, across the composite plastics of my angled surfaces. When he reaches for me, my hollow insides tense.

"Dude," he calls to his friend across the shop. "Dude, is there anything in here you want? Some of this stuff might be all right."

Being held by him is not unlike being held by his ex-girlfriend the shopclerk. His palm has the same warm elasticity of human flesh, his sweat the same tints of hope and despair, of longing and accusation.

I've been held by older people, picked up and fondled for a moment or few before returning, lonely and colder, to my shelf. But there is something in the scent of the young, something angry and delicious and unafraid. I tremble.

Just before he shoves me face down into the pocket of his jacket, I see what he holds in his other hand, the hand he has kept low, close to his side until now. It's a baseball bat, dinged, bands of colored aluminum faded and worn. From the confines of his pocket, my base exposed ignominiously to the cold night, my head buried in a small lint-filled fold of knit, I hear his friend answer from across the room.

"Nah," he says. "It's just a bunch of cheap import crap. Let's do this thing."

The sound of smashing plaster fills the air, and I picture Four-thumbs shattering, his large hollow head helpless beneath the force of the bat.

The sounds of smashing, breaking, tinkling, crushing go on for a long, long time. They go on for what feels like forever, and beneath it I hear the wail of dissipating polymer dust, and smell the burnt spice scents of exhilaration and shame.

The Pull of the World and the Push of the Sky

Gunh breathed deeply the mild morning air. He was pleased he'd convinced his tribe to follow the wooly mammoths farther north toward the perennial ice this spring. The grass was soft and pliant beneath his wide bare feet. Small purple flowers crushed under his toes as he walked, filling the air with sweet scent.

His brother Moogh complained that the perfume in the air—from grasses, from flowers, from soft whispering boughs of the green canopies of blossoming trees—inhibited his ability to hunt. He claimed he couldn't smell game for all the Fire-cursed flowers. But with the warmer summers of late, hunting was easier than ever, and there were more berries for the women to gather, and more beetles and small game, too. After listening for days to his brother's complaints, Gunh had finally suggested that perhaps Moogh's recent failures at the hunt had more to do with faulty equipment than with flowerscent in the air. He'd gestured toward Moogh's thick knobby club and sharp hunting stick when he'd made the handsign for *equipment*, but he'd stared pointedly at Moogh's head, wrinkling his own craggy sloping forehead and wiggling his heavy brows for comic effect. Everyone, catching the joke, guffawed and slapped their naked chests above the thick animal hides hanging from their belts, and the women that moonfall had shown a decided preference for Gunh's side of the fire pit. Moogh may have the stronger arm and the faster foot, but Gunh made the ladies laugh.

He knelt in damp grass to look more closely at the prints in the soft earth. Mountain herbivores, it looked like: small hoof-sign, top edges rounded into three segments. Good! Such game tended to grow big and move heavily when the grasses were greenest, especially here in the ice-river's valley where people had been scarce until the recent warming trend. The game wasn't always smart enough to stay away from boulders and from clumps of tall growth up on the valley ridge. A smallish man like Gunh could hide there for hours. He could sit still as rock until a beast strayed close enough for him to lunge upon and run through with his sharpened stick.

He always felt saddened by a kill, though he never told Moogh or the others. They found his Big Ideas about life and death tedious and useless, and never hesitated to tell him so. But much as he didn't care for the kill, he loved the wait. He loved crouching silent and still in the shadow of a large rock or low cliff, blending into the very air, invisible, seeming hardly to breathe for hours at a time. It was then he always came up with his best Ideas.

True, not all Ideas translated equally well into practice. His rolling travois invention had never become truly workable; the vehicles he fashioned and mounted on small spherical boulders inevitably proved more cumbersome and less swift than the lightweight contraptions women pulled behind them when they traveled. Gunh had dragged his heavy, unwieldy, boulder-mounted travois for three whole days, watching the rest of his tribe shrink smaller and smaller in the distance across the plains as they trotted along with their hides, their food stores, their babies strapped to the tops of bundled heaps, bouncing across the grasslands with seeming effortlessness. Gunh had finally abandoned his rolling boulder device with a heavy heart, sure he'd simply failed to arrive at the correct undercarriage formation. And he didn't even like to remember the fireshoes he'd had the Idea would keep his feet warm in winter. He had small blisters still around his ankles where the hides had burned through, and the laughter of the tribeswomen still haunted his nights.

But some Ideas were better than others. His boar tooth hunting stick was the envy of many. Even Moogh, whose ridicule always stung deepest and lasted longest, had recently mentioned to Gunh that he might allow his brother to show him how to rub a boar's hardened longtooth against hard sandrock until it honed to a point sharper than any tree branch; to chip notches from the base and strap it to the end of a hunting stick with strips of wet hide. Recalling that small victory made Gunh heft his own weapon with satisfaction. Sun glinted from its ivory tip, and he smiled.

Gunh crested the rise at the high rim of the ice-river's valley. Great Sun and Fire, but what a beautiful day! He breathed again the crisp air, felt the warmth of sunlight on his scraggy cheeks and jutting jaw. He gazed down into the verdant valley below, marveling at how much farther the solid ice-river had retreated since last spring. Each year it became visibly smaller, melting, shrinking back the direction from which it had flowed. Gunh wondered how long it had taken the ice to creep down from the mountain, and how long it would take it to melt back uphill, the length of the long valley all the way up to its high winter caves. Unfathomable numbers of seasons, he suspected.

He was about to turn away when something registered at the periphery of his vision. Shading his view from overhead glare, he squinted down into the valley. Far below, just at the edge of the wide rim of melting glacier, was an unusual shape, dark where the ice glowed blue-white in the sun.

He titled his head and tried to make sense of the splotch spread against the ice. Something seemed familiar about the sharp irregularity of the outline, but Gunh couldn't quite grasp what it was. He squinted again, inching closer to the cliff edge, leaning out over the steep vertical drop to better see into the valley below.

A huntbird startled him with its harsh cry from above. Gunh glanced up at the flying creature, whose wingspan was at least as wide as his own arms held out straight to his sides, but whose body was no thicker than the meat of his leg. Gunh closed his eyes and made the silent wish to the huntbird he always made when he saw one soaring free on the breeze. *Beautiful hunter of small things*, he signed in his mind without moving his fingers in flickering signspeak, *lend me some of your strength; from your vantage, you must see many grass-beasts and boar-beasts and great wooly mammoth. Point me the way, huntbird, and I'd be grateful.*

Since he'd been young enough to travel strapped to his mother's travois, he'd held such interior conversations: with birds, with trees, with the earth he bounced across; even with the sticks with which he'd played his child-games. He'd long ago learned to keep these private, though. The tribe thought him ridiculous enough as it was.

The huntbird dipped and soared on invisible breezes, its feathertips glinting in sunlight. It hovered, wobbled, seemed almost as though it would fall from the sky and plummet at his feet; but at the last minute swooped so close, Gunh felt air from its wings brush across his face. The huntbird's outline as it defied the pull of the world and the push of the sky lingered for a long moment, clear and distinct against the blue beyond, which made Gunh's eyes ache if he stared into it for too long. Lingering, floating, hovering . . . and then plunging. With no change discernible to Gunh, the huntbird dove from the sky, and fell and fell. It fell past him, silver wings outstretched, feathers practically ruffling the hair on his head, dropping through the air past the cliff ledge where Gunh stood and plummeting toward the frozen, unmoving ice-river in the valley beneath.

Gunh blinked against the sudden change of light to his eyes as he followed the bird's flight with his gaze. He scanned the pale blue ice far below, so different from the blue sky above, looking for the outline of the huntbird. There it was! A distinctive silhouette of outstretched wings, with a narrow pendulum body between and an elongated triangular head above.

But that wasn't right.

Gunh dropped his hunting stick and flopped to his stomach beside it. He propped himself on his elbows and cupped both hands around his eyes to focus on the ice in the shadow of the valley. The sun had risen, so that just as he squinted at the dark shape at the edge of the icemelt, morning light spilled over the valley rim to illuminate the scene from above. It was very clear to Gunh that if, from up on the ridge, a grass-beast walking the valley below would appear the size of a beetle, then the bird-shaped thing at the edge of the ice must be the size of two wooly mammoths standing trunk to trunk with their great curving longteeth locked together! It must be many, many times larger than a huntbird; much larger than Gunh himself; much larger even than Moogh! Never had he seen a creature with wings so enormous.

It was then that a Big Idea began to form in his mind. An Idea so Big, it almost hurt him to think of it.

He scrambled from the edge of the cliff and turned to make his way back toward the shallow caves of his tribe's summertime camp. The sun grew brighter and hotter as he went. He paused only briefly to gather a few fistfuls of roundfruits off low bushes so he wouldn't return completely empty-handed. He filled his hide sling nearly to bursting, though in his haste crushed almost as many roundfuits as he harvested. Distractedly, he munched these as he walked, the new Idea forming in his mind, though everything would of course depend on exactly what lay in the gorge at the bottom of the cliff. Just thinking of the possibilities made him lift his feet more quickly, his speed increasing as he covered the glassplains with his lolloping, bent-legged gait.

He reached the cave-riddled lowrise cliffs of grasscamp and headed for the narrow depression where Moogh slept. His brother stood near the entrance, animatedly describing his day's hunt to the beautiful Enkha in rapid signspeak. He punctuated his tale with satisfied grunts and howls, stabbing the air near her head with his new boar-tooth hunting stick, pausing to allow two nearby children to touch the sharp point with appreciative strokes.

"Moogh!" said Gunh, hooting in his excitement. "Moogh!"

Moogh's heavy brows bunched in annoyance, but Gunh launched rapidly into signspeak. He didn't give any details of his half-formulated Idea; he merely explained there was something in the ice-river at the bottom of the gorge with which he needed assistance.

Why don't you go by yourself? signed Moogh. *Why drag me with you on another of your stupid adventures? I have better things to do.*

He didn't elaborate on *better things*, but Gunh caught the slight nod in Enkha's direction. So did she. She stepped between the brothers, her back to Moogh. "Enkha will go," she said.

Enkha was the best mouthspeaker Gunh had ever met. His efforts at mouthspeak always felt clumsy and slow, and too inadequate to describe all the things he needed to say. Even his hands were sometimes too slow to keep up with his thoughts. His tongue was a disaster.

Moogh stepped around Enkha. Frowning heavily, he signed to Gunh, *Fine. I will go. This woman has children to watch.*

Enkha narrowed her eyes at him. Spinning on her wide flat heel, she reached down to the two children still fondling the tip of Moogh's hunting stick. The children each took one of her hands and the three of them crossed the trodden grass circle of camp to where Enkha's sister Ungha squatted, carefully sorting food beetles by the sizes and shapes of their colorful carapaces. Enkha marched back across the camp to Moogh's side, childless, and when she reached him she nodded once and said, more clearly than Gunh could ever hope to pronounce in mouthspeak, "Let's go."

They made a funny caravan. Though everyone found Gunh ridiculous, they also found him entertaining—it was rarely boring to watch Gunh struggling with some new Idea. But amusing as Gunh was, Enkha was the tribe favorite. Children and other women trailed along behind her wherever she went, and men vied for the honor of bringing her their furs and hides to soften and decorate. Her paintings and etchings on the pale, porous cavern walls of summercamp and on the dark basalt of wintercamp mountain caverns were famous among the tribes of several valleys.

If the day had not been so warm, the air not so heavy with flowerscent, the sun not so bright and high, perhaps the rest of the tribe would have kept busy at camp tasks. As it was, almost every member not too old nor too young to make a short trek to the ice-river valley trailed along behind Enkha and behind Gunh, who strode out across the soft grasses with eager, rolling strides. Moogh followed closely beside his brother, his hands occasionally flickering in muttered signspeak about the foolishness of summertime picnics. The children of the tribe laughed and tumbled on green ground, passing among themselves Gunh's full satchel of sweet red roundfruits. Behind, the women stretched out in a straggling line, often pausing to fill their own hide satchels with berries or nuts, sometimes pulling handfuls of flowers up from the field to braid into each other's hair as they walked. Several tribe huntsmen, spotting the group from far across the open plains, loped over to join the casual procession. Gunh couldn't remember a time when everyone had been so happy all at once, nor so relaxed. He sent up small thoughts of gratitude to Sun and Sky for making the world so beautiful.

Enkha was first to reach the cliffside. Daylight had moved with the march of the sun and now beat down into the ice-river's valley from directly overhead. The cold blue glow below clearly showed the stark outline of a massive winged creature at the edge of the ice, spread wide as though it had fallen straight from the sky to land as it had flown, wings outstretched. Enkha let out an excited bark of a laugh, and as the rest of the tribe straggled up to the edge and peered into the valley, fingers began to fly in speculation and appreciation. The silence of the sun and the morning breezes shushing across the steppe were only lightly sprinkled with tiny grunts and chuckles.

Gunh trotted off to the left, toward a navigable cut in the cliffside some distance away. First the children tumbled after him, squealing and signing to each other, bragging and betting and daring which of them would be first to reach the bottom of the valley. The women followed the children, and the hunters followed the women, and Moogh followed last of all, scowling as he trailed the loose procession wending its way down the steep sloping edge of the cut into the valley.

The valley was considerably cooler than the steppe above. Sun beat down from the very tip of the sky, warming the top of Gunh's head and shoulders, but the ice-river had resided in the valley for what Gunh thought must have been a very, very long time. He climbed over small hilly deposits of crushed, unsorted stone, left behind by the retreat of the melting ice-river. Cold wind blew gently off the ice, biting into Gunh's skin and making his feet ache. He began to fear the others would give up, would abandon their spontaneous decision to come help him implement his Very Big Idea. He hoped not. He needed them.

Up close, the bird shape looked like an enormous piece of hide stretched taut between gigantic, but slender, poles. It was dead, of course; long, long, longtime dead. Gunh had often gathered beautiful feathers when he came across them, studied them and tried to invent a hundred different uses for them other than decorating his shaggy hair and sleeping hides. He gave the prettiest ones to Enkha to paint with, or to the tribe's children, who bound them together with long grasses and named them and carried them everywhere as though they were children of the children.

The most shocking thing about the massive bird creature on the ice was that it hadn't a single feather on its entire leathery body.

It couldn't be a bird, then. It had wings, delicate yet oddly sturdy looking. It had a head, though the shriveled sharpness of its jaw was more that of a giant lizard's, looking not at all like a beak, but long and narrow in a manner Gunh had never seen on a bird. At the center of its outstretched limbs, beneath which lay the enormous rubbery webs of skin looking so much like bird wings, curled small articulated fingers with calloused knuckles and broken talons. It was as though the entire outstretched wing were supported by a single incredibly elongated knuckle and finger.

The body was nothing to the rest of the beast. It hung, a shriveled, relatively narrow thing, looking oddly deflated.

Agile as always, Enkha pulled herself up the side of the ice-river's edge, digging small pockets of rock and ice with her strong fingers to form handholds and footholds with confidence and speed. She reached the top of the frozen wall, and stood teeteringly beside the animal's elongated head. Balancing on the gritty ridge of the melt, she carefully leaned over the outstretched figure and grabbed one of its shriveled clawlike fists.

The unstable surface of the melting ice under her feet shifted. Pebbles and melting ice chips rained down. She flailed against the cold whiteness of the frozen river; against the not-bird; against the air with its nothing to hold onto, trying to keep her balance. A communal grunting cry rose from the throats of the watching tribe below. Gunh's shout was loud even to his own ears, as he lunged forward to break Enkha's fall.

But she didn't fall—not quite. Her whirling hands clutched at the not-bird. She gripped the edge of the leathery sheet of wing as she slid down the face of the ice-river, and the wing bowed out and away from the ice as she fell. It peeled from the surface of the frozen river like the skin of an overripe fruit peeling from its pulp. It seemed almost to catch the air; to fill up and ride the breeze like a hide tossed from the top of a cliff, or like a wide leaf falling from the top of a tree.

But only for a moment. The moment was so brief, Gunh couldn't be sure the event had happened exactly as he'd thought. Perhaps his mind filled in details colored with his own desires and his half-formed Big Idea. Either way, he was beneath Enkha when she slid to the ground, her fall a slow gliding decent, broken by the resistance of the not-bird and its leathery wings bowing in the air above her head as they came free from the ice. Gunh hit the ground, hard. Enkha landed on his chest, her head crashing into his with a teeth-jarring crack, the dark, cold body of the enormous ice-preserved creature landing heavily at Gunh's side, its leathery wing parts enveloping him in a cocoon of old hide and a musky, not unpleasant, animal smell.

Brief silence and complete stillness. Then the collective surge forward of the dozens of tribespeople, who ran to the base of the ice-river's frozen edge to tug the creature off Enkha and Gunh. Gunh blinked as the smothering leathery surface was removed and sun hit his face. He shifted so Enkha lay beside him rather than atop him, and rolled into a sitting position to inspect her head for serious damage. She brushed his hand aside and sat up, shaking her head as though to clear it. Gunh signed repeatedly, awkwardly and one-handed: *Are you all right? Are you all right? Are you all right?*

She plucked at his hand and laughed. She laughed as he'd never heard her laugh before—she laughed not as an accomplished artist, nor an upstanding member of the tribe, nor as the beautiful woman she was; she laughed not even as an adult. She laughed the pure, delighted laugh of a child.

"Did you see me?" she said, her hands flying in large exaggerated gestures like a mute echo of the words she spoke. "Did you see me?" she said again, looking up at the ring of people who stood around them, a cloud of concerned faces floating above. She laughed again, loudly. "I flew!" She reiterated with her hands: *I flew!*

Gunh smiled. Concentrating very hard, he said in the best mouthspeak he could muster, "Not yet. But maybe you can."

It took all of everybody—the hunters with their broad shoulders, long hairy arms, and barrel chests; the women with their wide hips and strong, bowed legs; the children with their tiny hands and sticklike arms—to carry the not-bird to the top of the cliff. Where they had trailed down the steep stone sides single file, they now shuffled back up with scuffling steps, all in a cluster around the edges of the great cold body of the long-dead beast torn from the melting river of ice. Gunh had feared the thing would be brittle, the way bodies of long-dead, long-buried things sometimes were. But it wasn't. It was supple, yet strong, like hides dried and beaten, and strung on frames of bound poles.

All the way up the cliff, Gunh turned over in his mind methods to bring to fruition his Big Idea. The creature was obviously made for flight. It was made for flight, and was sturdy enough to carry the body of a man. A man strapped beneath its belly, perhaps? With his man arms stretched out along the lines of the animal's bones, fastened somehow beneath the long sturdy fingerbones and the wings they supported. The creature's big, long fingerbones were visible, rounded and starkly apparent under the leather of the wings. Yet they seemed so relatively light, not heavy like wood, or like mammoth longteeth. Bones locked into fixed positions which left the beast's arms stretched out, keeping the wing portions spread open like enormous tent flaps, but hollow, perhaps? Animal bones were often hollow when Gunh snapped them between his teeth at the fire pit. Perhaps these were more hollow than most. Perhaps though they were big, they would float if laid upon water, or launched into the air. They certainly seemed very strong, supporting the expanses of the creature's rubbery skin.

The children tired, and let drop their sections one by one. When the group reached the top of the cliff, even the strongest hunters puffed with their efforts. Leaving the beast spread out under a tree like a collapsed hide tent with poles splayed at stiff angles, the tribe flopped in the shade almost as one. Hunters chewed on thick grass to moisten their mouths, and women and children sucked the remaining berries.

Gunh, rubbing the rising bruise where his head had collided with Enkha's, thought on how to strap himself to the underside of the great beast. With the bones locked stiff there'd be no way to flap, no propulsion through the air. But huntbirds didn't always flap. Sometimes, they glided.

Gliding. Gliding in the air like a huntbird, soaring far above the valley and the animals and trees and ground below. That was Gunh's Big Idea. It was the Biggest Idea he'd ever had.

Enkha was the first to recover from the climb. She walked around the large prone figure on the ground, prodding its oddly shaped head with her long artistic fingers, running her hand along the rounded ridges of bone under the hide-like skin. She looked up as Gunh approached. She tilted her head at him, shading her eyes against the bright afternoon sun though they stood beneath one of the few gigantic trees growing along the valley rim.

She squinted, then nodded. "Your Idea is good," she said.

You haven't seen my Idea yet, he signed.

She smiled. "Oh, yes I have," she said. "In here." She touched her head, where a bruise the size of a tortoise egg swelled from their collision. "And here." She pointed to a spot in the middle of her chest.

It was Enkha who organized the women, instructing them to weave together all available hide and leather into a large harness. She used the emptied berry satchels; she wove together the straps of everybody's belts, and demanded they relinquish their hides and furs, and that they cut everything into long lengths with the sharp stone knives they carried and the hardened tips of the hunters' sticks. Before long, the entire tribe stood naked in the light afternoon breeze under the trees, laughing and weaving and cutting their clothing into strips.

Only Enkha, thought Gunh, shaking his head and smiling to himself. Only Enkha could inspire the entire tribe to give up every scrap off their bodies. Only Enkha could convince even Moogh, glowering and sullen though he remained, to braid and weave his own garments into a thing with the sole purpose of helping Gunh fly.

The sun rode low in the sky by the time the harness was completed. It was a modified version of the rigging used to strap babies to travois for travel. With lots of calling and heaving and lifting, Enkha directed the fastening of the harness to the body of the once-frozen beast. Its large leathery expanse was no longer cold to the touch. The skin seemed to be tightening on the frame of the creature's impossibly long arm and finger bones. Gunh saw that as the thing dried out, it might become brittle. The wings might remain leather-like, but perhaps they would dry like dead leaves, and wither, and disintegrate into dust and nothing. It must be very, very old, this dead creature.

Working together, they gripped tight the edges of the beast all the way around, hunters toward the center where the body hung like a shriveled log. The women and children carefully lifted the outer edges of the wings, positioned along the delicate rims and the framework of hollow bones. When they reached the lip of the cliff, they set the large stiff thing, triangular and taut, gently onto the soft green grass.

Gunh turned to Enkha. *It's only because of you*, he signed. *Only thanks to you has this been done. It should be you to go.*

She pushed her long hair from her face. The breeze, turning slightly cooler as the sky slid into deeper shades, ruffled the hairs along the base of Gunh's spine, across his chest and on the back of his neck. Enkha reached to take his hands in both her own.

"No," she said. "It should be you."

She dropped his hands and flickered in signspeak: *It will be you, and I will paint it afterward. I will paint it over and over wherever we go, in caves and on hides, and everyone will know about the greatest Idea anyone ever had in the history of people everywhere.*

Gunh wanted to reach out and touch her, but she turned and began motioning to the others, directing the lifting of the not-bird and holding open the harness for Gunh to slip into beneath the large stiff triangle of the creature. Again, he was cloaked in the warm, very animal scent; a scent of dried grass and hot sand, which left a sharp underflavor of ground seeds and fresh hides on his tongue and in his nostrils.

Harnessed beneath the massive beast, barely held off the ground by the efforts of his tribe, Gunh had a moment of doubt. As they traveled slowly toward the edge of the vertical portion of the valley cliff, he felt small and vulnerable, strapped naked beneath the long-dead flying thing like a newborn baby to its mother's stomach, the grass close enough to tickle his nose. He almost called out for them to wait, to stop, to let him out. But then the edge of the cliff came into view and he could see the deep green living blanket of the valley, and the glowing snake of the ice-river, which looked no thicker than his arm from his vantage up on the cliff. The tops of trees growing below along the edges where the ice-river had retreated looked like small dark blooms, which Gunh might crush beneath his feet on a morning stroll. He saw a huntbird soaring way down there—seeming no larger than a flying insect—wings outstretched and locked into place, gliding, gliding, gliding on invisible breezes.

Yes, thought Gunh. *Yes*.

And then they launched him.

Together, all his people: Moogh and Enkha, and the children who laughed at his stories and ate his berries, and all the women and all the men whom Gunh had known his entire life—all ran together toward the edge of the cliff and as one, launched him out over the valley with a mighty heave. He heard the tribe's breath escape them behind him in a collective grunting sigh, and then the whistle of wind in his ears as he fell.

He rolled slightly to one side, his arms stretched out like the beautiful silver wings of a huntbird, locked straight like the enormous leather-covered frame above him. The wind caught, buoyed him, and he soared. He soared and he glided and he flew.

As the huge golden arc of the setting sun tinted the trees and valley and sky in gentle amber light, Gunh flew.

Laughing, he shouted into the wind as it rushed under him and toward him and away from him and around him. "Yes!" he shouted into the sky as he soared over the world. "Yes!"

Copyright Acknowledgments

Special thanks to Jessica Reisman for her generous assistance in proofing this text.

About the Author

Photo credit: S. Hazle

Camille Alexa grew up in Austin, Texas, under the auspices of a professorial Caribbean father, a bohemian painter mother, and a first-generation Norwegian grandmother with the best Science Fiction collection she has seen to this day. A recovering vintage shop owner, she is now the Poetry Editor for *Diet Soap*, the Flash Fiction Editor for *Abyss & Apex*, and she writes for *The Green Man Review*. When not on ten wooded acres near Austin, Texas, she lives in Portland, Oregon, in an Edwardian house with very crooked windows. *Push of the Sky* is her first book.